My Brother's Crown

Books by Mindy Starns Clark and Leslie Gould

COUSINS OF THE DOVE
My Brother's Crown

THE WOMEN OF LANCASTER COUNTY SERIES
The Amish Midwife
The Amish Nanny
The Amish Bride
The Amish Seamstress

Other Fiction by Mindy Starns Clark

THE MEN OF LANCASTER COUNTY
(WITH SUSAN MEISSNER)
The Amish Groom
The Amish Blacksmith
The Amish Clockmaker

THE MILLION DOLLAR MYSTERIES
A Penny for Your Thoughts
Don't Take Any Wooden Nickels
A Dime a Dozen
A Quarter for a Kiss
The Buck Stops Here

STANDALONE MYSTERIES
Whispers of the Bayou
Shadows of Lancaster County
Under the Cajun Moon
Secrets of Harmony Grove
Echoes of Titanic
(with John Campbell Clark)

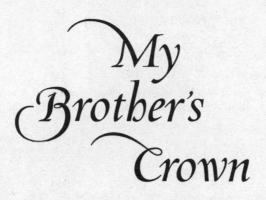

My Brother's Crown

MINDY STARNS CLARK
and LESLIE GOULD

HARVEST HOUSE PUBLISHERS
EUGENE, OREGON

Cover by Garborg Design Works, Savage, Minnesota

Cover photos © marzolino, darkbird, olly2 / Bigstock

The authors are represented by MacGregor Literary, Inc.

MY BROTHER'S CROWN

Copyright © 2015 Mindy Starns Clark and Leslie Gould
Published by Harvest House Publishers
Eugene, Oregon 97402
www.harvesthousepublishers.com

Library of Congress Cataloging-in-Publication Data
Clark, Mindy Starns.
My brother's crown / Mindy Starns Clark and Leslie Gould.
    pages ; cm. – – (Cousins of the Dove ; Book 1)
ISBN 978-0-7369-6288-9 (pbk.)
ISBN 978-0-7369-6289-6 (eBook)
1. Family-owned business enterprises—Fiction. 2. France—History—17th century—Fiction.
I. Gould, Leslie, – II. Title.
PS3603.L366M9 2015
813'.6—dc23

                                                    2015015758

Printed in the United States of America

15 16 17 18 19 20 21 22 23 / LB-JH / 10 9 8 7 6 5 4 3 2 1

Mindy

For the founders and many members
of the Starnes/Starns Triennial Association

You keep our history alive—
and our family connected.

Leslie

For Anaïs Edom,
a wonderful young woman of faith and strength

Thank you for your dear friendship
through these many years.

*Love and faithfulness meet together;
righteousness and peace kiss each other.*
PSALM 85:10

Historical Notes

*A*s authors we always strive to make our stories accurate, but when it comes to three-hundred-year-old history, sometimes even the most reliable sources disagree on the facts. In those cases, we have been forced to choose which version of the facts to use. Thus, though some elements of the history presented in this novel may be questioned, these facts are, to the best of our knowledge, correct—or as correct as information from the seventeenth century can be.

There is no official record that King Louis XIV and Madame Maintenon ever married, but it's generally agreed upon that they did. However, speculation as to when they were married is varied and includes dates in 1683, 1685, and 1686. Our research has placed the date of their wedding in the fall of 1685.

All of the characters in our story are products of our imaginations except for Louis XIV, Madame Maintenon, and Duchesse de Navailles (Suzanne). In our tale, we have stated that Suzanne's mother, Madame de Neuillant, was the godmother of Madame Maintenon, though some sources indicate that Suzanne was the godmother instead.

The persecution of the Huguenots varied from region to region and from time to time. The essence of the persecution we depict in our story is true, although the exact locations and times are fictitious. Statistics vary, but it's believed that as many as 400,000 Huguenots fled the country, and though many were assisted in their escape by others, the network of sympathizers depicted in this story is fictional, as is the Persecution Pamphlet.

This novel deals with a period of history when French Huguenots, also known as French Calvinists, were being persecuted for their faith. Though this was led by King Louis XIV in the name of the Catholic church, there is evidence that his true motives for this persecution were not so much about spiritual or denominational matters as they were about economics and power. We have striven to adhere to the facts of the period, which, while often brutal, also show that there were indeed acts of kindness and mercy by adherents to the Catholic faith, many of whom were sympathetic to the Huguenots' plight.

PROLOGUE

France
10 April 1685

*T*he boy stuck his head out the side window of the carriage and peered back at his home as it grew ever smaller in the distance. When he could see it no more, he withdrew and plopped back against the seat beside his two older sisters. Though Maman had called this their grand adventure, he knew that was not true. It was an escape, which was quite a different matter.

The trip was miserable, almost from the beginning. They covered a good distance that first day, but the next morning it started to rain, and as they traveled along a steep mountain pass, their horse slipped and injured his leg. They left him with an understanding farmer and were forced to continue on foot, carrying what they could and leaving their carriage and the rest of their belongings behind.

Papa said they should avoid the roads as much as possible, but he had no knowledge of the local footpaths, and as time passed it felt to the boy as if they were wandering with no direction. Finally, they came upon a village where they were deeply relieved to find a small Huguenot temple, one where they might seek refuge.

The pastor was kind. He provided food and a place to sleep, and he and Papa talked late into the night. The next day, the family set off again.

Still doubtful of his father's navigational abilities, the boy was surprised as the morning wore on and Papa seemed to be doing much better than the day before. He had some sort of pamphlet with him, a little booklet that must have come from the pastor. It looked like a simple collections of poems and illustrations, but judging by how Papa kept referring to it, it had to be some sort of guide for their journey. When the boy asked Papa about it, he tucked it away, ignoring the question.

They walked for three more days, staying off the roads and sticking mostly to field tracks when available, where they were less likely to be spotted by dragoons or informers. Thanks to the mysterious pamphlet, Papa seemed to know which strangers along the way would be willing to feed and house them, as well as which roads and paths to take and where to go once they reached their destination.

When they finally got to Lyon, they made their way under cover of darkness through the city and across the river Saône to a warehouse. They knocked softly on the back door, just once, and after a moment were greeted by a tall, lean man who seemed to have been expecting them.

"*Allons*," he barked gruffly.

He led them through a dark passageway by candlelight to what looked like a storage room. As the family of five waited among the shelves, the man moved to a side wall and pushed some sort of lever near the floor. As he did, a panel at the far end of the room began to slide upward. To the boy's surprise, the opening revealed a tiny chamber—a "vault," as Papa had said—with a table, chairs, a single bed, a small bureau, and various stacks of supplies.

As they stepped forward into the space, the man pointed out that there was enough food and drink to sustain them for two days, extra bedding to make pallets on the floor, a chamber pot in the front corner, and an oil lamp on the table. There was also quills, ink, paper, and a Bible for their use, though he warned them that the lamp held just one hour's worth of fuel, and that they were to light it only when absolutely necessary. The warehouse was a place of business during the day, he told them sternly, and they could not risk anyone spotting a glow along the floor seam of what was supposed to be the ordinary back wall of a supply room.

For the next two days, the family remained in hiding, spending most of their time in total darkness. All they could do was whisper and doze and try to stay strong for one another. With no windows, the only way for them to judge the hour was by the noises outside the panel door. When things seemed to spring to life, they knew it was morning. When, much later, the place grew quiet again, they felt sure it was evening.

They lit the lamp several times during the days, very briefly, just long enough to dole out food, and then they extinguished it again and ate in total darkness. The boy used those brief times of light to draw on the paper, one of his favorite pastimes. His hand moving from ink pot to the page and back again, he worked on a sketch of all they had left behind—their beautiful house, the stables out back, the big yard with his favorite tree, the one with a fat, knotted rope that hung down as a swing.

Papa lit the lamp and kept it on a bit longer in the evenings so he could read to them from the Bible. The boy found comfort in the words and in the soothing tones of his father's deep voice. He also appreciated that Maman did not stop him from drawing even during their worship time. He continued to embellish his picture, adding in a squirrel here, a bird there, until it was time again to extinguish the light and he was forced to put it away.

As the hours dragged by, all the boy could think of was getting out. He was so weary of this place, of its utter darkness. Of the constant need for silence. Of the stench from the chamber pot. Mostly, he was weary of wondering whether they were going to make it to freedom or end up imprisoned.

Or maybe dead.

He was also scared of the next phase of their escape. According to Papa, once they were released from this hiding place, they would be moved to another, even smaller one, stashed in narrow, hidden chambers under the floorboards of a special wagon, one designed for just this purpose. From the outside, it would look like a regular wagon, its driver bound for Switzerland. Only once they were across the border, however, would they be safe to climb back out again.

Of course, that was if all went as planned. If the driver did as he promised. If the people here could actually be trusted, which seemed to be the biggest risk of all. The boy had heard his parents whispering about it deep in the night, when they thought the children were sleeping. They talked about how the bounties for fleeing Huguenots had grown quite high, and how sometimes these supposed helpers were actually traitors in the end, turning over the Huguenots in their care to dragoons for a handsome fee.

That possibility was all the boy could think about when, at the end of the second day, he heard a rustling and a *thunk*, and then suddenly a quiet *whoosh* as the wall panel began to rise. There on the other side, in the supply room, stood the same man who had put them here two days ago. Again he held a candle—which seemed so very bright this time—and all around him came a rush of fresh air, sweet and life giving and so tangible the boy could almost taste it.

Papa stood, and the rest of them followed suit.

The man began to speak, his brows furrowed. Had they had enough food? Were they ready to get out of the vault and get on with their trip? They all nodded eagerly.

The man said they had ten minutes to stretch their legs and gather their things and then he would return to retrieve them and it would be time to go. "But the pamphlet stays here," he added sharply, pointing toward the small bureau. The boy watched as Papa pulled from his pocket the little booklet that seemed to have been their guide and set it there as directed.

Papa relit the lamp once the man left, and then the family went about straightening the vault and packing their belongings. Moving to the bureau, the boy slid open the top drawer and pulled out his sketch. Glancing down at the image of the house, the yard, the rope swing, it struck him that whether this next part of their journey brought them to prison or to freedom, one thing was certain: They would never be home again. That knowledge filled him with tremendous grief.

He folded the page and tucked it into his pocket. As he pushed the drawer shut, the pamphlet atop the bureau caught his eye, and he could not resist taking a closer look. Titled *A Collection of Verse for the Encouragement of Young Men and Women,* it had been written by someone named Father Écoute. The boy flipped through the pages, looking for the maps and instructions and such it seemed to contain. Instead, it was just a simple collection of poems and drawings—and the drawings were not even that good. He was studying a poorly rendered image of a rooster, wondering why it looked so odd, when he heard the noise of someone coming. He quickly put it down again.

"Time to go," the man said from the doorway.

Papa extinguished the lamp as he quietly addressed the children. "This last stretch will be the hardest," he told them with fear in his eyes even as he tried to reassure them with his words, "but it will be worth it in the end."

"*Allez!*" the man said impatiently. He led them back down the narrow passageway toward the door. As they went, the boy was intoxicated by the air. He wanted to run, to play, to yell. They were finally free! And they could see. The passageway was dark, yes, but not the kind of darkness they had endured for the past two days. This was a dark tempered by the moonlight streaming in through a high window, where he could actually see his hand in front of his face.

Spotting the exit up ahead, his joy began to fade. They were free now from the vault, yes, but for how long? What if this was, as his Maman had whispered to Papa late last night, only a trap?

When they reached the door to the outside, the man paused, one hand on the knob. Then he slowly pulled it open and waved them through, toward their future.

If, indeed, they had a future at all.

CHAPTER ONE
Renee

My transformation took place in a gas station bathroom off I-64 about five miles east of Richmond. Despite the cracked mirror and dim lighting, the acts of putting on makeup and styling my hair were the easy parts. The hard part was trying not to let my bare feet touch the floor as I changed from jeans, T-shirt, and sneakers to a white wrap-style blouse, gray pencil skirt, and black pumps. The obedient granddaughter in me wanted to show up at the bank looking the best I could, but the scientist in me knew the floor was always the dirtiest part of a public bathroom and could be a veritable stew of E. coli, coliform, staph, strep, rotavirus, and even MRSA.

Stifling a shudder, I managed to wriggle out of one set of clothes and into another, one side at a time while balancing on the opposite still-shoed foot. It wasn't pretty, and I was practically out of breath by the time I was dressed, but somehow I managed. If I were ever in this situation again, I decided as I took one last look in the mirror and smoothed back an errant lock of dark brown hair, I would take the time to find somewhere a bit more upscale first.

Soon I was back on the interstate in my rental car, one glance at the clock confirming I was still on schedule. Nana Talbot was a stickler for punctuality, whether the inevitable delays of travel were a part of the equation or not, so I was glad my flight from Seattle had arrived almost half an hour early. That bought me even more time to pick up the car and drive into town, including my stop for a quick lunch and a round of clothing gymnastics in that ceramic-tiled petri dish.

Now that I was back in Virginia, my mind inevitably went to thoughts of my grandfather, who passed away last November, just seven months ago. This was the first time I'd returned since the funeral, and though I was eager to see my grandmother, a big part of me hadn't been ready to come back just yet. My grief was still so strong, and I knew that being here in Granddad's world without him in it would only make things hurt more. At least I had a busy day ahead of me, which would provide a good distraction.

I'd been on a plane since eleven o'clock last night and had only managed to doze a little in transit, but there would be no rest for the weary. Between now and any hope of a bed, I had several important tasks that had to be accomplished, starting with this first one, a visit to the Richmond National Bank and Trust to meet up with my grandmother and some guy from her insurance company, a slick and weaselly type, no doubt. In this area, the Talbot name brought on an enormous amount of bowing and scraping—and attempted shystering—at least to those familiar with the family paper-and-printing empire.

Out in Seattle, on the other hand, even though I worked in a branch of the same company and was a member of the same family, my connection rarely registered. There, the Talbot name wasn't even enough to get me an extra shot in my latte at the company cafeteria. Not that I cared about that sort of thing—quite the opposite, in fact. I had a distinct aversion to being in the spotlight and was more than happy to fly under the radar whenever possible.

Traffic was heavy but moving, and in the end it took me less time to reach downtown than it did to find a parking place once there. At least I still had a good thirteen minutes to spare by the time I set out on foot, which meant I should arrive approximately ten minutes early. To me, that was an eon—though in Nana's world, of course, ten minutes early *was* on time—unless going to a social event, in which case "on time" was twenty minutes late.

Passing the dark glass of a storefront as I walked, I caught sight of my reflection, though it took a moment for me to realize what I was seeing. That tall woman in the professional-looking outfit with her straight hair hanging smooth and loose to her shoulders, her features enhanced with the just right amount of makeup, was *me*. Back home, I lived in lab coats over jeans and casual tops, my hair ponytailed, my face bare save for the occasional dab of ChapStick on my lips. But I couldn't do that here, not around my grandmother.

The only reason I even owned cosmetics in the first place and knew how to use them was because of Nana, who had insisted on charm school for each of her grandchildren upon the occasion of their thirteenth birthdays to mold them into "proper young men and women"— whether they wanted to go or not. I was just a few months older than my cousin Danielle, so at least we'd been able to attend the month-long summer session together. She and I had always gotten along beautifully despite the differences in our personalities. Where I was all science and facts and don't-rock-the-boat, she was art and spontaneity and rock-the-boat-till-it-tips-so-we-can-go-swimming. I still remembered how, during the girls' beauty lessons, the ever-artistic Danielle had taken the application of eye shadow to a whole new level, combining ten colors or more before she was done. A true creative spirit, she was genuinely puzzled when scolded for having used the makeup to give herself "Jezebel eyes," which was apparently worse than having no eyes at all.

My two brothers—one older, one younger—had each been forced to go as well, and though they had fought it, the lessons seemed to stick in the end as they were transformed from rowdy boys to polite young men. That made them a huge hit with the ladies, especially their eventual spouses. Though I, too, had emerged from the experience in a somewhat new and improved version—well, except for the cosmetics part, which only came into play when I was with Nana or had to do something very public, like present a paper—my good manners had not made me a hot commodity with the opposite sex, much less helped me land a mate.

Then again, even if proper etiquette had been for my brothers the behavioral equivalent of pheromones, it hadn't done a thing for me. I'd been a chemistry geek in high school, college, and grad school, and these days I spent more time flirting with leuco dyes or teasing out thermochromatic liquid crystals than I did with eligible men.

Correction. Quite a few of my colleagues were male, straight, and single, so technically they fit the term. But none of them were what might be considered viable options. On the rare occasion when I did actually cross paths with someone interesting, I was usually too inhibited to act on it. My job as a research chemist offered much in the way of intellectual stimulation and professional fulfillment, but it also gave me a good place to hide.

I reached the bank and again caught my reflection. Good thing the guys in the lab couldn't see me now, I decided as I broke the image by pushing open the door, or they might actually realize I was a girl.

Stepping inside, I spotted Nana right away, perfectly coiffed and dressed in a white linen suit, standing across the broad marble lobby and speaking with a brawny-looking fellow with neatly clipped sandy brown hair, wearing a suit and tie. Probably the head of bank security. As I advanced toward them, I was glad to have arrived ahead of the insurance man, as this would give my grandmother and me a few minutes alone. We hadn't been together since Granddad's funeral, and I wanted a minute to reconnect privately.

"Darling," Nana said, turning to greet me with a warm smile.

We embraced, and I closed my eyes as I breathed in the familiar woodsy-floral scent of her Calèche perfume. Though I had grown up on the other side of the country and spent only a few weeks here in Virginia every summer, somehow this was the smell of home.

We pulled apart, but before I could ask how she was doing, she turned and placed a hand on the security guard's muscular arm.

"Renee, I'd like to introduce Blake Keller of Eagleton Trust Insurance. Blake, this is my granddaughter, Renee Talbot."

I blinked, startled. *This* was the insurance agent? Whatever I'd been expecting, this mountain of a man was certainly not it. Trying not to let my surprise show, I met his gaze, only to realize that he looked equally surprised in return.

"The scientist?" he said, his tone almost doubtful.

"Yes. Nice to meet you." I offered a hand, but it took a moment for him to respond.

"Sorry," he said as he gripped it and gave a firm shake. "I..." His arms dropping back to his sides, he added, "Never mind. Nice to meet you too."

"Is something wrong?" Nana asked him. "You seem startled."

He gave an embarrassed laugh. "No. It's just that when you told me about your granddaughter Renee, the brilliant research scientist only three years on the job and already such a rising star..." His voice trailed off as he turned back toward me and added, "Well, let's just say I envisioned a different sort of look. My apologies."

I suppose I should have been flattered by what he'd obviously intended as a compliment, but somehow his assumptions seemed more egregious than mine. Had it really been that much of a stretch to align the body with the brains? Couldn't a woman be smart *and* attractive? Granted, the mad scientist look he'd been expecting was probably closer to my day-to-day appearance than this was, but still. I doubted he would have drawn the same conclusions were I a man.

Feeling uncharacteristically emboldened, I met his eyes. "Don't worry about it. I left my test tubes, safety goggles, and frumpy clothes outside." Before he could respond, I couldn't help but add, "Right next to your snake oil, actuarial tables, and scare tactics."

"Renee!" Nana scolded.

Blake just laughed. "Touché. Though you're probably thinking of a different department than mine. I'm in Security and Recovery. We don't deal much in snake oil."

I hesitated, our repartee interrupted by his surprising words. "Security and Recovery? For an insurance company?"

"Eagleton Trust, dear," Nana said. "They're one of the world's leading underwriters of fine art, among other things. The Persecution Pamphlet is insured through them."

"Okay." I turned back to Blake. "But what are you doing here?"

He shrugged. "Just providing a little extra security while the pamphlet's out of the vault. Protecting our interests."

I thought about that for a moment. Four years ago, the historical document Nana and I had come here today to retrieve had been appraised at more than a million dollars. I guess it made sense that the insurer might want to keep a close eye on it, especially when in transit.

The three of us were interrupted by the bank's manager, a smartly dressed woman with silver hair, blue eyes, and a melodious Southern voice. "Mrs. Talbot? You folks are welcome to come on back now if you like."

Glad to get things moving again, I took Nana's arm and we followed the lady, Blake trailing behind. She led us past the vault of safety deposit boxes and down a labyrinth of hallways until we came to a separate section. This area was protected by a sophisticated digital entry system and housed a specific type of safety deposit box storage, the kind rated by insurance companies as HPR for "highly protected risk." Climate- and humidity-controlled, with UV-safe lighting and extra security features, this art protection vault contained double-locked boxes that ranged from very small to quite huge, inside of which the wealthy of Richmond could safely keep their most valuable art, antiques, and documents when not in use.

Nana handed Blake her key, and then she and I watched as he and the manager attended to the locks. Moments later the small door was open, and Blake was sliding out a rectangular metal container.

The manager showed us to a viewing room and then excused herself as Nana and I took a seat at the table and set our purses on the floor. Blake moved into place across from us, leaning forward and holding out the container with both hands, as if he were a coachman presenting a glass slipper on a royal pillow to Cinderella. With a smile, Nana lifted the lid and removed from inside the two items that were its entire contents: a pair of white cotton gloves and a pale green, custom-made case about the size and shape of a VHS videotape holder.

"I'll be right outside if you need me," he said, and then he left the room, taking the metal container with him.

Glad to be alone at last, I ignored the case for a moment to speak softly to Nana.

"Are you doing okay? I know this must be emotional for you."

She blinked, looking away for a moment. "It is, but I'm fine, dear. Really. And it does feel good to be finishing what your grandfather started."

"Agreed." I gave her a reassuring smile as I slipped an arm around her slender shoulders for a quick hug.

"As for this," she said, the sparkle returning to her eye, "I'd just like to take a quick look to make sure it's okay. You can examine it more closely once we're home."

"Oh, I will," I said. There was something I wanted to look into, an idea that had come to me when I was thinking about the pamphlet late last night during my flight.

I pulled on the gloves as she carefully set the case on the table in front of me. Chemically stable inside and out, this preservation-grade polyethylene holder featured an alkaline buffer and a zeolite molecular trap, with a pH-appropriate, acid- and lignin-free interior. I only knew this because I was part of the team that designed it, four years ago, to hold one very special document. I'd still been in grad school, working on my doctorate at the time, but my grandfather had generously invited me to be a part of the process because of my field of study.

My gloved fingers were practically trembling now as I opened the case wide, reached inside for the familiar document, and held it up so both Nana and I could see it. Known as the Persecution Pamphlet, it was a mere eight pages long but contained a history beyond measure.

The cream-colored pamphlet had been created in 1685, and though it looked like a simple collection of French poems and drawings, it actually contained within its pages a coded guide that showed the way out of France for Huguenots fleeing the country in the face of religious persecution. At the time, multiple copies of the pamphlet had been printed and quietly distributed by a small group of Huguenot sympathizers to those in need, and the information it contained had helped dozens—perhaps even hundreds—of Huguenots make their way to safety. But in order to protect the identities of the Good Samaritans identified within, all copies had ultimately been re-collected and destroyed—except for one, which had been intentionally saved and passed down to future generations through the Talbot family. That one copy was what I now held in my own hands. Preserved for several centuries, it was a tangible reminder of the struggles the Huguenots endured for the sake of their faith under the reign of King Louis XIV.

"Looks good," I said.

"It does indeed," Nana replied, her eyes glowing. "Your grandfather would have been so pleased."

Though early details were sketchy, the pamphlet had ostensibly been created by one of our forebears or at least someone close to them and then passed down through the Talbot family, father to eldest son, for something like eleven generations over a span of more than three hundred years. It had become the property of my grandfather upon the death of his father back in the 1950s, but from the moment Granddad inherited it, he let it be known that the pattern would be broken upon his death. Rather than pass it down to my Uncle Finley, the eldest of his three sons and the father of my cousin Danielle, Granddad announced that he would be donating it to a museum instead. He felt that the time had come for the pamphlet to belong not just to one person at a time but to the whole world.

Uncle Finley agreed with the decision, and together he and Grand-dad chose the most appropriate recipient, the National Museum of American History, which was part of the Smithsonian in Washington, DC. Now the time had finally come to add the pamphlet to their collection.

In three days, at a Saturday ceremony during our annual Talbot family reunion, this priceless document was going to be handed over to the museum as a gift from the descendants of Emmanuel Talbot, the first of our male ancestors to come to America in 1704.

"What do you think, dear?" Nana asked. "Does it seem to have maintained its integrity since the last time you saw it?"

Before answering that question, I took a closer look, eyeing the front and back and then carefully opening it just a bit to turn the pages one by one till I reached the end. Its few small flaws had been there before, and otherwise it looked great, exactly the same as when it was authenticated and locked away in this vault four years ago.

"Seems fine. There's no degradation that I can tell. Between our custom, state-of-the-art casing and the controlled atmosphere of the storage vault, it looks like it's held up really well."

"I never doubted that it would."

Finished with it for now, I returned the pamphlet to its casing and sealed it shut, and then we were on our way.

We found Blake standing not far from the wall of double-locked boxes, his stance wide and his hands clasped behind his back. Looking at him now, I supposed he was quite handsome. *If* you went for that type.

"Ready to go?" he asked, flashing us an absurdly perfect smile.

"Not so fast," I said, for some reason feeling a surge of irritation. Who knew what kind of damage this behemoth's ignorant carelessness might wreak on our priceless but incredibly fragile treasure? Maybe he could protect it from being stolen, but that still didn't mean we could just toss it in the car and take off. There was the temperature problem, for starters, which I'd just begun to explain when he cut me off.

"Yes, ma'am. While you ladies were in the viewing room, I brought the car around and have it cooling to exactly sixty-four degrees. According to the portable hygrothermograph I brought along, the humidity's running about thirty-nine percent, which is slightly higher than optimum but shouldn't prevent us from moving forward, considering that we'll be at the house in under an hour even with traffic. As for the UV issue, I assume that's taken care of by the case itself, correct?"

I nodded, feeling simultaneously impressed and even more irritated than before. I was glad he was prepared to take care of the temperature issue, but did he have to be so smarmy about it?

"Have I forgotten anything, Dr. Talbot?"

I hesitated, almost wishing he had so I could bring him down a notch. "Just tact," I heard myself say, once again startled by my boldness. Never one to be snarky with strangers, I couldn't imagine where this was coming from.

Nana shot me a look of disapproval.

"Kidding," I said, though I hadn't been, not really. I met Blake's eyes, which held a look not of offense but amusement. He maintained my gaze until I looked away, realizing maybe I was the one with the more egregious behavior this time.

"Would you like to carry it?" I asked in a nicer voice, hoping to bury the hatchet.

He shook his head. "Actually, if it's safe to turn it vertically for a few minutes, I'd rather you put it in your bag till we get to the car. Hide it in plain sight, so to speak."

"Sure, whatever you think is best," I replied, glad my transformation into a professional-looking businesswoman had included trading out the small, raggedy purse I usually carted around for this elegant and roomy leather satchel.

We headed out after that, reaching Nana's Mercedes without any problem. And though I wouldn't be riding along with them, I climbed into the back so I could hand over the case in a less visible way. From there I watched as Blake helped Nana into the front, his strong hands surprisingly gentle as he supported her by the arm. It wasn't until she was in and the door was closed and he was moving past my window that the bottom flap of his suit jacket flipped back for a moment to reveal a startling surprise. At his hip was a black leather holster containing a gun. My stomach dropped as an old, familiar image filled my mind.

The body, just lying there on the cot.

The knife, buried in the chest, nearly to the hilt.

The blood, pooled on the ground below in circles of deep maroon.

I may have been only nine at the time, but even now, at twenty-eight, I still had a distinct aversion to all kinds of weapons—knives mostly, but guns and other types too—and likely always would. At the moment, just the sight of a firearm in such close proximity made me queasy.

"Can I give you a ride to your car?" Blake asked, startling me as he slid onto the driver's seat. I hadn't even realized he'd gone around to the other side or that he'd opened the door.

"No," I said, too quickly. Taking a deep breath, I tried to calm my pounding heart as I added, "Thanks, but no need. I'm parked just a few blocks over."

He eyed me strangely. "How about driving together? Did you want to follow us?"

"No, I'm good. I...I'll meet you there."

Flustered, I reached for the door handle and was about to give it a pull when he asked me if I was forgetting something. I turned and stared at him blankly.

"The document?" he prodded, a slight smile on his lips but a hint of concern in his eyes.

"Oh. Right." I could feel my face burning as I fumbled with the latch on my bag, got it open, and pulled out the case.

"Here," I said, holding it toward him until he took it from me. "See you at the house."

Then I gave Nana's shoulder a quick squeeze, got out, and walked away as fast as my legs would carry me.

Chapter Two

Renee

Needing time to think, I decided to drive the local roads northwest to Nana's rather than hop on I-64. That way I could ease more gradually into the inevitable, into what was really bothering me.

And I knew exactly why the sight of that gun had nearly generated a panic attack. It was because things were already heightened for me thanks to the knowledge of what I had to face next, what I always had to face when I came here: that first look at the "Dark Woods," as my cousins and I called it, where the long-ago "Incident" happened. Located next to my grandparents' house, the woods' proximity made it an inevitable part of coming here, a tangible presence and constant reminder of a trauma we'd rather forget altogether.

But the woods wouldn't let us forget. What happened had happened there, and as long as we wanted to visit our loved ones who lived in the house next to it, there was nothing we could do about that.

At least the woods and the estate were separated somewhat by a wide and impassible drainage gulley. Then again, all it took to get there was to walk toward the rear of the property and look for the wooden footbridge near the tennis court. That was how we'd always gone exploring as kids every year—my three cousins and I—over the footbridge and into the woods and all the way along the winding path to the old hunting cabin, where we loved to play house and pretend we were pioneers.

Not that we ever did it again, of course, not after it happened. Didn't go there, rarely talked about it with anyone else, didn't even like to look that direction, but there was no escaping its presence. Though the terrain in this part of Virginia was flat, in our minds the Dark Woods loomed large in the distance, like an avalanche about to give, or Mt. Vesuvius churning near Pompeii.

My cousins and I had not been victims of a crime back then, but we had been witnesses to one within the very cabin where we'd always gone to play. Ever since, for me, the challenge when returning here was in facing the initial sight of those woods, yet again, without letting the memories it awakened completely unnerve me. What other choice did I have, really? I couldn't stay away from my grandparents, nor from the annual Talbot reunion, which was always held here. And at least it had become a little easier with each visit—correction, with each visit that didn't include having a gun suddenly appear mere inches from my face.

I just needed to pull it together, put things back in perspective, and remind myself that what happened was a long, long time ago. There was much to do before tomorrow night, when the first families would begin to arrive for the reunion, and I was responsible for an important part of it this year. Surely I could find within myself the calm and reason that permeated every other area of my life except this one.

I turned up the radio, cleared my mind, and tried to focus on my breathing as I drove. Soon I did begin to feel better. It was nearly four o'clock by the time I reached the James River, and I crossed over it as slowly as I could, taking in the view on both sides. Less than five miles to go.

I exited the highway onto Huguenot Trail, happy as always to follow the pathways of my ancestors, and drove west, parallel to the river, enjoying the lush terrain that enveloped me. After several miles, I spotted the sign for Willow Lane and slowed for my turn. Other than the one home on the corner, there would be nothing else on Willow except for the Dark Woods—which started directly behind that house and ran for nearly a mile—and then, after that, the Talbot estate.

Clenching my teeth, I made the turn and kept going, driving past the corner house. Only once I was fully out of its sight did I slow down and pull over to the side of the road. I sat there for a long moment, preparing to confront the inevitable. *You love coming here*, I told myself in a quick pep talk. *You just need to deal with the memories as usual and then you can move on.*

Finally, I turned and looked. To my relief, the sight didn't feel any more traumatic than in previous years, despite the incident with Blake's gun. I guess the older I got, the better I understood that this place had nothing to do with what happened. It was just the setting, just the backdrop, nothing more than a collection of trees and brambles and brush. It had not been the one to wield the knife, nor the one to do what had come after. Feeling much better, I took a deep breath and started off again, continuing forward until the driveway of the Talbot estate came into view.

The house wasn't visible from the road, but it was obvious just from the elegant entrance that it had to be nice. And it was. Set back amid towering yellow pines, the stately redbrick home appeared after rounding the first curve on the drive, and its beauty caught me anew every time I saw it. A three-story Colonial, the house featured a large white portico at the front door, tall shutters at each window, and a row of dormers along the roofline. Twin chimneys rose from each end of the structure, flanked by a glass solarium to the left and a four-car garage to the right. Behind that garage, though not visible from here, were a guesthouse, pool, and huge yard beyond. Way out back was also a tennis court and the ever-present footbridge to the woods, though I wasn't going to think about that now.

I drove all the way around to the garage and parked, pulling to a stop behind several other cars. After turning off my rented Impala, I sat for a long moment, thinking through the rest of this day. It was time to get down to work, and though I would have dearly loved nothing more than to change into something comfortable first, I knew there would be other people around, which meant I couldn't exactly trade out my skirt for a pair of sweats lest I give Nana heart palpitations.

As I walked to the front door, I remembered yet again that this would be the first Talbot reunion since my grandfather's death. Ten years older than Nana, Granddad had been ninety-two when he died, but he was sharp as a tack all the way to the end. He was an amazing man, and his absence this weekend was definitely going to be felt. Tears filled my eyes at the thought, but I managed to blink them away. No mascara smearing allowed, I reminded myself.

At least Nana seemed to be holding up well. I found her in the kitchen, talking with the caterer about tomorrow night's dinner. The reunion was structured the same way each year, with immediate family coming on Thursday evening around six, sharing a big meal together, and staying in various bedrooms throughout the main house and the guesthouse. Considering that "immediate family" included four generations of Talbots, it was a miracle we could all still fit.

The larger reunion wouldn't begin until Friday morning and would run until Sunday afternoon, with events, meals, and activities scheduled throughout. No ordinary family gathering, this annual reunion was open to Talbot descendants at large and often brought in more than two hundred participants. Most of them stayed under a group rate at a hotel in town, with each day's events taking place either here at the estate or in a ballroom at the hotel.

Such a massive undertaking was no small feat, but thanks to a topnotch reunion committee, eager volunteers with years of practice, and a set of finely honed procedures, things usually went off without a hitch. The fact that Nana employed a veritable army of hired help to augment efforts behind the scenes didn't hurt either. By the time things kicked off Friday morning, her back lawn would have been transformed into a wonderland of white canopy tents, four separate buffet service lines, and enough activity stations to entertain participants of every age.

It looked as if Nana was going to be tied up for a while, so I just gave her a quick wave to let her know I'd made it and then returned to the entrance hall, which was wide and majestic and ran the entire depth of the house. Because the back wall was lined with windows and French doors looking out on the pool and grounds, the overall effect when coming in through the front door was striking and made the house feel even bigger than it already was.

Looking along the left side of the entrance hall and moving clockwise, first came the door to my grandfather's study, then the main staircase, the doorway that led to the dining room, and a half bath. Continuing on the right wall was the door to the laundry room and a mudroom beyond, and then finally, to my immediate right, was the large and sumptuous living room.

I loved the whole house, but for the next few days, my mind would be on the laundry room and mudroom. That's because we were going to turn them into a sort of mini museum, offering the first and final private viewing by the Talbot descendants of the Persecution Pamphlet before it would be given over to the Smithsonian. Connected by a swinging door, each room had its own entrance and exit, which made them the perfect choice for funneling through tons of people in an orderly fashion.

Knowing they would lose the use of these machines for a few days, the cleaning staff had tried to wash ahead of time everything that might be needed for the reunion. And though it wouldn't be as convenient, at least there was a small, stacking washer-and-dryer unit out in the guest-house should any emergencies crop up in the meantime.

Going into the main laundry room now, I found a worker up on a ladder mounting a projector to the ceiling and a man I recognized as Dr. Harold Underwood standing below giving directions. An academic and scholar, he specialized in historical documents and had been one of the members of the authentication team four years ago. He was short and stout with tufts of gray hair on a round, balding head. He'd been a valuable part of the team back then, and I was pleased to see him now.

He greeted me warmly with a double handshake and a smile. "Dr. Talbot, so nice to see you again. Very nice."

He dove right into an explanation of what he'd managed to accomplish thus far, and as he talked it was easy to hear the enthusiasm in his voice. I'd hired him to help transform these two ordinary rooms into a temporary viewing space where the pamphlet could be put on display without endangering it in any way. Happy to help, he'd been the one to design the layout and bring in the necessary equipment for maintaining appropriate conditions of temperature, humidity, lighting, and more that the pamphlet required. He was also working with Blake to keep the priceless document secure, starting with a locked and alarmed preservation-quality viewing cabinet. From the looks of things, Dr. Underwood and his helpers had already made a lot of progress.

As for Blake, he seemed to be in absentia at the moment.

The older man showed me the sketches he'd done of the basic layout, starting with black fabric panels that were now being hung around the perimeter of both rooms. Covering every inch of space except the doorways, the panels even hung in front of the washer and dryer, completely obscuring the fact that this was a laundry room. Next door, an extra wall of panels had been erected across the center of the mudroom, creating a buffer around the display area to protect it from exposure to any light that might come in when the exterior door was opened.

Entering in groups of about ten to twelve, guests would start in the first room, which would be set up as a viewing area, with a projector, screen, and two rows of folding chairs. There they would watch an eight-minute video Danielle had created for the occasion, one that explained the history of the pamphlet. After that, they would file through the swinging door into the mudroom, where they would weave around the protective black fabric panels to stand in front of the case and get a look at the document itself. Posters propped on easels would line the walls, providing further information that folks could view as they waited their turn. I felt our plan was doable, thanks in large part to the fact that these rooms were a bit more spacious than the average laundry and mudrooms.

Danielle had designed the posters using facts and photos I'd sent her, then she'd emailed the files to the local Talbot branch, where they'd been printed and delivered here. I hadn't seen them in person yet, so once Dr. Underwood finished his recap, he went back to what he was doing and I set about unpacking the posters so I could get a good look at them myself.

Of course, they were all great. Danielle was incredibly gifted, and it showed in everything she did. The facts-only information I had sent her had been pulled into bulleted lists and call outs with colorful arrows and lines and shapes that led the eye from one important point to the next. Most Talbots knew of the pamphlet's existence and some of the basic story behind it, but I doubted many of them had heard the whole tale, and almost none had ever seen the real thing in person.

I was arranging the posters on easels when Nana popped in, a small piece of paper in her hand.

"This is for you, dear. Blake's phone number. He asked that you contact him whenever the pamphlet is going to be out of the safe so he can be present."

"Even at the house? Is that really necessary?"

"His primary task is to keep that pamphlet secure until it's given to the Smithsonian on Saturday. We can't blame him for being diligent."

"Fine," I groaned, typing his number into my phone's contacts. "I guess it won't be too inconvenient."

"Oh, and one other thing." She gestured for me to follow her into the hall where we could speak privately. Once there, she said in a soft voice, "Will you be able to remember the combination to the safe if I tell it to you? I'd rather you not write it down."

"No need unless it's been changed."

"You still remember it? From four years ago?"

I nodded.

"But you only used it a few times, Renee. I know how smart you are, but still..."

"It's calcium silicate."

"Excuse me?"

I lowered my voice to a whisper. "That's how I remember it, Nana. Calcium silicate is made up of calcium, silicon, and oxygen. On the periodic table, calcium is twenty, silicon is fourteen, and oxygen is eight. Which is the combination, twenty-fourteen-eight. Calcium silicate. It even sort of rhymes."

I was proud of the clever memory aid I'd come up with, but Nana just gaped at me for a long moment, baffled and bemused. Then she simply shook her head and started for the stairs.

With a smile I went back to my mini museum and picked up where I'd left off. An hour later we were just finishing up when Dr. Underwood let me know he would be needing the pamphlet soon in order to determine placement and make his final adjustments with the lighting.

"No problem. I'll contact Blake," I said, and then I shot him a text asking him to come here ASAP if possible. *Butterfly needs to emerge from cocoon,* I added, smiling at my spy-talk and hoping he'd get the joke.

He responded soon after.

Be there in 15. Sustain diapause until my arrival.

I actually laughed out loud, amazed that someone like him would know the term. Diapause was an extended state of rest that organisms, including butterflies, sometimes entered into. By telling me to sustain it, he was saying to leave the pamphlet in the safe for now. Too thrown to come up with a clever reply, I texted him back a simple *Will do. Over and out.*

He showed up just as Dr. Underwood was dismissing his workers for the day and I was straightening the chairs in front of the portable movie screen.

"Thanks for waiting," Blake said as he came into the room. Then, glancing around furtively, he stepped closer and added in a low voice, jaw set and lips barely moving, "Imago may now emerge from chrysalis."

Again, I couldn't help but laugh. "Very impressive, Keller. Let me guess, you picked up the lingo during a previous assignment, one where you had to guard some rare species at a local butterfly conservatory?"

"Nope." With a sheepish smile, he gestured to his phone and added, "Once I realized we were playing secret agent, I just googled 'terms related to butterflies' and found some code words I could use."

"Clever. Very resourceful."

He shrugged modestly, sliding his phone into his pocket. "Comes with the territory. Kind of like it says in the Bible, I try to be all things to all people. You're a scientist. I can do scientist—or at least pretend well enough to hold up my end of the conversation."

His eyes locked on mine, and I felt an odd shiver. Quoting the Bible? Throwing out scientific terms in an attempt to speak my language? Maybe there was more to this guy than I'd first given him credit for. The thought surprised me, sending heat to my cheeks. Breaking our gaze, I managed to mutter, "Be right back." Then I turned and headed for the door, my pulse surging as I went.

I tried to talk myself down as I walked across the wide entrance hall toward the study. There was a big difference between googling and knowing. Anybody with a smart phone and half a brain could do what he'd done. Other than being adaptable and accommodating, there was nothing special about Blake Keller, nothing at all.

Except maybe those eyes, which were a deep green flecked with gold. And that hair, thick blondish-brown hair that almost made a person want to run their hands through it, if they went for that sort of thing.

With a groan, I forced myself to put such juvenile musings aside and focus on the task at hand. At the door of my grandfather's study, I paused for a moment then took a deep breath, pushed it open, and went in.

Granddad.

This had been his domain, and it still smelled like him, that familiar mix of teakwood and pipe tobacco and antique paper. The room looked the same as always, the dark leather swivel chair parked behind the massive wooden desk, rows of rare books lining the shelves along the right wall, and a pair of satin-upholstered antique chairs facing the desk.

Taking a deep breath, I padded across the lush beige carpet to the safe, which was located in a supply closet on the far side of the room. As I knelt and began turning the dial—right twenty, left fourteen, right eight—I could almost feel my grandfather's presence. What a fascinating man he had been, so intelligent, so generous, so paternal. He'd had eight grandchildren, but somehow he made each one of us feel especially loved and encouraged by him.

His inviting me in on the authentication process when I was still in grad school had meant so much to me. As a student of colloid and surface chemistry, my goal to work with security printing was about as cutting edge and future focused as one could get. Yet somehow he knew that involving me with this pamphlet from the past would have an influence on that work. The authentication had given me such perspective into the longevity, durability, and stability of not just ink but paper as well. It had been a valuable experience, both personally and professionally, and I would always be grateful for it.

Swinging open the safe's door now, I spotted the pale green case atop a pile of papers and some velvet jewelry boxes. I was just pulling it out when a man spoke.

"Your grandfather sure had varied tastes in reading."

Startled, I jerked my head around to see Blake standing in front of the bookshelves, perusing the titles of Granddad's collection.

"I like how he organized them, though," he continued, his eyes slowly scanning up and down. "Looks like he has them grouped by subject, then alphabetized by book title within those groupings."

"What are you doing in here?" I demanded, feeling utterly intruded upon. What made him think it was okay to waltz into a private office as though he owned the place?

"What do you mean?" he asked, his attention still focused on the shelves. "Of course I'm in here. Like I said before, wherever that pamphlet goes, I go. "

Pursing my lips, I turned back to the safe and closed and locked the door. Then I looked toward this unwanted protector and just stood there, clutching the case to my chest. How could one person be so appealing on the one hand, yet so obstinate and irritating on the other?

"Oh, wow," Blake said, oblivious to my thoughts. He was too busy reaching for a book and pulling it out to take a closer look. "*The Little Prince.* I loved this when I was a kid." He held it gingerly and turned the pages with care. "Such a great story. So many layers, you know?"

Seriously? We were going to stand here and discuss a children's book when there was work to do? I was about to say as much when he continued.

"What's the famous line? Something about learning to see with the heart instead of the eyes?"

"I wouldn't know," I replied. "I haven't had the pleasure."

With that, I started walking toward the door. If he wanted to go wherever the pamphlet went, then he was welcome to follow along—or not, his choice.

"Wait, what?" he said, quickly closing the book and sliding it back into place on the shelf. "You've never read *The Little Prince*?"

I kept going, and as I moved into the main hallway he fell into step behind me.

"Nope. Saw the movie version, the one with Shirley Temple."

He caught up and walked at my side. "No, no. That was *The Little Princess*."

"Oh, sorry. Well, at least I've listened to the music. I like Purple Rain."

"Purple Rai— That's *Prince*. The singer." Only then did he realize I was making fun of him. "Ah. Think you're smart, huh, Talbot?"

I shrugged, working hard to stifle a smile. "That's the rumor, anyway," I said before moving into the room and leaving him in my wake.

CHAPTER THREE

Renee

As Dr. Underwood pulled on his white gloves, Blake recounted for us the various steps he was taking to ensure the protection of the Persecution Pamphlet during the reunion. It sounded as if he had things well covered, including various alarms and cameras and even a security guard who would be standing watch during viewing hours.

"Of course, I'll be around that day myself too," he added, "to relieve the guard for breaks and make sure things are running smoothly. You know, keep an eye on stuff."

Why the thought of seeing him again on Friday wasn't exactly unpleasant was beyond me.

Turning toward Dr. Underwood, I opened the case and held it out. He gently removed the document and slid it into the cabinet. Under the warm glow of a UV-safe beam, inside the clear acrylic vitrine display box, the Persecution Pamphlet looked more regal than ever. As he went back and forth between adjusting its position and aiming the lights, I hovered nearby, ready to help, my eyes drawn to the sight of the treasure on display and its unwieldy title:

Un Recueil de Poésie pour l'Encouragement des Hommes et Femmes Jeune

"*A Collection of Verse for the Encouragement of Young Men and Women?*" Blake asked. "That's a mouthful for such a little booklet."

I shrugged, trying not to look surprised at his command of the French language. "Typical for the era."

He was quiet for a moment. "So why is it called the Persecution Pamphlet?"

"Long story," I said, waving away the question.

"No, really. I want to know."

Glancing at him, I could see he meant it, so I took a few moments to explain a little about the Huguenots' plight in seventeenth-century France, when Louis XIV was on the throne and he and his government were anxious to convert all the Huguenots to Catholicism.

"They sent out missionaries and offered financial incentives and things like that," I said, "but it wasn't enough to convert the masses. So as time went on, they got meaner about it and started imposing penalties and taking away certain rights and freedoms for those who refused to convert. When that didn't do it either, they instituted the dragoons."

"Dragoons. That sounds familiar. Weren't they military troops of some kind?"

"Yeah, but instead of fighting some foreign enemy, they were dispatched against their fellow citizens, the Huguenots within their own country. On orders from the king, the dragoons fanned out across France with the directive to make conversions happen, whatever it took. As you can imagine, the madness that ensued was horrible. They went way too far, ridiculing, tormenting, looting, torturing, raping, killing—you name it. They confiscated homes and businesses, burned down churches, all kinds of things. It was a terrible time of persecution, so bad that ultimately an estimated four hundred thousand Huguenots ended up fleeing the country. Some estimates put that number even higher."

"Wow. It couldn't have been good for France either, to lose so many productive citizens in such a short period of time."

"Oh, it was extremely damaging. The Huguenots were bankers, merchants, weavers, that sort of thing, with good job skills and educations. Some had titles of nobility. France may have confiscated many of their homes and money and businesses, but the skills and knowledge and work ethic the Huguenots took with them when they left were worth far more. Their departure created a serious brain drain."

"Where did they go?"

"Lots of places." I gestured toward one of the posters on the wall, which showed a map of their migration routes, with arrows leading to various other European countries as well as Africa and America.

He was studying it when Dr. Underwood interrupted to ask Blake if he would mind going up the ladder to adjust one of the directional lamps at the ceiling.

"Sure thing." He climbed up and began working with the lamp, twisting it in tiny increments until it was just right. As he started back down again, he asked me what happened to the denomination itself. "I mean, I see the word 'Huguenot' in this area all the time—on roads and historical markers and buildings and stuff. There's even Huguenot High School. But I've never seen any Huguenot churches. Is there still such a thing?"

"There's one in South Carolina, but that's about it as far as I know in this country, at least. Over the years most American Huguenots ended up assimilating into other reformed churches, other Protestant denominations—Episcopal, Methodist, Presbyterian, and the like."

He reached the ground and set the ladder aside. "So back to the original question, that's where the Persecution Pamphlet got its name? Because it was created to help Huguenots escape persecution?"

"That's what we always thought, but actually there's another reason. Did you notice the author?" I pointed to the object under the glass, reminding him that the word "Pére" was French for "Father."

Blake looked down and read off the name, which was printed below the title:

Pére S. Écoute

"This thing was written by a priest?" Blake asked.

"Supposedly. But look at it again. Really look at it. Do you see?"

Blake was quiet for a moment, and then he gasped. "Pere-S-Ecoute. *Persécuté*! The spelling is the same in English, minus a few accent marks. Persecute."

"Exactly."

Blake grinned. "So it's a play on words."

"Would you believe none of us noticed that except for Dr. Talbot?" Dr. Underwood interjected. "She spotted it during the authentication."

Blake looked my way, seeming impressed.

"Then again, she's also the one who discovered the 'mysterious markings,'" Dr. Underwood added, his voice dripping with sarcasm. I shot him a glance, but he was focused on adjusting the pamphlet inside the case.

"Markings?" Blake's eyes again went to the document under the glass.

I looked away, irritated. The Persecution Pamphlet contained several markings, tiny curved lines written in by hand near some of the letters. And though at first glance those lines looked random, as if caused by normal wear and tear, I'd always had a feeling they were intentional somehow, perhaps remnants of notes someone had jotted down as they were reading. The other members of the team had listened to my theory and studied the evidence, but when neither UV lighting nor Reflective Transformation Imaging had revealed anything, they dismissed the idea. In the end, I'd given up fighting them on it. Now even this man was trying to tease me about the matter, but I didn't find it funny.

Then again, I just might have the last laugh. Less than twenty-four hours ago, I'd thought of a way I might be able to prove those markings *were* intentional. It had come to me in the wee hours during my flight from Seattle to Richmond. I'd been thinking about the pamphlet and how I wished there was some way to uncover the truth once and for all. Then it struck me, a new method I could use to examine the markings, one based on the principle of interferometry. All I would need was a certain type of microscope and direct access to the pamphlet itself. And though I had no clue yet where I might get my hands on such specialized equipment, the document was mine to study at will—until Saturday, that is, after which it would be out of my hands.

Of course, I wasn't about to go into all of this now, not in front of Dr. Underwood. Instead, I simply answered Blake's question with a wave of my hand and a simple, "Long story. Hard to explain."

He nodded, watching me curiously, an intrigued glint in his eyes, a half smile on his lips.

And what nice lips they were, I thought suddenly, soft but firm, perfectly formed. Eminently kissable.

Startled by the very idea, I turned away, busying myself with smoothing a fabric panel. I was a scientist, for goodness' sake, not some googly-eyed teenager. What did it matter if he was good looking or not? We surely had nothing in common, not to mention we lived on opposite sides of the country. Gosh, for all I knew, he was married.

Was he married?

Feeling utterly foolish, I stole a glance at his left hand. No ring.

Not that it mattered.

Fortunately, I was saved from my ridiculous musings by Dr. Underwood, who was at last satisfied with the setup of the display. He showed me exactly how and where to place the pamphlet on Friday morning and then said I was free to return it to the safe until then. He was ready to go after that, so I saw him to the door.

As we went, I thought about casually asking if he knew where I might be able to procure an electron microscope with differential interference contrast, to use while I was in town. But I held my tongue, afraid he might figure out what I planned to use it for. If my theory turned out to be correct, of course I'd be sure to tell him all about it. But if I was wrong, I'd rather not advertise my intentions, especially not to someone from the original team who would gloat at having been proven right.

We reached the door, and after a quick thanks and a handshake, he was on his way. Retracing my steps across the entry hall, I thought about where I might be able to come up with the equipment I needed myself. I could always call around to some of the local universities, but even if they had such a microscope and were willing to let me use it, they would never allow me to do so away from the premises. They would likely offer me time on it there at the school, but the pamphlet had to be examined here at the house for security reasons.

I decided my best bet would be to go through the family company, Talbot Paper and Printing, which might have such a device available locally that I could borrow. Our Research and Development department, where I worked, was on the West Coast, and we were the ones with all the fancy scientific gadgets. But there was a chance one of the Richmond-area divisions, such as Quality Control, might have one too. I'd just have to make a few calls to find out.

For now I returned to the mudroom, where I found Blake leaning over the case, studying the pamphlet intently. He looked up when I entered, a strange excitement in his eyes.

"'It is only with the heart that one can see rightly,'" he said. "'What is essential is invisible to the eye.'"

"Excuse me?"

"That's the quote I was trying to remember from *The Little Prince*. I knew it would come to me."

I wasn't sure how to respond. My instinct was to scoff, not just because he was spouting quotes from a children's book as if it were fine literature, but also because the moment reminded me of every book nerd in high school who had tried to woo me by quoting some line from a poem.

But Blake wasn't trying to woo me, not by any means. He was just happy to have recalled a forgotten quote. As he returned his attention to the pamphlet, I decided that maybe for guys like him, ones far more physical than cerebral, a high-quality children's book *was* fine literature.

"So much history," he said softly, gazing down through the glass, "so much suffering, so much *bravery* preserved by this little document. It's a testament to a people who refused to give in to intimidation, even to the threat of death, in order to stay true to their faith. I have tremendous respect for that." He touched his fingers lightly to the glass. "It's one thing to look at this pamphlet with your eyes. It's another to understand its worth in your *heart*, just like *The Little Prince* says."

He seemed so sincere that I found myself repeating the words in my mind: *It is only with the heart that one can see rightly. What is essential is invisible to the eye.*

Okay, so maybe it wasn't so bad, as quotes go.

I was about to say as much when he stood up straight, shoved his hands in his pockets, and met my eyes. "I gotta tell you, Renee, it's an honor and a blessing to be the one in charge of protecting this thing."

I could tell he was sincere, and it struck me suddenly that he got it, the value of this pamphlet. Not just in a historical or monetary sense, but in a heart sense. Our eyes locked and held for a long moment, and though it probably shouldn't have mattered, it did. A lot.

"I guess as a man of faith myself," he added, "I can relate to their struggle."

A man of faith? My heart skipped a beat, pleased that my earlier suspicion had been confirmed.

With a smile, I gestured toward the pamphlet. "Guess we'd better get that thing back in the safe so you can get out of here."

"Sounds good."

I busied myself with pulling on the gloves while he unlatched the case.

"So what was that thing earlier, between you and Dr. Underwood?" he asked. "You sort of brushed it off, said it was a long story? Something about markings? Not to be nosy, of course."

I rolled my eyes, but not at him. "It's a sore spot. Dr. Underwood was trying to tease me, but I didn't think it was funny. Never have, never will."

Blake seemed intrigued, so I paused to explain, saying how there were some faint markings in the pamphlet, ones that everyone else said were random but that I thought were intentional and could be important somehow. "If I'm lucky, I just might be able to prove my theory very soon."

"How?"

Leaning forward, I carefully pulled the pamphlet from the display. "By viewing this thing through an electron microscope with DIC, that's how."

"DIC?"

"Differential Interference Contrast."

His brow furrowed as he held open the case and I slid the pamphlet inside.

"You didn't use magnification tools during the authentication?"

"Oh, we did." I took the case from him and clicked it shut. "But not at a microscopic level, and definitely not with the kind of depth that DIC can give."

"Why? What's so special about it?"

He seemed genuinely curious, so as we moved from the room and headed for the study I attempted an explanation that wouldn't be completely over his head. "Basically, DIC uses the principle of interferometry to reveal surface irregularities that are invisible under normal magnification." One glance at his perplexed expression and I took it down another notch. "Think 3D. With DIC, something that seems flat can actually be shown to have ridges and indentations because of optical density."

"Okay, that makes sense," he said. "Sort of. So do you have such a microscope at your disposal?"

I sighed. "Not here, but I'm going to check around and see if I can borrow one."

We reached my grandfather's office, and I locked the pamphlet inside the safe. Once that was done, there was no reason for Blake to stick around, though a part of me was reluctant to see him go. I walked him to the door, where he paused and gave me a look of concern.

"You know you only have access to the pamphlet for another two days, right?"

I smiled sheepishly. "Yeah, I know. But two days are better than none, right?"

Once he was gone, I returned to the study to make a few calls to people I knew personally at Talbot headquarters. In each case I got only voice mail, no actual humans, and I realized their workday must be over. Not wanting to leave my request in a message, I decided to try again in the morning.

Dinner wasn't for a while yet, so I used the time until then to unload the car and get unpacked. I didn't have all that much stuff, so it only took a single trip. Rolling my bag behind me, I moved around the garage, down the walkway beside the pool, and into the main door of the moderate-sized building.

Thanks to Nana's cleaning staff, the place was spotless, the scents of pine and lemon wafting my way as soon as I went through the door. Except for the fact that it faced toward the Dark Woods, I loved the guesthouse. It had a small kitchen, living room, bathroom, and three bedrooms, one of which was big enough to hold four beds. Known as the "Cousins' Room," that's where my three female first cousins— Danielle, Madeline, and Nicole—and I had stayed every year since we were little. Now that we were all in our twenties, it seemed kind of silly to keep sharing, but we wouldn't have it any other way.

Once I was unpacked, I thought about taking a nap but was so tired I feared I might sleep right through dinner. I ended up going for a nice long swim instead, which was the right call. By the time Nana and I finally sat down to eat, I felt totally refreshed, not to mention hungry. And the meal did not disappoint.

I'd always liked eating in the solarium, where the table was more appropriate for two instead of thirty. The room's three walls of windows also afforded the best view of the sunset, which started just as we'd finished the main course and were served coffee and a dessert of pears poached in honey and cinnamon. The scene our view afforded was truly lovely, the sky slowly fading from blue to orange to purple.

Nana and I lingered there until the show was over and it was completely dark. Then we moved to the living room, where I helped her work out the little five-minute speech she would be giving near the end of Saturday's ceremony. It took longer than expected, but by the time we were finished, we were both pleased with it.

She seemed so tired I insisted she go on to bed, saying I was just going to copy the speech over onto some note cards and then I'd be turning in too. We said our goodnights and she headed upstairs. Working in the quiet of the living room, I was almost finished when I got a text. To my surprise, I saw that it was from Blake.

You still up?

I smiled, typing a simple *Yes* in response.

Good. Got something for you. Okay if I swing by now and drop it off?

I hesitated, trying to imagine what this was about.

Sure. Text when you get here and I'll come outside.

Will do.

Five minutes later, I heard a soft knock at the door. Peering through the keyhole I saw that it was Blake.

"I told you to text when you got here," I scolded with a smile as I swung open the door. "My grandmother's asleep."

"Sorry. This thing's heavy, and I knew I'd need to carry it in anyway."

I realized he was holding a case about the size of a large microwave oven. Stepping aside, I invited him in and watched as he lugged it toward my grandfather's study.

"Probably best to put it in here," he said.

Only then did it dawn on me what he'd brought. My heart began to pound.

"That's not a microscope by any chance, is it?" I whispered, stepping into the office behind him and closing the door.

"A Newson 40XG with Phase Contrast and DIC. Your wish is my command."

I didn't ask where he had managed to come up with this thing out of the blue in such a short time. I was too busy removing it from its case, setting it up, adjusting the dials, and getting ready to take a 3D, microscopic-level look at the markings on the Persecution Pamphlet.

When the machine was all set, I slipped on the gloves, retrieved the pamphlet, and turned to the first marking. I smoothed the pages out carefully and then slid them into place under the lens. Fortunately, the flat area that held the slide, known as the stage, was wide enough to support the whole document safely.

Lowering myself to peer into the scope, I reached for the dials and worked in silence. It didn't take long to focus on the mark, and my heart began pounding in my chest as I peered down at what I saw.

Apparently, my theory was only partially correct. Yes, this first marking was part of something larger, something obviously intentional. But it had nothing to do with a note jotted beside the text, as I'd expected. It was instead the remnant of a *circle* around it—or, more specifically, around one letter. Though the rest of the circle's ink had faded away and only a fraction of it still showed to the naked eye, the entire *indentation* of the circle was still there, a clear sign of where quill or graphite had once been pressed down onto paper and dragged in a loop around one of the printed letters on the page.

I sat back and looked at Blake, my mind racing. Something about that sounded so familiar. A circle drawn around a letter...

"What is it?" he asked, trying to read my expression.

"Give me a minute," I replied. Thinking hard, I pulled out the pamphlet, turned to the next marking, and slid it back in again. Spent a few minutes scanning and focusing.

Same thing. This marking was also part of a circle that had been drawn in around a letter.

A circle around a letter...

I was still staring down at it when it came to me, and it was all I could do not to shout. Sitting up straight, I flashed Blake an exhilarated grin.

"What is it?" he repeated. "Can I see?"

"Help yourself," I said, rising and moving toward the bookshelves. "I have to find something."

As fast as I could, I ran my eyes along Granddad's collection, knowing his copy had to be here somewhere. It didn't take long to find it, thanks to his handy organizational system. It was in the section labeled "Ancestry," under *J* for *Journal of Catherine Gillet*, even though there was no spine to feature the title. It wasn't a book at all, in fact, but rather a stack of loose papers held together along one side with a pair of binder clips.

"Got it." I pulled the packet of pages from the shelf and started back toward the desk. "Can you slide that out of the way for minute?"

Blake was still peering into the microscope, but he quickly stood and did as I asked, carefully pushing the device over to one side of the desk.

"Thanks."

"I'm not sure what has you so excited," he said as he returned to his seat, "but it looks to me as if the marking is part of a circle around a letter. Is that significant?"

"More than you can imagine." I placed the packet of pages on the desk and settled into my chair. After removing the clips, I flipped through the stack and separated it into its two components—one written by hand, all in French, and the other printed out from a computer, in English.

I slid the stack of handwritten pages over to Blake as I explained. "That's a copy of a journal that was written by one of my ancestors back in the sixteen hundreds, a woman named Catherine Gillet. Dr. Underwood secured a copy of it four years ago when he was doing research for the authentication. The original is in a museum in Europe."

"Cool." Blake peeked at the pages as I continued.

"The journal entries start when she's a little girl and end when she's eighteen. They're sporadic—some years have only one or two entries, while the last few months have a whole bunch—but either way they make for a fascinating read."

"I can imagine."

"Anyway, the Persecution Pamphlet was created in the family print shop, and Catherine mentions it in the journal. Which made it a great supporting document for the authentication."

"I can imagine."

"Of course, she wrote by hand in seventeenth-century French, so Dr. Underwood had to have it translated first." Holding up the stack of pages, I added, "That's what this is. The translation of that."

"Okay," Blake said, setting down his own stack and looking to mine. "So where it talks about the pamphlet, does it say something about a circle written around a letter?"

"No such luck. But, well, you'll see..." My voice trailed off as I skimmed the first few journal entries. It didn't take long to find the one I was looking for.

"'Twelve October, 1676,'" I read aloud, and then I paused to do the math. "Depending on what month she was born, Catherine would've been about nine here. Oh, and she refers to a guy named Jules. That's her brother, who was a lot older." I held up the page. "Anyway, here goes. 'Jules came up with a new exercise today, one that's supposed to help with my reading and counting, only it's more like a game. It involves a secret code that he invented just for me. The way it works is that he hides a message within some discarded piece of printed matter from the shop, and then he gives it to me and I have to follow his counting rules to figure out what the message says. I found it quite fun and hope he does it again soon.'"

"Help with reading and counting skills?" Blake asked as I paused in my reading to find the next relevant entry. "That seems unusual for the era, considering she was a girl."

I shook my head, explaining that Huguenots had been big on education back then, even for women. Continuing my search, I found what I wanted, a paragraph written when she was about ten.

"'This one is from the following year. 'Got in trouble for running in church yesterday with some of my friends. We were playing around before the service and forgot ourselves—until we were reprimanded and forced to sit separately for the entire thing. That was bad enough, but today I got a secret message from Jules, and as it turned out, all he did was reiterate the scolding. So much work searching for circled letters and counting them off—'"

"Wait, what?"

I grinned at Blake, whose eyes were wide. I repeated that last part slowly. "'*So much work searching for circled letters and counting them off,* only to reveal in the end these words: *Young ladies walk, never run, especially at church.* That wasn't fair of him and no fun at all. I won't complain though, lest he stop playing the game. Except for this particular message, I still enjoy it very much, and I do believe it continues to provide good practice for my counting, handwriting, reading, and spelling.'"

"Renee, this is incredible. I think you're really onto something here."

Still smiling, I skimmed a few pages until I found the next entry, from when Catherine was twelve. "'This is about two years later. 'To my surprise, Jules gave me a coded message today, something he hasn't done in quite a while. It was hidden inside a booklet about cookery that was recently printed at the shop, and at first I thought he'd simply given me a copy of it for myself, as I have been working a lot lately on my household skills. But then I flipped through and spotted the telltale circled letters. Though I no longer need the decoding game as practice for my studies, I enjoyed it all the same. His message was an important one: *Our trip to the Plateau will be taxing on the animals. Do not forget that your horse is your responsibility. Keep an eye on her gait, which may alter if she is injured, and check her periodically for rubs, sores, swollen areas, and debris in her hooves. The sooner observed, the sooner attended.* It was a good reminder and managed to increase my excitement tenfold. We are leaving in less than a week, and I simply cannot wait.'"

When I finished reading, I set down the pages and looked at him. "If I recall correctly, that's the last mention of the code in the journal. But I think it's enough." Leaning forward, I worked through my theory, counting off each point on my fingers. "One, Jules gave Catherine secret messages by circling letters inside materials printed at his shop. Two, the Persecution Pamphlet has at least two circled letters inside it. Three, it was printed at his shop. *Voilà.* It seems obvious to me that Catherine's brother Jules must have given her a coded message in the Persecution Pamphlet via circled letters. Given the evidence, I think that's a fair and logical conclusion."

"Totally feasible," Blake agreed, nodding emphatically.

Setting the translation aside, I pulled over the microscope and again peered into the lens. If I was right, there would be other circles around other letters in the same pages, circles that had disappeared from normal view but would be visible under this microscope.

Blake grew quiet as I slowly shifted the pamphlet and searched for the same sort of indentations. Given the level of magnification, the process was slow and tedious, but if I found what I was looking for, it would be more than worth the trouble.

"One question," he said finally, breaking the silence. "I thought the Persecution Pamphlet was created in 1685."

"It was."

"But Catherine would've been eighteen by then. If the code was something from when she was a child, why would it show up in a pamphlet that didn't even exist until she was an adult?"

My eyes still on the lens, I thought about that for a moment. "Maybe the code was something they continued to share once in a while. As she said in that last entry, he did it even when she no longer needed it as practice for her studies. I'm thinking he probably gave her some message when she was grown, using the code from when they were younger."

Blake grunted in agreement. "Mind if I take a look at the translation?"

"Be my guest."

He picked it up and began slowly flipping through as I continued to scan for circles, micrometer by micrometer.

"I'm curious," he said. "I know you're really smart and all, but how could you possibly have remembered a few obscure references from a journal you read four years ago?"

I smiled at the compliment. "I've read it several times since then. I have my own copy at home. I love that journal. Catherine was my eleven-greats grandmother, you know. But even if she wasn't, I'd still find her story fascinating. Totally inspiring. You're welcome to borrow it. You should give it a read yourself."

I glanced his way, but his eyes were on the pages in front of him.

"Does she say anything in here about how the Huguenots were persecuted for their faith?"

"Yes, lots." I returned my attention to the lens. "The entries from the spring of 1685, when persecution was on the rise, are especially compelling. She was only eighteen then, but within the span of several months, it's like she went from an innocent and somewhat pampered girl of means to a wise and proactive woman. She was very brave. Far braver than I would have been in her shoes."

Blake began reading one of the passages aloud, but he lost me after the first few words. That's because at the other end of the lens I'd finally come across what I'd been looking for: another indentation surrounding one of the letters.

I gasped.

"What?"

"Another circle," I whispered. "That helps confirm it." I sat back, shaking my head in wonder. "Do you realize if we could find all the circled letters in this pamphlet, we could probably figure out Jules's code and read the secret message for ourselves?"

I met Blake's eyes and we shared a grin.

"Of course," I added, "finding all the circles wouldn't exactly be easy. We're talking about going through eight pages under the lens, one micrometer at a time. That's crazy. Super tedious and time-consuming."

"So worth it though, in the end."

I thought for a moment, going through the next few days in my mind. With so much already on my plate, I wouldn't have a lot of time, but I might be able to work on it in the evenings after everyone was in bed.

"When does the microscope have to go back?"

Blake checked his watch. "In about half an hour."

My eyes widened. "Seriously?"

He nodded. "I borrowed it from a buddy who works over at VCU Medical Center, but I have to return it before the end of his shift."

"Aw, man. I was assuming we had it for a few days. Can you borrow it again tomorrow night?"

"Highly doubt it. I had to call in a lot of favors just to get it this time."

"Okay. Let me think."

Looking at the sophisticated piece of machinery, I considered the situation and decided it was just as well. With so much else going on around here, there wouldn't have been enough time to get this done anyway.

"That's okay," I said. "I think I'll have to delegate. I'll call Dr. Underwood in the morning and tell him what we found. He should be able to help me figure it out from there."

Rising from my chair, I carefully removed the pamphlet from the stage and returned it to the safe. Blake attended to the microscope.

As he loaded it back into its carrying case, I thanked him profusely for what he'd done.

"Are you kidding me? This was fun," he said, pausing to meet my gaze.

"It was fun, wasn't it?" I replied, struck anew by the sparkle of his green-gold eyes. "And just think. If I hadn't been so stubborn about the markings, and you weren't so resourceful and helpful, those circles—that secret message, whatever it turns out to be—would've gone undiscovered forever."

Chapter Four
Catherine

Lyon, France
19 April 1685

athédrale Saint-Jean-Baptiste de Lyon was the last place Catherine Gillet should have been trying to go to on the Thursday of Holy Week—or any day, for that matter. Yet despite the risks she simply could not stay away.

With a tug at the black mourning veil covering her face, she stepped through the wide front center doors of the massive church, paused long enough for her eyes to adjust to the shadowy interior, and then angled toward the nearest row of chairs. After quickly slipping onto a seat, she took in a deep breath and forced herself to look toward the front of the sanctuary, to the sight of the coffin.

She could not believe her Uncle Edouard was gone. Yes, he had made some terrible choices in the past eight months, ones that had left him estranged from much of the family. But prior to that he had been a big part of their lives, and Catherine missed him. Now she was here to mourn his passing, whether that was against the rules or not.

She missed his daughter, Amelie, even more. Scanning the small crowd gathered near the nave, Catherine search for the beloved cousin she had not seen or spoken with since last summer. Sadly, it did not look as if she were present. Thus far, except for the monks seated together behind the coffin, the only people here were old, unlike Amelie, who was just nineteen.

Blowing out a breath, Catherine told herself to relax, that surely her cousin would arrive soon. The convent where Amelie had been sequestered was nearly prison-like in its protectiveness, but the powers that be had to let a young woman attend her father's funeral. To do otherwise would be unspeakably cruel.

Then again, Amelie's entire internment there had been cruel, the misguided act of a man who had convinced himself his decisions—to convert from his Huguenot faith, to send his daughter off to be cloistered following the death of her husband, to essentially cut off himself and Amelie from the entire family—was in all their best interests. Now he was gone, and here Catherine sat on this chilly April afternoon, waiting for his funeral service to begin.

Her brother, Jules, would be furious if he knew she was here, as would plenty of others on both sides. Huguenots were forbidden to attend Catholic services, but Catherine had never been one to follow rules if she believed them to be foolish. She deserved the right to observe her beloved uncle's passing, not to mention that she would not have missed this chance to see Amelie for all the world, not even under threat of capture and punishment.

And, really, what difference did it make? Life for Huguenots throughout France had been getting so much worse. The threat of persecution hung over her head almost constantly these days regardless of where she went or what she did.

Catherine's thoughts were interrupted by a strong scent tickling her nose. Turning, she saw two boys making their way down the aisle, waving incense. Behind them came Father Philippe, a friend of her brother's and the first person she had spotted here who would be able to recognize her. She turned her head away and tugged again at her veil, hoping it sufficiently obscured her features.

From the corner of her eye, she saw Father Philippe continue up the aisle without hesitation, his stocky form moving slowly behind the altar boys and their swinging orbs of incense. Either the priest had not spotted her or he was acting as if he had not. If the latter, she knew it would not be the first time he had turned a blind eye toward something he did not personally consider an infraction. Among her family at least, he was known to be sympathetic to the Huguenots' plight.

As Protestants, the Huguenots viewed the Christian life as simple belief in God centered around His sovereignty in salvation and all things. And though they avoided any semblance of ritual and pageantry, Catherine had always secretly enjoyed the beauty of the Catholic churches, which were so elaborately adorned.

For as long as she could remember, she had been curious about the inside of this striking cathedral and had peeked through the door several times over the years. But she had certainly never sat down and allowed herself to absorb it all, never attended an actual service. Her father would not have allowed it. Despite the fact that this was where King Henri IV, hero of the Huguenots because he believed everyone had the right to worship as they pleased, had gotten married eighty-five years before, Papa always maintained his conviction that this church was full of idolatry, that there was no hope inside, that God had no part in it.

Catherine disagreed, though she would never say as much aloud. Here she felt a rush of emotion along with an underlying sense of peace. *God's* peace. As a Huguenot, she may have disagreed with various tenants of the Catholic religion, but her sense of the Lord's presence told her that it was not up to her father or anyone else to determine which places God did and did not sanction.

She was also moved by the beauty of the statues. As the monks began to chant, she focused on an icon of the Madonna to the right of the altar. When she was a child, she had thought the statues of Mary were in honor of her own mother, who died when Catherine was just four years old. Her only memory of Maman was when she was ill, a shawl wrapped around her head and draping down over her frail body as she sat up to comfort her little girl. When Catherine first saw a figure of a Madonna soon after, she recognized not just the shawl but also her mother's pale, luminescent skin and sorrowful yet peaceful expression.

Catherine's gaze continued on to the astronomical clock, which stood as tall as three men behind Father Philippe. She loved the way the clock's hands moved, tick-by-tick, a reliable given in their rapidly changing world. She had heard once that the clock was built in the fourteenth century, long before her ancestors had broken off from the Catholic faith to become Protestants.

And though she dearly loved her own house of worship, the Temple de Lyon, it had been built in the simple, unadorned style of the Huguenots. There, no giant clock ticked along with their prayers. No blessed mother graced their worship.

Catherine returned her gaze to the Madonna up front, but the sight of the casket interrupted her thoughts. She could not believe Uncle Edouard was dead. Her own father had passed three years ago, when she was just fifteen, after which her only uncle had become a surrogate father of sorts, as loving to her as he had been to his own child—until, that is, he chose to convert and send Amelie away to a convent five miles out of town. Catherine felt sure his actions had come not from personal conviction but rather to protect his daughter's life in the wake of her husband's death as a martyr. Catherine suspected Uncle Edouard had also done it to save the family's printing business from the increasingly harsh, anti-Huguenot laws of the king.

"Convert or lose everything" was the refrain echoing across France, and many, her uncle included, chose to do exactly that. Uncle Edouard continued to work in the family business after the conversion, but otherwise, out of necessity, he had pretty much been cast from their lives. Jules had forbidden Catherine from having any contact with the man at all. She had not even been allowed to visit the family print shop or warehouse on the chance she might run into him there. And that was such a pity. Maybe if she had been allowed to speak with him when he was still alive, they could have found a way to make their peace. Perhaps she might even have convinced him to bring Amelie back home.

Thinking once more of her cousin, Catherine took another look around at the growing crowd of attendees and had to admit that Amelie still was not among them. She did recognize someone else, however, and the sight caused her to gasp. Her grandmother was there, sitting in a pew near the front, dressed all in black. And though her face was also obscured by a veil, Catherine knew without a doubt that it was she.

Grand-Mère's stately demeanor, elegant posture, and finely tailored clothing easily gave her away. How heartbreaking this must be for her, Catherine thought, to bury her last child.

Uncle Edouard's death had come as a shock to all of them, but especially to dear Grand-Mère. Uncle Edouard had stayed late at the print shop, alone, three nights before, and Jules had found him dead the next morning. The physician said his heart had failed.

Catherine dabbed at her eyes and focused on Father Philippe, who was now speaking in Latin from the marble pulpit. Thanks to her years of study in the language, she understood what he was saying, how Edouard's death was not the end, but that for the Lord's faithful, death meant life.

"This is the communion of saints," he continued, still in Latin, "that we profess our faith in the Apostles' Creed. We believe in the Holy Ghost, the holy catholic church, the communion of saints, the forgiveness of sins, the resurrection of the body, and life everlasting."

"Amen," Catherine whispered. She believed in the catholic—universal—church too. She just wished it did not involve so much conflict.

After several readings and more prayer, Father Philippe spoke specifically of Uncle Edouard, saying he had been a good man, a good father, and a good son. He did not mention Edouard's wife, who had died from consumption, the same illness that took Catherine's mother near the same time, fourteen years ago. The two had been sisters, coming when they were girls to Lyon from the Plateau Vivarais-Lignon in the mountains southwest of the city. The two sisters married the Gillet brothers, Edouard and Thomas, making Amelie and Catherine double cousins. They had been as close as sisters their entire lives until they were forced to part. Now that Uncle Edouard was gone, surely they would be reunited soon, whether Amelie had been allowed to come here today or not.

After the eulogy was communion, and then the service would be done. As parishioners rose to partake in the sacrament, Catherine glanced toward the doors behind her and wondered if she should slip out now. Even if Father Philippe had chosen to look the other way about her presence here, she did not want to force his hand. Besides, Grand-Mère would be startled to see her, so perhaps it would be best to connect elsewhere, away from prying eyes.

Catherine rose and moved quietly toward the narthex. She was not sorry she had come, for it had been important to her to have this final farewell. Now she needed to find out about the absence of her cousin, which had been both shocking and deeply disappointing. This was not the end of things with regard to Amelie, not in the least. In fact, now that Uncle Edouard no longer stood in the way, it was time to bring his daughter back home for good.

Catherine made her way through the dim light, opened the door, and slipped outside without too much noise. After softly closing it behind her, she turned to go—and stopped short, startled to see Pierre Talbot standing in the shade of a nearby tree, looking as if he had been waiting for her to emerge. Her heart stirred at the sight of him—at his broad shoulders, handsome face, and dark, wavy hair—even as she braced herself for the reprimand to come. Swallowing hard, she moved toward her betrothed, not lifting her veil until she was right in front of him.

"I thought I would find you here," he said, pulling off his hat as he stood up straight and locked his deep blue eyes on hers.

Rather than being upset, his expression held only compassion. She sighed in relief.

"Are you all right?" He reached out to brush his fingertips across the back of her hand.

Somehow, the kindness of his concern was nearly her undoing. She had remained stoic for the most part when she was inside the church, alone, but now that she was out here and face-to-face with someone who cared about her, it was all she could do not to sob aloud.

The man she had known and loved for years was now gazing down at her with such tenderness that she felt as if her heart might break. Turning away, she closed her eyes and took in a breath, a few tears slipping through as she managed to gain control.

He squeezed her hand and pulled her close until they were almost touching but not quite. Pierre was a gentleman, after all.

"I am so sorry." His voice was deep and steady. "At least you were able to see Amelie, *oui?*"

Catherine shook her head as the tears started to flow. He brushed his free hand against her face and then looked past her, toward the cathedral, and pulled it back.

"People are starting to stare. We can talk later."

She pulled her veil down again. "Yes. And you should be getting back to work anyway, I imagine."

"*Oui.*" He squeezed her hand again. "I'll see you soon."

She watched as he hurried back toward rue Saint Jean. She had thought since she was a child that she might marry him some day, but it was not until about two years ago that she *knew* she would, and that he desired the same in return. If not for all the upheaval and conflict and persecution of the Huguenots, they would have married by now. She hoped their day would come soon.

When Pierre disappeared around the curve in the narrow street, she turned her attention to the cathedral doors just as her grandmother emerged. Catherine managed to catch the woman's eye, and then she stepped back into the shadows to wait for grandmother to join her.

"What are you doing here?" Grand-Mère drew close, grasping Catherine's wrist.

"The same as you." She gave a nod toward the door of the cathedral. "I left a few minutes early, to be safe."

"I see." The older woman's lips pursed in displeasure, but she held her tongue, apparently seeing the hypocrisy in reprimanding her granddaughter for doing the very thing she had done herself.

"Amelie did not come," Catherine said.

Grand-Mère looked equally disappointed. "I thought for sure she would."

A horse plodded through the square, towing a wagon. The driver stopped it at the door of the church as six men carried out the casket.

Catherine pulled her grandmother close. Her uncle would be the first in three generations of the family not to be buried in the simple Protestant graveyard outside of town. "Are you going to the cemetery?"

Grand-Mère lifted her veil, revealing her silver hair, and peered intently at her son's casket. "There is no reason. He is gone."

Catherine nodded. "Which is why Amelie no longer has to stay in the convent."

"Shh." Her grandmother led Catherine to the side of the cathedral, back toward the garden. Once they were alone, Grand-Mère said, "Do not speak of it now. You do not know who may be listening."

"But how could they not let her out for her own father's funeral? That is unconscionable."

"*Oui*. I agree."

"Someone needs to go and get her, as soon as possible. And then we need to come up with a plan of escape. Obviously Jules is not capable of making a decision."

"Stop," Grand-Mère whispered. "It's not just us he is concerned about. Others would suffer too." Her expression was fierce for a moment before softening again. "We can talk back at the house. You will come home with me."

Catherine hesitated, for she had a different destination in mind. "I told Cook I would get bread."

"Then we will stop at the *boulangerie* on the way."

"*Non*," Catherine said. "I need the fresh air. We'll speak later."

Grand-Mère frowned. "What about the dragoons?"

Catherine reached up and pulled the veil back down over her face. "I'll be fine, see? The dragoons will think I am a good Catholic girl on her way home from mass and leave me alone."

The dragoons had recently grown in number in Lyon, under order of *le Roi Soleil*—Louis XIV—and though they were said to be converting Protestants back to Catholicism, they were, in fact, either by personal choice or a covert order, doing far more than that. Often obnoxious and cruel, they sometimes seemed no better than animals as they intimidated, tormented, and even outright tortured the Huguenots they encountered.

Catherine could not imagine how such behavior was allowed, much less sanctioned, by the king. There were those who claimed Louis's motives were pure, that he loved his subjects so much he wanted

them to share his faith. Others thought perhaps he just wanted everyone and everything to revolve around him, that because he was Catholic, everyone under his domain should be Catholic as well. Or maybe,
as Jules believed, his actions were solely about economics. With loans
from the Vatican came pressure to convert the Huguenots. And Louis
needed those loans to support his extravagant lifestyle, including his
expansion and remodel of the palace of Versailles.

Whatever the reason, the Sun King's handling of the situation had
become more and more unreasonable, wreaking havoc on Catherine's
friends and family. It was too late for Uncle Edouard, but it was time
to bring Amelie home. Then as soon as she was back with them, they
all could finally leave the country together and go somewhere new,
someplace where they would no longer be at risk of persecution simply because of their faith.

After helping her grandmother into the family carriage with the
assistance of their coachman, Monsieur Roen, Catherine hurried down
rue Saint Jean and into a *traboule*, one of Lyon's numerous interior
pedestrian passageways. Built for foot traffic only, the *traboules* were
paved in stone and mostly narrow, except where they opened up to
reveal sunny courtyards here and there along the way.

First created by silk weavers as a means for transporting fabric to
the river quickly and safely even in inclement weather, the corridors
bisected buildings across Lyon, allowing pedestrians to move directly
through the middle of long city blocks despite the structures that
would otherwise stand in the way. For Catherine, the *traboules* were not
just quicker but also offered a more discreet method for getting where
she needed to be. And though they were not guaranteed to be dragoon-
free, they still offered a better option than openly roaming the streets.

Catherine squinted in the dim light as she moved along through
the passageway. Just as her eyes had begun to adapt, she found herself
emerging into the brightness of an open courtyard. As she did, she
glanced off to the side and noticed a pair of young women, chatting

and giggling together. Moving back into the *traboule* and continuing onward, she thought of her beloved cousin and how the two of them used to be that way.

All through her childhood, Catherine had been closer to Amelie than to anyone else in the world. Both had the chestnut-colored hair, brown eyes, and grace of their mothers, although Amelie was a year older than Catherine and far more poised. The two girls had shared the same tutor, learning Latin and English, studying geography, their catechism, and the Scriptures together.

Thankfully, many in their faith valued educating women, claiming passages such as the one from Galatians that said there was "neither male nor female," that all were one in Christ Jesus. Even Jules agreed, regularly bringing home paper and ink from the shop and encouraging Catherine to practice her writing. "And your thinking," he often added.

Catherine and Amelie's education included more than books. Grand-Mère had taught them needlepoint, how to manage a household budget, and how to supervise the maids. The family owned farmland west of town, and that was where Monsieur Roen had taught them horseback riding, something Catherine deeply enjoyed. Under the protective eye of whichever male family member or friend or servant was willing to come along, the two cousins had roamed the hills near Lyon via horseback throughout their childhood. Learning, creating, and exploring had been a golden time for both girls. Amelie was cousin, sister, mentor, confidante, and best friend to Catherine.

If only they had known what a short time it would last.

The beginning of the end came the year Catherine turned sixteen. That was when Amelie met Paul Fournier, a handsome young Huguenot pastor who soon became the primary escort for their rides in the countryside. He and Amelie fell in love and were married as soon as Uncle Edouard allowed. Sadly, Paul died less than a year later, leaving his wife a widow at just eighteen. The tragedy changed all their lives.

Paul had been killed by some of the first dragoons in Lyon. He made the mistake of standing up to them when they threatened his small congregation on the southern end of town. The drunken dragoons beat him to death and then threw his body into the Rhône, threatening to do the same to Amelie. Reprimanded by their captain, the dragoons were ordered not to harm any more citizens—at least for the time being.

But Uncle Edouard, afraid of losing both the business and his only child, had responded almost immediately by converting to Catholicism and sending Amelie away to a convent. In one fell swoop, their whole family had lost so much. Catherine's own losses included her friend and in-law Paul, the companionship of her best friend and cousin Amelie, and the esteem she had always held for her uncle. She had also lost all sense of safety and security, stepping fully into adulthood with the knowledge that no amount of money or land or title could protect her or her loved ones from the king's cruel intentions.

A fresh sadness settling in her heart, Catherine reached the end of the final *traboule* and pushed open the door, stepping out of the dim light into the sunshine on the quai Romain. Adjusting her veil, she hurried north along the river wall to the stone bridge, where the reflections of the buildings on the other side shimmered in the water. The print shop was across the Saône, along the bend where the river turned for the last time before flowing into the Rhône.

Boats traveled the Saône and the Rhône, floating down the larger river all the way to the Mediterranean Sea. Lyon had long been a transportation hub, first established by the Gauls, then developed by the Romans, and now used by all of Europe.

The bells of the cathedral began to toll as she crossed the bridge. Feeling far too exposed, she increased the speed of her steps until she reached the other side, where she paused to take a look down quai Saint Antoine—just in time to see a roving band of dragoons coming straight toward her on their horses.

CHAPTER FIVE
Catherine

With a gasp, Catherine stepped back out of sight. Even though she appeared to be a grieving Catholic girl, she still did not want to be noticed or questioned by dragoons. She ducked over to the far side of the stone wall that ran along the river and continued on toward her family's warehouse. Though she would have to leave the protection of the wall soon, she would go as far as she could before taking that chance.

When she finally reached rue de Constantine, she glanced up the street again. Four dragoons sat astride their horses in the intersection. One spotted her. He alerted the others. She jumped down from the wall and into the grass, landing hard on her thin slippers, and then darted down the bank under the wooden bridge. Above, the thunder of hooves caused her to freeze.

What the dragoons would do if they caught her entirely depended on their mood. They might just humiliate her. Or scare her. Or beat her. Or drag her into a dark alley. All had happened to Huguenot women she knew, although the specifics of the horrors they had endured were not discussed.

She waited until the racket passed before climbing back up the stones, lifting herself up to the wall, and then jumping down the other side. She scraped her arm as she did and landed hard again on the street. She quickly shook out her skirts and then ran the rest of the way, her slippers pounding against the cobblestones.

Across the river, one of the dragoons pointed and shouted at her. Running faster, she darted up the next street and then turned to the left, racing toward the warehouse. Breathless, she pushed against the side door. It did not budge. She ran up the street to the shop and turned left again. The hooves of horses thundered behind her.

She rushed toward the main door, the beat of the horses' hooves nearly upon her. They would not dare pursue her into the building. There would be witnesses to be dealt with. Men who would protest the dragoons' treatment of her. A captain to be sought out and beseeched to reprimand his soldiers.

With a last burst of speed, she made it to the door and flung it open. She fell into the office and then slammed the door shut behind her, pushing the heavy bolt into place. Gulping for air, she pressed her forehead against the wooden slats "*Merci, Seigneur,*" she managed to say between gasps. She tore the veil from her face and wadded it in her fist around the comb that had held it in place.

The dragoons stopped outside. Her heart began to race even faster. Perhaps she had thanked the Lord too soon. She held her breath, terrified they would break down the door. But they must have decided against it, for after a long moment she heard the sound of their horses' hooves slowly fade away,

Catherine finally exhaled.

"Stupid, stupid, stupid!"

She turned to find her brother, wearing an ink-stained apron around his thin frame, standing in the archway to the shop. "*Seigneur, aie pitié.*"

Lord, have mercy was right. And may her brother show mercy too.

Behind him stood two men she did not recognize, one older and one younger, so similar in appearance they were surely father and son.

"*Pardonnez-moi,*" she said, discreetly slipping the veil and comb into her purse. To Jules she added, "I've come to speak with you."

"I'm busy."

"It's fine," the father said. "We need to be on our way while we still can."

The son added, "We'll consider your offer and—"

"*Chut*," Jules snapped, cutting him off. "Don't discuss business matters in front of my sister."

"Ah, your sister." The son stepped toward Catherine. "Mademoiselle Gillet. I'm so pleased to meet you." He kissed her hand. "I am Monsieur Audet."

"*Bonjour*, Monsieur." Catherine bowed.

"We're from Le Chambon-sur-Lignon," he added. "It's just a small village on the river, a good two days' ride from here, but I believe your family has a connection with the place?"

"Of course," she replied, her polite smile growing more genuine. "Our mother and aunt, God rest their souls, both grew up there." Not wanting to seem a braggart, she did not add that Jules owned property in Le Chambon, inherited from their mother's father, or that Catherine had once visited the region herself. Then again, they may have known that already as well.

"So you are the makers of the paper that comes from the Plateau?" she asked.

They both nodded.

"*Merveilleux.* Yours is my favorite of all the paper used here. The quality is outstanding." She hoped they knew she was being sincere and not merely polite. Though most of the print shop's supplies came from Grenoble, she much preferred the paper from Le Chambon when she could get it.

Smiling, they accepted her praise even as Jules began wrapping things up. They said their farewells, and then he escorted them out through the warehouse.

"We'll look for the shipment in a few days," she heard him say as they went. "And I'll send an answer with the rag peddler by the end of next week."

Wondering what her brother was up to, she stepped through the archway between the office and the shop and paused there, taking it all in. The printers mostly ignored her as they worked, except for Monsieur Talbot and Eriq—Pierre's father and brother—both of whom waved from the far corner. She smiled and waved in return.

The business was co-owned by the Gillet and Talbot families and consisted of the print shop in front and a warehouse behind. She'd missed the place so much since being banished. The hive-like busyness that went on nonstop. The smell of the ink. The hum of the press as the wooden arms moved up and down. The blocks of letters. She cherished everything that had to do with this place—the ink, the writing, the letter setting, the reading. The leftover paper.

That thought reminded her they were running low on paper at home. She would need to take some with her today.

Catherine had been writing on those leftover pieces for as long as she could remember. Notes to herself. Narratives about her day. Her feelings. She'd held onto many such pages over the years, collecting them into a journal of sorts, which she stored in a bottom drawer of her grandmother's writing desk.

These days, she also wrote letters. Lots of letters. As Grand-Mère's eyes grew weaker, Catherine managed all of her correspondence.

While Catherine waited for her brother to come back so they could talk, she turned her attention to stacks of printed pages lined up along the wall to her left, ready to be taken to the warehouse. First was a pile of Protestant Scriptures, printed in folios and needing to be folded. Next were bank notes. Then a stack of Catholic homilies.

She stepped closer, reading the invoice and seeing that Father Philippe's name was on it. Other Huguenots may have refused to print for Catholics, but Jules was a pragmatist. He always had been.

The last pile was also for Catholics it seemed, a stack of thin pamphlets written by a priest, though Catherine did not recognize the man's name, Écoute. She picked one up and flipped through it, stopping at a poem about a horse, one that dreamed of "galloping in the noble meadows by moonlight" before coming to rest "in a grand place that fits like a glove." How odd. She put the pamphlet back. The printing was nicely done, as usual, but the poetry was abysmal, as were the drawings.

"Catherine." Jules had returned and was now standing in the middle of the print shop facing her, his arms crossed and eyes blazing. "Go to the office and wait for me there."

She obeyed, slinking back the way she had come.

Moving into the relative quiet of the print shop's office, her eyes went to an unusual sight atop her brother's cluttered desk: a blueprint, held flat at its corners by a bottle of ink, a jar of feathers, and two iron paperweights. She took a closer look, tilting her head as she tried to orient herself to the diagram. It was of the warehouse. Perhaps Jules planned to make modifications? Eight years ago, when the business acquired the vacant land next door, he had drawn up the design for the large structure himself despite being just seventeen at the time. That may have been a surprising feat for others his age, but not for Jules Gillet, who had been a prodigy in both math and science his whole life. Fortunately, the design that seemed good on paper turned out to be excellent once built, a useful addition to their printing business.

His intelligence extended to entrepreneurial matters as well. Not only did he manage the print shop, but about a year ago he had purchased a promising rag collection company, and now he had his own troop of rag peddlers out buying old cloth from both city dwellers and peasants, which he then sold to paper mill owners throughout the region. As the demand for paper increased, it took more and more old rags, the main ingredient, to satisfy the growing need.

Now he was interested in acquiring a paper mill? Truly, his mind and interests never stopped. Ordinarily, Catherine would have appreciated such initiative, but this was a time when they should have been liquidating their holdings, not acquiring more. She did not understand his thinking at all. Unless...

She gasped. That couldn't be it. Surely Jules was not planning for them to relocate to the Plateau. Her mind reeled. She'd heard rumors about Huguenots seeking refuge in the elevated region known as the Massif Central, where stoic farmers minded their own business and dragoons had not yet penetrated.

She couldn't imagine a more miserable existence, not to mention the area couldn't remain safe for Huguenots forever. No, only one choice remained for them, to leave the country entirely. In the end, anything less would surely condemn them to prison or death.

Catherine's mind was churning when Jules joined her in the office at last. As he came through the doorway, she eyed him suspiciously.

"Why are you buying a paper mill, especially one so far away?"

"That is not your concern."

"But if you're determined to branch into yet another business, why bother to buy theirs? Why not just build a new paper mill here in Lyon?"

He hesitated before answering. "The chemistry in the rivers is wrong. Too much calcite."

"But Le Chambon? It's so far away."

Jules shook his head. "As I said, this isn't your concern."

"My concern," she replied, her tone verging on disrespect, "is that you are taking on new businesses when you should be doing the exact opposite. You know it's true."

"Catherine—"

"My concern," she repeated, even more angrily this time, "is that you plan to move us to the Plateau to live. Please, Jules, tell me it isn't so."

His eyes flashed. "I will not discuss this now," he hissed, his jaw tight as he glanced toward the print shop.

Catherine lowered her voice. "The walls don't have ears, Jules. Surely you can trust everyone here."

Whether that was true or not, she could tell by the glare he gave her that she had pushed things as far as she could. Better to calm down and focus on why she'd come in the first place, in order to discuss the retrieval of their cousin from the convent. The Plateau they could talk about later, in the privacy of their home.

Jules sighed and gestured toward the exit. "You should be going. You know you're not supposed to be here."

"But that was because of Uncle Edouard. Now that he's gone, your rule about my staying away no longer applies, *oui*?" She hoped the mention of the man's name might soften Jules's heart toward Edouard's now-fatherless daughter, Amelie.

"What do you want, Catherine?" Jules asked wearily.

She exhaled slowly, gathering her thoughts. "I need your help."

Jules shook his head.

"I have not even asked you yet—"

"Whatever it is, it's not a good idea."

Catherine met her brother's dark eyes and saw a rigidity there, one that told her she no longer held sway over anything he may or may not do. Thanks to the seven-year difference in their ages, the two of them had never been very close, though they had gotten along well enough when she was younger. He had even seemed to value her opinion at times. But since their father died—thrusting Jules into the position of family patriarch, legal guardian to Catherine, and manager of all their business holdings, properties, and finances—he'd begun to shut her out. These days, barely a civil word passed between them. And the further he continued to go down the wrong path, enmeshing them within a country that was growing harsher toward Huguenots by the day, the wider their rift became.

"Very well," she said at last. "Then I shall ask Pierre to help me instead." She turned and left the office. Several of the printers paused to watch as she crossed through the shop, including the oldest one, who had worked for her family since he was a boy. He gave her an encouraging smile and she nodded in return. Just as she reached the passageway to the warehouse, the door swung open and Eriq appeared.

"Catherine!" Jules scolded from behind her.

She kept going, ignoring him.

"What is wrong?" Eriq asked. "Can I help?"

Catherine shook her head. "*Non, merci.*" He was just a boy. What could he do?

"Catherine!" Jules demanded again, his voice even louder this time.

Behind Eriq, Pierre appeared in the doorway.

"What is going on out here?" he asked, his brow furrowed as he looked from Eriq to Catherine to Jules.

She gestured for him to come closer. After pulling the warehouse door shut behind him, he did as she asked, the four of them clustered there together in the passageway between the two structures, where they could speak in relative privacy.

Keeping her eyes on her betrothed, Catherine straightened her shoulders, drew in a deep breath, and spoke directly to him in a voice that sounded calm yet determined.

"We need to retrieve Amelie from the convent," she whispered. "Now that Uncle Edouard has passed, there is no reason for her to stay."

Behind her, Jules let out a groan. "You have no idea what you are asking."

She turned and gave him a glare. "If you're not willing to help," she snapped, "at least do not interfere."

"You don't understand the legalities involved. It's not as if we can march up to the place, knock on the door, and tell them we want her back. It's far more complicated than that."

Catherine's jaw clenched. "So file a petition, or write a letter, or do whatever it takes to undo the mistake Uncle Edouard made by sending her there in the first place. It is a convent, not a jail. You are her guardian now, Jules. They cannot hold her there against your will. Surely our solicitor can help. The law must be on our side."

His eyes widened, and Catherine realized he was looking at her with something almost like pity, as if she were too ignorant to grasp the complexities of the situation.

"The *law*? We no longer have any redress from the law."

"I know Huguenots are no longer allowed to bring cases into the courts, but perhaps—"

"Catherine," Jules barked, cutting her off. "I'll take the proper steps when the time is right. Not before."

"But what if there comes a point where we have no choice but to—" Catherine had been about to say "flee the country" but thought better of it at the last moment and held her tongue. Maybe some walls did have ears.

Still, they all knew what she meant. "Amelie needs to be with us," she said.

"For now, she is better off in the convent."

"She would be safer with us."

"Oh? And how safe do you feel these days, little sister?"

Catherine cringed, hating the way he turned his last words into an insult instead of a term of endearment.

Leaning forward, she dropped her voice even lower. "If we are forced to flee—"

"Do you not understand?" he hissed. "This must be handled with great thought. It's not just our family who would be cast off into the unknown. So would everyone associated with us."

"That is not my concern right now," Catherine said. It was not that she didn't care, but there was nothing she could do. Nothing any of them could do in the long run. "My concern is Amelie. If she is not with us, and we are forced to...go...we will we have no choice but to leave her behind. She will be lost to us forever."

With a heavy sigh, Jules looked over her shoulder to Pierre, as if to say, *You talk sense into her. I cannot seem to get through.*

Turning back, Catherine's eyes met those of the man she loved. Yet by the expression on his face, she realized almost immediately that he wasn't going to take her side. Her heart sank, for she couldn't stand how easily he was influenced by her brother. The two men owned equal shares in the business, but he seemed to follow, without question, every one of his partner's mandates. True, Pierre was five years younger than Jules, but how could he not have a mind of his own when it came to matters of such importance?

"Catherine," Pierre said, hands raised in a gesture of futility. "You must understand—"

"What I understand is that my cousin is being held against her will in a place run by agents of the king, the very ones who would just as soon see every Huguenot wiped from the face of the earth."

Though she had spoken in a whisper, her words hung in the air between them.

"Even so, I cannot take part in this," Pierre said, shaking his head sadly. "Your brother is moving carefully in this matter, and that takes time." He hesitated, and then he added, "You cannot *steal* away and do this, at least not *as soon as you leave here.*"

His emphasis on the words "steal" and "as soon as you leave here" confused Catherine for a moment, but then she realized he was trying to give her a private message by using words only she would understand. He wanted her to go to their secret place, the vault hidden behind the supply room, where they could discuss the matter further in private. She appreciated the thought, but this was of concern to all of them, Jules included.

"It's not as if I would go in blindly," she said, turning once more toward her brother. "I have a plan."

Jules laughed. "Oh? And exactly what does this plan entail? Do you think you will be able to sneak Amelie past the Mother Superior as one might smuggle a criminal past his jailer?"

"If necessary."

"And if no one will help you?"

"Then I shall do it by myself."

"Oh?" Her brother's eyes were mocking now. Cruel.

"That's enough," Pierre objected, though he didn't outright contradict Jules's position on the matter. "Catherine, you could not free your cousin now, not for all the money in the king's *vault...*"

"Yes, Pierre, I understand!" she snapped, tired of his attempts to end the conversation now when she knew full well he was only going to maintain his same position once they were alone. Regretting the harshness of her tone, she met his eyes and gave him a knowing nod.

Then she made one last appeal to her brother. "We owe it to Amelie to free her. And yes, Jules, I will do it alone if no one will help me."

"*I* will help you."

The voice was Eriq's, who until now had been silently listening to the entire exchange.

"What?" she asked in surprise.

"I'll help however you want."

She swallowed hard, considering his offer. Though Eriq was only a little more than a year younger than she, Catherine had always thought of him as a child. Now that he was seventeen, however, even if his general demeanor was still not fully that of an adult, at least he had the physique—and clearly the heart—of one more mature. Maybe what she needed most was simply brawn, which he had, as well as the reckless bravery of one who still saw the world with idealism and innocence. Perhaps his help *would* be enough to get the job done.

She stepped toward him. "*Merci*, Eriq. It's good to know that *someone* here still understands the difference between right and wrong."

She had more to say, but this was not the time or place. Instead, she simply took the young man's arm and suggested he see her out. Despite her frustration with Pierre, she paused long enough to flash him a look, one that assured him she would meet him as requested, though not until she had a chance to chat with his younger brother first.

And though Catherine expected to hear objections from both Pierre and Jules as she and Eriq started off through the print shop, neither man said a word.

Once they were in the office and she had pulled the door shut behind them, Catherine spoke to Eriq in quick whispers, saying he could pose as a rag peddler, which would be a plausible cover as long as he dressed the part. He would need to bring along a cart and rags, which could be used to steal Amelie away from the convent.

"You plan to hide her under the rags in a cart?" he asked, his eyes wide. The often filthy cloths were used for everything from diapers to corpse wrappings before being collected and thrown, still soiled, into the wagon.

"If I have to," she said, knowing she would even climb down in there with Amelie herself if it meant bringing her cousin home.

In the end, they agreed to meet at six that evening on the west side of passerelle St. Vincent. He was to come with the cart and in disguise so they could head straight to the convent from there.

"We can do this," he said when their scheme was set, almost to reassure himself as much as her.

She gave his hand a squeeze. "Yes, we can. See you in five hours."

With a final nod, the young man returned to the shop. Catherine watched him go and then waited there for a long moment, expecting Jules to come in and try to talk some sense into her. When he did not appear, she finally turned to go to meet Pierre in the vault.

First, however, she had to get herself outside and all the way around to the back of the warehouse, which put her once again at the risk of being sighted by the dragoons. Before going out, she retrieved her headpiece and reaffixed it to her hair. Tugging the veil securely over her face, she unbolted the door, wondering if either Pierre or Jules realized what had happened today, that the youngest among them had been the only one willing to stand up and act like a man.

CHAPTER SIX
Catherine

The dragoons were nowhere in sight when Catherine stepped out of the print shop. She closed the door and headed out, moving along the side of the building as quickly as possible. When she reached the end, she took a moment to glance around and then darted into the alley that ran behind the warehouse.

Moving past the stables, she spotted Jules's black gelding in one of the stalls. The papermakers were gone, and there were no other unfamiliar horses or carts in sight. In the equipment shed beside the stable, she noted that the space for the delivery wagon was empty, as were those for the rag carts. That was as it should be for this time of day. All would be returned later in the afternoon in plenty of time for Eriq to pull aside one of the drivers, make arrangements to borrow cart, rags, and clothing, and still meet up with her as planned.

Her stomach clenching at the thought, Catherine tried to calm her nerves as she reached the back door of the warehouse and slipped into the building. Thanks to a large pallet of boxes stacked in the delivery area, she was able to make her way unseen to the entrance of the corridor on the far right. The passageway was dark, barely illuminated by a small window near the ceiling about halfway down.

She pressed forward, confident of her steps as she made her way through the damp, dingy space. She had spent so much time here as a child that she could easily maneuver around, even in the dark.

All of the children had played hide-and-seek in the warehouse when it had first been built. As the youngest, Eriq's small stature had left him at a disadvantage, and he would often stomp off in frustration. But the rest of them—Amelie, Pierre, and Catherine—would play there for hours, their fathers and Jules oblivious as they worked nearby.

Catherine had been the one who first found the hidden vault off the supply room, behind the sliding panel, and she had shared her discovery with the others as proudly as if she had uncovered a cache of gold. Not only had the secret space made a perfect hiding place for their games, but over the years it had also come to serve as an occasional refuge whenever the print shop or warehouse grew too noisy and chaotic and she felt like slipping away somewhere quiet simply to read or write.

As she grew older and she and Pierre began to think of each other in a whole new way, he sometimes teased her about the two of them meeting there so that he could steal a kiss.

"But if I give it voluntarily, how can you call it stolen?" she had teased in return.

Not surprisingly, their first kiss had ended up happening exactly there, in the privacy of the vault, when she was sixteen and he was eighteen. As a proper young woman, sneaking away to a hidden spot for a romantic encounter with a handsome young man was not something she made a habit of doing, not even after that man became her betrothed. But in the two years since that first kiss, they had managed to meet up in the vault for brief moments of privacy now and then, each time Pierre asking if he might steal a kiss and each time Catherine replying that he need not steal it, for it was a gift.

Smiling at the thought, she reached the end of the corridor now and paused to listen for any telltale sounds. Then she took another couple of quick steps and slipped into the supply room, quickly moving past shelves of paper until she came to the side wall. In the dim lighting, she found the lever at the floorboard, pushed it, and then stepped back as the panel hiding the vault slid upward with a soft swish, propelled by the power of the pulley system her brother had designed. She stopped the door once it had risen by several feet, bent low, clutched her skirts around her legs, and ducked inside.

Catherine reached for the panel and manually pushed it back down until it was an inch or two from the floor. Even if Pierre would be along soon, she dared not leave the panel open more than that lest someone else happen into the supply room and spot the strange opening.

Though the windowless vault was nearly pitch-black with the door down, she had never been frightened in it as a child, nor was she now. She moved farther into the darkness to wait for Pierre. Originally designed to serve as storage for important documents, the vault was small, perhaps four paces deep by five paces wide, and it was usually empty except for business cabinets. But this time, after a few steps, she banged into something hard. Stifling a yelp, she took a step back and rubbed her hip before leaning forward to slide her hands over the object she had run into, deciding it was a table. Going by feel, she moved around the obstruction and then tried to keep going—only to bump into something else. When she put her hands down to feel what this item might be, she realized it was not a table but something softer and made of fabric, perhaps a chair or couch.

Before she could explore more, she heard footsteps in the supply room. Though she knew it had to be Pierre, she spun around and held her breath as she watched the sliver of light at the base of the panel door. That door once again swished open, the glow of a lantern preceding the man who held it as he bent low and stepped inside.

"Catherine?" Pierre whispered in his deep baritone.

"I'm here."

Standing straight, he pushed down the door and held up the lantern as he moved closer. In the glow she saw that the first thing she had walked into was indeed a table, with a basin and pitcher on top of it. Glancing behind her, she realized that the second item she had bumped into was neither chair nor couch, but instead a small bed tucked against the wall.

Catherine was startled. She had no idea why this previously functional room had been turned into some sort of bedchamber, though she had a feeling that with all his long hours of late, her brother had needed a place to rest. Regardless, the presence of that bed now made her meeting alone here with Pierre not just borderline inappropriate but positively scandalous.

"I cannot stay," she said, feeling her cheeks flush as she turned back to face him.

"This shouldn't take long," he replied, clearly oblivious to the source of her concern. "I just wanted to say how sorry I am that I can't help you with Amelie. There are things that…things I can't speak about right now. I'll be able to explain later. You must trust me."

Catherine took a deep breath, aware of his usual scent, a mix of turpentine from the ink, linen from the paper, and sweat from his hard work. She tried to ignore it, just as she was trying to ignore the warm, inviting bed directly behind her.

"I do trust you, Pierre," she whispered, forcing herself to focus on the matter at hand. "But I don't have time to wait. Amelie must be rescued sooner rather than later."

"Don't be foolhardy, Catherine—"

"Foolhardy?"

He set the lantern on the table. *"Oui.* You and Eriq need to cancel whatever grand rescue the two of you have cooked up and wait instead for Jules to decide how the situation should be handled."

Catherine understood what he was saying, but she was tired of waiting on Jules's decisions when it came to anything important. If a matter was business related, he could move on it quickly, but if it had to do with the family, he couldn't seem to make up his mind. With everything progressing so slowly, they would all be broken on the wheel before he had perfected a plan. There were stories of Huguenots tied to wagon wheels and then beaten, as the large wheels were turned, until their limbs were broken. The torture always ended in death.

She shuddered. *"Non,* we will not cancel our plans. You must listen to me instead."

Pierre bristled. "Are you saying I need to bend to your will?"

"Non. You don't understand." Catherine stepped away from him, bumping against the table again. "I'm trying to figure out what is best for our families, starting with rescuing Amelie."

"We are all trying to figure out what is best for our families—"

"*Non*. You and Jules are trying to figure out what is best for the business."

"Catherine," Pierre said, stepping closer. "It's not that simple." He reached for her hand. "Give us more time, please. We are working on it. Will you trust me?"

Her heart skipped a beat. She wanted more than anything to trust him.

Leaning even closer, he placed a hand on her cheek, his breath on her face warm and sweet. "I know you think you have it all figured out, but things are complicated. You don't understand all the nuances—"

She pulled away. She did understand, full well, what was happening. Jules and Pierre lived as if they were men in a fire but denying the flames all around them. "You must not be so rash," he said.

Rash. That was a word Jules sometimes used in referring to her. He felt she had been given too many privileges as a young woman and expected too much now, in return. It wasn't true, but she feared Pierre was beginning to think the same. Once again, he had been influenced by his older friend and business partner.

Her face grew warm this time with anger. "I didn't come here to argue with you, Pierre. It's time for me to leave."

He was quiet for a moment, and then he said simply, "Fine. I shall walk you home."

"*Non*. You should go back to work."

He shook his head. "It's not safe for you to travel alone."

"I managed to get here, didn't I?" She pushed against his shoulder. "Go." She didn't want to spend another minute with him.

He seemed ambivalent, but finally he handed her the lantern, saying he would leave first, through the doorway to the front of the warehouse back to the shop, and she should wait five or ten minutes to exit through the back, using the corridor, the same way she came in. "Put the lantern on a shelf in the supply room," he added.

Then he turned to go, listening at the panel for a long moment before sliding it up, slipping out, and quickly pulling it back down again.

Catherine exhaled, glad he was gone. Was that normal, to feel this way about the man to whom she was betrothed? She simply didn't know.

Putting such thoughts from her mind, she set the lantern on the table and waited for what seemed like an excess of five minutes, left the vault, extinguished the lantern, and set it down in the supply room as directed.

By the dim light from the high window, she grabbed a stack of paper—the good kind—from a shelf and tucked it under her arm as she hurried to the corridor.

Catherine made it safely across the bridge without spotting a single dragoon. Retracing her earlier steps, she walked at a brisk pace through the *traboule* and out the other side, past the cathedral.

A few blocks from home, she came to La Boutique de Lyon, a dress shop owned by friends who were Catholic. Glancing into the show window as she moved past, she came to a complete stop at the sight of a magnificent Parisian gown. The dress was breathtaking, made with cut velvet and pinked silk, its waist tiny, its skirt full. Though her family certainly had the money to afford such a dress, she knew it was never to be. As a wealthy Huguenot, all of her clothing was well tailored but far less ornate—and almost always gray or black.

Catherine sighed, so weary of modesty and simplicity. She thought of the splendid stained-glass windows and statues in the cathedral and could not believe God wanted her to live such a drab existence in comparison. What was the point of being French, of living in the most elegant country in the world, if she could not dress fashionably?

Of course, as soon as the question popped into her mind she felt bad about it. She also realized she was still standing on the street, gazing in wonder at the beautiful gown on the other side of the window. Even amid potential danger, the fact that she could be completely stopped by the sight of finery was shameful. Good thing Grand-Mère had not been with her, she told herself as she turned away, or the woman would have recited Bible verses to her about the love of money and the root of all evil.

Catherine was nearly to the end of the block when she heard what sounded like several horses *clip-clopping* together along the upcoming side street. Her view was blocked by a building on the corner, and she could not see who it was, but fearing it might be dragoons, she quickly back-tracked to the boutique and dashed inside. Shifting her stack of paper to her other arm, she took a deep breath and told herself to calm down.

"May I help you?"

Catherine turned to see her friend Janetta holding a bolt of satin in her hand, her blond hair piled atop her head, her blue eyes bright.

"*Bonjour,*" Catherine said in relief at the sight of a familiar face. "When did you get back?"

Janetta stared at her, blinking. "*Excusez-moi?*"

Catherine took a step toward her friend, only then remembering her veil. The moment she reached up and pulled it from her face, Janetta's demeanor changed.

"Ah, Catherine! *Bonjour*! I'm sorry. I did not recognize you in those clothes." Janetta moved forward and greeted her with a kiss.

The clatter of horses' hooves startled Catherine, and her head jerked toward the window. Three young men went racing by, shouting at each other in fun. The sound that had driven her inside had not come from dragoons after all.

She turned back toward Janetta and tried not to seem flustered as she added, "Did you have a good trip?"

"*Oui.* London was wonderful." It was Janetta's third visit to England with her father, who was a silk merchant. "You would love it there. It doesn't compare to Paris, but at least there are not these hostilities against Protestants. You could probably live a normal life for a change."

Catherine couldn't help but smile. Janetta always said exactly what she thought.

"And the meals were much better than they used to be. They are adopting more and more of our food. *Salades. Ragoûts. Fricassées.* And fresh fruits and vegetables are finally becoming popular in England—all because of the French influence, of course."

Catherine smiled again.

The young woman kept talking. "The fashions are not Parisian.

They are a year behind at least, but still they appreciate good fabric. There is hope for them yet."

Now Catherine could not help but laugh. "*Oui*, but is there hope for me?"

Janetta sighed, but then she smiled. "There is always hope for you. In fact, you look rather nice today."

"I was posing as a Catholic girl for my uncle's funeral."

Janetta's smile faded. "Oh, I am sorry. I heard he passed. How is Amelie?"

Tears stung Catherine's eyes. "I don't know. She wasn't there."

Before she could say more, someone from the back room called out Janetta's name, probably her aunt who ran the shop, overseeing the tailors who worked for them.

"Oh, dear," Janetta said. "I had better go." She held up the satin. "We are deciding on what fabrics to carry for summer. Then it's on to Rome in September. Father says it would be too hot to travel any sooner. He's going to start trading Italian silk along with the *Lyonnaise*. Everyone is asking for it. Business keeps getting better and better."

"That's wonderful. Congratulations." With a another kiss, Catherine bid her friend *au revoir* and stepped back out to the street, her heart heavy as she resumed her walk toward home.

As a Catholic, Janetta was able to live a life Catherine could not. And while she was truly happy for her friend, she had to admit that she coveted the girl's freedom. Her adventures. Her clothes. All of it.

Immediately, thoughts of Grand-Mère again came to mind. If she were here at the moment, she would quote from the Scriptures, *A sound heart is the life of the flesh: but envy the rottenness of the bones.* Catherine said the familiar verse to herself instead, trying to push envy aside and focus on the idea of London—not as a place of business, but one of refuge.

Perhaps that was where her family and the Talbots should move, Catherine decided. As Janetta said, in London, being Protestant would not be a problem at all. They would simply join the other Huguenot refugees who were already there and live among them, free of harassment.

They could open a print shop, and she and Pierre could finally be married. It couldn't be that complicated to immigrate. They all spoke English. And London was a *city*, far, far larger than Lyon and infinitely bigger and better than the Plateau. Having grown up in Paris, Grand-Mère was a city girl at heart. She would be happy there. So would Catherine.

True, leaving France would be painful, but the sooner they went the better. And at least London was more sophisticated than Switzerland or Germany, or the New World, or any other place Huguenots were fleeing to. People were leaving so often that on any given day another Huguenot home was found abandoned, its occupants having slipped away under cover of darkness. Had they obliged the king's command to abandon their faith, they could have stayed. Many Huguenots, Uncle Edouard included, had done just that. But Catherine would never convert, no matter what, and neither would any of her loved ones.

It was not until she crossed the street a block away from the family home on rue Juiverie that the dragoons reappeared, taking her by surprise. With a gasp, she ducked into the *boulangerie* and quickly secured the comb in her hair. Then she draped the lace of the veil back over her eyes and approached the counter, ordering baguettes from the baker. Wishing to stall for a moment, she pretended to search for a coin in her purse, keeping her back to the window.

When her order was filled and paid for and she could delay no longer, she reluctantly left the shop, glancing up the street to see one lone dragoon still there, sitting on his horse. Before she could react, he raised his firearm as if in greeting and then turned and rode away.

Puzzled, she stood there for a long moment. Then she heard a commotion and turned to see that the other dragoons were now at the cobbler's shop down the block, harassing the owner, a friend and fellow church member at the *Temple de Lyon*. Catherine said a quick prayer for him and then hurried away in the opposite direction, toward home, her mind returning to the odd gesture of the dragoon.

Why had he not pursued her?

CHAPTER SEVEN
Catherine

As Catherine neared their home, she found herself trying to empathize with her brother, who seemed to hold on so tightly to it. It took up an entire block. Inside the stone wall were the house, a stable, and a courtyard with a beautiful old chestnut tree.

Instead of going around to the front, she tried the wide gate that led to the stables. It was locked. Grasping the stack of paper in her left hand, she banged the bronzed doorknocker against the sheet of brass with her right, hoping Monsieur Roen would hear. He did—immediately. One side of the big double door creaked as it swung open.

"I hoped it would be you," he said, his pale blue eyes smiling. He waited for her to enter and then secured the door before heading back toward the stables. He had worked for Catherine's family as coachman for as long as she could remember.

She took off her veil as she passed under the golden-green leaves of the chestnut tree and stopped for a moment, overcome with relief at being safe within her family compound at last.

She loved this house as well as the farm. The country property had been passed down from baron to baron until four generations ago when her great-great-grandfather chose to move into town. He stud-ied the law and became the mayor of Lyon, a distinction that would have made the family nobility if they had not been already. True, the title of baron was not as high as count or marquis or duke, but it had afforded the family privileges and distinction for centuries, not to men-tion resources. Once he'd become mayor, he'd acquired this land on rue Juiverie and built the original structure. Everyone in Lyon knew of it.

His son, Catherine's great-grandfather, also studied the law and had added to the house, creating a rambling mansion and elegant gardens. He'd been the one to convert to the teachings of Jean Calvin soon after his comrade King Henri IV issued the Edict of Nantes, a grand ges-ture that guaranteed religious liberties to Protestants. Catherine's great-grandfather ventured to Henri's court several times and continued to gain favor with the king as well as the people of Lyon. All in all, peace and prosperity reigned regardless of faith.

Over time, the family had become used to city life, so eventually her grandfather, who bucked family tradition by not studying the law, instead partnered with the Talbot family and started a printing busi-ness. A caretaker was hired to oversee the farming of the country estate. That was where Catherine used to go riding, and every morning milk, butter, and eggs were delivered to the house from the farm.

She left the tree and walked to the well in the corner of the court-yard closest to the kitchen. Placing her things on a nearby table, she washed her hands in a basin of water.

Sighing, she acknowledged to herself that it would be hard to leave this all behind. And Grand-Mère was right—it was not just their fam-ily who would suffer. All of the poor families, Protestant and Catholic alike, for whom Grand-Mère regularly provided food, clothing, and medicine, would miss her care. Grand-Mère often quoted a particu-lar Scripture from Proverbs when it came to her work, saying, *He that giveth unto the poor shall not lack: but he that hideth his eyes shall have many a curse.* Catherine knew most of those living in poverty, and she often worked alongside Grand-Mère—though, she feared, with not nearly as much grace.

Jules was right too. It was not just their family who would be cast

off into a new life—it was all of their employees as well. At the farm.
In the house. At the shop.

Catherine sighed again. Jules had accused her of being simplistic.
That was not true. Though their departure from Lyon would be a hard-
ship for those who were dependent upon them, they still needed to get
themselves to safety. If they were imprisoned or dead, they would be of
no use to anyone. How could she make her brother—and Pierre, for
that matter—understand?

She dried her hands on the cloth left beside the basin and then ran
it over her face and neck to take off the dust of the day. It was a few
years ago that Louis XIV, disregarding his grandfather's pledge to the
Huguenots, began to slowly reverse the Edict of Nantes, although he
had not revoked it outright—at least not yet. But almost everyone felt
it was merely a matter of time. Property was being seized from Huguenots in the south, and men had been arrested and sent to the galleys.
Families were being torn apart. So far, in Lyon, only Amelie's husband,
Paul, had been murdered, but more killings were bound to happen.

Catherine stepped into the empty kitchen and put the baguettes
on the center table. A pot hung over the fire, and the hearty smell of
boiling meat filled the room. A basket filled with bread, herbs, cheese,
and vegetables sat on a side table. Grand-Mère had not made her deliveries yet.

Catherine left the kitchen and headed down the hallway, all the way
around to her grandmother's *appartement.*

"Grand-Mére?" she asked, tapping on the door.

"Is that you, *ma petite fille?*"

"*Oui.*" Catherine pushed open the door and stepped inside. Grand-
Mère was there in the sitting room at her desk, past the settee and
chaise lounge.

She turned toward her granddaughter. "Where have you been all
this time? I was worried sick." Grand-Mère squinted as she spoke. Her
eyesight was growing worse. For a time a pair of spectacles had helped,
but in the last year the problem was from the clouding of her eyes and
could not be corrected.

"I took a detour across the river."

Grand-Mère shook her head. "Catherine, why?"

"I wanted to ask Jules to help me bring Amelie home."

Grand-Mère folded her hands in her lap and met Catherine's gaze. "And?"

"He said he would not. As did Pierre, though Eriq agreed to help me."

"*Non, chérie.*" Grand-Mère sighed. "That will not do."

Catherine wrinkled her nose, wanting to challenge her grandmother but remaining silent.

"You know it is forbidden for you to go to the shop. Did you apologize to your brother for disobeying him?"

"Uncle Edouard is gone. There is no reason for me not to go anymore."

"That is not what I asked."

Catherine shook her head and put her stack of paper on the edge of the desk.

"Then you must apologize to Jules."

Catherine could not think of anything worse—at least not at the moment.

Grand-Mère was adamant. "You *must* ask your brother's forgiveness when he gets home."

Catherine knew God commanded that children honor their parents—or guardian in this case—no matter if he was right or wrong. So she said with a sigh, "I will." And then, because she couldn't help it, she added, "But he shouldn't be so unreasonable. It wouldn't surprise me if he decided to convert to save himself, just like Uncle."

Grand-Mère clucked her tongue. "Edouard did what he thought he needed to do for all of us."

"Well, he was wrong to do it."

"Catherine." The disappointment in her grandmother's voice was humbling.

She blushed. She had not meant to be disrespectful to her uncle—and on the day of his funeral, no less.

"Did the dragoons bother you?"

Catherine shrugged. "Some. I wish they would be called back to Paris."

"They are not all from Paris. I have heard the newer ones are from around here."

"The king should be embarrassed. And so should his church. What happened to common decency? And freedom?"

"*Oui*, the king is responsible. But not everyone in the church. Many are ashamed by what is going on."

"Who?"

"Father Philippe, for one."

Catherine already knew that. "Who else?"

Grand-Mère picked up an envelope from her desk. "Suzanne."

"A letter came?"

"*Oui*."

Catherine wrote regularly to Duchesse de Navailles on Grand-Mère's behalf. Sometimes she added a few words of her own as well, which the duchesse seemed to enjoy. Long ago, back when the king's father was young, both Suzanne and Grand-Mère's parents had been members of the court, and the two girls were close in age and had become friends. Suzanne's father was a duke, his title passed down through his family for generations, while Grand-Mère's grandfather had been knighted after having done some extensive legal work for Louis XIII. When Suzanne's mother fell ill, she stayed with Grand-Mère and her family and the girls had formed a close bond.

Suzanne married the Duc of Navailles, had seven children, and remained active in the court for many years. Her mother was the god-mother of Madame de Maintenon, Louis XIV's current *favourite*, and had in fact been the one who introduced the two of them in the first place.

Though Catherine abhorred the king because of his treatment of the Huguenots, stories of Paris intrigued her, as much as did high fashion or the pageantry of the church. Letters with Suzanne were the closest she had ever come to any kind of court experience, even though her family was nobility.

"I will read it to you," Catherine said, taking the letter and sitting down in the chair on the other side of the desk. It began with a warm greeting to Grand-Mère and an inquiry about her health. After that, Catherine continued on with the next paragraph, keeping her voice deep and rich in an attempt to imitate what she imagined Suzanne's sounded like.

"'I have been at Versailles for the last couple of weeks and will remain here for several months. All is well with His Majesty and even better with Madame de Maintenon. Yvonne, you should come to visit me at Versailles. It has been years since you have been to Paris. I know your brother would want you to stay with him. In fact, I saw Laurent last night and he said as much. We both agree you should bring your dear *petite fille* as well.'" Catherine smiled, pleased that the invitation had also been extended to her.

"Continue," Grand-Mère said.

"'As for your son...'" Catherine's voice trailed off at the mention of her late uncle, not just because of his death but also because Suzanne had never been told of his conversion to Catholicism. *Too complicated to explain* had been Grand-Mère's response when Catherine had asked if she should write about it last year. The fact that Grand-Mère had left the Catholic church to become a Huguenot had always been a sore point with Suzanne. Perhaps Grand-Mère believed the woman would interpret Edouard's conversion as a victory for all who shared the king's opinions about religion—including Suzanne.

"Tell her about Edouard when you respond," Grand-Mère directed now, interrupting her thoughts. "Just that he died."

Catherine nodded and then started at the beginning of the sentence again. "'As for your son, be sure he comes too for protection along the road. I am also enclosing a letter of passage for your coach that a captain of His Majesty's soldiers assures me will bring you here safely.'" Catherine flipped to the second page. It was the letter of passage.

She turned back again and continued reading. "'I treasure your friendship and long to see you. Write back as soon as you know when you will be coming to Paris. There is no need for you to await my reply. Once you have arrived, send word with the exact date you plan to visit Versailles, which is only three hours away, and I will be here to greet you with open arms. Your loving friend, Suzanne.'" Catherine looked up. "There's a postscript."

"Go on."

"It's to me."

Grand-Mère smiled. "Of course it is." She paused. "Well, are you going to read it?"

Catherine lowered her head again. "'*Ma petite* Catherine, convince your grandmother to make the trip and bring you with her. It will be worth it to all of you. You are a woman now. I would like nothing more than to have a chance to meet you and see what you have to offer.'"

Grand-Mère frowned.

"What does she mean?" Catherine asked, folding the letter.

"Suzanne is known for her matchmaking. She may have someone in mind for you, which is a ridiculous thought."

Catherine returned the letter to its envelope. Ridiculous, *oui*, but she could not help but be flattered.

"A trip to Paris is a lovely idea, but now is not a time for the frivolities of travel," Grand-Mère pronounced with finality, taking the envelope and placing it on the desk. "I am sure my old friend knows that."

"Now is *exactly* the time," Catherine replied emphatically, hoping her enthusiasm did not come across as disrespect. "*Absolument.* This visit with Suzanne must happen as soon as possible."

"Oh?" Grand-Mère lifted an eyebrow. "And why is that?"

"So you can ask her to help us."

"How could she possibly help?"

"By securing passage for our family to London."

Grand-Mère pursed her lips. "It's not safe. Refugees are being murdered on the beaches. Those who make it into a boat are killed crossing the Channel."

"Only some of them," Catherine said. "Many refugees have arrived on England's shores unharmed."

Grand-Mère's eyes filled with tears. "Still, the risk is too great," she whispered.

"Then perhaps Suzanne could make the dragoons leave us alone here."

Grand-Mère shook her head. "Suzanne knows the king, but she does not have that sort of favor. In fact, you might say she is one of his least favorite people and has been for many years."

Catherine blinked. "I don't understand. How can she be a member of the court without the approval of the king?"

"Many years ago, when the king was much younger, she opposed him in a matter of...propriety...which he greatly resented. He had her removed from court, but the Queen Mother implored him to bring her back. Which he did, eventually."

"Oh," Catherine said, hoping for more details but knowing not to ask.

"Yet...perhaps there is a chance Suzanne could help us," Grand-Mère added. "A slight one."

"It's worth a try. We both know that if things continue to get worse, we may have no choice but to flee to another country."

Grand-Mère's eyes filled with fresh tears as she struggled with that notion. "I do not want to leave France."

"So you would have us relocate to the Plateau instead? It may still be France, but it's in the middle of nowhere. You would be miserable there, Grand-Mère, just as I would. You grew up in Paris, not in the wilds. You need to be in a city, even if that city is somewhere other than France."

"*Oui*. You and I are both used to all a city has to offer."

"Besides, there are likely dragoons there too—or, if not already, eventually there will be. Why go to the trouble of relocating to the Plateau now if we will only be forced to flee again later?"

Grand-Mère dabbed at her eyes with a lace handkerchief. "I agree. But do not worry. No one is considering the Plateau as an option."

Catherine blinked. "*Non*? Then why is Jules negotiating the purchase of a paper mill in Le Chambon?"

Grand-Mère's eyes widened. "What?"

Catherine's head jerked back. "I thought you knew. Monsieur Audet and his son, the makers of the paper we like so much, were at the shop today, discussing a sale with Jules."

Grand-Mère's face grew pale. "*Non*."

"*Oui*."

"To live on the Plateau..." She paused. "I have never been, of course, but from what I understand it is a desolate and lonely place."

Catherine nodded. As a child the rugged landscape of that area held a certain appeal for her, but she could not fathom living there as an adult. There were far better places to relocate. She'd been twelve when she visited the village of Le Chambon-sur-Lignon, situated in a mountainous region southwest of Lyon known as the Plateau, where her mother and aunt were from. The purpose was to see the property Maman's father, who had recently died, had left to Jules. Together Papa, Uncle Edouard, Amelie, Jules, and Catherine had traveled by horseback. That part had been a grand adventure, but once they got there, she had not been impressed by the provincial village at all—especially not when she learned how much snow fell in the region in the winter. Mostly, it had made her sad to be where her mother had grown up and even sadder not to remember her, except for the one image. Everyone else spoke about Maman and her sister nonstop, all while Catherine listened in miserable silence, longing to return to Lyon and Grand-Mère.

"Do you not think London would be a better place to settle?" Catherine asked now. "Perhaps we could make our way to La Rochelle and find a ship there instead of going north and trying to cross at the Channel."

Shaking her head, Grand-Mère placed her hand on the desk and leaned against it. "I cannot imagine leaving my homeland. Surely the family name of Gillet will protect us here."

Catherine felt just as sure it would not, but she held her tongue. Certainly, the Gillet name would have made no difference to the dragoons who had followed her earlier.

"All I know is that the point may come when we have no choice but to move, wherever that move will be. That's why I must rescue Amelie right away. If Jules whisks us off while she is still at the convent, she will never be able to find us should she ever get out."

Grand-Mère was quiet for a moment. "Perhaps we *do* need to get Amelie," she said, the closest she had come to admitting what likely lay ahead for them all.

Relief flooded through Catherine.

"As for Suzanne," Grand-Mère continued, "write her back for me."

"I will tell her we hope to come soon."

"We?" Grand-Mère fixed her eyes on her granddaughter. "You certainly cannot go with me. Paris is no place for you, much less Versailles."

Catherine's heart fell. "And why is that?"

"Too many temptations."

Catherine shook her head. "You know I would not do anything immoral."

"Not even covet?" Grand-Mère asked. "You have that tendency you know, to be drawn toward the nicer things. You always have."

Catherine's cheeks flushed with heat as she remembered her thoughts just a short while ago at Janetta's boutique. Grand-Mère knew her so well. "I promise I will not. I am content with how we live, truly I am."

Grand-Mère's eyes narrowed as she leaned forward and studied her granddaughter. Straightening her shoulders, Catherine tried to return her gaze with quiet confidence, fully aware that the woman would never take her along if she believed such a trip might endanger her soul.

"Will you consider it, at least? Please? I'm not a little girl anymore, Grand-Mère. I know the dangers of bright and beautiful things. But that is all they are. *Things*. I prefer to store up my treasures in heaven. And I would never be interested in whatever young man Suzanne might think would be a match for me. I am committed to Pierre." Even if he was annoying her right now.

Grand-Mère considered her a moment longer and then finally gave a nod. "*Bien.* I will ask your brother."

"*Merci,*" Catherine whispered, knowing he would not like the idea but grateful that her grandmother was willing to ask.

Chapter Eight

Catherine

*H*ours later, when Catherine left home again, she wore an old cloak over a simple dress and apron, with a maid's cap covering her head. Clouds had rolled in over the hills and hung heavily above the city. She hurried toward the river, thankful that the dragoons were nowhere in sight. When she reached the Saint Vincent Bridge, she stopped for a moment. There was no rag cart on the other side. Perhaps Eriq had parked on a different street.

She kept going, pausing again at the end of the bridge, unsure as to what to do next. Going to the print shop was not an option. Jules would stop her.

Perhaps Eriq had not been able to find the ragman. Or perhaps the ragman didn't want to loan him the cart, even though the Gillet family owned it. Surely Eriq would think to offer him a coin in exchange.

The thunder of hooves drew her attention back to the bridge. Dragoons, the same ones as earlier, raced toward her. She ducked her head, hoping they would ignore her.

They did not. The first one stopped. "Sister?"

Perhaps he didn't recognize her from before.

"You should move along," he said. "Get on home."

"*Oui,*" she answered, turning her head toward the water, hoping he would think she was a shy maid. "I just stopped to catch my breath."

"Do not dawdle," he said, waving to the others to keep moving. "Be on your way."

She started to shuffle along, her head down until she thought they had all passed. They had not. The one remained.

He gave her a puzzled look. It was the soldier who had raised his firearm to her earlier.

He looked familiar, and suddenly she remembered who he was—a fellow named Waltier, a friend of Pierre's who used to live in Lyon. Several years ago, Waltier's father had lost his trading business and the family had left the area. Wherever they had gone, Waltier was back now—as a dragoon. Catherine could scarcely believe it. He had been such a nice boy.

A glimmer of recognition in his eyes and a reddening in his cheeks indicated he recognized her too. She took a sharp breath, sure he would alert the others, but he spun his horse around and took off after his comrades.

Catherine forced herself to return to her shuffling. With no Eriq in sight, she decided to proceed toward the shop and perhaps petition one of the ragmen herself.

Ahead, in the middle of the street, a horse whinnied. She looked up to see Waltier passing a cart—a rag cart. To her relief, he gave it barely a glance and kept on going.

She quickened her step. The man driving the cart hung his head, his face hidden by a tattered black hat. Catherine gave a discreet wave to make sure he saw her. He nodded and then lowered his head again.

When she neared the cart, however, she realized it was not Eriq after all. It was Pierre. Perhaps Jules had sent him to take her home.

"Get in," he grunted.

She hesitated.

"Catherine, do you want the dragoons to come back?"

She shook her head and climbed up onto the seat beside him. Immediately, she had to resist the urge to pinch her nose shut from the stench of the rags behind them. He turned the horse to the left, down an alleyway in the opposite direction of the river. Perhaps he planned to take her to the convent after all.

She didn't speak until the nag reached the outskirts of the city and started to climb the hill. "Why did you decide to come?"

"I knew that if you were determined to do this no matter what, then it should be with me."

She exhaled slowly. "*Merci.*"

They rode in silence until he finally said, "What is your plan?"

"I will go to the convent door and ask if they have any rags to sell."

Pierre shook his head. "They will never take you for a rag lady. Besides, how will you get them to let you see Amelie?"

"I am going to say I knew her growing up and heard she was at the convent. I will ask for a quick visit."

"And then what?"

"When we are alone, I will tell her we have come to take her home."

"You think they will allow her to simply walk out the door."

Catherine didn't answer.

Pierre persisted. "Even though your brother is her guardian now, Mother Superior will not see it that way. She will not allow Amelie to leave the convent to go live with Huguenots. She has the law on her side."

"Then we will sneak her out."

Pierre shook his head, not saying anything more—but at least he kept going. A half hour later the cart crested the hill and then rolled down the road into the forest.

Twice last autumn Catherine had ridden her horse out to the convent, hoping to catch sight of Amelie. The last time a group of nuns and students had been in the garden, harvesting the final crop of squash, but her cousin was not among them. Although Uncle Edouard had taken Amelie to the convent, it was not uncommon for Huguenot girls to be torn from their families and forced into a convent to be reeducated, this time in the state religion.

As the wind picked up through the trees, Catherine feared rain was on its way. She pulled her cloak tighter as the cart rounded a bend in the road and the convent came into view. The sunny days had dried the mud, but rain might make it hard to get home.

"I will stop there, under that tree," Pierre said. "Grab a bag from the back."

"*Merci*," Catherine said again as she jumped down from the cart. She truly was thankful for his help. Maybe there was hope for him yet. She bent down and rubbed her hands in the dirt and then wiped it across her apron, her face, and her forearms.

Pierre had only a halfhearted smile for her, but his eyes lit up at the sight. "You still don't look like a rag lady—and you certainly don't smell like one."

She smiled in return, grabbed a bag from the back, and marched toward the side door of the convent.

"Do you have money to pay for the rags?"

She stopped and turned around slowly.

He held out a coin, his eyes dancing in the dimming light. She walked back and took it, muttering, "*Merci.*"

By the time she reached the door, the rain had started. She knocked and waited. Then pounded and waited. Finally, a maid responded.

Catherine held up the bag. She was not sure of the rag collectors' routes, but she knew they traveled deep into the countryside around Lyon. She hoped one had not been by the convent recently.

"Come in. I will check with the housekeeper," the young woman said.

Catherine stepped into the warmth of the kitchen and waited by the door as the girl hurried on through to a hallway. A pot simmered over the fire, and three loaves of bread waited on the tabletop. A woman—probably the cook—entered from a side door with a crock in her hands, humming as she walked.

"Oh!" she said, stopping when she saw Catherine. "You startled me."

Catherine held up the bag. "The girl went to find the housekeeper, to see if there are any rags."

The cook continued on to the table. "There might be. I wouldn't know." She put down the crock and then began slicing the bread. When she finished she picked up a piece and offered it to Catherine.

She almost refused but then remembered that a rag collector would take it. Her mouth watered. She was hungry.

"*Merci.*" Catherine took a bite and then said, "I knew a young woman back in Lyon who I heard is here now."

"Oh?" The cook busied herself with the next loaf.

"Her name is Amelie Fournier. Her family name was Gillet."

"*Oui,* she is here."

"How is she doing?"

The cook stopped slicing the bread. "How do you know her?"

Catherine could feel her face grow warm. She glanced down at her dirty apron. "My family..." Her voice trailed off, hoping she implied a reversal of fortunes, which was not entirely false. Their misfortune, so far, just did not happen to be monetary.

"I see," the cook said, putting down the knife. Perhaps she knew of Amelie's Huguenot background and assumed that was the connection. "The poor dear has not been well, not since her confinement."

Catherine swallowed hard, trying to hide her shock. Her *confinement*? Amelie had had a *baby*?

Catherine's mind was spinning as she did the math, terrified that her cousin had been compromised somehow after being sent away from the family. But then she realized that the child could be Amelie's late husband's, depending on when it was born. Paul was killed eight months ago. Perhaps she had been newly pregnant at the time, though she wouldn't have realized it yet.

Had Uncle Edouard been told? "Can she have visitors?"

"I wouldn't know," the cook said as the girl returned, followed by an older woman.

"No rags, I am afraid. We use everything we can here."

Even before Catherine could thank her for her trouble, the cook said, "She is a friend of Amelie's. She was wondering if she could see her."

The housekeeper stepped closer to Catherine. "Did you know she has been ill?"

"*Non,*" Catherine said, hoping the alarm she felt did not show in her face. "I had no idea. I thought I might bring her news from home."

The cook began piling the bread on a tray. "It might do the girl good to see an old friend." Without looking up, she added, "Do you not think?"

The housekeeper wrapped her hand around a ring of keys at her side and stared at Catherine. Then she said, "I should check with Mother Superior, but she is resting now. I will take you instead. But not for long. It is almost time for our dinner."

"*Merci*," Catherine told her, crumpling the bag in her hand.

The light was dim in the hallway but grew brighter on the stairs and even more so on the landing. The housekeeper gave a knock on the first door and then pushed it open, saying, "You have a visitor."

Catherine followed the woman into the room, hoping her cousin would not be so shocked and excited at the sight of her that she would react in a way that aroused suspicion.

She need not have worried. Amelie was sitting on a chair, a babe in her arms, and when she looked up, her eyes simply filled with tears.

"Now, now," the housekeeper said. "She cannot stay long. Make sure the visit does you good and not harm."

Amelie nodded. "*Oui*. It has done me good already."

Catherine knelt at her side as the woman left, waiting for the click of the door before she gave her cousin a long hug and then spoke. "You had a child. When?"

"A month ago."

So it was Paul's. *Merci, Seigneur.*

"And you have been sick?"

Amelie swiped at her eyes with her free hand.

Tears filled Catherine's eyes too as she reached for the *bébé*. So many times they had imagined, as girls, raising their children together, all living together in the Gillet family home, Catherine and her brood established on the first floor and Amelie and hers on the second, both sharing the ground floor lounge and dining room, just as the families in the house had always done. How could their lives have changed so dramatically in so short a time?

"Her name is Valentina," Amelie said softly. "After Paul's Italian grandmother."

"Hello, Valentina," Catherine cooed softly, gazing down at the little one in her arms. The baby peered up at her, eyes wide. She had a full head of dark hair, but she was small for a month old, too small. Catherine looked again at Amelie. "Did Paul know?"

Amelie shook her head. "Neither of us had any idea." Tears filled her eyes again, and she brushed them away. "I did not realize I was expecting until I had been here for a couple of months. I assumed with all the stress of his death and then being sent away..." She shook her head. "The prospect never crossed my mind until Mother Superior pointed out the tightness of my clothes and my never-ending appetite."

Catherine pursed her lips. At some point along the way, that appetite must have waned, because Amelie had never looked thinner. Or paler, for that matter.

"We need to get both of you out of here."

"Father will never allow it."

Catherine hesitated, unable to keep the shock from her face. "You don't know?"

Amelie stared back at her, brow furrowed.

"He...he passed away. Your father was buried this afternoon."

Amelie sank back against the chair, tears spilling down her cheeks. "*Non!*"

Catherine's heart ached for her cousin. "They didn't tell you? When you missed his funeral today, I assumed they refused to let you go. I never imagined they withheld the truth from you entirely."

"Today," Amelie echoed, looking even paler than before. "You say he was buried today?"

"*Oui.* I slipped into the service at the cathedral—as did Grand-Mère. They laid him to rest at the *cimetière des catholiques* afterward."

Catherine would have liked to give Amelie a chance to digest the news of her father's death, but she feared they might be interrupted at any moment. She rose to her feet, clutching the baby, and took her cousin's hand. "I need to take you home."

"Mother Superior will not allow it."

"Then we will sneak you out while the rest are eating."

She shook her head. "Take the baby. Put her in your bag."

"She will scream," Catherine said.

Amelie's brow furrowed. "Maybe not at first. Not if you move quickly..."

"I don't think we should risk it," Catherine said, gently swaying the baby. "Are there guards here?"

"Two. Though they are usually drunk in the garden by now."

"And if it's still raining outside?"

"Then they will be doing their drinking in the shed, out back."

"Very well." Catherine began to pace as she adapted her plan to accommodate the infant. "Pierre is waiting outside with a rag cart not far from the kitchen door. I will go out first and tell him we need to stall for a few minutes. You come with the baby soon after. If anyone inquires what you are doing, just say you needed to tell me one more thing before I go. Don't wear your cape or bring any possessions. They cannot suspect you're leaving." Catherine picked up a blanket from the bed and wrapped it around the infant. "Come to the cart, and we will hide both of you under the rags and go. God willing, the guards will be too busy with their drinking to notice."

Amelie was quiet for a long moment as she considered Catherine's words. "Is Jules aware of all this?"

Catherine shook her head as she adjusted the blanket around the baby and then lifted the little one to her shoulder, brushing her chin across her soft head, ignoring her cousin's question.

"He does not have any idea?"

Catherine shrugged. "Of the proposal, yes. Of the particulars, no. But Grand-Mère does and she encouraged it. She will know what to do to get you strong—and the baby too."

"But even if your plan works, even if we manage to make it all the way home..." Amelie shook her head, as if trying to collect her thoughts. "Once Mother Superior realizes we're gone, what is to stop her from having the authorities come to the house and simply retrieve me?"

"Jules is your guardian now, Amelie. And your father sent you here voluntarily. It's not as if you were a young girl forced into a convent by the state. Surely your family should be allowed to be responsible for both you and your child."

A rap on the door and a brusque "Time to go" interrupted the women.

Quickly, Catherine slipped the baby back into her cousin's arms, whispering, "Pierre and I will be waiting."

The door swung open to reveal the housekeeper. "Mother Superior is feeling better. You need to leave."

"Very well," Catherine replied. Then she turned back to Amelie and added in a casual tone, "It was good to see you. My deepest sympathies on the loss of your father."

Catherine tried to act completely normal as she thanked the housekeeper, stepped out of the door, and headed for the stairs.

When she reached the kitchen, the cook nodded toward her as she ladled soup into a bowl but did not speak. Catherine nodded in return and kept going. Once outside, she wiped her sweaty palms on her apron as she approached Pierre, who had thought ahead and was now facing the road, under the same tree where he dropped her off, about ten paces from the door.

"We need to buy some time," she said softly when she reached him.

With a nod, he hopped down from the cart and knelt beside the wheel, pretending to examine it. Rain dripped through the leaves overhead. Catherine stood nearby, growing wetter by the moment as she glanced around for any sight of the guards. The wind picked up even more. She shivered in the chill, pulling at her cloak and wishing Amelie would hurry.

After a while, Pierre gestured for her to draw close, so she leaned forward and pretended to study the wheel alongside him.

"Are you sure she is coming?" he whispered.

"Patience," Catherine scolded, as much to herself as to him. "They will be here soon."

"They?"

She was about to explain when the back door opened and Amelie stepped out, Valentina in her arms.

Catherine rose and moved to the back of the cart, where she pushed the rags aside and gestured for Amelie to hand her the baby and then climb in.

Amelie pointed to the filthy rags and made a face.

"*Oui*," Catherine said, "but it's our only choice."

Amelie nodded and climbed into the wagon.

"*Voilà*," Catherine said once her cousin was safely inside, giving the tiny blanketed bundle back. "Now lie down and I will cover you both."

Thanks to the rags, it was not difficult to conceal them, and a moment later Catherine hopped up onto the bench seat beside Pierre and whispered fiercely, "Go! Now!"

"There is just one problem," he replied, frozen in place.

She followed his startled gaze to see two guards standing a short ways in front of the cart, blocking their path.

"Go anyway. They will scatter." When he still did not move, Catherine reached over and grabbed the reins from his hands, slapping them on the back of the horse.

"What are you doing?" he demanded, taking the reins back from her even as the nag obeyed and began moving forward.

To her dismay, the guards responded by pulling out their swords and yelling, "Halt!"

Pierre pulled the horse to a stop, just inches from the armed men.

"What have you got in the back?" one of them demanded.

"Just rags," Pierre answered.

"And?" The guard remained where he was but craned his neck to look. "You might as well tell us the truth. We saw the girl."

Pierre handed Catherine the reins and climbed down, walking around to the front of the horse. "Let us handle this in a civil manner," he said. "The young woman's father just died. She needs to be in the care of her family."

"Then why the need to sneak her out?" the larger of the two guards asked.

The other one stepped around to the side of the cart and began poking the rags with his sword.

"Stop that!" Catherine said.

The guard laughed. The smell of wine was heavy on his breath. Amelie's head popped up.

"Good girl," the guard said, stepping back.

Amelie sat up and clung to the side of the wagon, her arms empty, the baby still hidden.

"Get up," the guard commanded, his eyes on Amelie.

Catherine realized that they must not have noticed what was in the bundle Amelie was carrying when she made her escape, and she prayed that Valentina would not start crying and give herself away.

The guard repeated his command, so Amelie stood, swaying slightly as she tried to keep her balance. Catherine was about to turn on the bench seat and take her cousin's hand to steady her when the sound of hooves caught her attention. A rider approached from up the lane. She glanced toward the guards, who had also noticed and were moving forward.

Seeing an opportunity, Pierre turned toward Catherine and hissed, "Get in the back." Then he quickly clambered up onto the bench and grabbed the reins.

She hesitated, looking again at the rider galloping toward them on his horse. With a jolt, she barely believed what she saw. It was Jules atop his black gelding.

She did as Pierre commanded, astounded to realize that her brother was so opposed to her plan that he had actually come to sabotage it. At least Pierre was still on her side, ready to make a dash for it now that the guards were distracted by Jules's appearance.

"Amelie! Sit!" Catherine commanded, but her cousin remained standing there on the wagon bed, frozen in fear and confusion.

Catherine looked forward to see Jules's horse gallop past the guards and veer straight for the wagon.

Pierre turned to her. "Get her down!" he hissed, gesturing toward Amelie.

The larger guard shouted, "Halt, all of you!" and then swung his sword toward the cart.

Catherine lunged toward her cousin, but just as she was about to grab Amelie's hand and jerk her down, Jules wrapped an arm around

Amelie's waist and lifted her to his side. At that moment, Pierre snapped the reins and yelled for the horse to move. The cart lurched and began rumbling forward as both guards yelled profanities. Frantic, Catherine scrambled under the rags for the baby until she found her, lying near the front of the cart bed under a mountain of filthy torn cloths. Beyond the gates now and out of sight, she lifted tiny Valentina and checked to make sure she was okay. Then she clenched the babe tightly to her chest with one arm as she lay down and yanked rags over them both as best she could, holding her breath as she did.

Jules may have prevented the rescue of Amelie, but at least he had not stopped them from saving Valentina.

CHAPTER NINE

Renee

*S*unlight streamed through the window as I climbed out of bed the next morning, grabbed my toiletries, and headed for the shower. I was excited about seeing everyone, especially Danielle, who would be arriving before the others, in just a few hours.

The rest of the immediate family—all twenty-one of them—would be coming later, starting around five or six p.m., with dinner promptly at seven. Between now and then, my primary objective was to contact Dr. Underwood and somehow set in motion the task of going through the Persecution Pamphlet and finding all of the circled letters, whether by arranging to do it myself or hiring someone else. Beyond that, I would need to finish getting things ready with the display rooms, in particular making sure the setup for Danielle's video worked to her satisfaction. Otherwise, I would be pitching in as needed, helping to prepare not just for the closer relatives coming tonight but also the two hundred more Talbots arriving tomorrow.

Excited about all that lay ahead, I finished getting dressed and ready for the day and then did a final mirror check, pleased to see I was once again fully Nana-ready in pressed khaki slacks and a pale blue top, my hair shiny and straight, my makeup perfectly applied. I couldn't fathom how women found the time to go through such tediousness every single morning. As far as I was concerned, anything other than jeans and T-shirts was just too uncomfortable, and makeup was for the birds.

Speaking of birds, they were tweeting away like crazy when I stepped out of the guesthouse and pulled the door shut behind me. Looking around, I was struck anew by the beauty of this estate, the expansive crystal-clear pool, the wide flagstone patio, and the shady oaks, maples, and pines that dotted the immaculately trimmed grounds. It was all so peaceful and inviting—which said a lot considering that the Dark Woods were just beyond the perimeter.

As I headed toward the main house, I realized it was already hot, much hotter than at home. I didn't mind. That was part of coming here, especially when the high temps were exacerbated by humidity. Seattle's climate was so moderate, which was preferable for the day to day, but something about this kind of sweltering heat was part of the whole Virginia vacation experience, the steamy air evoking lazy morning brunches on the patio, afternoon dips in the pool, and evening chats rocking on the porch to the chirp of crickets and the sparkle of fireflies. Not that we'd have time for any of that today, but it was pleasant to imagine.

Because I'd never come early to the reunion before, I never realized how much work went into hosting two hundred plus people for a weekend, even if most of them would be staying at a hotel. I'd intended to pitch in where I could, but after sharing a quick breakfast with Nana, I ended up spending the next two hours on the phone, talking with Dr. Underwood about last night's discovery and trying to make arrangements to have the entire pamphlet analyzed as quickly as possible.

Despite our efforts, neither one of us was able to locate a reputable lab to do the job, much less on a rush basis, nor was there an electron microscope with DIC available for me to rent or borrow. In the end, our only solution was to talk with the folks at the Smithsonian and see if there was anything they could do. Intrigued by my findings, they said they would definitely examine the pamphlet for circles themselves once it was in their possession, and that they would be more than happy to let us know what they found.

But that meant giving the pamphlet over to them before we even knew what its message said. I didn't like that idea at all. Then again, what other choice did we have? We couldn't exactly postpone the ceremony, and in the end we'd still be donating it, message or not. Bottom line, I guessed we'd just have to go with it and trust that the Smithsonian people would keep us in the loop.

Sadly, because I was flying home Sunday and they couldn't even get started on it until Monday, Blake and I wouldn't be able to solve Jules's code together, something I'd really been looking forward to. Decoding secret messages was probably right up his alley, and working on it side by side with him would have been a lot of fun.

With a sigh, I gave up trying to find any other options, put away my notes, and turned my attention to preparations for the reunion. There was still much to do, and as I went from one task to another, I started thinking about my three cousins and how excited I was to see them.

I was closest to Danielle, but I also adored Madeline, who was just a year younger. I loved Maddee's little sister, Nicole, too, though things with her were always a bit more complicated as she tended to specialize in chaos, recklessness, and bad decisions. Nicole had been only six the year of the Incident, and in a way it had hit her harder than any of us. As she grew older and eventually "went wild," as Nana liked to put it, I'd often wondered how much that long-ago trauma played into Nicole's current issues. Regardless, we four cousins shared a bond born of family ties and annual gatherings and forged at a young age by our common trauma in the Dark Woods. Drama or not, I loved getting together with her and the others each year at the reunion.

I took a break in the early afternoon and threw together a quick lunch in the kitchen of the guest house. I was settling in at the table, just about to take the first bite of my turkey sandwich, when the door to the patio slid open with a bang. I looked up to see Danielle standing there, a duffel bag slung over one shoulder and a wide grin on her face.

The next hour flew by in a nonstop gabfest. My favorite cousin and I talked as I ate and she got unpacked, talked as we went to the main house and I showed her the display rooms, talked as she took a look at the projector and realized she could run the movie from a flash drive rather than from her laptop.

She grew quiet, and I watched as she dug one out from her bag, inserted it into her laptop, and copied over the file. With her blond, flyaway hair, perpetually dreamy expression, and just-a-little-outré clothing, Danielle always looked the part of the artist. It wasn't hard to imagine her out in a field of wildflowers, palette and brush in hand, poised in front of a waiting canvas. But now I was reminded that she was equally adept behind a camera or at a computer, using her skills with whatever medium applied at the moment.

Once she was finished with her last-minute edit, we sat side by side in the darkness of our little ad hoc movie theater and watched the story unfold on the screen in front of us. I'd had no doubt that the video would be visually appealing with a nice mix of photos and graphics and transitions worthy of a Ken Burns documentary. But I was more than a little impressed with the other elements as well, including the editing, pacing, and writing. I guess I shouldn't have been surprised. Creative types like Danielle often possessed talents across the board. She was even musical, yet one more skill that was as foreign to me as my world of colloid chemistry and security printing were to her.

We differed in other ways as well. She was lighthearted and silly where I was studious and somber, creative where I was scientific, absentminded where I was laser focused. Yet for all our differences, we got on so well together and always had. The fact that she'd been working with me on this important educational exhibit made it even that much better. Currently, Danielle's day job was as a freelance "visual merchandiser," which according to her was just a glorified term for window dresser. She liked her work, but her dream was to be a museum exhibition designer and eventually a curator, goals I had no doubt she would end up achieving. I'd seen pictures of her work, and even her most modest window designs were so good they practically belonged in a museum themselves.

Once we were finished with the movie, she and I spent a little time on the final touches of the display rooms and then passed the rest of the afternoon back outside, doing what we could to help.

Maddee showed up just around the time most of the workers were wrapping things up, so after the requisite squeals and hugs, Danielle and I called an end to our workday as well and the three of us headed to our room, arm in arm, to get cleaned up and ready for dinner. In the distance, we could hear the slam of car doors in the driveway and the chatter of excited voices as more relatives began to arrive. But except for a few hugs for my brothers and their families when they showed up at the guesthouse to drop off their bags, I was happy to start with just my two cousins for now and worry about greeting everyone else later.

A tall and striking redhead, Maddee was the prettiest of the cousins—and that was saying a lot. A classic ugly-duckling-turned-swan, she'd been perpetually freckled as a child, her reddish-brown hair a frizzy mess. As a teen, she shot up to nearly six feet tall and for years was all arms, legs, elbows, and knees—and braces. Thank goodness for Nana's etiquette classes, because at least Maddee learned at a young age to stand up straight and hold herself in a regal manner. It wasn't until she was nearing her twenties that she finally began to fill out and sort of grow into herself, and these days, she looked like a fashion model. The fact that she dressed with style and flair—often sporting three-inch heels without a second thought—only served to enhance her appearance. Still, even with all of that, the loveliest things about her were her sweet personality and maternal ways. Perhaps because she'd come to her beauty relatively late in life, she possessed not one ounce of divaness, which was refreshing in one so lovely.

After working outside in the heat for much of the day, I needed to start over with a shower, so once Danielle and Maddee were dressed and ready, they sat on their beds in our room and kept me company while I did my makeup. The topic of Nicole arose right away, as she had yet to appear.

Maddee sighed. "We never know what she's up to these days." She looked from me to Danielle and then down at her hands. "She may not be coming at all."

"*What?*" Danielle cried, her tone echoing my own surprise. It wasn't unusual for Nicole to be late, or to show up with alcohol on her breath, but she'd always come eventually. She'd never missed the reunion before. None of us had.

Maddee caught us up on her little sister's latest drama, but after a while I tuned it out and focused on finishing my face. It was always the same story, back to drinking, probably drugs as well, living with some guy—a classic tale of self-destruction. Maddie had contacted Nicole a few weeks ago to see if she wanted a ride to the reunion. Nicole had said no, that she was going to have to "play it by ear" this year. Both Maddee and her mom had tried reaching out several times since then, but Nicole had stopped answering their calls or responding to their texts a few days ago.

"That tells me she's going to be a no-show," Maddee added, "and that she just doesn't want to hear it."

Saddened by our conversation, I was glad when we moved on to another subject. Once I was ready, the three of us clustered together and Danielle snapped a selfie. We looked good, if I did say so myself, but an odd thought struck me as I glanced at my two cousins. Between the delicate, ethereal loveliness of Danielle and the tall, striking good looks of Maddee, they were both certain to catch Blake's eye tomorrow when he came to guard the display. To my surprise, the muscle man had really started to grow on me, and the thought that he'd soon be sharing witty repartee with these two beauties made me feel oddly...disappointed.

Putting such thoughts from my mind for now, I fell in step as we headed to the main house. Inside was happy chaos with everyone greeting each other and doing the how-are-you, you-look-great thing. Once all were present and accounted for, we gathered around the massive dinner table for our first big family meal since the one following Granddad's funeral seven months ago.

Nana asked Uncle Finley to lead us in prayer, and when he was finished, she rose to give a toast.

"To this amazing family and its brave spirit," she said, holding up her glass of iced tea. "And to the weekend ahead. May it be full of love, joy, and unity."

There were "hear, hears" and clinks and sips, and a whole lot of smiles and even a few hugs around the table.

Nana remained standing, and once things quieted down, she raised her glass a second time.

"And to the man," her voice caught for a moment, but she swallowed hard and then started again. "To the man who should be in the chair at the end of this table," she said, holding up a glass toward that empty seat, as if Granddad were still there and doing the same in return.

We all grew more solemn as we joined in, the words "to Dad" and "to Granddad" echoing all around. Nana sat and we began our meal. But as it went on, I couldn't stop my eyes from wandering again and again to the second empty chair here, the one across from me, where Nicole should have been sitting and was not.

The next morning I was awake and ready for the big day before either of my roommates even stirred. Blake would arrive at eight, and the relatives would start piling in at nine, so I was glad for the extra time to grab some breakfast, get fixed up, and tend to last-minute details.

As soon as I stepped outside I realized that today was as hot as yesterday but not nearly as muggy—not yet, anyway—which was good. We almost always had nice weather for the reunion weekend.

I entered the house through the front door. Everyone attending the event would come this way to pick up their welcome packet and sign up for a time slot on the Persecution Pamphlet viewing schedule. Then they would move through the entrance hall and out the French doors to the festivities beyond. Those who signed up to see the pamphlet were to return to the laundry room at their designated times, and they would enter in groups of ten to watch the video in the first room, view the pamphlet under glass in the second, and then exit through the mudroom door to the outside.

Excited for the day to start, I grabbed a welcome packet myself and carried it to the dining room, which was blessedly empty and quiet for the moment. Today's lunch would be served outside, with chefs in tall white hats at carving stations and servers in crisp uniforms hurrying back and forth replenishing the buffet. But this breakfast, a much more modest and mostly unattended spread, was only for those who were staying here at the house, to be eaten at our convenience. I helped myself to a bowl of oatmeal from a steaming Crock-Pot and then topped it with nuts and raisins and a shot of milk.

I would have preferred to eat in the solarium, but I could hear workmen in there, probably hanging up the giant family tree the committee rolled out and added to each year as needed. Instead, grateful to have the room to myself for the moment, I sat facing the windows at one corner of the dining table, said a silent grace, and then enjoyed my breakfast as I looked out on all the preparations.

The grounds beyond the pool area were starting to buzz with activity as a bunch of green-polo-shirted workers from the rental company swarmed across the yard, setting up large white canopy tents that would provide extra shade. Others were bringing in rented tables and chairs that would go under them.

I turned my attention to the welcome packet, pulling out the contents and skimming through everything. It all looked great, as usual. There was a map of the house and grounds showing the various activity stations and a schedule of events packed with all sorts of fun, including the Talbot Family Olympics and the Annual Talbot Talent Show. This year's main event, however, was the ceremony. It would be held tomorrow, in the backyard, with our top dignitaries seated on a rented dais and everyone else watching from chairs under the big white tents.

So that the pamphlet would not have to be exposed to the elements, I'd made a facsimile of it, and the plan was for Uncle Finley and Nana to symbolically present that to the director of the museum during the ceremony. Then, once it was over, a few of us were to proceed to the study, where we'd retrieve the actual document from the safe and hand it over for real.

Just the thought of that special moment brought bittersweet tears to my eyes. Blinking them away, I finished my breakfast, cleared my dishes, and headed for the viewing rooms—or at least that was my intention. It wasn't yet eight a.m., but already the check-in ladies were assembling in the main hallway, and between them and the aunts and uncles and cousins who were coming down to eat, I was waylaid several times.

Nana was there too, impeccably dressed and coiffed as usual, and though she seemed excited, there was a distinct sadness in her eyes. Impulsively, I pulled her in for a big hug.

"I miss him too," I whispered before letting go.

We shared a teary smile—what was it with me and tears this morning?—and then she surprised me by placing a hand on my cheek and holding it there for a long moment, soft and papery and cool, as she gazed lovingly into my eyes. She'd never been overly demonstrative, so the tenderness of the gesture made it even more special to me.

Our moment was interrupted from one direction by my parents, who were just coming down for breakfast themselves, and the other by a fresh batch of volunteers feeding in through the front door.

I loved seeing my family like this each year, but making pleasant conversation with so many people at once was draining for me, especially when I still had things to do. It didn't help matters when some of the youngest relatives, excited to be together again, started running up and down the broad hallway, weaving in and out between our legs, giggling all the while. Feeling flushed and overwhelmed, I longed for the quiet of my lab back home but was willing to settle for the display rooms right now—if only I could get to them. Attempting again to extricate myself, with one last dash I finally made it.

Pulling the door shut firmly behind me, I sat in the nearest chair in the empty room, closed my eyes, and tried to catch my breath. I was starting to feel better a few minutes later when Danielle came in from the outside door, looking lovely in a pale pink sundress and strappy sandals.

"Hey, you," she said, wiggling a flash drive at me. "I added some last-minute tweaks to the movie and wanted to run through part of it again on the big screen. Is that okay?"

"Of course."

"I'm not interrupting? You look like you're in the middle of something."

I smiled. "Yeah. I was recovering."

"From?"

"Let's see. 'Oh my goodness, you're getting so much older!' 'Honey, you're just so thin, do you ever eat?' 'Looks like you've put on a few pounds since last year, Renee. Are you eating too much?'"

Danielle laughed. "Oh, boy. I can't wait." Glancing around, she spotted the ladder, now propped against the wall, and moved it over under the projector.

"And then there's my favorite," I continued. "'Are you seeing anyone?' I got that three times. This last time, they added, 'Are you seeing anyone? Because you're not getting any younger, you know.'"

With a groan, Danielle started up the ladder. Moving closer, I held it steady while she worked.

"So are you?" she asked after a moment.

"Am I what?"

"Seeing someone? I noticed you didn't volunteer any info last night when Maddee and I were dishing about our love lives."

For some reason I found myself hesitating. The answer was no, and yet not only was that word suddenly stuck in my throat, but I could feel my cheeks turning a vivid red.

In the the absence of a reply, Danielle glanced down at me and then did a double take. Mortified, I turned my face away.

"Renee!" she cried eagerly, abandoning her task and climbing halfway down. "What are you not telling me? I know that expression. There *is* someone, isn't there?"

"No!" I blurted out, the word finally popping from my throat like a piece of bread after a Heimlich maneuver.

She came down the rest of the way and stood her ground in front of me, hands on her hips. "Oh, yeah? This is *me* you're talking too, cuz. I see all, I know all, remember? Now spill."

I let go of the ladder, taking a step back. "I'm not dating anybody, I promise."

"But..."

This was so embarrassing. "But...okay, fine. I did meet someone just recently who seems kind of interesting. "

"Mm-hmm," she said, her eyes narrowing. "And what's his name?"

I pinched a finger to my thumb and slid them across my lips like a zipper.

"Got it. So you think what's-his-name is 'interesting' but otherwise nothing's happened? You haven't gone out yet?"

I shook my head, feeling fourteen. "We only just met."

"Yeah, but what's the real holdup?"

I shrugged. "I don't know. He's not my type. Like, not at *all*."

"How so?"

To my relief, she turned back toward the ladder and began to climb it again.

"Well, he's kind of...um...well, *built*. Really built. Like big muscles, big neck, big arms. All brawn, no brains, you know? At least, that's what I thought at first. But then we started talking and..." My voice trailed off as I realized how ridiculous I was sounding. I hardly knew anything about the man. "It's dumb. Really. I doubt it's even mutual. Besides, he doesn't live near me, so it's not like we could date or anything."

At that moment, the door to the hallway swung open and there stood Blake Keller. Silhouetted against the bright morning light pouring in from the windows behind him, he looked like some sort of Adonis poised on the horizon. Then he moved further inside the room and shut the door, turning back into himself again.

Not that he wasn't an Adonis in his own right.

Chapter Ten

Renee

"Good morning," I said to Blake, drawing on every speck of summer etiquette camp I could muster to stay right where I was rather than walk away and start fiddling with the pleats on the nearest fabric panel or straightening the rows of chairs.

"Good morning, Talbot," he replied, his eyes sparkling as they lingered on mine.

Ignoring the flirty nature of his gaze, I turned toward Danielle, who had come back down the ladder and was waiting for an introduction. "Blake, this is my cousin Danielle Talbot. Danielle, this is Blake Keller."

"Nice to meet you," he said, turning that handsome gaze toward her. He was looking good—maybe too good—in a slim-cut navy jacket, light blue shirt, and subtly striped tie.

"You too," she replied, shaking hands and giving him her prettiest smile.

Oh, who was I kidding? He could never be interested in someone like me with someone like her around. And the minute Maddee showed up, well, that would seal the deal. Not that either one of them were man-stealers by any means—nor that this guy was even mine to steal in the first place. But still. It was ludicrous to believe he might look my way again once he'd met the two of them.

Feeling disheartened but trying not to let it show, I explained to Danielle that Blake was with Nana's insurance company and had been charged with protecting the Persecution Pamphlet until tomorrow's ceremony.

"Cool. Like, standing guard and everything?" she asked, her eyelashes looking ridiculously long and full.

"Actually, I have a guy to do that, but I'll be spelling him once in a while. Otherwise, I'll be sort of here and there, just keeping an eye on things."

He flashed me a quick smile, but I found myself incapable of giving him one in return.

"Danielle is the one who did the posters," I said instead, trying to cover my awkwardness. "And the film too."

"Oh, so you're the artist, huh? Your grandmother mentioned you. I have to say, you look almost exactly like I expected you would." With a quick glance at me, he added, "Then again, I'm kind of uncanny that way. I always know what to expect when meeting new people."

I waited a beat. "Yeah, it's his superpower," I said dryly, a flutter running through me at our shared private joke.

We were interrupted by the ding of an incoming text. Blake pulled out his phone and glanced at the screen before excusing himself, saying his "guy" had arrived. With that, he went out the way he'd come in, leaving behind a silence so loud I could almost hear the grass growing outside.

"Lots to get done!" I said quickly, turning on my heel and moving as fast as I could into the other room.

"Yeah, like that's going to save you," Danielle replied with a giggle, hot on my heels.

My face burning, I reached behind a fabric panel to grab a rag and the bottle of cleaner Dr. Underwood had left for me, and then turned and went to town on the display cabinet.

"Honey. Seriously. You call that 'interesting'?" Her tone was hushed but eager. "I call that prime rib with lobster on the side. Are you *kidding* me? He's *gorgeous*. And *totally* into you, by the way."

"No, he's not." My hands went still, but I couldn't meet my cousin's eyes. "Is he?"

I expected to hear something sweet, something encouraging and kind.

Instead, her voice was sharp and scolding. "Now you listen here, missy."

When I didn't meet her eyes, Danielle leaned forward and placed both hands squarely on top of the case I was trying to clean.

"Hey—"

"Renee," she barked, cutting me off. "This is serious."

I stopped cleaning and stepped back. "What?"

Looking me deeply in the eye, she spoke succinctly. "Do. Not. Mess. This. Up. Not again."

I looked away.

"Oh, like you don't know what I'm talking about? Every time you meet a guy who is actually smart enough and cute enough to catch your eye, you end up running him off."

"Come on—"

"Either you're snarky or condescending or, worst of all, you do the buddy thing, where you act more like a sister than a girlfriend."

Ouch. Her words hurt, but we both knew they were true.

We were quiet for a long moment. When she spoke again, her tone at last was gentle. "I don't know what it's going to take to make you change," she said softly, "but at least you have to try." After a beat, she smiled and added in a high-pitched, nasally voice, "Because you're not getting any younger, you know."

As it turned out, Blake's guy was a grizzled older fellow with a gravelly voice and steely blue eyes who introduced himself as "Ingles"— though whether that was his first name or last, I wasn't sure. He was wearing a navy uniform with all kinds of things strapped to it, including a Taser, a flashlight that could double as a billy club, and a big, shiny gun. I wasn't exactly thrilled at the sight, but at least I didn't have a panic attack. Unlike yesterday outside the bank, I was prepared this time.

Blake instructed Ingles on logistics and procedure while I finished the last of my preparations, and then it was time to retrieve the pamphlet from the study. Only then, however, did I realize I had made one important miscalculation: Between here and there were tons of relatives, even more than before. I explained to Blake that we were going to be waylaid, probably over and over. He thought for a moment and then looked to his buddy.

"Guess we can do a Swift?"

"Sure," he replied, standing up straight and placing a hand just millimeters away from his gun barrel.

My pulse surged. "What's a swift?"

"A Taylor Swift," Blake explained. "Her tour came through Richmond last month, and Ingles and I were in charge of getting her in and out of the coliseum. We got it down to a science."

I blinked, about to ask what on earth they were doing escorting a pop star to her concerts when he added matter-of-factly, "Her legs are insured by our company."

"Ah. I see."

"Anyway, here's how it works," Blake continued, taking my elbow. "The two of us flank you real tight and then we walk three across, moving with speed and purpose directly from here to the study in as straight a line as we can muster."

"If anyone tries to engage," Ingles added, "we just pass 'em by. No eye contact, no response. Nothing. Got it?"

Behind me, Danielle clapped. "Fun, Renee! You're a rock star."

I couldn't imagine anything I less wanted to be, but the pamphlet was in there and we needed it in here, so I reluctantly agreed. Then we were off.

By the time we returned, I could barely control myself. As Ingles pulled the door shut behind us, I burst into laughter.

"Unbelievable," Blake said, laughing as well, though his cheeks were tinged with pink.

Ingles merely gave a growl and then marched into the next room.

"What happened?" Danielle asked, wanting in on the joke.

As soon as I caught my breath, I replied, "Let's just say the most rabid of Taylor Swift fans has nothing on Aunt Cissy."

"No! Not Aunt Cissy."

"Oh, yeah, and she's in fine form. 'I will *not* step aside, young man,'" I said in my best imitation. "'I don't care how big your muscles are. I haven't seen my great-niece in months and I am going to give her a hug whether you like it or not.'"

Blake gave an exaggerated shudder. "Feels like I've stared death in the face...and lost."

He was just joking, but his words fell on Danielle and me like ice water.

Our smiles instantly fading, we both looked away, a familiar, surprising *thud* hitting me square in the chest. Danielle wasn't much better. After mumbling a quick, "Excuse me," she turned and left, going out through the same door she'd come in.

Poor Blake. He had no way of knowing what he'd done wrong, of knowing that that's exactly what she and I had done when we were just children. We had stared death in the face, and in many ways, we had lost.

Ignoring his perplexed expression, I forced a smile and held up the pale green case. "We'd better take care of this."

I headed for the next room, Blake coming right behind me. Ignoring him, I turned on the UV-safe lights that were directed toward the cabinet and turned off all of the others. As I worked, I heard him ask Ingles if he would give us a minute.

Without a word, Ingles left, and then Blake and I were alone.

I managed to avoid his eyes as I handed him the case and retrieved the white cotton gloves. Once the gloves were on, I gestured for him to open it up, but instead he pulled it away, holding it beyond my reach.

"Blake—"

"Renee." His voice was soft and deep, possessing a tenderness that surprised me. "What happened out there just now? I obviously offended you or hurt your feelings in some way, but I don't know how. And for the second time too. I'm thinking if you could bring me up to speed, maybe I can stop doing whatever it is I keep doing."

I sighed, wishing I could tell him, that I could just blurt out the story as if it were no big deal. But it wasn't that simple.

Even so, he was a decent fellow, and I felt bad that he thought these odd moments were somehow his fault. I wouldn't go into everything, but maybe he did deserve at least part of the story.

"It's not you, I promise," I said, forcing my voice to sound calmer than I felt. "I was...I have...My cousins and I, when we were kids, we went through something traumatic. And it left a few scars, that's all."

His eyes widened.

"Emotional scars, I mean. The kind that make a person overreact to a perfectly innocent comment, like what you said in there about looking death in the eye. You were just joking, and you couldn't possibly know your words would hit so close to home. It's not anything you can stop or change. It's just a problem of ours. Of mine. I appreciate your asking, but please don't worry about it. Really."

His eyes narrowed. "And Wednesday? In the car, outside the bank? What did I say wrong that time? After you practically ran away, I started to ask your grandmother what I'd done to offend you, but she immediately changed the subject, and I could tell she didn't want to talk about it."

Of course not. She never wanted to talk about it, not even back when it first happened.

I shrugged. "Well, thanks to the same incident, I'm sort of paranoid about weapons. I happened to see your gun as you were walking past the window, and it startled me. That's all. I was fine afterward. I just had to calm down a little." Gesturing toward his hip, I added, "I mean, I'm sure you're wearing it now and see? I'm okay. It's all about expectation and not being caught by surprise."

"Oh. Huh." He thought about that for a long moment. "So, if I may ask, what happened to you that was so traumatic? Though if you'd rather not talk about it..."

I hesitated. "It's a long story. Basically, my cousins and I were off playing when we happened upon a crime scene, someone who had recently been murdered in cold blood."

Blake's eyes widened again.

I decided to elaborate just a little. "We'd gone hiking in the woods next door, all the way to an old hunting cabin where we loved to play. As soon as we walked inside, we saw a man lying on a cot across the room, a big knife buried in his chest, and pools of blood splattered on the wall and pooled all over the floor."

Blake sucked in a breath. "How old were you?"

"Danielle and I were nine. Madeline was eight. Nicole was six."

"No wonder it left scars—on all of you, I would imagine."

I nodded, wishing I could tell him the rest of the story, the part that had been in a sense even more damaging, the part about how we ran screaming toward home, told our parents, and waited till the police arrived. How by the time we got back to the cabin, the body was gone. In the space of maybe half an hour total, someone had come in and removed the corpse and completely cleaned up the scene. To make matters worse, they had also set things up to look as if our dead body was a pile of blankets, the knife was a stick poking out of them, and the blood was just a puddle of rainwater from one of the leaks in the roof.

I couldn't tell Blake about that, which was something I'd learned the hard way. I just couldn't bear that inevitable moment when I laid it all out for someone new and saw a flicker of doubt in response, a millisecond of *maybe it really was just a blanket and a stick and a puddle.* Whenever that happened, I'd feel as betrayed as I had that day, when the police and our parents decided we'd merely been the victims of our own overactive imaginations. Some of our male cousins had even dubbed us the "Liar Choir," a nickname the four of us found infuriating.

I'd spent the past nineteen years trying to understand what happened out there in the woods, nineteen years knowing that what we saw was real, and knowing the adults who were supposed to be our advocates did not believe us. Eventually, they grew so tired of our histrionics that they even made us stop talking about it.

The biggest concession I'd ever gotten from anyone had come from a counselor I saw in college. "I believe that *you* believe that's what you saw," she'd told me. It wasn't enough, and I didn't go back.

Now, Blake was looking at me expectantly, and I could tell he knew there was more that I wasn't saying. But he didn't press, much to my relief. Instead, he simply gave a nod and told me, "Okay. Well thanks for explaining. I appreciate it. And, hey, you have my number. If something concerns or frightens you, feel free to text or call, okay?"

I simply nodded my head, unable to speak.

Then he held the case toward me and gave me a warm, encouraging smile, his signal that our talk was over and we could get on with the business at hand.

Oddly, now that he knew at least part of the truth, I felt better. Lighter, somehow. Maybe it was because he was so big and muscular, but being with him made me feel safe—despite the gun at his hip.

Returning his smile, I took the case, opened it up, and turned my attention to the pamphlet inside. I pulled it out and cradled it gingerly in my gloved hands. Blake opened the back of the display cabinet for me, and I gently slid the Persecution Pamphlet inside, laying it atop the slanted linen-wrapped prop box the way Dr. Underwood had shown me. It took some trial and error to get the pamphlet in just the right spot at just the right angle, even with Blake's assistance, but I was satisfied at last. Stepping back, I gestured for him to take it from there, and then I watched as he closed the back, bolted it shut, and activated the cabinet's alarm.

When he was finished, we took a final walk around both rooms. Blake put away the ladder and got Ingles back at his post while I tucked the case and the gloves into a cubby behind one of the fabric panels. Once we were all set, Blake checked his watch.

"Well, look at us," he said with a grin. "Ready for the masses with a good ten minutes to spare."

To my relief, the setup I'd been responsible for worked out great, with family members filing in to watch the film, continuing on to see the actual pamphlet, and then exiting from there. I'd known many of them would enjoy the experience, but what I hadn't anticipated was the word of mouth that would ripple through the crowd whenever a new group emerged from the rooms. By early afternoon, I'd had so many more requests from people who hadn't signed up in the first place and were now regretting it that I had to add on an additional hour and a half of viewing slots.

The rest of the reunion seemed to be flowing along well too, with folks chatting and laughing everywhere, as usual. When I wasn't busy with my mini museum, I was mostly hanging out with my first cousins—minus Nicole, who still hadn't shown up. Now and then during the day, whenever I saw Blake, I would feel a surprising surge of electricity deep in my chest. Eventually, I had to admit the truth. I found him intriguing and appealing, and I really would like to get to know him better.

At one point Danielle had to put in her time as a helper in the children's craft area, leaving Maddee and me to wander around alone. We played one round of horseshoes and then decided it was too hot and headed for the much cooler solarium inside the main house. That was where all the family displays were set up, starting with the "What's New?" section, where people could put any Talbot-related photos or facts or documents they had managed to unearth since the last reunion. Some of these folks were hard-core genealogists, and this gave them the opportunity to display the fruits of their labors each year. Though I had great respect for our family's history, I'd never really gotten into tracing my roots beyond the limits of an ancestry app on my phone, so I always appreciated that they were willing to share.

After that came my favorite display of all, the Talbot family tree. Printed on a massive sheet of vinyl that covered an entire wall, the original version of the huge sign had been created years before I was born and was updated—with new spouses, new babies, new information about previous generations—by hand, written in a neat print with a permanent marker, each year. The design featured the faint image of a tree in the background, its trunk running nearly from ceiling to floor, its widest limbs stretching almost the full span of the wall. In the foreground was the biggest, most fully constructed name chart I had ever seen, one that had grown bigger with each passing year.

I started, as always, by finding my own name, which sat just under my parents and alongside my brothers. Seeing it there always made me feel so connected to the extended Talbot family.

Except now it struck me for the first time how little space I took up compared to my siblings. I had one nameplate total: Renee Michelle Talbot. No spouse. No children. My two brothers, on the other hand, took up *seven* spaces between them. Seven.

To my one.

Refusing to dwell on that thought, I turned my attention to the top of the tree, to the man we considered the founding father of the family, Emmanuel Talbot. He'd been the first male Talbot to come to America, in the early 1700s, though I seemed to recall hearing that one or two of his sisters preceded him. Emmanuel's mother was Catherine Gillet Talbot, the one who had written the journal. Ever since I'd read her story in her own words four years ago, I'd felt a sense of kinship with the woman—and, by extension, her son.

"This thing is just about full," Maddee said, pointing to the bottom.

Taking a look, I realized she was right. There was room for just a few more names, and then this lovely family tree was going to be out of space.

"Not that they'll ever need any room for my sake," she added, an odd sadness in her voice.

I glanced at her, confused for a moment, and then it came to me.

Of course. The old baby hunger, an affliction Madee had suffered forever. I'd never really understood until a few years ago when I held my first nephew in my arms and gazed into his precious face. A sudden, sharp longing for a child of my own startled me in its intensity. In the three years since, the feeling would reemerge now and then, such as when I helped out in the church nursery or shopped for a Mother's Day card or rocked my niece or nephews to sleep.

Then again, I knew I had nothing on Maddee. A born mother, she reportedly tended to her classmates' needs when she was still in kindergarten. By age twelve, she'd already chosen the names for her future children—all six of them. By seventeen, she'd started sewing baby clothes and tucking them away for the future.

"God is the one who gave you all your mommy instincts," I said. "I'm sure He has something wonderful in mind for you."

"Yeah, I know. But I'm ready *now*. It's terrible, Renee. Sometimes I think I should just marry the next man I see."

As if on cue, a male voice called out to us. "Hey, Talbot, there you are. Got a minute?"

We turned to see Blake striding toward us across the solarium.

My heart sank. This was perfect. Not only had the inevitable moment arrived when he was to meet the most beautiful of my young and eligible cousins, but he couldn't have been given a better setup if he'd tried.

"Sure," I said, my voice strained as I made the introductions. He and Maddee greeted each other, but then he simply took me by the elbow and asked if he could borrow me for a minute.

"No problem," Maddee replied. "She's all yours."

Ignoring her bemused smile, I allowed Blake to lead me into the dining room.

"Your Aunt Cissy is looking for you," he said softly once we'd come to a stop, "to ask if she can sing the National Anthem at the ceremony tomorrow. I wasn't sure if that would be a good thing or a bad thing, so I decided to give you a heads up."

I groaned. "Oh, that would be a bad thing, a very bad thing. Thanks for the warning."

He smiled. "Want me to head her off at the pass?"

I thought for a moment. "Nah, that's okay. I'll just tell her the only way we could fit it in would be to cancel somebody's speech, but that I wouldn't feel right doing that on such short notice."

"Ah, that should work," he said, eyeing me shrewdly. "See? That's why I like you, Renee. You're not just book smart, you're people smart too."

With that, he turned and headed for the door, leaving me to watch him go.

His words stayed with me the rest of the afternoon and into the evening. They were still on my mind once the day's events finally came to an end. Even after Blake was gone for the night and I rounded up my cousins and we set to work dismantling as much of the mini museum as we could—taking down the fabric panels and putting away the chairs and the screen—five words kept ringing around in my head.

That's why I like you. That's why I like you.

What did he mean, exactly, by the word "like"? As a friend? As something else? There was definitely chemistry between us, but did he actually *like* me?

Just as important, did he realize I liked him?

Of course, I got nothing but torment from my two cousins later that night once we were in our room. Like a pair of teenagers, they kept swooning and giggling and teasing me about Blake until finally my older brother knocked on the door and asked us for the third time to please quiet down and go to sleep. Chagrined, we did as requested, turning off the light and climbing into our beds and eventually falling silent.

I thought I'd be awake half the night, my mind swirling with thoughts of Blake. But the exhaustion of the day soon caught up with me, and I was relieved to find myself drifting off to dreamland.

Chapter Eleven
Catherine

After traveling for what seemed like hours, Catherine felt the cart slow. She laid as still as possible under the rags, clutching the whimpering baby to her chest, praying that whatever had caused them to move from a gallop to a trot would not end up with them being apprehended.

"Catherine? Are you okay?" Pierre asked softly, but she didn't dare reply. After a moment, he said it again, this time adding, "You can speak. We're alone on the road. How are you doing? Is the baby all right?"

"We are both fine. What's going on? Why have we slowed down?"

"We're nearing the city and need to travel at a normal speed. We don't want to appear as if we're fleeing."

"But we are," she said. "Please hurry, Pierre. Surely the guards have horses and will be along to catch us soon."

"No, I believe we're safe. Jules is the one who has Amelie, so our hope is that they will follow him. He'll easily outrun them."

Lying there in the darkness, under the rags, the small weight of the infant atop her chest, Catherine's mind reeled. So Jules had come not to sabotage but to *assist*?

She could scarcely believe it.

The rain started up again, the drops plopping softly against the rags above her, the water eventually making its way through the cloths to her face and body. Instead of acclimating to the stench from the soiled rags, she nearly retched from the smell. Carefully, she shifted her cloak so it covered the infant and would perhaps keep her dry a bit longer. A quarter of an hour later, Catherine could tell from the sounds and the movements of the cart that they were nearly home.

They came to a stop, and she could hear Pierre jump down to open the courtyard doors. Beyond, the bells of the cathedral tolled, commemorating Jesus's Last Supper with His disciples. The bells would not ring again until Easter Sunday.

Seigneur, aide-nous, she prayed as the wagon shifted under Pierre's weight and they inched forward into the courtyard.

She waited for the telltale *clunk* of the gate before finally sitting up, still clutching the whimpering baby to her chest. Rain pelted her face as she leaned forward, trying to protect Valentina.

Grand-Mère's voiced called out, "Where is she? Where is the *bébé*?" Catherine breathed a deep sigh of relief. If Grand-Mère knew about Valentina, that meant Jules and Amelie had arrived ahead of them.

Turning, Catherine lifted the child toward the side of the cart and into her grandmother's waiting arms. She had never been so relieved in all her life. Not only had they all made it safely home, but now someone with experience could take over with the infant.

"*Merci,* sweet Jesus, *merci,*" Grand-Mère cried, holding the babe close to her face for a good look and then tucking the little one's head under her chin. As she moved toward the house, she called out, "God bless you, Catherine. You did the right thing."

Overwhelmed, Catherine nearly fell back into the rags.

"Come on," Pierre said, reaching for her hand. "You need to get dry and warm."

Water dripped from his hat.

"You too," she said, taking his hand and rising to a standing position. He gripped her waist and swung her down to the ground. Their eyes met and held, and in that moment Catherine could see the love in his expression. But there were other emotions there as well, primarily consternation—perhaps even regret—for what they had just done.

"Trust me, Pierre. It was the right thing to do. Now that we know she had a *bébé*, our actions were even more justified."

He gazed into her eyes and seemed about to pull her into an embrace when Monsieur Roen emerged from the stables.

"I will take care of the horse," he said, seemingly unaware that he had interrupted their moment.

"I need to return the cart," Pierre answered, taking a step back and running his hand across his wet face.

"Can't it wait until morning?" Catherine asked.

Pierre shook his head. "I promised the rag peddler—"

"There is a dragoon across the street," the coachman whispered as he drew closer.

"*Oui*, I saw him," Pierre replied. "He is an old acquaintance, Waltier Chaput."

Catherine grimaced. "I recognized him earlier today."

"I believe he will look the other way." Pierre turned to Monsieur Roen. "I will return the cart in a little while."

The man nodded. "I will feed the horse in the meantime." He clucked his tongue. "You two did a brave thing tonight."

Tears stung Catherine's eyes. Pierre took her hand, leading her into the house. Even in the cold rain, his skin was hot against hers, and she longed to wrap her arms around him. She resisted, all thoughts of their earlier conflict far from her mind at the moment.

Cook stood by the fire, stirring the pot. "I have a *ragoût* on," she said as they entered, dragging her plump forearm across her brow. "Get cleaned up and then come eat."

"Where is Amelie?" Catherine asked.

"In your grandmother's apartment."

Together, Catherine and Pierre moved from the kitchen into the hallway. When he paused at the door to the study, she braced herself, knowing Jules was likely inside and it was now time for her chastisement.

"I need to check in with your brother," Pierre said, calming her fears. "I will find you before I leave."

Catherine gave him a nod and then hurried down the hall toward the sound of a crying baby. She pushed open the door and moved through the sitting area to the bedchamber. By the dim light of the candles, Catherine could see that the drapes of the canopy bed were open, and Grand-Mère was helping Amelie into one of Catherine's nightgowns. The baby was crying loudly, her face red and scrunched up as she wailed on her blanket on the end of the bed. Catherine could not help but smile, grateful that the infant had withheld such a racket until they were safely home, almost as if she had known to be quiet for their escape.

"I have dry clothes for you," Grand-Mère said to Catherine. "On the chair."

Catherine stooped to pick up the baby.

"Leave her," Grand-Mère said. "I will attend to her in just a moment."

Catherine washed her face and hands, undressed, dried off, and then slipped into fresh undergarments and a housedress. Then she wrapped a shawl around her shoulders.

When she turned back again, Amelie was tucked under the covers and Grand-Mère had the baby unwrapped and was examining her, clucking her tongue as she did. "She is scrawny."

"I was so ill at first that they brought in a wet nurse for a time. But then as soon as my fever passed, they let the girl go, insisting I was well enough to nurse her."

"Clearly they were wrong," Grand-Mère said, her eyes still on the baby.

Amelie sighed. "I tried to convince them to either bring the wet nurse back or find another one."

Grand-Mère clucked her tongue again, pulling the cloth from the little one's bottom. With her other hand, she unfastened the ring of keys from her skirt and handed it to Catherine. "Go get rags from the housekeeper's cupboard."

Catherine obeyed, although she hated to leave. As she headed down the hall, she heard a low rumble of voices in the study, their words becoming clearer as she drew closer.

"We should not have been there at all," Jules said as she passed the closed door, causing her to pause and listen. "Now I will need to petition our solicitor to prove that my guardianship of Amelie supplants what rights those at the convent have over her." He sighed, loudly. "Not to mention Catherine risked Amelie's life—and her own. And the baby's."

"*Oui,*" Pierre replied.

Catherine's stomach clenched. Nothing had changed. Jules may have shown up after all, but apparently it had been against his will and his better judgment. Worse, Pierre—who had been so heroic just a short while ago—was again acting as Jules's most dependable pawn.

"But God worked good of it," Pierre added after a moment. "*Oui?*"

At that, Catherine's heart softened just a bit. Perhaps he was not so much a pawn as a knight, which was another thing entirely.

She did not hear Jules's response over a pounding sound from the kitchen.

She turned that way and had only taken a few steps when Cook yelled, "Monsieur Gillet!"

Moving back toward the study, Catherine called out, "Jules!"

The door swung open. The two men emerged and headed toward the kitchen. She followed, stopping in the doorway. Three dragoons, including Waltier, stood in the middle of the room. They each wore white trousers, a brown coat, and red vest. Monsieur Roen stood behind them.

"*Merci,*" Jules said to Cook. "You may go on to your quarters. I will deal with this."

"I would rather not," she said.

Jules put his hand on her shoulder. "I insist." He gave her a gentle nudge and pointed in the direction of the stairs to the servants' floor.

When Cook left, Jules asked what the dragoons wanted. Waltier stepped forward. "We have been assigned to *billet* in this home."

Jules laughed, something he rarely did, and then asked, "Our home?"

"*Oui,*" Waltier responded.

Jules turned to Catherine. "Go help Grand-Mère."

She wrinkled her nose but darted to the housekeeper's cupboard, unlocked the door, grabbed a handful of clean rags, relocked it, and headed back to the hall. She paused for a moment, hoping to hear more, but Jules spoke so quietly she could not make out his words.

Catherine found Grand-Mère sitting on the edge of the bed, the baby in one arm and her other hand on Amelie's forehead. "What is going on out there?" Grand-Mère asked. "Is that the physician already? I sent the footman after him, but I did not expect them back so soon."

"No. It's dragoons." Catherine handed over one of the cloths. "They have been assigned to our house."

Grand-Mère groaned.

"One of them is Waltier Chaput." She put the other rags on the table. "Do you remember him, Amelie? He was a friend of Pierre's."

Amelie nodded but did not answer. Her hair was pulled back from her ashen face. It seemed her brown eyes had grown bigger in the last year and her cheekbones sharper.

"Go get your things from your room before they head up there," Grand-Mère said to Catherine. "You will stay in here with us."

Catherine grabbed one of the candles from the table and followed Grand-Mère's instructions, running up the stairs and then quickly gathering clothes from the pegs along the far wall and from her chest, shoving all of them into a large basket. Someone—probably the house-keeper—had already closed the wooden shutters over the windows, blocking her view of the courtyard. There were shouts below. Waltier and the other dragoons were probably forcing Monsieur Roen to care for their horses. As badly as she felt for their loyal coachman, she was grateful for the extra time the ruckus was bringing her.

She gathered up her books, her collection of writing tucked inside her leather satchel, and her pens and ink, wedging them along the sides of the basket. Then she hurried from the room, the basket under one arm and the candle in the other hand.

She made her way to the staircase as the flickering flame cast her shadow along the stone wall. As she started to descend, voices startled her.

"We will take any room we please," one of the dragoons said and then laughed.

Holding back a gasp, she leaned against the stairwell to steady herself.

"I will escort you," Jules said.

"No need," the same dragoon replied.

Grateful her brother was there too, Catherine started down the stairs again, moving as quickly as she could. But before she reached the halfway point they started up, the loud one first. He leered at her. She kept barreling down the steps, but he stopped and spread his arms wide.

"*Excusez-moi*," she said.

"Take the basket back upstairs."

"*Pardonnez-moi?*"

He stepped closer. She turned her face to the side, away from his foul breath, and wedged the basket between them.

There was a scuffle at the bottom of the steps and then Pierre's voice, calling out, "You will act like gentlemen!"

The dragoon laughed.

"Let her pass," Waltier said.

The loud dragoon's face grew hard, and he pressed against the basket. "You will soon see how this works. This is not the first Huguenot house I have billeted in—and to think there are two young ladies here. And both are ready to be married." He laughed as he stepped back, without warning. Catherine fell forward, past him, and against Waltier. The basket slipped from her arms and tumbled down the steps, her belongings scattering.

The first dragoon stomped up the stairs, still laughing. Waltier muttered, "*Désolé*," as he righted her. "It's only temporary until we are assigned south of here, along the Rhône." As he followed the other dragoon, he hissed, "Basile, stop acting like a brute."

Catherine bent down to grab an underskirt and then a pen. Pierre helped her collect her things, much to her embarrassment. Once they had gathered it all, Jules told her to go directly to Grand-Mère's apartment and not come back out again.

Looking to Pierre, he added, "You should go. What if dragoons have arrived at your house too?"

Pierre exhaled. "You're right. Mère would not handle that well at all."

Catherine reached out to take the basket from him, but he insisted on carrying it for her. They walked together down the hall to the apartment, and when he handed it to her at the door, she looked up into his deep blue eyes.

"*Merci*," she said. "Not just for this. For everything."

A gentle smile came into his eyes as he gazed down at her and gave a slight shake of his head, as if to say *I only did it because I know how stubborn you are.*

Their gaze lingered for a moment, and then with a final nod, she took the basket from him and slipped quietly into her grandmother's rooms.

The footman returned, saying he had left word for the physician but had no idea when he would come. Amelie tried to nurse the baby during the night, over and over, but the infant's cries became increasingly frantic. Before dawn, Grand-Mère stole out of the bedroom door. Catherine scooped the baby from the bed and followed her, thinking that maybe Amelie could get some sleep without all that crying in her ear.

Cook was stoking the fire when Catherine followed Grand-Mère into the kitchen. The baby stopped screaming for a moment, her eyes darting to the massive timbers overhead darkened by smoke and then to the flickering light from the lamp on the table.

Monsieur Roen sat at the end of it but stood in a hurry when they entered. Grand-Mère waved her hand at him and he sat back down.

"Has Jules already left for the day?" Catherine asked.

Cook nodded and reached for the baby. "Poor, miserable little thing," she cooed, her mouth against Valentina's dark hair.

"We need a wet nurse." Grand-Mère sounded exhausted.

"Of course you do," Cook answered, her head still down.

"Do you know of one?"

Both servants shook their heads, but then Cook turned toward Monsieur Roen. "What about the young woman from mass, the seamstress whose husband passed away back in January? Did she not just have her *bébé*? I know she is struggling to make ends meet. Perhaps…" Her voice trailed off as their eyes locked and something unspoken passed between them.

"Perhaps," Monsieur Roen replied, though he sounded far less certain.

Grand-Mère interrupted. "Could you send word to the girl that I would like to speak with her about a job?"

Monsieur Roen pinched his lips together, his cheeks suddenly flushing a bright pink. When he did not reply, Grand-Mère glanced at Cook, but she busied herself by bouncing the squalling baby in her arms. Catherine realized what was going on. Obviously, Grand-Mère understood as well.

"Perhaps being paid for two jobs at once would be worth the risk of associating with Huguenots," she said, an icy edge to her voice. "Tell her she would be allowed to do her regular seamstress work between feedings."

Everyone was quiet for a moment until finally Monsieur Roen spoke. "I am not sure how to get in touch with the girl, but I will go see Father Philippe. He will direct me."

"*Merci*," Grand-Mère whispered. "As for our other problem, the matter of the dragoons…" Her voice trailed off as she stepped forward and took the baby from Cook. "I am aware of the extra work their presence is creating for both of you. More mouths to feed. More horses to tend. Perhaps you could each hire a temporary helper or two?"

Again, both Cook and Monsier Roen averted their eyes, responding to Grand-Mère's offer with shrugs and mumbles of "That is not necessary." Obviously, no one would be willing to take on such a job—and all four of them knew it.

"Very well." Pulling Valentina close, Grand-Mère turned to go but then paused and looked back at the two servants. "Both of you have worked here all these years, and I feel as if I need to be the one to say this. I understand if you would rather seek employment elsewhere."

Cook kept her eyes on the fire. "Are you wanting us to leave, Madame?"

"Of course not. I do not want trouble for you. That is all."

Monsieur Roen stood. "I am staying here."

"So am I," Cook said.

Grand-Mère nodded in response but did not speak. Then she hurried from the room, no doubt before they could see the tears of gratitude their loyalty had brought to her eyes.

The dragoons left the house just after sunrise, telling Cook they would be patrolling the other side of the Rhône all day but would be back in time for dinner.

An hour later Monsieur Roen returned, and Catherine traipsed after Grand-Mère, the crying baby in her arms, into the kitchen. A red-eyed and red-faced young woman stood on the stoop. She was young, perhaps a year or two younger than Catherine.

"I am here for the job," she said in a voice barely above a whisper. "My name is Estelle."

"*Merci* for coming, Estelle. And your *bébé*?" Grand-Mère said. "Where is she?"

The girl looked down toward the floor, her eyes suddenly filling with tears. "He," she whispered.

"He, then. Did you not bring him with you? Because the two of you will have to move in here for as long as—"

"He has passed, Madame."

Catherine's heart lurched. Her baby died? She and her grandmother shared a look of consternation.

"I am so sorry for your loss," Grand-Mère said, turning back toward the girl. "But perhaps you did not understand correctly. We are looking for a wet nurse."

"*Oui*," the girl replied, barely audible now. "I am...I can...it just happened, two days ago. It's not too late."

Grand-Mère nodded. "So was it an illness of some kind?" Her tone was gentle, but the question had to be asked.

The girl shook her head. "He just came too soon, more than a month early. So small, so helpless..." She did not need to go on.

"I am sorry," Grand-Mère said again.

"*Oui*, Madame," the girl replied, dabbing at her tears with the hem of her apron as she tried to pull herself together.

Without another word, Grand-Mère reached out and took Estelle's hand, pulled her inside, and sat her down at the table. Next, she dished up a bowl of gruel, spread jam on a piece of bread, poured a cup of tea, and then shooed everyone else from the room, including Cook.

Catherine retreated down the hall to Grand-Mère's apartment, bouncing the baby as she walked. Amelie sat up in bed, a bowl of untouched gruel on the table beside her. "Is someone here?"

"*Oui*, the wet nurse. Grand-Mère is speaking with her now."

Amelie sank down into the bed, clearly relieved. Catherine started to add the second bit of news, that the girl's own baby had died, but she decided to wait for the time being. Valentina was still so tiny. Her mother needed no reminders that all too often babies did not survive.

For a moment Catherine longed to settle down on the bed across from her beloved cousin and simply talk. There was so much they both needed to catch up on, but the baby was wailing loudly, so Catherine set that notion aside and took the child back out to the hall. She paced up and down, wishing she felt as comfortable as Grand-Mère and Cook seemed with Valentina even when she was crying. The housekeeper made a brief appearance, bustling down the stairs and heading toward the empty study at the end of the hall, but otherwise Catherine was alone with the baby.

Finally, after what seemed like forever, Grand-Mère came around the corner, followed by the wet nurse, who kept her eyes down as she passed by. Grand-Mère motioned for Catherine to follow, and the three women entered the apartment. Amelie opened her eyes as they stepped into the bedchamber.

"This is Estelle," Grand-Mère said.

Amelie reached for the young woman's hand. "*Merci*," she whispered.

Grand-Mère retrieved one of her own simple gowns for Estelle and directed her to the washbasin in the corner. After the girl cleaned herself up, Grand-Mère brushed out her light brown hair, pinned it to her head, and then placed a covering on top. No one spoke over the hollering of the baby.

Finally, Estelle sat down in the chair along the wall and gestured for Valentina. Within moments, the baby's screams ended so abruptly that they seemed to echo in the silence. Grand-Mère and Catherine both let out a sigh, the smile they shared fading only when they looked over at Estelle and realized she was crying again, the tears rolling down her face even as she nursed the hungry babe.

Grand-Mère shooed Catherine out of the chamber. "Ask Cook if she needs your help. The kitchen maid quit this morning." The butler had quit the week before, claiming he was moving to Grenoble. None of them believed him. More likely he wanted to get out of the Huguenot household—and he could not be blamed, not at all.

Catherine retrieved her cloak in hopes that she could manage to convince Cook to send her on an errand. As she stepped into the hall, she realized the physician had arrived and the footman was leading him her way.

She curtsied as he greeted her, grateful that the man was finally here. Then she kept going and continued along the corridor to the kitchen, where she found Cook kneading a mound of bread dough with vigor. Outside the open door of the kitchen, Monsieur Roen walked Catherine's mare. The entire household seemed to have settled back down.

Catherine took the market basket from the shelf.

"*Non*," Cook said. "It is too dangerous."

Catherine reminded her that the dragoons were on the other side of the Rhône for the day. "I cannot stay inside for the rest of my life. Grand-Mère told me to help you, and I know everyone would rather have me do the marketing than the cooking."

"Be quick then," Cook said, rattling off a shopping list and pulling the money from her apron pocket. "I got off to a late start, but I will have the bread baking by the time you get back."

As Catherine hurried over the slate of the courtyard, she looked toward the pen outside the stable, into which Monsieur Roen was leading her horse. Catherine missed her riding time, but just a week ago Jules had forbidden her from riding at all, saying it was no longer safe. Perhaps tomorrow she would take over the animal's care instead.

For now, she pushed through the door to the street and walked toward the market, slowing at the window of La Boutique de Lyon and squinting into the shop. A girl from the neighborhood examined a bolt of cloth with her mother. A beautiful coral silk. Janetta was nowhere in sight.

Catherine hurried on until she reached the market, which was located in the shade of Saint-Jean-Baptiste. As she neared the poultry cart, Madame Berger, the pastor's wife, came around the corner, glancing over her shoulder as she walked.

"*Bonjour,*" Catherine called out. "*Comment vas-tu?*"

"*Très bien,*" she answered, again peering over her shoulder.

"Are you looking for someone?"

Madame Berger shook her head and whispered, "There is a dragoon at the edge of the market."

Catherine rose to her tiptoes but did not see a soldier.

"Two moved into our home yesterday. They are sleeping in the loft," the pastor's wife confided.

Catherine could not imagine it. The Bergers lived in a small house. As a family of five, they were crowded even without dragoons.

"I left the boys at home." The three Berger sons ranged in age from five to nine. "I thought the dragoons were gone for the day, but I just saw one—although I cannot be sure if he is one of the ones staying with us or not."

Catherine grabbed her hand, pulling her past the herb seller and a stack of flour bags to the fishmonger. She asked for three of his largest pikes. Then she whispered to Madame Berger, "Where is Pastor today?"

"He had an appointment."

A woman cried out across the market as Catherine was paying for the fish. She looked up to see that a dragoon had her by the hand. But then, from across the crowded square, he seemed to spot Catherine—and he let the woman go.

"He is coming," Madame Berger said. "But I do not recognize him."

Catherine started marching toward the cheese cart. "I do," she said. It was the drunk one from the night before. She stopped and asked for a wheel of hard cheese. The *fromager* took her money and handed her the wheel.

There was another commotion, this time at the fish cart.

Catherine ducked toward the cathedral.

"Stop!" the dragoon commanded.

"Leave me," Catherine whispered to Madame Berger. "Go on home."

The woman glanced at the soldier again. "I am afraid the others may have come back too."

"Of course," Catherine said. "Go home to your sons. Maybe Pastor will be back by now." Her legs trembled and she grabbed her skirt with her free hand, hoping she sounded braver than she felt. She could not imagine that Madame Berger would be any safer at home. How were they to protect themselves?

"Go," she said, pushing against the woman. "You have little ones to think of."

Madame Berger obeyed, walking away with her basket still empty, leaving Catherine to fend for herself.

CHAPTER TWELVE
Catherine

Catherine continued on to the egg cart, pulling the smaller basket from the larger one. Cook had used more eggs than usual recently, and the farmer had not delivered enough. As she stopped, the dragoon rounded the corner on his horse. "There you are." He sneered at her and then laughed. "Surprised to see me, *non*?"

She ignored him and ordered two dozen eggs, passing the basket to the farmer.

His hands shook as he filled it. When he returned it to her, the dragoon swung his sword up underneath the basket, sending it spiraling into the air, eggs flying in all directions.

Catherine stepped backward, covering her head with her free arm as the eggs rained down. The horse reared. The farmer hurried to the back of his cart. A woman screamed and shoppers scattered.

"That will teach you to ignore me." The dragoon brought his horse back down. He slipped from the saddle, holding tightly onto the reins, his eyes beady in the morning light. "Come here," he commanded Catherine. She took another step away from him but slipped on a broken egg. She reached for the cart behind her to steady herself but accidentally upset it instead. A mountain of greens fell on top of her as she landed on the ground, her back crashing hard against the toppled cart.

The dragoon stepped toward her.

Ignoring her pain, she scampered to her knees and stood, grabbing at her skirt.

She took a step toward the cathedral.

"Stop!" the dragoon yelled.

She hurried on. A peasant moved out of her way, and she stepped into the barrel chest of someone wearing a brown tunic.

"Catherine." Father Philippe, with Pastor Berger behind him, put his hands to her shoulders. "What is going on here?" the priest boomed over her head.

Catherine turned toward the dragoon, who had his sword drawn. He slowly put it back in its scabbard.

"For the love of God, these are good people." Father Philippe pulled Catherine behind him and stood face-to-face with the dragoon. "You will treat them with respect."

The dragoon spread his feet apart. "I am only following the king's orders."

"No one has ordered for women to be mistreated."

The dragoon crossed his arms.

"You will treat the women of this town as you would the women in your own family. Do I make myself clear?"

The dragoon glared at the priest.

"Then I will speak with your superior," Father Philippe said. "Today."

The dragoon's eyes darkened even more, but he remounted his horse. His beady gaze fell on Catherine, and then he spurred his mount and headed back toward the river.

"*Merci*," Catherine said, going weak in the knees as Pastor Berger stepped to her side and steadied her.

"*Oui*," the priest responded. "Do not come out by yourself anymore. It is not safe."

She nodded, finding her footing. "I thought they were gone for the day."

"Perhaps they told us that to lure us out," Pastor Berger said, releasing his hold on her arm.

She nodded. He was probably correct.

The farmer began trying to upright his cart. Father Philippe and Pastor Berger stepped forward to help. As they did, Madame Berger appeared and quickly grabbed Catherine's basket, stuffing the fish and cheese back inside.

"Go straight home, Catherine. Tell your grandmother what happened. That dragoon is the worst I've seen."

"*Oui*," Catherine said as the men righted the cart. In a lower voice, she added, "Would you believe he is one of the dragoons currently billeted at our home?"

Madame Berger's eyebrows raised in alarm. "*Vraiment?* That's terrible!"

With a solemn nod, Catherine bid the woman *au revoir*. As she turned to go, Pastor Berger gestured for her to wait. He stepped close and spoke softly, saying they would not be meeting at the church for the evening's Good Friday service.

"We considered meeting at the home of the Talbots, but Pierre's mother is too afraid," he added, "so it will be at our house."

"But the risk—"

"The dragoons will be at mass. Father Philippe has assured us of it. They are commanded to go by their captain. We will be safe."

Catherine didn't tell Grand-Mère what had happened, but she and Cook both guessed anyway, thanks to the look of the basket and the egg yolk on her dress, crusted with a bit of shell.

"I will send Monsieur Roen," Cook said, sighing. "I need the eggs for the custard."

Catherine leaned against the table. "I am sorry."

"*Non,*" Cook said. "What was I thinking to let you go? I heard the talk this morning. They are incorrigible. The worst of them found his way to the wine cellar last night. If he keeps this up, it will be bare in no time."

"Oh, dear," Grand-Mère said. "I will lock it. I never thought of it last night."

"He will just make you unlock it later, Madame. It's probably better to let it be."

Grand-Mère shook her head but then stopped. "You may be right. Tell the footman to move the best of it into the root cellar, and we will water down the rest."

Cook grinned. "That's the spirit."

Catherine shook her head and walked out of the kitchen with Grand-Mère toward the corridor. "What did the physician say?"

"He thinks the illness Amelie had soon after the baby was born was scarlet fever. Even though the infection is gone now, it may have damaged her heart. If she is not better in the next week, he will consider bloodletting, but he said with rest she may heal on her own."

Catherine hoped it would not come to that, but she knew the physician would only do it if he needed to.

"Did he say anything else?"

"Just that we should have an idea in a week or so how she will fare in the long run."

"What about the baby? Did she have scarlet fever too?"

Grand-Mère shook her head. "Probably not. According to him, babies don't often get it, thankfully. He said Valentina is malnourished, but he thinks she will be fine once she gains more weight."

The two women stepped into the apartment to find Estelle resting on the chaise lounge in the sitting area. They passed through the room quietly and quickly.

In the bedchamber, the baby was tucked beside a sleeping Amelie, the drapes around the bed pulled back to let in fresh air. Flames roared in the fireplace, making the room almost unbearably hot.

"Ah, peace," Catherine whispered, quickly taking off her cloak.

"Momentarily," Grand-Mère responded.

Catherine relayed Pastor Berger's words about the Good Friday service. Amelie stirred. Catherine lowered her voice even more. "I will stay
here so you can go."

Grand-Mère shook her head. "You will go."

Catherine nodded. She hadn't expected her grandmother to leave
Amelie. She certainly could do without the dragoons in the house, but
she was enjoying the camaraderie of staying in Grand-Mère's room
with Amelie and now Estelle too.

Catherine took her covering from her head and shook out her hair.
"Perhaps this would be a good time to write to Suzanne." She sat down
at the desk and then glanced up at her grandmother. "What should I
tell her?"

Grand-Mère put her hand to her chin. "Say I hope to go see her. I
know it has been years, but she is still a dear friend. Maybe she will be
able to help us."

Her eyes met Catherine's and they shared a look of anticipation
mixed with concern.

"Such a trip would depend on Amelie's recovery, of course," Grand-
Mère continued. "And the dragoons...I will not leave if I think that
would put Amelie and Estelle at risk."

"Of course not," Catherine murmured.

"I suppose...tell her about Amelie and the baby, and that I must wait
to decide about traveling until Amelie is well. Write that if I can travel
I am not sure who would come with me. Say that I need to speak with
her about...our current situation."

Catherine nodded, taking a feather from the jar on the desk and
running it along her cheek. Then she began to sharpen the quill with
her small knife.

"Tell her I would like her advice." Grand-Mère sat in the chair next
to the desk. Catherine met her gaze. "If I cannot come in the next few
weeks, I will put the matter in a letter, but I would much rather speak
to her in person."

Catherine set down the feather and opened the bottle of ink.

"Add more. Make it interesting. Your letters bring her joy."

Suzanne had lost her husband the year before, and it clearly warmed

Grand-Mère's heart to know that Catherine's letters comforted her friend.

Grand-Mère stood and turned toward the bed. "After you are finished with Suzanne's letter, write to my brother in Paris and tell him I am considering a trip—nothing more." Grand-Mère yawned then, her eyes watering a little. "I am going to rest while the baby sleeps," she said. "There is a reason God gives newborns to the young and not to the old." A few minutes later, she was on the other side of Amelie, tucked under the covers too.

Catherine thought through each sentence and chose her words carefully. She wrote everything Grand-Mère asked and then added more, about how beautiful the spring flowers were and about the walk across the river the day before. She left out being harassed by the dragoons—both times—though she did mention the dress shop and talked a bit about Janetta. *My friend has been to Paris and London too. She will go to Rome in the autumn.*

Then she wrote about the market. She described how big the fish were and how pretty the greens looked in the farmer's cart.

Finally she told Suzanne that she hoped to meet her in person someday, but they would all have to trust God with the possibility of a trip and that she would write again soon.

As the ink on the last page dried, Catherine stared at Amelie and the baby. Grand-Mère once said she had always longed for a house full of children. When only the two of hers survived, she still hoped for a house full of grandchildren. But then both of her daughters-in-law died, leaving only Jules, Catherine, and Amelie between them. As neither of her sons remarried, that seemed to be the end of it—until now, at least, with the addition of a great-grandchild, tiny Valentina.

Jules used to say that Catherine had been spoiled after their mother died and that as the youngest she always got her own way—coercing her cousin Amelie to ride all over the countryside with her, visiting the print shop whenever she pleased, and speaking her mind all too often. He had teased her about it when they were younger.

But he had not held her independence against her then. In fact, he had encouraged it—just as he had encouraged her education. When

Catherine was fifteen and Jules twenty-two, their father died, saddling her brother with so much responsibility that it changed him into someone harsh and impatient and almost always angry. That was the man she knew now. But once upon a time, before all of that, he had actually been a pleasant sort, one who sometimes teased her, yes, but who also treated her with love and kindness.

Back then he was always playing the role of headmaster, making sure she was learning her lessons, giving her books to read, and expecting her to report on them. And then there was his secret code. When she was nine, Jules invented it to help her with studies. At the time, she believed him when he said it was unbreakable, though in retrospect she realized it had not been all that sophisticated. Pulling from surplus copies of booklets and pamphlets at the shop, Jules would take some leftover printed matter and a piece of graphite and then go through the text circling certain letters. When he was finished, he would give that text to her, and she would have to go through it herself, find each of the circles, write down their corresponding letters on a piece of paper, and then use Jules's formula—a designated pattern of counting off and crossing out various letters—to decode them.

If she did it all correctly, once she was finished she would have a secret message he had created just for her. Usually it was something silly, such as "...on the Bridge of Avignon, we all dance in a ring..." a line from a children's song she loved. Occasionally, though, it would be something more serious, such as a brotherly reprimand: "Young ladies walk, never run, especially at church." Sometimes it was something exciting. "Look in the hall cupboard for a *petite gateau*." She would run off to find a little cake he had hidden there for her earlier.

His plan worked. She mastered reading and writing and counting in no time and gained more independence in both thought and action because of her skills. Jules was quite proud of her. One time she caught him bragging about her to a client in the shop, saying how smart she was. "Too bad she is a girl," he had added, "or we could use her to proofread our galleys before printing." The fact that such a thought had even crossed his mind was a tremendous compliment.

She sighed. She missed those days. Now he was too serious to joke or tease at all. Or teach her anything new or even reminisce about their childhood.

The baby stirred. Grand-Mère sat up and reached across Amelie, taking the little one in her arms before settling back down.

Catherine knew Grand-Mère did not want to leave Lyon. Did not want to leave the house she still longed to see filled with children. Did not want to leave those she employed and served. But unless by some miracle the persecution of the Huguenots came to an end, soon she would have no choice.

There was no denying the family was on the cusp of change. Catherine had been writing about their lives, little narratives on this and that, for as long as she could remember. She'd hung on to many of those pages over the years, keeping them together in a stack in the bottom drawer of the desk.

For now, she retrieved a fresh piece of paper to pen a new journal entry. When she was done, she slid open the drawer and added it to the pile, face up so that it wouldn't smear before the ink was dry.

It wasn't long before Grand-Mère was up with the baby. "Go tell the housekeeper we need another cot in here for Estelle. Get more cloths for Valentina and ask when she will attend to the soiled ones."

Catherine found the housekeeper in the lounge, cleaning out the fireplace. The two maids had left a month ago, afraid to continue working for a Huguenot family. This housekeeper would likely soon follow suit, though if she did, Catherine would not be critical of her. Leaving would be the prudent thing to do.

She relayed Grand-Mère's instructions to the woman, who looked up from the floor with an expression of despair spreading across her face. "I still have the rooms upstairs to see to and your grandmother's chamber, plus all the sweeping and the other fireplaces. And the mending to do."

"I will help," Catherine said.

The housekeeper gave her a withering look.

Ignoring her implication, Catherine added, "The wet nurse is a seamstress. I will ask her to assist with the mending."

"I'm not sure what your grandmother will think…"

"She'll be fine with it. Our lives are changing. It can't be helped." Grand-Mère's eyes were too poor to sew anymore. Catherine could offer her assistance, but she had not mastered the skill enough to do finishing work. She hoped Estelle would be willing to lend her talents to the cause.

The housekeeper told Catherine to look on the top shelf of the cupboard in the hall for more cloths. "Then get the mending in the basket on the bottom."

"*Merci.*"

A short while later, Catherine and Estelle were settled down at one end of the kitchen table with the mending while Cook sat at the other end, peeling parsnips to roast and serve with the fish. "The men do not want to be traveling back and forth between here and the shop," Cook said. "So they will not be home for the noon meal. We will dine in the late afternoon, before church."

"*Très bien,*" Catherine said, and then she added that her church would be gathering in a home tonight instead of at the temple.

Cook raised her head from her peeling. "Has it come to that already?"

Catherine shrugged. "At least for now."

"What about your Easter service?"

"Oh, I hope it's at the temple." Their building was simple and plain compared to the cathedral—too plain, in Catherine's opinion—but it was all they had. "Surely we'll be safe in the daylight."

"Who knows anymore," Cook said, picking up a carrot. "Except God. And why He is allowing all of this is beyond me."

Catherine agreed with Cook but held her tongue, not wanting to sound heretical.

Estelle was quick with her needle, working on Jules's shirt while Catherine mended Amelie's chemise. After a time, Grand-Mère came for Estelle, who put away her mending and went to the bed chamber to nurse the baby.

"And perhaps a bowl of broth for Amelie," Grand-Mère added,

turning to Cook. "She says she is not hungry, but she needs to eat something."

Cook dished it up from the pot over the fire.

When Catherine entered the chamber a half hour later, the baby was fed and in Grand-Mère's arms while Estelle held the bowl of broth for Amelie, trying to coax her into taking just one bite.

CHAPTER THIRTEEN

Catherine

Grand-Mère chose to have dinner in her room with Amelie and Estelle, leaving Catherine and Jules to eat alone in the dining room.

"We need to hurry or we will be late for the service," he said as they took their places across from each other at the table.

Catherine reached for the bell to signal the footman, which was usually Grand-Mère's job, but Jules snatched it away from her. Catherine narrowed her eyes at her brother. He was like a little tyrant, grabbing more and more control of both the business and the household. Worse, he could not see what he had become.

After he put down the bell, Jules bent his head in prayer. "*Merci, Seigneur,*" he prayed, "for Your sacrifice, for this food, and for loving us. Help us to love each other. Amen."

Catherine wrinkled her nose. He seemed so hypocritical. Grand-Mère would chastise her if she said such a thing out loud, but she did not understand how her brother could be so cold one moment and then speak to God with such sincerity the next.

"Do you think it's safe for us to leave Grand-Mère and Amelie here?"

"I have the dragoons under control," Jules answered.

Catherine raised her eyebrows. Did he fancy himself a miracle worker now? "Pray tell."

He shook his head. She had thought him in denial, but this seemed more like pride to her.

"Did you speak with our solicitor today about Amelie's situation?" Catherine asked.

"*Oui.*"

"And?"

"It's none of your concern."

Of course it was her concern, but she chose not to respond. The guards from the convent had not come to the house today to try to take her cousin back. Perhaps the solicitor had sent a letter to Mother Superior already.

They dined in silence after that, and when they had finished, Jules rang the bell once more. Catherine excused herself and headed down the hall to retrieve her cloak.

Grand-Mère was in the sitting room, holding Valentina and talking with Estelle. Watching them, Catherine thought about both women losing sons in the past week. Grand-Mère had lost other children in her life as well—several babies, a toddler, a daughter at age ten. Papa three years ago. Two daughters-in-law. Catherine did not know all the stories of the earlier deaths, just bits and pieces. Just enough to know Grand-Mère had treasured Amelie and Catherine as her own from the moment they were born. And now she had Valentina to love.

"You should go," she said to Catherine. "Monsieur Roen will have the carriage ready."

"*Oui*, I just need my cloak." She stepped into the bedchamber.

Amelie sat up in bed, appearing more rested than she had all day.

Catherine sat down beside her. "Are you feeling better?"

"Some." Amelie reached for Catherine's hand. "How was dinner?"

"Quiet."

Amelie smiled wryly. "I take it Jules was off somewhere in his thinking, far from you."

Catherine sighed. "If only I could get a glimpse of what goes on in that mind of his." She squeezed her cousin's hand. "He said he spoke with the solicitor, though he would not give me any details."

"I thought that might be the case. Either that, or the guards came for me and you scared them away."

"Any of us would." She kissed her cousin on the forehead. "You are well loved."

"I cannot tell you how grateful I am to be home." Tears filled Amelie's eyes. "God used you to answer my prayers. I do not think Valentina or I could have lasted much longer."

"Hush," Catherine whispered. "Do not speak in such a way. You are safe now."

Grand-Mère called out. "Jules is waiting, *chérie*."

Catherine kissed Amelie again and then jumped to her feet, grabbing her head covering, cloak, and Bible. She bid her cousin *au revoir* and headed through the sitting room, waving to Grand-Mère and Estelle as she went.

Jules was standing by the carriage, and he climbed inside after Catherine. Then Monsieur Roen took the reins and they were off. As they pulled through the gate and onto the road, Catherine found herself thinking again about all of those deaths. It was one thing for Catherine to lose her mother as a young child and to search for her in every Madonna she saw, but it had been quite another thing to have lost Papa eleven years later when she understood death so much more clearly.

Her father had been kind and gentle. He was as relaxed as Jules was intense, and as much of a feeler as Jules was a thinker. Papa was her security, her anchor. Once he was gone, had it not been for Grand-Mère's continual infusion of Scripture and life lessons, Catherine was not sure how she would have survived that time of emotional upheaval. It was Grand-Mère's constant presence and, in the past two years, the hope of a future with Pierre that had kept Catherine grounded.

The ride to Pastor Berger's was short, and once they arrived Jules told Monsieur Roen to go on to mass. "Give Cook a ride home, would you? We can walk." Then he led the way into the house with Catherine following behind.

The furniture had been pushed to the sides of the kitchen and living area, and the members of the congregation who had dared to venture out stood around the room. Pastor Berger greeted them at the door. Above, in the sleeping loft, the boys and other children had gathered. The youngest Berger child, five-year-old Jacob, leaned against the railing and smiled down at Catherine. She winked in return. For the moment, with the dragoons gone, the children seemed relaxed, although the adults were clearly on edge.

Pierre entered the house a few minutes later, just as Pastor Berger began with the hymn "All Mortal Flesh Be Silent." The melody, sung softly by the congregants, reverberated to the open timbers of the house.

Next Pastor Berger read the crucifixion account from the Gospel of Mark. Catherine followed along in her new Bible, which fit into her apron pocket, a small one her brother had printed in the shop and given her a few months before. Then Pastor Berger admonished the congregation to remain strong in the face of persecution. Before closing, he announced that for Easter they would meet in the temple. "The good Lord told us not to fear," he said. "We will carry on with our usual practices after tonight."

Once the service ended, Pierre stepped to Catherine's side as she warmed herself by the fire.

"Why are your parents and Eriq not here?" she asked, keeping her voice low.

"Mother heard about your ordeal at the market today. When she found out the Bergers have dragoons lodging with them too, she didn't want to come." He leaned his shoulder against the stone mantle. "She's afraid we will have dragoons living with us next." He lowered his voice even more. "She and father are talking about leaving." He shook his head. "Father is taking steps to make that happen."

"Leaving? For London?" Catherine asked, hope rising inside of her.

Pierre shook his head. "Switzerland."

Catherine took a step backward. "Do you plan to go with them?" Her heart raced at the thought of him leaving without her.

"I have no idea what I plan to do. It's very complicated, more than you can imagine."

"But is going to Switzerland something you're considering?"

She did not add the more important questions—*What about me? What about us?* Catherine was devastated. She loved Pierre, but she couldn't commit her life to someone who didn't value her input enough to include her in such a monumental decision, or at least to keep her informed of his own thinking in the matter.

Before he could reply, however, Jules called out to Catherine and motioned toward the door.

"I have to go," she said. Turning back to Pierre, she added, "And so should you while it's still safe out there."

Again he was about to speak when he was interrupted by Pastor Berger.

"I am coming with you," the man said to Catherine. "To see Amelie and the baby."

"Now?"

He nodded, his hat in his hand.

"What about your family? The dragoons should be returning soon."

"Pierre has offered to stay until I get back."

Catherine looked at her betrothed, not at all pleased. She wanted the Bergers to be safe, yes, but not at the risk of Pierre's safety.

"Amelie is too ill to convert just yet," she said quickly to the pastor, unsure how else to stop him from coming with them. She wanted Amelie to do so, of course—but not at the cost of Pierre's life. What if staying here now and going home later ended up putting him in harm's way? The streets of Lyon were no place for a Huguenot to be after dark.

"I just want to encourage her," Pastor replied, oblivious to her concerns.

There was nothing more Catherine could do. Looking to Pierre, she whispered, "Be careful."

Then she turned and followed Pastor Berger out the door, praying for a time when they would no longer have to watch over their shoulders in terror every time they ventured onto the streets.

⁓

Amelie again appeared exhausted as Catherine led Pastor Berger into the bedchamber, but she managed to sit up and even seemed to rally some, to the point of asking if he could baptize the baby as long as he was there. "And I would like to convert back," she added. "To the faith of my family."

"Right now?" he asked, shooting Catherine a dubious glance. He obviously was mindful of her warning that Amelie was too ill to do so just yet.

Catherine felt torn between wanting the baby's baptism and Amelie's conversion to happen and wanting the pastor to get on home so Pierre could leave before the dragoons returned. She turned to Amelie and tried to gauge her strength. "How are you feeling? Do you need to lie back down?"

"*Non*," Amelie replied, a surprising—and heartwarming—look of vigor in her eyes. "Both of these things are important."

Catherine nodded, still concerned for Pierre but thrilled nonetheless to see a hint of the old spark in her cousin's eyes. Just the thought of what was about to happen—the baptism, the conversion—felt like a soothing salve on a deep wound, one inflicted by Amelie's father the day he turned from the faith.

Everyone gathered in Grand-Mère's bedchamber for the event. Amelie, who had quickly dressed in one of Catherine's gowns, managed to stand—the bed just a few feet away in case she felt faint—as Pastor Berger led her through the recantation of her conversion to Catholicism. When he finished, he said, "And you desire that your daughter be baptized in the name of the Lord Jesus Christ?"

She nodded.

"Has the child been baptized before?"

"*Oui*. Mother Superior had it done while I was ill."

Catherine knew that meant the baby was on the Catholic rolls and they would not be able to get her off. No matter. This baptism could still be done in the name of faith.

Pastor Berger asked, "Whom have you chosen as godparents for the little one?"

"My cousin Catherine," Amelie said.

Catherine felt the corners of her mouth rise in a modest smile even as she blinked away the threat of tears.

"And my cousin Jules," Amelie added.

Catherine's smile faded. She found herself wishing she'd had a chance to discuss that choice with Amelie beforehand. Her cousin knew enough about Jules's peculiarities to joke about him, but she had no idea what kind of person he had become.

The pastor took a sleeping Valentina from Grand-Mère. The baby stirred but didn't fuss. She was dressed in the christening gown that both Amelie and Catherine had worn as infants and which Grand-Mère had kept in the trunk at the end of her bed all these years.

He held the baby up and away from him and said, "Baptism is a sign of the covenant, of engrafting the babe into the church." He turned to Amelie. "Do you vow to bring up your child in the nurture and admonition of the Lord?"

Amelie nodded.

He turned to Catherine and then to Jules. "Do the two of you vow to help raise Valentina in the knowledge of the Lord?"

They both agreed.

Grand-Mère stepped forward with the washbasin, presenting it as a font. Pastor Berger dipped his hand into it and quoted from Ezekiel, "'Then will I sprinkle clean water upon you, and ye shall be clean...I will put my spirit within you, and cause you to walk in my statutes.'"

He flicked his hand over the baby and water fell to her head and trickled down to her face.

Valentina squawked and turned red. Then she began crying, but this time, everyone smiled or chuckled at the sight. Amelie leaned against the bed. Pastor Berger handed the baby to Catherine.

Their smiles faded as the little one began to scream, scrunching her eyes closed. Catherine looked to Grand-Mère, but the old woman seemed serene. Catherine looked for Estelle, but she was nowhere to be found. Jules stepped back, away from her, with his hands up, as if surrendering, and Pastor Berger headed for the door.

"Tell Pierre to be careful going home," Catherine called out to him over the howling of the baby. She remembered all too well the fate of Amelie's husband.

The pastor nodded as if he had heard her, but the baby was crying so loudly she did not see how he possibly could have. She followed him to the hall, saying a prayer for Valentina's health as the little one continued to wail. At least caring for the baby was not up to her. Thank goodness for Grand-Mère and Estelle. Catherine had had no idea a baby could be so tyrannical.

She found Estelle in the kitchen with Cook, who was arranging cheese and bread on a plate. Three bottles of wine rested on the table.

"Are they ready for the toast?" Cook asked over the baby's cries.

"Nearly," Catherine said, "but Valentina is not."

"I'll take her." Estelle reached for the baby. "She'll soon be fine."

"*Merci,*" Catherine said, releasing Valentina and gathering up the bottles.

By the time the wine was poured, the baby was fed and now content in Grand-Mère's arms. Again, everyone gathered around Amelie, who was sitting in bed now, propped up by pillows. Estelle and Cook stood in the open doorway, wine in their hands too.

Jules nodded to Catherine to go first. She had never been a godmother before and had no idea what to say. She had not paid attention to any of the christenings she had been to in the past, at least not beyond enjoying the cuteness—and sometimes the antics—of the infants involved.

Catherine started by addressing Amelie. "You mean the world to me, and now your daughter means the same. I will instruct her to honor her dear, deceased father, you, and our Lord. I will, along with you and this entire family, raise her in the faith." Catherine lifted her glass. "And I will pray for your health every day and do all I can to see you well again."

"*À la santé,*" Amelie said as everyone toasted. Then she turned toward Catherine and whispered, "*Merci.*"

Jules cleared his throat and everyone turned toward him. "This is a momentous occasion. Our family has suffered great loss this week— and great gain. We are blessed to have a new member, a fatherless and grandfatherless baby that I swear to protect with my body, mind, and spirit." He looked toward Valentina, and Catherine was surprised to see something like tenderness flicker in his eyes for just a moment. He turned and gave Amelie a somber nod. "I know nothing about *enfants,* but you have my word that I will serve your daughter with my very being."

Grand-Mère said, "*Santé!*" as she crossed the room, the baby still in her arms, and kissed Jules on one cheek and then the other. "*Merci,*" she said to him, tears trickling down her face. "She could not have a better protector."

Catherine looked away, her heart sinking. Grand-Mère was wrong. How would Jules protect Valentina? Even if he did seem to have a fondness for the baby, he'd never been known for courage, compassion, or valor. Given the current situation, she doubted he could protect himself, much less the women in this family, much less a helpless *enfant.*

The dragoons returned to the house around midnight, just as Catherine had finished writing down the events of the evening in her journal by the light of a lone candle. She feared the loud one's shouting would wake the baby, but only Grand-Mère stirred. A pounding on the sitting room door startled Catherine.

"Stay where you are," Grand-Mère said to Catherine, slipping from the bed. She tiptoed into the room, Catherine following despite her command. Her grandmother stopped at the bolted door but didn't raise the rod.

Basile, the loud one, cursed and then someone else, probably Waltier, said something and soon the racket subsided.

They left midmorning of Holy Saturday, long after Jules had headed to the print shop. Catherine stayed in Grand-Mère's sitting room until they were gone. She felt for Cook and the housekeeper, who now had a smaller staff but more responsibilities. Grand-Mère would not let Estelle leave the apartment until after the dragoons were gone either, but as soon as they left she sent both the young women out to help. Cook sat them down at the table to polish the silver.

The hours progressed uneventfully until the early afternoon, when the butcher's apprentice delivered a rack of lamb to the cellar. He was a young man whose family also attended the Temple de Lyon.

When he came in to collect payment, he spotted Catherine at the table.

"How is Pierre doing?"

"*Excusez-moi?*" Catherine replied.

"Well, that was quite a fright he had last night," the young man said.

Catherine straightened her back. "*What?*"

"Getting harassed by the dragoons like that. He is lucky he didn't end up in the—"

"That's enough young man," Cook interrupted. "I know you have plenty of other deliveries to make. You need to be on your way."

Catherine was on her feet, sure her heart had stopped. "What happened?"

The man was blushing now. "I shouldn't have said anything. He's all right. At least that's what the butcher's wife told me."

Catherine dropped the polishing rag on the table and started toward the door.

"Stay where you are, Mademoiselle," Cook said. "Your brother would have told you if something was wrong."

"I'll be fine," Catherine said. She could see through the open window that a light rain was falling. She needed her cloak and started down the hall. As she neared the apartment, she could hear Valentina crying. The door opened before she could reach it, and Grand-Mère appeared.

"Tell Estelle it's time for the baby to be fed."

"*Oui,*" Catherine said. "I just need my cloak."

"You are not going out..."

"Just to the shop."

"*Non.*"

"Something happened to Pierre last night. The dragoons—"

"I said *non*, Catherine." Grand-Mère swung the babe to her shoulder. "What good will it do for you to be accosted too?"

Catherine hesitated.

"Don't be rash, *ma petite fille*," Grand-Mère said, putting an end to the conversation.

Catherine stayed as silent as possible the rest of the afternoon as she waited for Jules to return. When he finally arrived home, she was cleaning up after finishing the polishing. By the time she made it down the hall to his study, Grand-Mère was already there, deep in conversation with him. Neither saw Catherine as she stopped to the side of the doorway.

"I don't think it's prudent to buy another business," Grand-Mère said.

Jules's voice was so low in response Catherine could barely hear him. "What other choice do we have?"

Grand-Mère sighed. "We could leave once Amelie regains her strength."

Catherine's heart lifted a little.

"*Non*," Jules said. "That would be a mistake."

"The businesses no longer matter, Jules, not in comparison to our lives."

"What will we live on once we are out of the country? The kindness of others?"

"We will have to leave our home and business behind, of course, but there must be money as well, *oui*? Surely we could manage to bring most of that with us."

"Much of our money is tied up in investments..." His voice trailed off, as if he were not sure whether to say any more or not.

Catherine was holding her breath, hoping he would, when suddenly Jules appeared in the doorway and his eyes fell on her.

"For shame," he said. "Here you are, eavesdropping again."

"*Non*. I was not trying to eavesdrop, Jules, I swear. I came to ask about Pierre but did not want to interrupt."

"Since when have you not wanted to interrupt?"

"Jules," Grand-Mère said, scolding him for the first time in years. "Stop."

Catherine felt a brief flush of victory—until Grand-Mère breezed past and shot her a withering look as well, one that said, *He is right. You were eavesdropping.*

Catherine's face grew warm. Once Grand-Mère had disappeared down the hall, she turned to her brother. "What happened to Pierre?"

"Dragoons stopped him last night a few blocks from his home. They tried to scare him, but they did not hurt him. He is fine. "

"The butcher's assistant did not sound like he was fine."

Jules shrugged. "He was at the print shop before I was this morning. He seemed well enough to me."

Unconvinced, Catherine turned and walked away. She would have to wait until church the next day to find out for herself.

CHAPTER FOURTEEN
Catherine

Easter morning, Cook put breakfast on the table and then headed to early mass with Monsieur Roen and Estelle. The plan was for them to be back in time to care for Amelie and Valentina, freeing everyone else—including Grand-Mère—to go to their own Easter service, which would start later in the morning.

"Those of you who can should go," Cook had said before she left. "You don't know how much longer you'll be able to meet together."

Even so, Catherine felt sure her grandmother would not leave Amelie's side. That was why her mouth flew open a few hours later when she realized Grand-Mère was climbing into the carriage after her.

"Don't look so surprised, Catherine," Grand-Mère scolded as she settled into her seat. "I would trust any of you in the care of Cook. And I believe Estelle is just as trustworthy. Besides, Amelie seems stronger today."

After that, no one else spoke the rest of the way. When they arrived, there were only a handful of other carriages nearby. Perhaps the majority of people had been scared away by the dragoons.

Eager to see Pierre and know for certain that he was all right,

171

Catherine was the first one out, and she took off quickly the moment her slippers hit the ground.

"Wait," Grand-Mère called after her—not because she needed an arm, Catherine felt sure, as she had Jules for that. No, she was trying to stop her granddaughter from rushing into the building like a frantic girl rather than walking in at a normal pace like a lady.

Reluctantly, Catherine complied.

Grand-Mère caught up with her at the bottom of the steps as Jules ambled ahead of them and opened the door. A few people greeted one another in the foyer. Pierre was not among them. With a pat to her grandmother's arm, Catherine left her with her friends and continued on into the sanctuary alone, her eyes and mind frantic even if her movements were not. A group of women sat on the middle benches, while men were scattered on the rows outside. A couple of people sat in the balcony, though clearly from preference rather than necessity, as so few members were present.

Pierre was nowhere in sight, nor was anyone else from his family.

Catherine turned in a full circle, again scanning the entire sanctuary. What if he had left the country without her? Would he do that to her? She was afraid he might, especially after how frustrated she had been with him lately.

She continued to stand even as the others began filing in from the foyer and taking their seats. She saw Grand-Mère go all the way to the front, where she joined a friend in the first row. Madame Berger sat with them as well.

The benches in the temple were backless and made of the same pine as the timber beams overhead. The most ornate woodwork was the balcony railing—and even that was quite simple. The temple was as different from Saint-Jean-Baptiste as could be.

Pastor Berger stepped up to the barrel-shaped wooden pulpit—nothing like the marble one at the cathedral. He led the congregation in singing Psalm 68, a favorite among the worshippers.

Catherine slipped onto the last bench and forced herself to sing along with the others even as she kept turning to look toward the door, waiting for the arrival of her betrothed.

"May God arise, may his enemies be scattered; may his foes flee before him."

A rustling overhead distracted Catherine, and as she looked up, her heart leaped. Pierre! He had come with Eriq, though she didn't see their parents. The two men found seats in the first row of benches in the balcony, and then Pierre caught Catherine's eye. Relief flooded through her. She had been so worried, but he really was all right.

He smiled, causing her heart to lurch. She could not bear to think of what might have happened. He nodded, as if to reassure her, but when he turned his head toward the pastor, she saw a scrape on the left side of his face. Her heart lurched a second time, but she forced herself to calm down. At least he was alive.

Turning back toward the front, she tried to focus on the music.

After another song and a prayer, Pastor Berger began reading about the resurrection from Luke 24. "'Now upon the first day of the week, very early in the morning, they came unto the sepulcher ...'" He paused for a moment and looked up. Catherine turned her head toward the door. Something was going on out in the street. Ignoring it, Pastor kept on reading, "'...and they found the stone rolled away from the sepulcher. And they entered in, and found not the body of the Lord Jesus.'"

The back door burst open with a crash of hooves and the snort of animals. Basile raced in on a horse, a burning torch in his hand. Waltier entered next, also astride a horse, and then a third dragoon followed, this one a captain that Catherine had not seen before.

Pastor Berger climbed down from the pulpit and stood at the front of the church as several congregants fled out the back. Catherine rose, searching the balcony for Pierre, but both he and Eriq were gone.

The captain shouted, "By order of King Louis XIV, the congregation of the Temple de Lyon must vacate these premises and never return. No services of any kind will be allowed, either in this building or in homes or in gatherings outside. All members of this congregation must convert to the eldest daughter of the Church, the Roman Catholic Church of France, and join his Majesty in the one true faith of our great country."

Catherine started down the aisle toward Grand-Mère, but Eriq was suddenly at her side, his hands gripping her elbow as he dragged her in the opposite direction.

"*Non,*" she said, yanking away. Frantic, she looked around for Jules, who was blocked by the dragoons, also unable to get to their grandmother.

Eriq grabbed Catherine again, and again she pulled away, crying, "Grand-Mère!"

"Pierre has gone for her, Catherine! I am to see to you."

Basile wove his torch around, spying the banner above the pulpit, the new one with the Huguenot cross embroidered on it, that had been a gift from a southern congregation in Nîmes. He jerked his horse around to the front of the church and lit the fabric on fire. Someone screamed.

Next Basile headed up the aisle, torching the benches as he went. The burning banner fell from the pole onto the pulpit.

Desperate, Catherine searched through the thickening smoke for her grandmother and finally spotted her coming toward them, Pierre helping her along. Turning, the four of them headed for the door— but then Basile moved his horse into their aisle, blocking the way. They stopped. Catherine grabbed Grand-Mère's hand and started leading her sideways along a bench, to the other aisle. Eriq followed, as did Pierre.

Flames now engulfed the front of the sanctuary.

"You must vacate the temple immediately!" the captain shouted. "The doors will be barricaded. Anyone left inside will perish."

Catherine handed off Grand-Mère to a friend, and as the two of them continued on to the door, she turned and looked for her brother. She did not see him anywhere. Closer to the front Madame Berger shouted, "Where is Jacob?"

Catherine saw Pastor Berger still standing at the front of the church, searching the balcony.

"Jacob!" Madame Berger yelled.

The next youngest boy ran from behind the burning pulpit.

"Get out!" Pastor Berger cried. "All of you!"

"Jacob!" the distraught mother yelled again.

"Maman! Up here." Through the slats of the railing, five-year-old Jacob peered down at all of them.

Pierre took off running toward the stairs.

Catherine tried to go as well, but Eriq caught her by the wrist and dragged her toward the door. Even as she kicked at his shin with her foot, he held on, and he was much stronger than she would have expected.

"Get out!" Pastor Berger was shouting to his boys and wife. "I will help Pierre."

Catherine quickly shifted her weight, trying to yank herself free some other way. She could not but managed to twist enough to see Jacob still kneeling in the same place up in the loft, along the railing, his arms outstretched through the slats. The older boys, who had encircled their mother, were moving toward the door as instructed, Basile waving his torch behind them. Smoke completely filled the sanctuary now and burned Catherine's eyes until Eriq wrapped an arm around her waist and forced her out the door.

Stumbling forward and trying to catch her breath, she spotted her grandmother a short way off, huddling with some of the others. Jules stood beyond them, his arms crossed. Disgusted with his inaction, she noticed Waltier, sitting on his horse on the street below. He looked away.

"Do something!" Catherine shouted at him. "Pierre was once your friend! Now you would have him die?"

Waltier ignored her, but a pained expression flickered across his face.

As Madame Berger and two of her boys came through the door, Basile jumped from his horse and slammed it shut.

Finally free of Eriq, Catherine ran toward the side of the church, through the passageway. Surely the back door would be unlocked. But it was not. It had been barred from the inside.

"Pierre!" she yelled, banging on the door. Eriq joined her. Glass broke overhead and Catherine stepped back, sure heat from the fire was blowing out the windows.

But a small leg appeared and then another. Then the rest of Jacob.

"Over here," Catherine yelled to him. "Come to the edge of the roof, in the corner. You can climb down the trellis." She expected Pierre to be right behind the boy, but he was not, nor was the child's father.

Terrified he might slip on the tiles and fall from the high roof, she started toward the trellis herself, intending to climb up and get him.

"Catherine," Eriq yelled, grabbing her arm yet again and stopping her short.

She struggled against him until she saw Pastor Berger climbing out of the window and onto the roof. He took Jacob's hand, and together they inched across the roof toward the corner.

Smoke started billowing through the broken window.

"Where is Pierre?" she shouted.

Without looking down, Pastor Berger yelled, "He is coming!"

A moment later another set of legs appeared at the window and then Pierre, his face covered with soot, emerged. He paused a moment, his hands on his knees, as he sucked in air and then coughed. Relief flooded through Catherine even as her legs began to shake.

The trellis held as first Jacob and then Pastor Berger climbed down. Catherine scooped the sooty little boy up into her arms and held on tight until his father made it all the way down. Then she lowered Jacob to the ground, and he grabbed hold of his father's leg.

By the time Pierre reached the trellis, the members who had not fled had gathered in the back with them, including Grand-Mère, though Jules was not among the small crowd.

Once Pierre was nearly down, Catherine took in the sight of the church as a whole. Flames shot from the roof now. It had not been fancy, but it had been theirs. How she wished she would have valued it more.

"All is lost," she said to Grand-Mère.

"*Au contraire.* Nothing is lost. *We* are the Lord's temple, Catherine, not some building."

As soon as Pierre hit the ground, Pastor Berger wrapped him in an embrace. Then, as their leader, he instructed everyone to leave the premises before someone was injured. "You will hear from me soon," he said, his voice quiet and raspy. "*We* are the church, not this building," he added, echoing Grand-Mère's words. "Remember that, my brethren."

People began to scatter, though Catherine remained where she was, watching as Pierre tousled Jacob's hair and then, almost shyly, raised his head toward her.

She exhaled, tears filling her eyes. She tried to blink them away, but it was no use. They spilled down her cheeks, surely making dark streaks on her face.

Seeing her tears, he came to her, wrapped his arms around her, and pulled her close despite propriety. Given the circumstances, not even Grand-Mère objected.

"I thought I had lost you for sure this time," Catherine whispered.

"You cannot get rid of me that easily," he replied, burying his face in her hair.

After a long moment, Eriq stepped over to join them, so finally they pulled apart.

"My brother, the hero," Eriq teased, slapping Pierre on the back. Though he seemed proud, Catherine thought perhaps he was a tiny bit jealous as well.

"You were a hero too, Eriq," she said, remembering how strongly he had held on to her despite her frantic thrashings. "*Merci* for coming to save me. I'm sorry I fought you."

"*Oui,*" Pierre added, his eyes twinkling, "I saw it happening. I do believe Catherine was a foe nearly as fierce as the fire."

"And I'll have the bruises to prove it," Eriq agreed, grinning as he rubbed his shin.

Grand-Mère stepped closer and quietly asked Pierre how his parents were.

His smile faded, his expression growing somber. "On their way," he replied softly.

Catherine gasped. "Out of the country?" How could he not have told her?

He glanced around and then nodded.

"I suspected as much," Grand-Mère said. "*Ah, bien.* You and Eriq join us for Easter dinner. We have much to discuss."

"Easter dinner?" Catherine snapped, her sudden anger with Pierre falling onto her grandmother instead. "Who can eat at a time like this?"

"Mind yourself, Granddaughter," she replied, then she turned and moved away.

Chagrined, Catherine directed her attention back to Pierre.

His parents' departure for Switzerland had an impact on her life too, yet he had chosen not to share that with her. She could not trust him—and he did not seem to think he could trust her either.

Pierre and Eriq had walked to the temple, so they crowded into the carriage with the Gillets. As they drove away, a fire wagon sped by, most likely to protect the surrounding buildings. It was too late to save the temple, even if the dragoons would have allowed them to try. Already the roof was falling in. Soon the walls would collapse.

All was not lost, however, Catherine reminded herself. No one had been killed, and everyone was safe—though how the group of believers would continue on and worship together after this was beyond her comprehension.

Feeling the loss, she turned to her brother, who sat across from her. "You certainly didn't exert yourself to help."

"Granddaughter!" Grand-Mère scolded for the second time that day.

Jules shrugged. "The situation was under control. There was nothing I could do."

Catherine swallowed hard to keep from responding. Always the pragmatist, her brother. How very different he was from Eriq and Pierre.

Once they reached home, they all eventually gathered in the dining room, and Catherine found herself appraising the two brothers. Their faces were clean again, and though Eriq was still in his own clothes, Pierre was wearing a simple pair of too-short trousers and a white shirt drawn tight across his broad shoulders. She hadn't realized how much bigger and more muscular Pierre was than Jules until she saw him in her brother's clothes. When he turned to speak to Grand-Mère, Catherine noticed a smudge of soot still behind one of his ears, and she found herself fighting the urge to reach out and wipe it away with her finger-tips. As upset as she was with him, she could not deny her attraction, which never seemed to go away.

They settled in at the table, but Catherine found the scene disturbing. How could everyone just sit here and share a meal as if it were any other ordinary Easter? Didn't they understand that after today nothing would ever be the same? If burning the churches did not make the Huguenots convert, then who was to say that the next step would not be to burn down their houses?

Finally, as the food began to come in from the kitchen, she could not hold her tongue any longer despite Grand-Mère's previous warning. Working hard to keep her tone from sounding in any way disrespectful, she waited until the footman left and then turned to her grandmother.

"How can you have an appetite after what we have all just been through?" she asked, and then she looked to the others. "All of you. How can you sit here and share a feast when our precious temple has been burned to the ground—very nearly taking Pierre with it?"

They all grew quiet for a moment until finally Grand-Mère responded, quoting a line from the twenty-third Psalm.

"'Thou preparest a table before me in the presence of mine enemies,'" she said, her tone strong but her eyes kind.

Catherine understood. Then she picked up her fork, somehow finding her appetite on the strength of God's Word.

Over their dinner of salad, rack of lamb, and spring beans, Pierre revealed more about his parents' departure—information that Jules obviously already knew. Monsieur and Madame Talbot had left early yesterday morning. If all went as planned, they would have crossed into Switzerland by now, headed for Bern.

"Mother has been terrified," Pierre said. "Her great-grandparents were both killed before the Edict of Nantes. Unfortunately, she grew up with that horrible story."

"I hope they won't stay in Switzerland," Eriq said.

Jules shrugged. "It's as good a place as anywhere else. They want to see what the business climate is there, especially for printers."

"They will write when they can," Pierre interjected. "They finally decided it best if Eriq and I came later, after they have a place for all of us to settle."

Catherine cringed inside. So Pierre had agreed to Switzerland without having bothered to discuss it with her at all.

"We'll help here, with the business, as long as we can," Pierre added.

Madame Talbot was an anxious woman. Perhaps she feared if the boys did not stay, the family would not get their fair share of the printing shop if it sold.

"We should all be leaving," Catherine said. She bit her tongue to keep from adding that they should be going somewhere besides Switzerland, somewhere with more opportunities. "The sooner the better."

"*Oui*," Eriq said, and she flashed him a grateful look.

Jules answered, "It's not something to rush into."

"Rush?" Catherine shook her head. "There is no worry about that."

"That is enough," Grand-Mère said as the footman entered to clear the plates without the bell being rung.

Catherine leaned back in her chair.

All were silent until the footman left again.

"This is larger than just us, as I have said before," Jules uttered quietly. "We must think of the future with regard to the Lord's work, our families, our employees, and our country."

Catherine wished she could freely speak her mind. For all his talk, she knew what he was really placing above all else was money, business, and profits—and nothing more.

After a dessert of crispy *bugnes* and stewed pears, Pierre asked Catherine to join him in the courtyard. Sunshine warmed the area, and the two sought a bright patch on the other side of the chestnut tree.

She asked him what he planned to do.

"Jules has an idea he's working on."

"One that includes buying the paper mill on the Plateau?"

Pierre's face reddened.

Catherine crossed her arms. "Why would you encourage him in

taking any sort of business risk now? He is too buried in obligations as it is. I love my brother, but he's not a man of action except when it comes to expanding the business."

Pierre shrugged.

Catherine felt her resentment growing. "I don't care if he thought the situation was under control today. Why was he one of the first to leave the church? He didn't even risk going around to the back to see if he could help."

Pierre shook his head. "He was right. We didn't need any more help—"

"He *would not* have been any help is what you mean. He is the least courageous person I know."

"I cannot agree with you, Catherine." He stepped back. "Not at all."

"His priorities are wrong, Pierre. Why else would he plan to buy another business when we should be fleeing the country as your parents have? I know how it works. I have heard the whisperings. I know people are willing to help us along the way."

His eyes widened. "Then you also know that there are those who pretend to help but in the end do the opposite. Would such a risk be worth it?"

She exhaled, ignoring the question as she came at the issue with a different approach. "Eriq doesn't want to sit around and wait either. He said so today."

"Well, he hardly wanted to flee to Switzerland when he was given the chance." Pierre leaned toward her. "You and Eriq are a lot alike, actually. It troubles me."

"What are you talking about?"

Pierre sighed. "I heard of your plan to go to Versailles."

"Who told you?"

"Jules."

Catherine hadn't said a word to her brother, which meant Grand-Mère must have. Perhaps, because Amelie was better, it might be a possibility soon. "We're only going in order to secure help—safe passage—from Grand-Mère's friend. That is all."

"Are you sure?"

She turned to face him more directly. "What are you insinuating?"

He shrugged. "Like Eriq, you have always yearned for the finer things, for what a refugee could never have—"

"My faith is the most important thing in my life!"

He nodded, but he didn't look as if he quite believed her.

"You have a great-uncle in Paris, *non*?" he said. "Perhaps he will ask you to stay."

"Do not be ridiculous. I would never do that."

He motioned toward the house. "You wouldn't stay in Paris even if the alternative was giving up the luxury you are used to? Not if your only other option was moving to the Plateau? Or fleeing to Switzerland? To perhaps live in poverty the rest of your life?"

Catherine hesitated. "Is that what Jules has planned for all of us?"

Pierre frowned. "I'm not at liberty to speak for your brother."

"First, if we are able to make the trip, we will see if Grand-Mère's friend can help us. My family has many connections. It's hard to imagine someone not protecting us."

Their eyes met, but Catherine looked away, aware that she hadn't really answered his question. If her only choices were Paris or the Plateau, which would she choose? She belonged with her family and her fellow Huguenots, even if that meant the Plateau. In her mind there was no doubt.

In her heart, however, she was not quite so sure.

Footsteps fell on the other side of the chestnut tree and then Eriq appeared.

"We should get going, if we still have a home to go to."

Pierre nodded. "We will walk past the temple on the way to see if anything is left."

"Be careful," Catherine said. Surely the dragoons would not still be there.

Eriq gave her a parting smile, which she returned. He had been brave today. She was sure he would have gone after the pastor's son if Pierre had not. And his arms had been so strong around her, forcing her out of the church for her own safety.

"*Merci*, again," she said to him.

"For?"

"All that you did today."

"It was nothing." He smiled and then followed Pierre across the courtyard and to the street.

When Catherine returned to the house, Grand-Mère had retreated to her apartment with Amelie.

Jules was in his study, the door open. "Catherine," he called out as she passed by. "Come here for a moment."

Reluctantly, she stepped into the room. He sat at his bare desk, his hands folded on top. "What would you have me do?"

"About?"

"All of this."

She placed her palms down on the wooden surface and leaned forward. "I would have you do *something*. Anything!"

"Monsieur Talbot didn't have much of a plan except to get his wife to a safer place. I want to do better than that."

"You have had enough time to plan, Jules. *Now* is time for action."

"Action. Such as?"

Catherine felt the heat in her cheeks. "Going north and crossing the Channel to England. Or...something."

"We have a sick cousin."

That was true.

"And a newborn baby. How would we travel to the Channel, let alone cross it? And what money would we use once we made it out of France?"

"Do we not have savings?"

"Most of it is tied up in the courts right now due to Uncle's death. And then there is this house, as well as the family estate. I cannot liquidate these assets if we leave the country. They would simply be seized instead. Is that what you want? To lose everything our family has worked for? To live as paupers because you were too impatient to do this the right way? We can leave Lyon if need be, Catherine, but we cannot leave France. At least not yet. If we do, we lose everything."

"And so we relocate," she said softly, her mind spinning from all he had shared with her. "To the Plateau."

"Perhaps." Jules sighed. "I don't know yet, for sure."

A sense of shame overcame her. Jules was right. Her impatience could cost them everything. She considered apologizing until she thought of the paper mill in Le Chambon.

"One moment." Her voice wavered as she spoke. "If you hope to liquidate our holdings, then should you not be trying to sell the businesses we have instead of buying more? Not even Grand-Mère thinks the paper mill is a good idea."

Jules blushed, something he never did. "I'm trying to be pragmatic."

Catherine put her hands on her hips. "Like Henri IV?" He had been raised Huguenot but converted to Catholicism to become king. That was ninety years ago, but for the Huguenots it was a pivotal event, one that had kept them safe until Louis XIV's recent proclamations.

Her brother shrugged. "His politics paid off and brought years of peace for us."

If only Louis XIV shared his grandfather's commitment. "Would you do the same?"

"Convert?"

She nodded.

"Uncle Edouard did, and I thought no less of him for it."

"Yet you forbade me to see him."

Jules shrugged, and she feared he was actually considering conversion as one of the options available to him.

"I have no idea what I would do—or will do," he said. Before she could object, he added, "What I *do* know is you have heard more than is wise."

"You need to stop treating me like *une enfant.*"

"You need to stop acting like one," he replied, meeting her gaze.

Years ago, when he had been proud of her, he used to tease her and tell her to act her age, saying it in Latin, knowing she understood even as a young child. He meant it as a compliment, implying that she was mature beyond her years.

Now he accused her of the opposite.

Catherine did not bother to wish her brother *au revoir.* She just turned and walked out, marching down the hall to Grand-Mère's apartment. When she reached the door she paused for a long moment, trying to get her emotions under control. Bringing her temper in with her would only serve to make Amelie upset and Grand-Mère disappointed. Better to calm herself for now and deal with Jules and his ridiculous ways later.

When she finally felt ready, she continued on inside and found Estelle feeding the baby in the sitting room and Grand-Mère and Amelie resting on the bed.

Amelie opened her eyes and reached out her hand to Catherine, pulling her close. In a whisper she said, "Tell me about Pierre. I thought the two of you would be married by now."

Catherine shook her head. It felt impossible to explain the last year to Amelie—how they had felt after Uncle Edouard left the church and sent her away. How the king's edicts were slowly eroding their confidence. How she and Pierre agreed this was no climate in which to be married and start a new life. Better they settle the questions of their future first and then take that step. They had weathered the strain as best they could, but she felt as if the last couple of days may have pushed their relationship too far.

All of that would be nearly impossible to explain, but it was still comforting to have her cousin, best friend, and life-long confidante ask her about it.

Catherine sat down on the edge of the bed. "There have been complications."

"Oh?"

Catherine didn't want to alarm Amelie. She shrugged. "*C'est la vie, hein?*"

"What is going on?"

Catherine hesitated and then said, "He and I have not been getting along well, that is all."

Amelie smiled. "You will work things out." She took a deep breath and exhaled slowly. "I overheard you and Grand-Mère talking about Suzanne's letter. You should go soon and ask her for help."

Catherine shrugged. "Not yet. Not with the dragoons still here."

Amelie peered at her for a long moment. "You mean not while I am still so incapacitated."

Catherine looked away as Amelie continued. "Please, *chérie,* do not wait on my behalf. I am feeling much better. I would be fine. And I have Estelle to help with the baby. We will make do while you are gone."

"I do not know…"

"Please go," Amelie said. "Write to Suzanne. I will speak to Grand-Mère. I want to get Valentina out of danger before it's too late."

Amelie grew silent after that, and when Catherine turned to look, she realized that she had fallen asleep. Just like that, the window had closed again, the old Amelie disappearing back inside the new, ailing version they had rescued from the convent. With a heavy sigh, she rose and went to the desk, where she pulled out a sheet of paper and then selected a quill from the jar. It did not take her long to pen the letter. She simply said they would come as soon as they could and would send a message once they arrived in Paris.

When she was finished, she took another piece of paper and recorded the events of the day in her journal. She stopped a moment and ran her fingers along the feather. She knew she needed to trust God with her future—she had been taught that her entire life. But sometimes He seemed like the men in her family—a little slow.

She shook her head, frowning at her own blasphemy. Was she going to choose not to trust the Lord? Was that the sort of woman she was becoming?

Perhaps Jules was right and her impatience would end up being the ruin of them all.

Chapter Fifteen

Renee

My cousins and I may have kept everyone else up way too late Friday night with our giggling and talking, but we got our comeuppance the next morning, when we were awakened noisily in return. Between kids running through the hall, pots and dishes clanging in the guesthouse kitchen, and the general volume of voices all around, the three of us were rudely roused from sleep. I had a feeling the noise was intentional, but I supposed we deserved it.

At least the commotion helped get me up and going. I had lots to do before today's ceremony, so I hit the shower first and was ready and done, all decked out in a sleeveless sheath dress with a lace overlay, before my two cousins were even out of their jammies.

Wanting to avoid the noisy crowd in the guesthouse kitchen, I headed for the main house instead, where I was able to enjoy a much quieter breakfast from the family buffet. The rental company showed up just as I was finishing, so I went outside to supervise the setup for the ceremony.

The morning passed in a blur. Amid all my preparations for the event, the reunion recommenced with its influx of relatives ready for more activities. Eventually, our dignitaires started to arrive, and then it was time for the ceremony to begin. As everyone headed to their seats, I handed the black leather holder containing the facsimile of the pamphlet to Uncle Finley, who was to be the event's emcee and would also be the one to present it at the end, along with Nana.

To my great relief, the ceremony went off without a hitch. The crowd seemed a little restless at first, probably because of the heat, but Uncle Finley was a gifted speaker, and soon his witty opening and warm welcome had helped settle everyone down and give the event just the right tone.

For the most part, the various speakers—the president of the local Huguenot Society, a woman from the DAR, and the director from the Smithsonian—stayed within their allotted time slots. The congressman, to whom I had given the largest single chunk of time, ended up providing the perfect keynote, his talk moving skillfully from lighthearted to serious to downright touching, and it even brought tears to more than a few eyes. Once he was finished, he stayed in place at the podium in order to recognize the efforts of those involved. When he got to me, I had to rise and give a little wave from my seat in the front row while the crowd applauded. As I sat back down, my eyes went to the handsome man standing off to the side, watching me. Thanks to a sexy and expensive-looking pair of sunglasses, I couldn't see Blake's eyes, but by the smile on his lips, it seemed he was impressed—maybe even proud of me.

The congressman acknowledged Nana last, saying that though she may not have been a Talbot by birth, she had become one through marriage and was a vitally important part of the family's legacy.

That brought a standing ovation, during which Uncle Finley helped Nana to her feet and they strode together to the podium. As the applause died down, the two men sat and she remained standing.

She looked regal and beautiful, and as she began to speak, her voice was surprisingly strong and sure. She started by thanking the congressman, the Talbot family both immediate and extended, honored guests, members of the press, and everyone else who was here today helping to celebrate this momentous occasion.

"When Douglas Talbot got down on one knee back in 1956 and asked me to marry him," she said, her eyes twinkling, "I knew I had landed a real catch."

The audience laughed, pleased by such a proper woman's use of the vernacular.

"What I hadn't realized at the time was that along with him came a set of extended relatives that numbered not in the tens or dozens but the hundreds."

More laughter, more cheering, just as I had hoped when we'd written this speech.

"What a wonderful thing that turned out to be, and what a blessing all of you have been to me, especially in this last difficult year." Her voice nearly broke, but she pressed through. "I would give anything to have my husband still here beside me, but today is about faith—the faith of the brave Huguenots who fled France more than three hundred years ago in search of religious freedom. That same deep faith is what sustains me now, for I know that I *will* see him again someday, in heaven."

Nods and murmurs came from the crowd.

"In the meantime, I will honor his memory by joining with our oldest son in donating this important gift to the Smithsonian. Thank you."

I blinked away tears as Nana turned and gestured for the Smithsonian representative to join her. Uncle Finley stepped forward as well, the black folder in hand. He and Nana stood side by side, facing the man together, Uncle Finley leaning toward the microphone.

"In accordance with the wishes of my late father, Douglas James Talbot," he said, his tone deep and somber, "and on behalf of all the descendants of Emmanuel Talbot, the first of our ancestors to come to America, I now present this historic document, known as the 'Persecution Pamphlet,' as a gift to the National Museum of American History."

The crowd erupted into applause and another standing ovation as Uncle Finley pulled from the folder the facsimile of the pamphlet, held it up for all to see, and then handed it to the museum's director, who accepted it graciously.

Uncle Finley closed out the ceremony with a prayer, and then we were done. Standing beside my seat, I exhaled, thrilled that everything had gone well but so very glad it was over. After a moment, Blake joined me. I expected some sort of sarcastic remark, but I realized his expression was serious.

"Have I mentioned how great I think this whole thing is, your family giving that document to the Smithsonian? In my business, I don't usually pass judgment one way or the other on our clients' valuables, but in this case I can't help it. It's a really generous and special thing to do."

His words were so sweet and unexpected that they brought tears to my eyes. Glancing around for the purse I had left in my room, I ended up having to wipe them away with my hand as they spilled down my cheeks.

"And now I've made you cry," he said. "Sorry, I take it all back. This was a terrible thing you guys did, just horribly rude and selfish."

I laughed even as the tears kept coming. "It's fine. I'm just..."

My voice trailed off. Blake held out a neatly folded tissue, and I took it from him gratefully, dabbing at my cheeks and hoping I didn't look like a raccoon from all the mascara. I managed to pull myself together long enough to shake a few hands and head for the main house behind Nana and the museum director, Blake at my side.

Of course, the waterworks nearly started up again once our little foursome went into the study. I removed the real case from the safe and gave it over to Nana, who paused just a moment before handing it on to the museum's director.

I felt both deep loss and great joy. Granddad had done the right thing in donating our family treasure, I knew that, but tears threatened at the back of my eyes as I grappled with the thought that it would never belong to us again.

Somehow, I managed to keep it together, and soon the director was shaking my hand goodbye and once again thanking me for all I'd done to help make the donation possible. Nana walked him out, and then Blake and I were alone.

With a heavy sigh, I collapsed onto one of the chairs in front of my grandfather's desk, glad at least that my responsibilities had come to an end.

"You okay?" Blake asked, taking the seat next to mine.

"I'm fine. Just exhausted."

"I can imagine." He clasped his hands together behind his neck and leaned back in his chair.

"At least my work here is done," I added.

"Yeah, mine too," he replied happily. "The butterfly has flown."

I glanced at him, surprised at the relief that filled his face. Was he really that thrilled to be finished and out of here? Did he expect me to be happy about that?

"Well, good for you," I managed to mutter, looking away.

"And for you too, I would hope," he replied. "I mean, think about it. Now that you and I no longer have a professional relationship, it's perfectly appropriate to consider some other kind."

I turned back to look at him.

"Just one question," he added with a grin. "If we go out on a date, do I have to leave my gun at home?"

A date. My heart surged with pleasure at the thought. I took a moment to reply, trying to sound matter-of-fact as I held in my smile. "Only if you want to get within ten feet of me. I mean, we could still go out, but if you insisted on bringing the gun, we'd have to take separate limos. Separate tables at the five-star restaurant. Separate boxes at the symphony. You get the idea."

"Oh, I see. So what you're saying is, separate bicycles, separate booths at McDonald's, and separate couches while we watch NASCAR?"

"Um, something like that."

"Ten feet with the gun, huh?"

"That's right."

"Okay, so let's say I leave it at home. How close does that get me?"

He sat forward in his chair, sending all witty repartee from my mind.

"About as close as you are right now," I managed to say.

"What if I want to get even closer?" He leaned forward, closing the distance between us.

Any closer and I just might do something stupid, I realized, like reach up to brush the hair off his forehead or bury my face against his broad shoulder. He was so close, I couldn't think.

It was all I could do to breathe.

Slowly, he reached up and touched one finger to my cheek, running it lightly along my chin line.

"Blake, I don't think you know what you're getting into here," I said softly. "Trust me, I'm no prize."

I didn't know what made me say that, but even as the words came out of my mouth, I realized I meant them. I had too much baggage, too many fears, too many unresolved issues in my life. With other guys I dated, that hadn't really mattered. But this time, with this guy, it did.

It mattered a lot.

"I don't understand," he said, backing off just a little. "You're the most amazing woman I've ever met, Renee. Beautiful, smart, funny..."

"...emotionally unavailable. Hypersensitive to anyone who doubts me on anything. Scared of my own shadow..."

"Stop. Come on, Talbot. We all have issues."

I shook my head. "Yeah, except with me it's more than just that. Maybe I didn't realize how bad it was until this weekend. Until I read Catherine's journal and was reminded how brave she was." I forced myself to meet his gaze. "Until I met you and...wanted to be better. To be whole." Perhaps I was being a little too honest, but suddenly I didn't care. If letting him know how he'd affected me sent him running, then he wasn't the guy I thought he was after all.

"Is this about seeing that dead body in the woods? 'Cause it's understandable why something so traumatic might stay with you. You were young."

I took in a deep breath and let it out slowly as I settled back in my chair.

Then I launched in, telling him the whole story, in detail, including the part he hadn't heard yet, about what happened later when we went back and the body was gone. Halfway through, it struck me that I was probably testing him or looking for an excuse to reject him. Either way, he couldn't win, not if even a millisecond of doubt was visible in his eyes.

When I was finished, there *was* something in his eyes, all right, but it wasn't doubt. It was more like a deeply smoldering anger.

"That is wrong, so wrong," he said, shaking his head. "Just because you were kids doesn't mean you made it up. What were they thinking?"

"I don't know. But my cousins and I were the ones who paid the price for their disbelief. We were all deeply affected by it. Look at Danielle. She spends most of her time lost in her art, pouring all her pain into the things she creates. Maddee tries to make it all better by living some fantasy of the perfect life she's going to have 'someday.' Nicole's a hot mess all the way around. And then there's me, with all my stuff."

"What if we did something radical? Is the cabin still there?"

"What do you mean?"

"We could investigate. We know there was a body, and then it was gone, the scene wiped clean. That's not a closed case. That's a cold case, whether the police believed you or not. You're a scientist, Renee. You must know all about fluorescene. Luminol. Haven't you ever gone back to the cabin and done any testing? If there was blood on the floor back then, I guarantee you there are chemicals that can help us find it even now, all these years later."

There was an excitement in his voice that both thrilled and frightened me.

"I've thought about it," I admitted. "When I was getting my doctorate, I did some work on the absorption spectra of nanocrystals, and that got me to wondering...I mean, I would never have had the nerve to go there myself, but I considered hiring a private investigator or a retired cop to run tests for me. I called Granddad to find out who owned the woods next door, thinking the first step was probably to get permission to be on the property."

"So what happened with that?"

I shrugged. "The call went really bad. Granddad was *not* happy about the idea and told me to let it go. I guess his reaction sort of dredged up all that old stuff."

"I can imagine. What did you do?"

"I did as he asked. I tried to let it go, at least for the time being." I glanced at Blake, thinking he would understand better if he'd actually known my grandfather. He was a good man, but going against him in a disagreement was like trying to walk up the James River against the current after a hard rain.

"Shortly after that he invited me to join the authentication team, and I enjoyed myself so much I didn't want to rock the boat by bringing up the matter of the Incident again."

"You have a right to know what happened over there. All four of you do."

The way he said it, so resolutely, made me realize he had no doubt about the matter at all. He believed me. Not only did he believe me, he wanted to help me.

"What do you say, Talbot? Want to validate what you've known all along to be true? Just say the word and we'll go there and take a look."

I swallowed hard, my heart pounding with fear and excitement.

"You would do that for me?"

He smiled, melting my heart in an instant. "Sounds to me like you need to resolve the past so you can move on with the future. If this will help you do that, then nothing would make me happier."

I waited until the day's events were over with before I talked to my cousins. We were in our room, on our beds, the familiar "slumber party" vibe flowing between us. But I had something to ask them that wasn't the wanna-play-truth-or-dare or anybody-up-for-a-facial-mask kind of question. It was serious—and possibly life changing.

I started by inquiring about their schedules and what they were like over the next few days. Both lived close enough to come here by car, and though Maddee had ridden with her parents, Danielle had driven herself. If they were to stay an extra day or two, I knew Danielle could take Maddee home on her way.

"Why?" Maddee asked, her eyes narrowing. "What's up in that complicated brain of yours, Renee?"

I swallowed hard. "I have something I want to propose to you guys, but part of it depends on whether you're in a position to stick around a little longer. I am. I've already talked with my supervisor and let her know I'm taking some extra time, and I changed my flight and extended my car till Wednesday."

They looked at each other and then back at me.

"There's something I want to do," I continued, "whether you guys can be a part of it or not. But I'd rather not do it without your blessing. And ideally I'd rather you stick around and be a part of it too."

"This is totally your serious face," Danielle said, sitting up on her bed. "What is it, Renee? Talk to us. I can swing an extra day. I'm not sure about more than that, but I could try."

Maddee nodded. "Same here as long as Danielle can get me home." "Of course."

Maddee again fixed her compassionate gaze on me. "Whatever it is, honey, if you need us, we're here for you."

Danielle nodded. "We got your back, girl."

I exhaled slowly. "I really appreciate what you're both saying, but don't speak too soon. This...thing I want to do, it isn't just about me. It's about all of us."

I sat up straight and tucked pillows behind my back, buying time as I tried to think of the best way to jump in. Finally, I decided to start within my own comfort zone and explain the science of what I wanted to do. I asked if either of them had ever heard of chemiluminescence. They both shook their heads.

"How about luminol?"

Maddee frowned. "Isn't that what they use on *CSI* to find blood at crime scenes?"

They shared another glance, their expressions growing wary.

"Probably." Pressing on, I gave the simplest explanation I could, telling them how the chemical luminol could be put into a spray bottle along with several other substances.

"Blood contains hemoglobin," I added, "which contains iron, and when blood is sprayed with the luminol mixture, the iron becomes a catalyst." Resisting the urge to go into the full explanation about cyclic peroxide and electron transfer and 3-aminophthalate, I just said that the reaction increased energy, which was then released as photons of light, resulting in blue chemiluminescence.

"Earth to Renee," Danielle interrupted. "Can you bring this down a notch for us regular humans?"

I smiled. "Fine. There's this really cool chemical, and if you spray it on a surface where there has been blood—even if that blood is no longer visible to the naked eye, even if it's been decades since the blood was there—chances are a chemical reaction will occur, and for about thirty seconds the residual iron from the blood will cause the luminol to light up as a distinct blue glow."

Maddee scooted to the edge of her bed, dumbfounded. "You want to test the floor of the cabin in the Dark Woods."

Looking from her to Danielle, I nodded. "Blake has offered to help."

Their eyes began to light up at the thought. After all these years, would we finally be vindicated?

"I'm in," said Maddee.

"Me too!" said Danielle.

"Wait," I said, holding up a hand. "There's one more thing. To see the glow, it needs to be dark. Which means going there at night."

I wasn't sure why, but I expected discussion or debate or outright refusal. Instead, both of my cousins just grew quiet for a long moment.

"If Blake can get things squared away in time, the plan is to do it tomorrow night," I continued, speaking into their silence. "But bear in mind that luminol does have its disadvantages, including that it doesn't always work. Though considering the amount of blood there that day, I feel it's worth a try. So I guess the first question is, is it okay with you guys if he and I do this?"

They both nodded enthusiastically.

"Okay, second question. Do you want to be there when we do?"

It took about ten more seconds of silent thought before Danielle spoke.

"Yes," she whispered.

Maddee sucked in a breath and blew it out. "Yes."

"Good," I said, giving them a nod.

As if recognizing the importance of our decision, Danielle surprised us by sitting up in bed, raising her right hand, and declaring,

"From this moment forward, we will no longer be called the Liar Choir. Henceforth, we are to be known as the Truth Sleuths."

Maddee and I cheered softly and then we all hugged and cried a little. We spent the next half hour lying on our beds and whispering about what this would mean if it actually worked.

Chapter Sixteen

Catherine

*C*atherine was determined to make the trip to Paris and Versailles a reality. She knew their options were rapidly dwindling and that Suzanne was their last hope. Wanting to build a spark within Grand-Mère's heart, she kept bringing up old, oft-told stories in conversation, ones about her grandmother's youth in Paris.

Grand-Mère had grown up Catholic, but when she was sixteen she met a printer from Lyon at the pond in the Jardin du Luxembourg. He was staying with friends not far from her parents' grand house across from the gardens, and they met every day for a week on the edge of the pond in front of the Luxembourg palace. On the second day they met, he told her he was Huguenot. There were not many Protestants in Paris, and Grand-Mère was surprised that the young man she had so quickly grown fond of did not share her faith. But by Sunday she was willing to sneak away from mass at her family's church, Saint Germain, to boat down the Seine with him to the Temple de Charenton, outside of the city.

That very day she fell in love with both the young man and the Savior the pastor preached about. "I could have come to know that same Christ through my childhood faith," she had said. "But somehow I had missed Him. It was not the fault of the nuns who schooled me or the priests who taught me. I think hearing it in a new way is what touched me."

She converted and married the man and moved to Lyon, into a home that far exceeded his humble description. She'd had no idea the position his family held in the city, even though her parents had discovered the Gillet family was nobility.

But neither Grand-Père's family's stature nor their wealth swayed Grand-Mère's mother and father into accepting her husband. They said she had disgraced them by marrying a Huguenot. In the few times my grandparents visited Paris after their marriage, Grand-Mère's parents had been cordial to her husband but never warm.

Grand-Mère may have left the Catholicism of her girlhood, but she brought her Holy Days with her, teaching them to Catherine. "There is a lot to learn from the rhythm of the days," she said. Catherine liked that every single one not only had a number but also a name. This was the first Monday of the Octave of Easter. She liked the thought of it being the *first*. She hoped it was the beginning of something new in their lives.

The physician came to examine Amelie that afternoon. On his way out, he also checked Valentina and said he was pleased with how she was improving. "She is filling out already. Amelie is better too."

Catherine nodded in agreement. "Do you think they are strong enough for us to consider going away for a time and leaving them behind? Grand-Mère has been invited to Versailles to visit an old friend."

"Medically that would not be a problem as long as there are others to care for them here. My bigger concern would be your safety, Catherine, in Paris and on the road. And Amelie's safety here in the house, with the dragoons..."

"Of course. We will not go unless we can assure there is protection both here and on our journey."

"Very well," he said, smiling kindly. "Then I wish you Godspeed."

Once he was gone, discussion of the trip continued, with Amelie urging them to go but Grand-Mère still resisting.

"Our temple has been destroyed." Amelie's voice was much stronger. "We are running out of time."

"I will not leave you, not with the dragoons here," Grand-Mère answered.

"They are not staying," Estelle chimed in from the doorway to the sitting room, the baby still at her breast.

Catherine turned toward her. "What?"

"Waltier told me. Last night. Father Philippe made an arrangement with the captain. The platoon was already going south, down the Rhône, for the next several weeks. Father Philippe convinced him to send them ahead of schedule."

Amelie managed to walk to the dining room at dinnertime. The first thing she asked after sitting down was if it was true that the dragoons were leaving for a time.

Jules nodded. "I confirmed it with Father Philippe this afternoon. They should be gone soon." He was obviously pleased to have Amelie join them for the meal. After the food was served, he said, "Our prayers are being answered. You have come home, our solicitor assures me the Mother Superior has no claim on you, and you will soon be well."

She leaned toward her cousin. "I am so much better that Grand-Mère and Catherine can leave for Paris soon."

Jules nearly choked on his beef. He took a drink of wine and then said, "No one is going anywhere, at least not that far. Besides, I know you think Suzanne can help, but why? She is a friend of the king's mistress, *oui*? What power do you think she has? Certainly none over Louis XIV."

"It is worth a try, *non*?" Amelie said softly.

Jules shrugged. Catherine knew he would have a hard time saying no to their cousin. She had forgotten that, what it was like to have an ally around to sway him when nothing else could.

"They will need someone to accompany them," Amelie continued. "What about Pierre? Could he go?"

Jules shook his head. "I need him to look at the mill on the Plateau. We are going down there soon."

Catherine's heart sank until he added, "Perhaps Eriq could

accompany you if you absolutely insist on going. I can spare him. Thanks to the king's latest manipulations, we are short on orders."

Though Catherine would have far preferred Pierre, at least her brother's suggestion of Eriq meant he was willing to help make the trip happen.

"What if Eriq went with you to the Plateau instead?" Amelie asked. "Then Pierre would be free to go with Catherine and Grand-Mère."

"*Non.* Eriq has no experience with these sorts of things. And I do not—"

A commotion in the kitchen kept him from finishing his sentence.

"The dragoons," Grand-Mère said, sighing. "God willing, we will only have to put up with them for a short time."

After a moment, a drunken Basile burst into the room, followed by Waltier, who appeared embarrassed by his comrade's behavior, as usual.

"Come in," Grand-Mère said. "You will be served shortly."

As Basile took a seat at the table, Jules escorted Amelie from the room. Catherine tried to slip out as well, but Basile commanded her to stop.

She kept going. "Get her!" Basile shouted, and before she could reach the end of the hall, Waltier grabbed her by the arm. "Play along," he whispered.

"I do not want to play anything with him," she hissed.

"I will protect you."

"Really? Like you did Pierre yesterday, at the fire?"

He dropped his eyes. "I will do my best."

"Let her go," Grand-Mère said quietly to Waltier. "You are heading south soon, *oui*?"

Waltier nodded.

"I will give your colleague a couple of bottles of our best wine," Grand-Mère whispered. "That should distract him for another night."

Waltier shrugged but let go of Catherine.

"Basile," Grand-Mère said, stepping back into the dining room. "I have something for you. I need the help of my granddaughter in the wine cellar." She jingled her keys as she came back into the hall. Then, before turning for the kitchen, she gave Catherine a push toward their rooms. She reached the suite and closed the door behind her, locking it.

"I take it the dragoons are back," Estelle said from the chaise.

Catherine exhaled. "They cannot leave soon enough."

"Oh, I do not know," Estelle said. "Waltier is not that bad."

Catherine frowned. "Not compared to the other one, *non*, but he is still doing the work—"

"That he has been assigned to do," Amelie said. "All of us have our burdens to carry, Catherine. This is clearly a burden for Waltier."

"Then why does he not quit?"

"He would be hung for treason," Amelie said, sighing. "None of this is easy. Not for any of us."

"Except for people like Basile. Or the king," Catherine interjected. She had no sympathy for either.

Amelie sighed again. *"Non,* we cannot guess at what demons torment them."

Estelle stood with the baby in her arms and started toward the cradle.

Catherine helped Amelie into bed, and she could see in the weariness of her body the cost of having taken dinner at the table with the family.

"I wish you could go to Paris too," Catherine said softly.

"I have never wanted to go. You were the one interested in fashion and the court, remember?" She leaned back against the pillow. "And traveling and adventures. All I wanted was a husband and a family." She turned her head toward Valentina, her eyes shiny with sudden tears. "I just want to get well and be able to care for my daughter. And for all of us to keep her safe."

Catherine sat down on the side of the bed and held her cousin's hand. That was what they all wanted.

On Wednesday, on the Feast of Saint Mark the Evangelist, Grand-Mère took Catherine to Janetta's shop and ordered two gowns, one brown and one gray. Both would be a little lower in the bodice than the ones she had and much fuller in the skirt. Both would be more appropriate for older, married women, Catherine was sure.

"You are going to Versailles?" Janetta asked as she measured Catherine.

"We may," Grand-Mère said.

"No one wears this sort of thing there," Janetta said, stretching the measurement string down Catherine's back.

"*Au contraire.* We just had a letter that this is the latest fashion, set by Madame de Maintenon."

Janetta laughed, dropping the string on the floor. As she retrieved it, she said, "Certainly it's the latest fashion for a fifty-year-old favorite, but it isn't for an eighteen-year-old beauty." Catherine expected Janetta to laugh again, but she did not. "She needs a colorful dress and, I'm afraid, a lower neckline. She will be laughed out of Paris, not to mention Versailles. As lovely as she is, she will be ridiculed. You do not want that."

Catherine's face grew warm, though whether at the compliment or the warning, she wasn't sure.

Grand-Mère pursed her lips together and then said, "It's a chance we will take. Our goal is not to have Catherine accepted into Parisian society but to speak with my friend—and keep our integrity."

Catherine was grateful for the dresses, she really was. But Janetta's words caused her concern. Maybe she had been wrong about Paris.

After Janetta assured them the dresses would be done in time, they left to continue their preparations for the trip.

On Thursday of the Octave of Easter, Catherine and Grand-Mère took a chance on going out in order to deliver soup and bread to several elderly people in the area. They heard dragoons had been harassing the cobbler again, so on the way home they went by his shop. It was closed. Catherine peered in the windows, but there was no sign of anyone.

"Perhaps he got away," Grand-Mère said.

"Where do you think he went?"

Grand-Mère put her finger to her lips, and they continued on in silence. As they neared the house, a shout startled them. Two men were pointing down the street. Catherine turned to see what the commotion was about. Jules approached them on his black gelding.

"It's him!" the larger of the two men exclaimed.

Catherine's knees grew weak. They were the guards from the convent. They began to run toward Jules. He slowed his horse to a trot and then stopped in the middle of the street.

"We have come to take the young woman and baby back," the younger man said. "Mother Superior sent us."

"Impossible," Jules said. He opened his leather bag and pulled out a piece of paper. "I have a document preventing that prepared by my solicitor and already signed. I am the guardian of both Amelie Fournier and her daughter, Valentina."

The older man squinted at the document and then snatched it from Jules's hand.

He glanced toward Catherine and Grand-Mère and then nodded toward the gate as he said, loudly, to the guards, "I have already sent a copy of the document to Mother Superior. Check with her. It should have arrived by now."

The second guard looked over the first one's shoulder at the document and shrugged.

Grand-Mère looped her arm through Catherine's and pulled her to the gate.

"If Mother Superior has any questions, tell her to contact my solicitor," Jules added. "In the meantime, may I give you a bottle of wine to compensate you for your useless journey today?"

Thankfully, the gate was unlocked and Catherine and Grand-Mère slipped through. On the other side was Monsieur Roen. He must have overheard the ruckus. Grand-Mère gave him the keys to the wine cellar. "Would you?" she asked.

"Of course," he answered, closing the gate but not locking it.

Grand-Mère went inside the house, but Catherine waited by the well until the wine was delivered, Jules was safely inside the walls, and he had left his horse in the stable.

"When are you and Grand-Mère leaving?" he asked as he approached.

Catherine blinked. "I don't recall your giving us permission."

He shrugged. "Well, then, I'm giving it now. Though you would go whether I said you may or not."

"That's not true," Catherine answered, genuinely hurt. She tried so hard to respect and honor him, yet he thought so little of her in return.

"Go," Jules said.

"What about your trip to the Plateau?"

"We will postpone it as long as possible. Someone needs to stay with Amelie, especially if those guards come back."

"Who signed the document?"

"Father Philippe."

Catherine smiled. "Would his signature stand up in court?"

"It's confusing as far as the law. Completely open to interpretation. I'm hoping Father Philippe's involvement will impress Mother Superior, though." He leaned against the well. "Still, I'll stay here as long as I can."

Catherine shaded her eyes from the afternoon sun as she looked up into her brother's face. "So we have your blessing to go?"

"More or less." He stepped toward the house but then stopped and turned back toward her. "Eriq has agreed to go with you. It's the best I can do. I know you would have preferred Pierre."

Catherine nodded, keeping her expression somber, but inside she cheered. Amelie was improving. Jules had thwarted the guards from the convent. And he was allowing them to go to Paris. True, she found it disappointing that Eriq would be the one going with them instead of Pierre. Then again, the way their relationship had been lately, perhaps some time apart would be good for both of them. She stepped into the house, already composing letters in her mind to both Suzanne and her great-uncle.

The rest of the week was spent in preparation. Jules suggested that they arrange the trip through a business that ran coaches all the way to Paris instead of taking their own. That would make their travel much faster because there would be fresh horses to use along the way, whereas Monsieur Roen would have to rest their horses and not be able to travel as far each day. The arrangements were soon made for a private coach that would deliver them to the home of Catherine's great-uncle, Sir

Laurent Delecore, in Paris. Grand-Mère and Uncle Laurent's grand-father had been knighted by Louis XIII, transforming the Delecores from a wealthy Parisian family into a rich and noble one.

Jules made sure Eriq had a musket with him and was prepared to use it if needed. "The driver will have one too," he said one afternoon in Grand-Mère's sitting room while Amelie lounged nearby, the baby in her arms. "And both men will have swords." Catherine knew her brother had a musket too, a relief if the guards from the convent came back. So far they had not. She would not be surprised if they did return, though. At least Jules saw Amelie's safety as a higher priority than his trip to the Plateau.

Catherine marveled at the thought of actually going to Paris.

"What Bible do you plan to take?" Jules asked.

"I hadn't thought about it," she answered. She had put a lot of consideration into her wardrobe but that was as far as she had gotten.

"Take your little one. You can hide it in your bun, under your covering."

Catherine frowned. That sounded uncomfortable.

"The dragoons would never think to look there." Jules stood. As he passed Amelie and Valentina, he reached down and patted the top of the baby's head. She yawned and stretched, causing him to pause. Something in his features seemed to soften.

Catherine could not believe it. Was that actually a smile coming to his face? How long had it been since she'd seen her brother smile?

But then Valentina opened her eyes and began to cry, at which point Jules immediately backed off, stiffening again into the man he always was these days.

"You frightened her," Amelie teased, shooing him away. "She is not used to having men around."

Catherine couldn't imagine her brother ever having children of his own, let alone a wife. Their father had been so different. Tender. Loving. Simple. Nothing like his complicated son.

～⌇～

On Divine Mercy Sunday, the family worshipped at home. That afternoon the dragoons finally readied to leave. Waltier certainly knew it was coming because he had told Estelle. And Father Philippe knew because apparently he suggested it.

But Basile did not know until their captain gave the order that afternoon. He came back to the house in a rage, tearing through the kitchen and upsetting the soufflé Cook had made for dinner before heading upstairs to gather his things.

"Don't be sad to see me go," he called loudly as he came back down again and spotted Catherine hovering near the end of the hall.

She held her breath. He marched toward her and then stopped a pace away. "It will not be long until we return. I know you think you are far above me in station, but we could wed and save your home." He showed his teeth. "Or perhaps your infirm cousin would be better suited to me."

Catherine had never heard anything as appalling in her entire life. She bit her lip to keep from responding. He laughed and then walked away.

Regardless of Basile's inane proposal, the last day of the Octave of Easter ended on a high note. The dragoons were gone, and the trip to Paris would begin the next day.

CHAPTER SEVENTEEN
Catherine

The day of the trip, Pierre arrived with Eriq as Catherine carried the basket of food Cook had prepared for them out to the courtyard, placing it near the well. As Eriq busied himself with his bags, Pierre reached for Catherine's hand and pulled her over to the chestnut tree.

"You came to tell me goodbye?" she said with deep relief.

He nodded. "Well, that and it was easier to drop Eriq off now than to find some way to get the horse home later."

Her smile faded.

"Not to mention, Jules wanted me to go into the shop with him early," he added, oblivious to the good his words were undoing.

"Why?"

"Some...decisions need to be made." He shrugged. "But I *am* pleased to be here to say goodbye. I will miss you." He moved around to the far side of the tree, taking her with him.

Catherine looked up into his blue eyes. She would miss him too.

He tucked a loose lock of hair behind her ear. "I'm glad, though, that you will have a chance to visit Paris. And I'm looking forward to seeing the Plateau."

"But the two of you are not going there until we get back here, *oui*? The dragoons could return. Amelie needs protection."

"It depends, I think, on the message Jules receives from the owners of the mill."

Catherine put her hand on her hip. "He said he would not go yet."

"If it's not safe to leave Amelie, then he will not. But that is for him to decide, not you. Or me, for that matter."

Catherine frowned. He almost sounded as if he wanted to go, as though the Plateau were somewhere a civilized person might choose to visit. Even though she had only been there once, she remembered every detail—every village, every stop—and there was really nothing there. Just small villages and fields and a river. And cows. Lots of cows.

He took her hand. "I know you are annoyed with me, Catherine, but please be patient."

Patient? What did he think she might do? Run off with someone she met in Paris? Convert? Flee to London on her own? "Is that how everyone sees me? As impatient?"

"*Non*," Pierre said, but then he smiled. "Well, *oui*, at times."

Her face grew warm. "I know things are complicated right now, and I'll be patient, Pierre, I promise. But do not let Jules make decisions for all of us. Grand-Mère doesn't want to live on the Plateau and neither do I. We could easily make a life in London. If we stay in France, I fear we will all be killed and thrown in the river like Paul. Or drug from the back of a cart."

Pierre winced and then said quietly, "We received a message from our parents."

She sucked in a breath. "Are they safe?"

He nodded. "They are over the border and headed to Bern. They asked Eriq to join them as soon as possible. Of course, he will have to wait until he gets back from Paris, but then he will have to go."

"What about you?"

"They want me to come too as soon as things are settled here."

"And?"

"And you as well, of course." He said it so simply, as if how she felt about the matter was of no importance whatsoever.

She stepped back, against the tree, pulling her hand away from him. "Have you considered at all what I might want?"

From across the yard, she heard Jules calling for Pierre.

He glanced in that direction and then returned his attention to her. "*Oui*, of course I have. But there are so many layers to this situation you do not understand. So many...opportunities. So many risks. So many dangers. We have to move very carefully. As I said before, you need to trust me."

"Pierre!" Jules yelled again. "We have to get to the shop." From the look on Pierre's face, Catherine could tell he was glad for the excuse to end the conversation.

"Go," she said. "We will speak when I return. We will know more then." Perhaps the time apart would clear both of their heads.

Hidden as they were, Catherine allowed her betrothed to give her a quick kiss goodbye, though she turned her head at the last moment so that it landed on her cheek and not her lips. Then, avoiding his gaze, she stepped out from behind the tree, calling to her brother, "Here he is."

Jules squinted into the rising sun as he stepped forward. "*Bonjour,* Pierre."

"*Bonjour,*" Pierre answered and then turned back to Catherine. "You are all set, then. I hope Eriq will be of help. He promised he would."

"He will," Catherine said. "He has become quite dependable. Quite grown-up."

Pierre raised his dark eyebrows, but she could not tell what he was thinking. Did it bother him that she and Eriq would be spending so much time together? Sharing this adventure, seeing so much along the way, strolling side by side in the most romantic city in the world?

Though Catherine hoped Pierre knew he could trust her, a part of her also hoped he was at least a tiny bit jealous.

"We need to hurry." Jules nodded toward the stables. "Father Philippe is expecting us."

And so of course Pierre did as he said, giving her a final nod and then heading for his mount. He always did as her brother said.

Catherine stayed where she was, watching the two men ride out of the courtyard, listening to the *clip-clop* of their horses' hooves fade in the distance. None of this made sense to her—not Pierre's thoughts or his intentions and certainly not her brother's actions. Swallowing hard, she brushed at the tear that threatened to spill from her eye.

Then, with a heavy sigh, she turned toward the house. Eriq stood at the back door, waiting for her.

"I'm so glad you're going," Amelie said when Catherine came to tell her goodbye. She was sitting in a chair, holding Valentina, while Estelle made the bed. "Write about it so you will remember to tell me everything."

Catherine picked up her satchel, where she had already packed quills, ink, and paper. "I will."

Amelie smiled, a teasing glint in her eye. "I have no doubt about that. You write down everything these days."

Catherine gestured toward the desk. "I am keeping a journal of all that has been happening to us. I believe it is important." She could not help but hope someone would read it someday. "Whatever happens from here, none of our lives will ever be the same."

Amelie paused for a moment, taking in Catherine's words. "That is good, very good. Someday Valentina will be able to read our story and know what we went through to ensure her safety when she was still *une enfant*."

Catherine treasured the thought of the baby reading her journal. The two young women both gazed down at her, and then they looked to each other.

"I'll miss you every day I'm gone," Catherine said. Her heart ached at the thought of leaving Amelie. For the first sixteen years of her life, they had been inseparable. The time they had been forced to spend apart these past months had been the most terrible.

"Well, do not pity me," Amelie said, trying to be comforting. "I'll miss you too, but I do not wish I were going with you. I am content here."

Catherine nodded. Though she found it hard to understand why, her cousin had never been as adventuresome. It was Catherine who would beg Amelie to go on horseback rides in the hills and out to the family estate west of town. It was Catherine who wanted to play with the boys and learn geography and English. Amelie only went along with her plans to appease her cousin.

And though Amelie was just one year older, she had grown up so much faster, Catherine had to admit, marrying and starting a family and then enduring so much heartbreak and misery with stoic grace. In the past year, Amelie had suffered the death of her husband and banishment to a convent, given birth to her baby, and lost her father—yet she was the one who seemed the least burdened of all.

Meanwhile, Catherine was still clomping around like a sullen girl, fighting with her brother, trying to get her own way, and struggling with her desires for the things of this world. Looking at her beautiful cousin now—at the curve of her neck framed by her loose hair, her arms cradling her baby, and the peaceful expression on her sweet face—Catherine realized this was what she wanted to be like too, not some overgrown child but rather an adult, one who exhibited all the fruits of the Spirit and a maturity beyond her years.

After Catherine hugged Amelie, kissed Valentina, and told Estelle goodbye, she hurried down the hall with her satchel. Again, she wiped a tear from her eye.

Cook handed her yet another basket once she reached the kitchen. "The best wine is for Madame Gillet's brother, *oui*? We do not want him to think you are simple country folk."

"*Merci*," Catherine said. "For everything."

"Do not worry," Cook assured her. "I'll take good care of both Amelie and the baby."

Catherine nodded, forcing a smile. "I know you will."

By the time she reached the courtyard, the hired carriage had arrived. It was larger and newer than the Gillets' more modest carriage and was pulled by four horses rather than two. The coachman had loaded their luggage and Grand-Mère was already inside, but Eriq waited for Catherine. He put out his hand for hers and held it as she climbed up, and then he slipped in after her, taking the bench across from her and Grand-Mère. Catherine had to admit that it had been wise of her brother to arrange for the carriage. The benches were padded and much more comfortable than theirs, and glass filled the windows rather than mere blinds.

They were off in no time, making their way down the street. As they passed the cathedral, the bell tolled seven times and parishioners hurried in for morning mass. Doves flew from the bell tower, and farmers set up their produce at the market.

According to Grand-Mère, the ride from Lyon to Paris would take nearly two weeks, and they would stay in inns along the way.

The road outside of the city led through rolling fields. Wildflowers bloomed in the grass. Sheep grazed in a field. Around every few curves in the road, the Saône came into view. After a while, Eriq put his head back against the seat and closed his eyes. Grand-Mère took Catherine's hand. "It's a dream come true, *non?*"

Catherine nodded and squeezed her grandmother's hand, causing the woman's ruby ring to dig into her finger. It was the second Monday of Easter, one of the best days of Catherine's life. The only thing that kept it from being perfect was the fact that Eriq was here instead of Pierre.

Looking over at the dozing young man now, she told herself to make the best of it. At least he was a friend, not to mention that he was tall and muscular and brave, a good choice for the role of protector.

They spent the first night in an inn north of Villefranche-sur-Saône. Dusk was falling as they arrived. Eriq stepped down from the carriage and then turned to help the women disembark as well. The innkeeper came out and assisted the driver in wrestling the trunk from the top of the carriage, nearly dropping it on the ground as they did. Eriq helped carry it into the inn, while Grand-Mère and Catherine followed.

After a dinner of lukewarm *ragoût* and dry bread, the two women retreated to their upstairs room while Eriq stayed down in the eating area, speaking with a friendly fellow who had introduced himself to the three of them earlier as a Monsieur Olivier, from Paris. Around forty, he was smartly dressed in a black wig, ruffled blouse, gold coat, and high-heeled shoes. Catherine imagined King Louis dressed in a similar, though likely even fancier, manner.

Grand-Mère insisted that Catherine wrap in her cloak to sleep instead of placing her body directly on the bed. Grand-Mère did the same, flicking something off the bed to the floor as she said, "Who knows when the bedding was last washed."

When they descended the stairs the next morning, Eriq was again deep in conversation with the same gentleman.

Once they were back on the road, Catherine asked what the two of them had found to speak about that was so compelling.

"He is a businessman, dealing in property. He has quite a few contacts with noblemen and visits Versailles from time to time. His home is near your great-uncle's. He is on his way to Lyon on business for a day or two, but then he will head back. He said I should look for him while we are in Paris."

Catherine tilted her head. "*Pourquoi?*"

"He might come in useful." Eriq shrugged. "You never know."

After a while, the rocking of the carriage lulled Grand-Mère to sleep, her head resting against the corner of the carriage. Catherine leaned forward to ask Eriq exactly what Monsieur Olivier did concerning property.

"He finds buyers. For example, if a nobleman is selling off part of his estate, Monsieur will find the right person to purchase it."

"Why would a nobleman want to sell his property?" Unless he was a Huguenot. She knew the answer for that.

"There are many reasons. Maybe he doesn't want to maintain it. Or perhaps he has fallen into debt."

"Oh." Catherine certainly did not think her family was in debt, although Jules had said their money was tied up. Perhaps there were things she did not understand.

Eriq leaned back against the bench, his eyes heavy, but Catherine was not finished with her questions. In a whisper, she asked, "Did you mention the properties of our families to Monsieur Olivier?"

He waved his hand in front of his face. "In passing only. I have no control over any of that."

Catherine leaned forward again, her elbows on her knees. "But you are part of the business."

Eriq leaned toward her until their faces were just inches apart. "I am the second son, Catherine. I stand to inherit nothing. And as things are now, everyone expects me to go to Switzerland as soon as possible to take care of our parents." His face grew serious. "I want to honor my parents, but I have no desire to follow them to Bern. No one asked me my opinion about any of this."

Catherine nodded. "I understand."

He smiled, just a little, his gray eyes still heavy. "I know you do." He reached for her hand and gave it a squeeze before quickly letting it go. "If I could come up with a viable business plan on this trip, then I could earn a living and send money to help my parents instead of going myself." He leaned back against the seat again. "That is what I hope to accomplish, anyway."

"But in France, Eriq? Surely you do not think it will be safe to stay."

"I would prefer to stay in France, but of course London is probably more realistic, with some sort of French connection."

Intrigued, Catherine held his gaze for a long moment. So he had not come along solely as a protector. He was more complex than that— and more appealing.

She smiled. "Will you stay in the business of printing?"

He shook his head. "I've never enjoyed working in the shop. Printing does not interest me. And papermaking certainly does not." He shuddered. "Have you ever been around a paper mill? The pounding of the cloth in that big vat of water is enough to turn a person into a lunatic."

Catherine laughed softly. She'd heard it was a noisy proposition.

"Besides, I want something that is my own. Something separate from Pierre." He spoke with conviction. "I respect my brother, but I need to become my own man."

"I see," Catherine said. And she did. Eriq's relationship with his older brother was in some ways even more difficult than Catherine's was with hers. Eriq was required to earn a living and support a family, while Pierre would be handed his future on a silver platter. At least Catherine would one day marry and be out from under her older brother's influence.

Then again, she realized, if she married Pierre, that would not hold true at all. Pierre would always be aligned with Jules, which meant as Pierre's wife, Catherine would never be out from under her brother. She found the thought nearly suffocating.

She was impressed with Eriq's initiative and wished she'd realized earlier what it was like for him, always being in Pierre's shadow. She did not blame him at all for wanting to break free and become his own person.

If she were a man, she would too.

CHAPTER EIGHTEEN
Catherine

*T*he journey continued on through the countryside. They passed vineyards, large manors, and fields of rye, oats, and barley. Despite the glass windows, dust from the road seeped through the cracks of the carriage. The next night they stayed in another inn. This time Eriq wrestled the trunk down by himself. He met another businessman, this one from Orleans, and spoke with him through dinner.

Catherine could not help but admire his gift of interacting with others and gathering information. Clearly, Jules and Pierre had both underestimated Eriq's skills. She was sure he could be an asset to the business if they only gave him a chance.

The next day, Grand-Mère suggested to Eriq that he might prefer less confinement during the day and he should ride up top with the driver. He took her advice. "He used to be so annoying, but he has grown up after all," Catherine said as the carriage lurched forward.

"*Oui*, most people do," Grand-Mère replied. "But I want you to be careful with him."

Catherine leaned back. "Have I acted inappropriately?"

"*Non,* not at all. I just...Jules has some concerns. He fears that the young Mr. Talbot may have a bit of a crush on you."

Catherine laughed. "Why would he think that?"

"Apparently, Eriq was all too eager to step in as our protector and go on this trip with us. Your brother said the he was practically giddy at the thought. Such behavior seemed suspicious, is all."

"Eriq was excited for Paris, Grand-Mère, not for me," Catherine replied with a huff. She wanted to add that he had also been eager for the business opportunities he knew the trip would afford him. But he had shared that fact with her privately, and it wasn't her place to tell his secrets. "Jules trusts no one."

"He trusts Pierre."

"Pardon?"

"Jules. You said he trusts no one, but that's not true. He trusts Pierre implicitly."

"Ah. That's because Pierre does not think for himself."

Grand-Mère shook her head. "Catherine, you know very well that Pierre is his own man. He simply trusts Jules's judgment enough to go along with his plans and decisions for now."

"Who can know for sure?" Catherine turned her head toward the window. Grand-Mère adored Pierre, not to mention Jules. Of course she would defend them both.

They continued on in silence, an emerald sea of wheat rolling gently in the wind. Beyond, a row of poplar trees swayed back and forth. Tears stung her eyes. She missed Pierre, the old Pierre who was more than just an echo of her brother.

She missed his caring blue eyes. His strong shoulders. His quick smile.

A heaviness settled in her chest.

They continued on day after day until, on the third Monday of Easter, the seventh of May, they reached Auxerre, two-thirds of the way to Paris. As they drove through the village, Grand-Mère pointed to the temple. It was even simpler than the one in Lyon had been—but at least it was still standing. That was a good sign. "More than a hundred years ago, this village was captured by the Huguenots," Grand-Mère said. "It has been a safe place ever since. I hope it still is." Catherine heard about the Religious Wars through the years. She knew Henri IV had stopped them. It was all so long ago that growing up she could not imagine what they had to do with her—until now.

They stopped at an inn on the far side of the village. This time Eriq found a Huguenot man to talk with as they sat around the simple table. While Grand-Mère spoke with the innkeeper's wife, Catherine found herself eavesdropping on the men. The Huguenot man spoke with Eriq about planning to sell his home and business, and the need to do so as soon as possible so they could leave the country for good. He was in Auxerre looking for a buyer.

"I wish you could convince my older brother of that," Eriq told him, shaking his head, a mix of sadness and disgust on his face.

Catherine agreed, so wholeheartedly in fact that she nearly said so out loud.

"He is being so stubborn," Eriq added. "Sometimes I wonder if something else is going on with him, if he has other motives."

Other motives? Catherine did not know what he was implying, and the men's conversation headed in a different direction, but the words rang around inside her head long into the night, even after the lights were out and everyone else was asleep. *Other motives.*

She would not question her fiancé's character again in front of her grandmother—or anyone else, for that matter. But as soon as she had an opportunity to speak with Eriq alone, she was going ask him exactly what he meant.

They journeyed onward the next day. The sky was gray and ominous, the land around them bleak. But it was not just the weather and the terrain that weighed on Catherine. It was the thought of what Eriq had said the night before.

Eriq must have been thinking about the same thing, for at one point, as he gazed mindlessly out of the window, he commented on how difficult it must be, even once a decision had been reached, to actually make it all the way out of the country. "There should be places along the travel routes, safe places where Huguenots could seek respite without having to fear for their lives."

"*Oui,*" Catherine replied, "but even if there were such things, how would one recognize them? A home that is safe and one that is dangerous look the same from the outside."

Eriq turned his attention to her and held her eyes for a long moment, but she could not read his expression. "One might say the same of people."

They finally reached Paris after several more days of travel, rolling into town at four o'clock on the third Friday of Easter. They had not been stopped by dragoons or by marauders or any other villains. Eriq had not had to use his musket or his sword and neither had the driver. It had been a successful trip all the way around.

The day of their arrival was bright and warm, almost too warm in the carriage. Both Catherine and Eriq had their noses pressed to the windows as they entered the city. First manors gave way to houses, and then the streets narrowed and tall buildings appeared, five and six stories high. "These are the medieval neighborhoods," Grand-Mère explained. "They are overcrowded and dangerous. The people have little means of providing for their families and sometimes grow desperate. I used to come here with *ma mère* with baskets of food."

A man dressed in rags slept against a post. Above him, a metal lantern hung.

"Night watchmen—archers—patrol through here," Grand-Mère said, looking at Eriq. "This is miles from the home of my brother. Do not wander down here."

Eriq nodded in agreement.

A man pushed a cart with a broken wheel, loaded with stones; a miller peddled bags of flour from a wagon; a young woman strung wash on a line outside her window, high above the street.

A little girl in a filthy frock held out a cup to a woman in a red dress, but the woman hurried on by without noticing her. A boy, nine or ten, darted through the traffic, chased by an older boy. It was clear they were not playing.

Catherine took her handkerchief from her bag and dabbed at her nose. Dust was not coming through the chinks in the carriage now. Odors were. Open sewage. A vinegar plant. A butchery.

"How many people live in Paris?" Eriq asked.

"Last I heard, around five hundred thousand," Grand-Mère answered. That explained the smell of unwashed bodies also coming through the openings of the coach.

Grand-Mère pointed out the other side of the carriage. "Look, the Seine."

Catherine followed her grandmother's hand and sighed in relief at the sight, her mood growing remarkably better. The dwellings changed again. Single homes made of quarried stone now lined the streets. By the time they reached the river, the gowns of the ladies strolling along the sidewalks had grown more and more elaborate. The dresses were made of bright colors—green and sapphire, yellow and pink. Catherine glanced down at her drab dress. Janetta had been right.

"Across the river is the Palais du Louvre," Grand-Mère said, squinting as she spoke. Catherine strained her neck to see. The massive building went on for blocks. Beyond she could make out the spire of a church.

"Is that Notre-Dame?"

"*Oui*," Grand-Mère answered. Joy had slipped into her voice.

At the next street the carriage turned right and made its way down the narrow streets of the Latin Quarter, filled with carriages and handcarts rolling over the cobblestones. Boutiques, butcheries, and pastry shops filled the bottom levels of the buildings. Flowers spilled out of pots on the balconies.

Catherine glanced at Grand-Mère, who held her head high, her hands folded in her lap.

"Have things changed since the last time you were here?" Catherine asked.

"*Oui*. There are more bridges on the river. There are more flowers. More beautiful clothing on the street."

The carriage turned right onto a main street and then left, along a park.

"Is this Jardin du Luxembourg?" Catherine asked.

Grand-Mère nodded. A block later, the carriage stopped. Eriq descended first and then assisted Grand-Mère and Catherine. They stood for a moment at the foot of the stairs to the three-story house before them, la maison Delecore, Grand-Mère's childhood home. It was large but not as big as the Gillet residence in Lyon. It was made of quarried stone, as were all the houses opposite the park. The white-washed shutters were flung wide, the windows open to the warm day.

A butler stepped onto the stoop and then opened the door wide, saying to Grand-Mère, "Madame." She led the way to the entry, with Catherine following her. Eriq waited behind to help with the luggage.

The butler paused in the front hall to hand Grand-Mère a letter that had come for her and then led them up to their rooms. The suite for Catherine and her grandmother was ornately decorated and filled with light, thanks to numerous large windows that lined two walls.

Grand-Mère went to the biggest window and Catherine joined her there.

Jardin du Luxembourg spread out before her. The palace. The pond. The gardens of flowers. The trees, planted in groupings.

"Did you not first see *Grand-Père* by that pond?"

"*Oui*. Every day after that for a week I met him there."

"And then you visited the temple with him." It was a story Catherine knew, but she loved to hear it over and over.

"And I learned about the Lord in a new way. A way that touched my heart. I was doubly blessed that week."

"But was it not hard to leave Paris?" Catherine asked. She could not imagine.

"*Non, chérie.* I never looked back. I enjoyed the few visits I made through the years, but I was always ready to return to Lyon. That was my home. That was where my family was. That was where I learned even more about my *Saviour*."

She sat down on the edge of the brocade settee and handed Catherine the letter. "Would you read this, please?"

"Of course." Catherine opened the envelope and pulled it out,

reading quickly. It was from Suzanne, saying she would not be able to
see them for another week.

Catherine relayed the information to Grand-Mère. "I see," she said,
clearly disappointed. Catherine did not share her disappointment, but
she withheld comment.

After bathing and dressing in their best gowns, Grand-Mère and
Catherine headed downstairs. As they passed through the foyer, Eriq's
voice came from the next room.

Grand-Mère led the way into the lounge. A bouquet of lilies sat on
the table, along with a bottle of wine and four glasses. Behind the table
stood an older man and Eriq.

The man turned. "Yvonne!" he exclaimed, moving toward her
around the table.

He kissed both of her cheeks and then hugged her as she said, "Laurent." Catherine could tell her grandmother was genuinely pleased to
see her brother.

Once he released her, he said to Catherine, "And my grandniece."

Catherine nodded and curtsied. He kissed both of her cheeks,
"*Enchanté*," he said. He was a stocky man—or maybe just well fed.
Though he was shorter, something about his bright eyes and long face
reminded her of her father, who had been this man's nephew. Unlike
her father, however, her great-uncle was wearing fancy clothes and a
white wig.

After asking about the trip and the rest of the family, he glanced
from Grand-Mère to Catherine to Eriq and asked why they were still
in their traveling clothes.

Grand-Mère smiled and said with dignity, "This is our dinner attire."

Uncle Laurent shook his head. "Surely not."

Grand-Mère smiled again, her eyes dancing as she spoke. "We actually had them made for this trip."

"That religion of yours is so austere." He sighed. "I was afraid of such.
You, Yvonne, can get by with black and gray, but not even brown will
do for the young lady." He took another look at Catherine. She was
wearing her new gown from Janetta's shop.

"There is a boutique just a few blocks away. My butler will take you first thing tomorrow."

Grand-Mère protested.

Uncle Laurent shook his head. "You all look like church mice. It's mortifying. I insist, and I will pay. Two gowns for the young lady and one for you, Yvonne." He shifted his gaze to Eriq. "And a new coat and breeches for the young man."

Catherine's face grew warm.

Uncle Laurent added, "You would be the laughingstocks of Versailles if you made an appearance in such drab clothing."

Grand-Mère appeared as if she were biting her tongue, but then she simply said, "*Merci.*"

Uncle Laurent turned toward the table and began pouring glasses of wine. "Nearly all the Huguenots have fled Paris. I find it odd that they are leaving and yet you have come to visit." He handed a glass to Grand-Mère.

She gave him a wry smile.

"I know, I know," he added, handing a glass to Catherine. "Suzanne asked you to come. I have seen her quite a few times at Versailles lately. The fact that the king is allowing her there now shows how taken he is with Madame de Maintenon. Louis *loathes* Suzanne."

"*Oui,*" Grand-Mère said. "We are looking forward to seeing her. Although not until next week."

"*Très bien,*" Uncle Laurent said as he handed a glass to Eriq and then took the last one for himself. "You will have decent attire by then."

He led the way toward the dining room, and as he passed through the open double doors, he said, "Clothing is one thing, but your future is quite another, and it's a problem much more difficult to solve." He stopped at a large table set with fine china and crystal. "We will discuss it over dinner."

CHAPTER NINETEEN
Catherine

*I*n the end, the only solution Uncle Laurent had was for all of them to renounce their faith and convert immediately. He even insisted there might be some money in it for them, that some Huguenots in the area had been offered all sorts of financial incentives to convert. Catherine could not imagine such a thing. As far as she was concerned, converting for money was even worse than converting because of persecution.

"You can send for the rest of the family and live here. They can open a print shop. Parisians like to read too, you know." He chuckled. "Although we have much more to compete for our time than the Lyonnais."

Grand-Mère shook her head. "There has been no talk of anyone converting."

"Edouard did. He wrote to let me know."

"Well, yes," Grand-Mère said. "I certainly was not trying to hide that. But no one else is considering it."

Eriq shifted in his chair. Catherine gave him a questioning look, but he didn't meet her eyes. Did he know something he hadn't told her?

Something about Pierre? Or Jules? One of the main reasons Uncle

Edouard had become Catholic was to protect the print shop from being confiscated by the state. Now that he was dead, that protection was gone. Both Pierre and Jules claimed to be looking for ways to handle the problem, but what if their big solution was to convert? The thought broke her heart. She hadn't had the chance to speak with Eriq alone since she had overheard his words the other night. Once she did, however, she planned to ask about this as well.

"Edouard wrote to me, asking my advice about protecting the business." Uncle Laurent shrugged. "Whatever he did must have worked. The business is still in the Gillet family name, *oui*?"

"That's correct," Eriq said. "And in the Talbot name too."

Uncle Laurent shrugged again. "No matter how protected you feel in Lyon, make no mistake. The business will soon be taken from you. And your beautiful home as well."

The next morning was spent with obtaining new clothes. Janetta's shop paled in comparison. This boutique displayed at least a hundred gowns.

The owner suggested different fabrics, several that Grand-Mère vetoed after closer inspection. She finally agreed on a rose-colored silk and a purple-and-gold brocade for Catherine's two gowns and a navy blue one for her.

"You will be presentable," the shop owner said to Catherine when they were ready to leave. "In fact, with your beauty and your uncle's connections, you could be the talk of the town if not for your religion."

Catherine's face grew warm. It sounded as if she already was the talk of the town.

"Such a waste," the woman said to Catherine as she followed Grand-Mère to the door of the boutique. She called after them, "I will have the garments delivered by the next Wednesday."

The next morning Eriq was not at breakfast, and Uncle Laurent explained that the young man had gone out on his own.

Grand-Mère frowned. Catherine did too. On a Sunday morning?

"He is with a businessman he met during your travels," Uncle Laurent said. "He asked me to pass on his regrets. Unfortunately, it was the only time the man could see him."

Catherine was disappointed in Eriq, but a small part of her could not help but envy him and his freedom to roam the city as he pleased.

An hour later, Grand-Mère and Catherine rode with Uncle Laurent in his carriage to île de la Cité, the island in the middle of the Seine that was home to Notre-Dame. He dropped the two of them off at the stairs and they headed down toward the water.

Catherine took Grand-Mère's arm. A handful of boats were moored along the docks and others moved up and down the river, carrying people and cargo.

"Our boat should show up soon," Grand-Mère said.

"What if it doesn't stop here anymore?" Catherine asked.

Grand-Mère smiled. "It will."

Catherine was not so sure. It had been a long time since Grand-Mère had gone to the Temple de Charenton.

The boat did come, half filled with people. Several others boarded after Catherine and Grand-Mère. Cool air wafted around them as the boat veered away from the dock, and Catherine caught a fishy smell. The air grew colder as the boat picked up speed. Catherine tipped back her head, taking in the magnificence of the cathedral. Perhaps later she could see the inside too.

Soon the rowers began singing, "This is the day which the Lord hath made; we will rejoice and be glad in it." Catherine and Grand-Mère both sang along for the next stanza, then more joined in, their voices rising up above the river through the final line. "O give thanks unto the Lord; for he is good: for his mercy endureth forever."

The words and unity of the singers brought tears to Catherine's eyes. She did not know a single one of these people other than her grandmother, but they sang the same songs. They held to the same beliefs. They shared the same worries. The group continued to sing all the way down the river.

When they disembarked, several people greeted them, and once they learned Grand-Mère and Catherine had come all the way from

Lyon, they peppered them with endless questions about the level of persecution there and how the two had managed to travel all the way to Paris unharmed. Finally, Catherine took Grand-Mère's arm and they excused themselves, walking up the dock to the embankment. Ahead was the temple, three-stories high.

Inside were two sets of balconies, both filling up with people. They sat near the back and Catherine continued to gaze around the temple. The gowns of the women were fancier than what she was used to. Brighter colors—teal and even red, and much fuller skirts. Much fancier than the black gown Grand-Mère wore now and Catherine's brown one. Janetta had been right, that was for certain. Thank goodness Uncle Laurent had already intervened. They did not even fit in at the temple.

She leaned her head back and began reading the Apostles' Creed, printed on a banner hanging in the front of the church, until a hand fell on her back, interrupting her. She turned her head. It was Eriq. Smiling, he sat down beside her. "Thankfully, my meeting did not take long."

She raised her eyebrows.

"You remember the man from the first inn, Monsieur Olivier?"

"*Oui*," Catherine said.

"He had some business ideas for me."

"On a Sunday?"

Eriq shrugged. "I am here now, am I not?"

The service began, so they grew quiet. Once it was over, as the congregation left the temple, it was to find dragoons on horses circling around the building and weaving in and out of the trees. Catherine took Grand-Mère's arm. "Do not look them in the eye," Eriq whispered, stepping close to Catherine.

She did not. They moved swiftly forward, down the embankment, and then along the dock to the boat. The dragoons did not follow. The vessel filled quickly and was soon on its way. "I am surprised they have not yet burned this temple," Catherine whispered to Eriq.

"I'm sure they will soon enough."

After a delicious dinner of duck, fresh beans, bread, and *crème moulée*, Grand-Mère went upstairs for a nap and Catherine visited the garden behind the house. She strolled a bit, taking in the herbs and greens and irises that were just starting to bloom. Then she sat on a bench at the far end, next to a fountain, and watched a cat slink along the top of the wall.

Footsteps fell on the stones nearby. Catherine stood as Eriq came toward her.

"I am going for a walk. Would you like to come?" He went on to explain that he was heading over to the far side of the Seine.

And though she was tempted, she declined, not wanting Grand-Mère to wake and find her gone. "But before you leave," she added, "may I ask you about something?"

"Of course."

"When you and the Huguenot man spoke back in Auxerre, I overheard a little." Her face grew warm but she persisted, reminding him of their conversation and asking what he'd meant when he said Pierre might have "other motives."

Eriq took a long moment to respond, "I didn't mean to be disrespectful."

"You were not. I just feel I have the right to know…"

"Of course." He peered around the fountain and then sat beside her, shifting his gaze to the ground. He spoke so softly she had to concentrate to hear him. "Someone in our community, back in Lyon, has been functioning as eyes and ears for the crown, betraying our people. They trick them into thinking they will help them escape— providing food and shelter and a place to hide—only to end up turning them in to the dragoons instead."

"*What?*"

Eriq nodded. "I couldn't imagine who would do such a thing until one day when I needed to look something up on a past order. I couldn't find it and decided to check the documents stored in the old vault, but when I got there, I saw that it had been turned into a bedchamber, of sorts."

Catherine's face colored. She had already seen that for herself, but considering that she had been alone with Pierre at the time, she didn't admit as much now.

Eriq clasped his hands together as he continued. "I hesitate to say this, Catherine. It sounds ludicrous, I know. But after much thought I've come to believe that the vault is that hiding place I have heard about, the one used for betrayal rather than deliverance. Worse, I think that Pierre and Jules are the ones who are the betrayers."

Grand-Mère ended up resting the entire afternoon, giving Catherine time alone to think about what she had learned. She was dumbfounded by what Eriq had told her, but somehow she managed to get through the rest of day and evening without anyone noticing that her whole world had been turned upside down in the space of a single conversation.

The following day, Grand-Mère was more of herself again. The morning had been wet, and although the rain had stopped, clouds still filled the sky as the two of them took a walk. They strolled through the Latin Quarter toward the Seine, Grand-Mère pointing out this and that as they went. Trying to take on her grandmother's exuberant mood, Catherine linked arms with her and forced all other thoughts from her mind except this place with this person.

Grand-Mère squeezed her hand in return. "I am so happy to show all of this to you, *ma petite fille*. I did not realize until we arrived how much I wanted to see it again."

"Does it make you wish you could stay?"

Grand-Mère's eyes grew watery but she shook her head. "*Non*. I am just happy God made it possible for us to visit."

On the Pont Neuf they paused at the base of the statue of Henri IV, bareheaded on his horse, posed as if in motion.

"What a contradiction he was," Catherine said, gazing up at him.

"Such a good king, and yet his personal life..." She shook her head as her voice trailed off. He was rumored to have had more than fifty mistresses in his lifetime.

Grand-Mère sighed. "The relationships of kings can be very complicated."

Catherine nodded. Was not Madame Maintenon's relationship with Louis XIV proof of that?

"We have tried to shelter you as much as possible."

"Grand-Mère, I know how the world works."

A wry smile fell across Grand-Mère's face. "Goodness, I hope you do not entirely know how the world works. I hope you never will."

On the way back, they stopped by Notre-Dame so Catherine could take a quick peek inside. The cathedral was indeed beautiful, but she did not feel the same warmth there as she did in Saint-Jean-Baptiste in Lyon. Or the harmony she had felt at the Temple of Charenton.

When they arrived back at the house, they found Eriq and Uncle Laurent in the lounge, waiting for them.

"Madame Gillet," Eriq said to Grand-Mère, looking tall and confident as he rose to greet the two women, "I have your brother's permission to take your granddaughter on an adventure. If she is interested, that is."

He gave Catherine a sparkling smile, and she realized with a start that he was no longer a boy. Somehow, he had transformed into a man without her even noticing—until now.

"*Oui*," she said, looking to her grandmother for permission. "I am interested."

"It's all very safe, Yvonne," Uncle Laurent added. "Eriq has run the entire plan by me and I approve."

Grand-Mère seemed ambivalent, but she gave her assent. Thus, after taking a few minutes to freshen up, Catherine found herself back on the street, this handsome man at her side.

"Mademoiselle?" he said, crooking his elbow toward her.

Suddenly shy, she took his arm. "*Merci.*" As they started walking, it struck her that *he* was the one she wanted to be with in this moment.

Whether his brother was a traitor or not.

Chapter Twenty
Catherine

As Catherine and Eriq made their way along the busy Paris street, she grew even more self-conscious about her dowdy gown. "Where are we going?"

"We have one matter of business and one of pleasure," he replied happily. "Business first, of course."

As he didn't seem to care that she was the most somberly dressed young lady in Paris, she would do her best not to think of it either.

They walked along in front of the Louvre, and at the end of the palace grounds, they entered a formal park which Eriq said was the Jardin des Tuileries.

"I met Monsieur Olivier here yesterday. We only had a moment—he was on his way to mass—but he said to come back today and bring you with me."

"Why me?"

Eriq shrugged. "You impressed him when he saw you at the inn. He was interested in your family. He remembers your grandfather."

Halfway through the garden, past the first pond, Eriq pointed to a bench. They sat and chatted as they watched people, mostly couples, stroll by. The women were all dressed much more fashionably than

Catherine, but none of them seemed to notice her, although a few stole looks at Eriq. He had definitely blossomed in the last few weeks away from Lyon. Away from his brother.

Finally Monsieur Olivier approached, apologized for being late, and, after kissing Catherine's hand, thanked them both for meeting with him. "This is strictly informal, understand. But after Eriq told me about the family property in Lyon, and once I found out you are Sir Delecore's great-niece...well, I had to see you again. Of course, I remembered how beautiful you were from when we met on the road."

Catherine, taken aback by the flattery, gave Eriq a questioning look.

"Under normal circumstances, I would not be able to help you, but because you are the niece of a respected solicitor, and a nobleman at that, perhaps I can," Monsieur Olivier said.

Catherine shook her head. "I have no need of your help."

Eriq took her hand. "I told him about the print shop and warehouse."

"I was only in Lyon for a day, but I took the liberty to go by the property and your family home also." Monsieur sat on the other side of Catherine.

Her face reddened, and she pulled her hand away from Eriq. "I am not at liberty to discuss any of this." Her heart raced at the thought of Monsieur Olivier spying on her home. "And you should know I do not have any influence with my brother in regard to these matters."

Monsieur Olivier leaned closer. "Women always have influence. Especially beautiful sisters who need to be kept safe."

A knot began to form in Catherine's stomach. "You would have to speak to my brother."

"I plan to." He smiled. "I will be back in Lyon next month. Would you be willing to introduce me to him?"

"Perhaps..." Catherine stood. She wanted her family to go to London, and she knew their properties would need to be sold in order for that to be possible, but she was not sure she trusted the man. Maybe Eriq had not grown up as much as she thought. She turned toward him. "It's getting late. We should be going."

After a moment of silence, Monsieur Olivier said, "My dear, forgive me, I have intruded, obviously, and made you uncomfortable. Please reconsider, for I do believe I can help your family. But I cannot do so without an introduction from you or your grandmother. Or perhaps from Sir Delecore?"

Catherine shook her head. That was the last thing Grand-Mère would want, she was sure.

"I see." Monsieur Olivier turned toward Eriq. "Speak with your own brother and Mademoiselle's family too, though that will slow the process, which may prove to be a tragedy." He shrugged. "Feel free to contact me if the circumstances change." He thanked her again, kissed them goodbye, and then excused himself, saying he had another appointment.

Catherine remained silent until he was out of hearing distance. Then she said, "I cannot speak for my family."

"Of course not," Eriq said. "I am just exploring options. I wanted to include you, that's all."

Catherine took a deep breath and exhaled slowly.

"I simply thought if we came up with a buyer, then Jules and Pierre would be more likely to agree with us," Eriq said.

She appreciated that. Perhaps it was not as bad of an idea as she had initially thought. Besides, she had to admit that it was refreshing to be consulted on something —anything. Pierre hadn't even bothered to talk to her about moving to Switzerland, yet here his little brother had been considerate enough to bring her in on a business matter.

"It's fine," she said, and she meant it.

Eriq offered her his arm again and she took it. Dusk began to fall as they strolled out of the park and continued on to the bridge and across the river.

"What do you think it would be like to live here?" he asked as they went.

"In Paris? It's a beautiful city—more so than I ever imagined." If she did not think about the poor. "And it's wonderful not to have to worry about the dragoons," Catherine added. "Although if we stayed for long, they would figure out who we are. We would put Uncle Laurent in a perilous situation too."

"Not necessarily."

Catherine narrowed her eyes. Did he know something she did not?

Before she could ask more, he came to a stop and announced that they had reached their destination. "Dinner at the most exclusive new café in town," he told her, "compliments of your great-uncle. He knows the owners."

"What?" Uncle Laurent had already paid for the clothes. Now he was treating them to an expensive meal too?

Eriq opened the door and they stepped inside.

Students and businessmen lined the tables. A few women—ladies, to be sure—sat with the men. The waiter led Eriq and Catherine to the back. "For young lovers," he teased as he showed them to a small table by a window, pulling out the closest chair for Catherine as her face grew warm. She sat, tucking her skirt around her.

Eriq ordered wine. After some discussion with the waiter, he also ordered *hors d'oeuvre, rôti de boeuf, legumes, salade,* and *fromage.* Catherine worried about the cost, but Eriq did not seem concerned.

They talked easily as they ate, and she found herself admiring his sense of adventure. Clearly they had a lot in common, as Pierre had said, but she realized now that that was a good thing, even if her betrothed had meant it as a caution. The meal was more sumptuous than she could have imagined, but when they were finished, the waiter surprised them with the most delectable treat of all, a special dessert called *pots de crème au chocolat.*

"*Très bien!*" Catherine cried as he set it on the table in front of them. She'd heard of chocolate from Janetta, but she'd never dreamed of actually tasting it herself.

As the waiter took the lid off the pot, a rich, sweet smell enveloped Catherine. She took a bite of the creamy mixture, and it tasted even better than it smelled. The two ate every drop in silence, it was that good.

"*Merci,*" she said to Eriq when they were finished. "For all of this. It was simply *délicieux.*"

Clearly he was pleased. After instructing the waiter to put the dinner on Uncle Laurent's bill, he led Catherine from the café into the warm spring evening. As they slowly strolled back to the house, she linked her arm in his. Her only regret was that she had not had one of her new gowns to wear on such a special evening.

The next day it rained again and Eriq stayed home, spending time with Catherine in the lounge, playing chess. Jules had taught both of them as children. They were evenly matched and traded games back and forth for most of the morning.

Grand-Mère spent hours with Uncle Laurent in his office, finally coming out when it was time for luncheon, but she gave no indication as to what they had been discussing.

Wednesday dawned bright and sunny. After breakfast, Eriq said he was going out and asked Catherine to join him, but Grand-Mère shook her head in disapproval. She hadn't been happy about the expense of the dinner at the café, citing how many families back home they could have fed with that money.

Later that morning the boutique owner's assistant dropped off the new clothes. Eriq returned at dinnertime, and Versailles quickly became the topic of conversation. Uncle Laurent had sent a message to Suzanne, saying they, including himself, would visit the next day, Thursday. Grand-Mère seemed none too pleased that her brother planned to accompany them, though Catherine was not sure why.

"Suzanne didn't extend an invitation to spend the night," Uncle Laurent added, "which means it will be a long day, considering that it's a three-hour carriage ride each way."

"Better that than spend the night in another questionable inn," Grand-Mère replied. "We will have enough of that on the way home."

Unable to contain herself, Catherine asked, "Will we see Madame de Maintenon? Or the king?"

Uncle Laurent chuckled. "I wish I could say His Majesty will join us, but he will not, and I doubt that Madame de Maintenon will either. Do not get your hopes up, my dear."

Grand-Mère didn't seem the least bit upset by that, but Catherine felt disappointed. She certainly hadn't expected to actually meet the king, but she had hoped to at least glimpse him at a distance.

The next morning the maid entered the suite at first light to start the fire and bring in pitchers of warm water. Grand-Mère and Catherine both bathed and put on their corsets and petticoats. The maid then helped Grand-Mère with her hair, which did not take long. Then she helped Catherine, first circling her locks with an iron that she heated and then piling them atop her head, leaving a large strand in the back flowing over her shoulder.

After Catherine was dressed in the purple-and-gold brocade gown, Grand-Mère said, "Do not look in the mirror. I don't want you to grow vain."

"Grand-Mère." Catherine's hand went to her throat as she turned toward the glass. The purple fabric made her skin appear creamy, and the gold brought out the auburn highlights of her hair. She turned away, knowing she was presentable at most but certainly not beautiful. Grand-Mère was biased.

Uncle Laurent met them at the bottom of the stairs and seemed deeply pleased at the sight of her. "It is a shame, really—"

"*Chut,*" Grand-Mère said.

Eriq's footsteps thundered down the stairs. Catherine turned toward him. His gray eyes, highlighted by a sky-colored jacket, lit up when he saw her.

"We should be on our way," Grand-Mère told them, nudging Catherine toward the door.

The sky was overcast as they started out in Uncle Laurent's carriage, its ride even smoother than the stagecoach, but by the time they reached the outskirts of Paris, the sun began streaming through the clouds. Grand-Mère stayed quiet most of the way, but Uncle Laurent and Eriq spent the time chatting. They talked about different businesses, including several silk markets Eriq had seen. Catherine stopped listening, concentrating on the farms that now lined the road, but when Uncle Laurent asked Eriq about their printing company, she focused on their conversation again.

"What role do you play?"

"Pawn," Eriq said, and then he grinned.

"You seem to have a head for business. Why do they not give you more responsibility?"

Eriq shrugged his shoulders.

Catherine leaned forward and said, "Because my brother is witless."

Grand-Mère put her hand on Catherine's back and said, "He is not, not at all. He is brilliant. Eriq and Catherine have no idea what all Jules has done for both of our families."

Catherine stiffened. She had not meant to offend her grandmother.

"Perhaps he is behind the times, though? Maybe too provincial? Too focused on religion?"

Grand-Mère shook her head again. Looking from Catherine to Eriq, she said quietly but firmly, "We will not speak of private matters in a careless way."

Uncle Laurent raised his eyebrows, Eriq shrugged, and then they all continued on in silence. Catherine was not used to her grandmother being testy. She turned back toward the window and watched the fields and woods pass by.

It was late morning by the time they arrived at Versailles. Catherine pulled back the blinds and strained her neck to see the enormous palace and endless grounds. Both seemed to go on forever. Uncle Laurent's driver dropped them off at the back. The coachman helped them down and then a butler escorted them into a large foyer.

"I will join you shortly," Uncle Laurent told them. "Believe me, I will not miss anything important. Suzanne will prattle on for at least an hour about her own life before she is ready to speak of anything or anyone else."

The butler led the way to a staircase and then up to the second floor. Most of the doors along the corridor were closed, but one was open as they passed by. The room was beautiful with plush furniture, gold wallpaper, and heavy red drapes. At last they came to the end of the hall, and the butler rapped on a door and then opened it.

A woman in a white wig and black dress came toward them, her arms outstretched. In her late fifties, she was striking if not exactly beautiful.

Grand-Mère stepped forward.

"Yvonne!"

"Suzanne!"

The women exchanged kisses and then held each other at arm's length.

"You have not changed a bit," Grand-Mère said.

"Oh, do not be ridiculous. Of course I have. And you have too."

"Well, I have a head start on you," Grand-Mère said.

"*Oui*," Suzanne said. "And you are a great-grandmother now."

Catherine was pleased to know the woman had read all of her letter.

"How is Amelie?"

"Better. So is the baby. And this is Catherine."

"Finally," Suzanne said, giving her a kiss. "I am absolutely delighted to meet you at last."

After introducing Eriq as well, Grand-Mère thanked Suzanne for allowing the visit.

"It's providential that you came when you did. I will be leaving Versailles soon. It has been good to be back though." Lowering her voice, she added, "No thanks to Louis, I might add."

Catherine realized she was speaking about the conflict that had occurred between her and the king many years ago, the one that ended with him sending her away.

Suzanne lowered her voice even further. "He may have intially reinstated me to please his mother, but the king was not happy with me until Madame de Maintenon became his new *favourite*. Now he tolerates me at least."

Catherine wondered if Jules had been right when he said Suzanne would be no help to them because she held no sway with the king. Perhaps they had come all this way for nothing.

Suzanne led them to a plush sitting area and then addressed Catherine once they were settled. "Did your grandmother tell you why the king despises me so?"

Catherine's face grew warm. "She said only that you opposed him in a matter of propriety and he resented you for it."

Suzanne laughed. "Yvonne, you are too discreet. You were welcome to share the details."

Grand-Mère folded her hands in her lap without responding, obviously uncomfortable, especially once Suzanne turned back to Catherine and began her tale.

"There was a secret door the king had installed to the sleeping room where the young ladies stayed," she said. "The king would…well, to put it delicately, make frequent visits. Being a woman of morals, I couldn't tolerate the way he was taking advantage of the innocent girls."

Catherine sat straight and kept completely still as her face began to grow warm.

"Perhaps I was presumptuous to do so, but because of my position with the Queen Mother I dared to have the door removed one day and filled it in with a wall to protect the young women. The king discovered what I had done late one night." She smiled a little. "Of course, he was furious. That is why he banished me and my husband."

"Oh, my," Catherine managed to say. She could not help but wonder what had happened to the young ladies. Perhaps the king had the door put back in. Or perhaps he was shamed into behaving. But she doubted it.

"Given all of that…" Suzanne turned back to Grand-Mère. "I am guessing you're here because you want my assistance. I will do what I can."

"*Merci*," Grand-Mère murmured and then said, in a clear voice, "Is Madame de Maintenon sympathetic at all?"

"To the plight of the Huguenots?"

Grand-Mère nodded.

"She is conflicted but agrees with the king that a certain stubbornness is involved. Would converting be that much of a problem?"

Grand-Mère smiled but did not answer.

"Madame is in a precarious situation," Suzanne added. "She fears if she asks for protection of the Huguenots that it may lead her enemies to claim that she is still a secret Protestant." Suzanne waved her hand as if that would never happen. Then she smiled. "You will be happy to hear she is the reason the king has been more virtuous, both in his actions and his faith. Also the dress in court has become more modest under Madame de Maintenon's influence, and others are copying her *fontage*, or top-knot, as she likes to call it." Suzanne touched her own headdress. "And her darker gowns. Of course, the younger women still dress in a provocative manner, although they are wearing the top-knots too."

Suzanne turned her attention toward Catherine. "In fact, I have a headpiece that would look fabulous with your gown. It has gold roses wired onto purple lace. I will be right back."

Catherine shot Grand-Mère a questioning look but only received a shrug in return. Eriq gave her a smile, though. Suzanne returned a few minutes later, carrying a top-knot made of lace, wire, gold ribbon, and roses. It was at least six inches high.

"Put it on," Suzanne said, handing it to Catherine. "Because I am in mourning, I cannot wear it for another year. It will be out of style by then."

Catherine did as she said, securing it on top of the half bun that the maid had fixed that morning and arranging the lace in the back.

"Lovely," Susanne said. "Please take it."

"*Merci.*" Catherine had never worn anything like it before and felt as if her head might fall forward. She sat up as straight as she could.

Suzanne paused to straighten a vase of irises on the table and then retook her seat. "Yvonne, back to what we were speaking of...I spoke to Madame de Maintenon this morning about your predicament."

"Oh?"

"She was sympathetic. Perhaps she will be available later..."

"She is here now?"

"Of course. She's down the hall, but just for a short time. The politics...well, they tire her. She has a home nearby."

"I see."

"An artist—Jean-Charles Nocret, the son of Jean Nocret. He is working on two portraits of her." Suzanne's eyes twinkled conspiratorially. "In fact, she has promised me the smaller of the paintings. She said if my mother were still alive, she would give it to her, so she wants me to have it."

"How marvelous," Grand-Mère said.

A smile spread across Suzanne's face. "It may be worth something someday if the king actually marries her. Of course, then he might not be in favor of me having one of the portraits..."

Grand-Mère nodded.

Eriq shifted in his chair.

"Oh, goodness," Suzanne said. "I have gone on and on. We were discussing your safety." She leaned forward. "It is rumored that the Edict of Nantes will be completely reversed."

Grand-Mère grew pale. "I was afraid of that. When?"

"At least by next year. Maybe even by this autumn." She clasped her hands together. "I am very worried about you—" She glanced from Grand-Mère to Catherine to Eriq. "All of you, honestly."

Grand-Mère gave a slight nod.

Suzanne sighed. "But I know you are as devoted to your faith as I am to mine."

Grand-Mère nodded again, this time more noticeably.

"Well, then, what do you want me to do? Find a buyer for your property? Help you secure passage out of the country?"

Catherine took a deep breath. Suzanne *could* help them.

"I appreciate your kindness," Grand-Mère said. "But what I hope for is a broader letter of protection, similar to what you wrote before but to give me unhindered mobility and not just for this trip."

Catherine's mouth dropped open, but then she remembered her manners and closed it. She knew better than to voice her concerns out loud, but why was Grand-Mère not asking for more help than that? What about their plans to leave the country? What about London?

"It would need to include protection from the dragoons."

"Of course," Suzanne answered

"*Merci*," Grand-Mère said. "And could you include that any others in my care will not be accosted either?"

Suzanne gave her a puzzled look.

"I am thinking of my great-granddaughter. The *bébé*, specifically."

"Of course," Suzanne said, rising and stepping across the room toward a desk.

Perhaps Grand-Mère would ask for more assistance once the letter was written. As Suzanne sat at her desk and retrieved a piece of paper and a pen, Uncle Laurent entered the suite. After greeting him, Suzanne said she was writing a letter of protection—two actually, so that they could keep one with them and have the other stashed away in a safe place.

Suzanne held up her index finger and then turned toward Catherine and Eriq. "The young people would most likely prefer to look around. Wouldn't you rather do that than just sit here waiting while we draft this letter?"

Eriq nodded.

"Go out into the gardens," she said. "Come back in a half hour. We will have luncheon then."

Catherine gave Grand-Mère a questioning look and was answered with a nod.

As they left the suite, her mind returned to the lecherous tale of the king. She shook her head, but then her top-knot started to sway and she put her hand up to stop it.

"I don't know who would think of touching you with that thing on," Eriq said, as if reading her mind.

She laughed at his words, patted the top-knot, and cooed, "My protector." But then she took it off, afraid it might plummet from her head.

Eriq turned serious. "You know I would not let anyone hurt you."

She did know but was not sure what to say in return, so she remained silent. They continued halfway down the hall until they heard voices, and then Eriq stopped just before they reached an open doorway. A woman sat in a chair, her back to them, with her elbow on the arm and her head resting on her hand. She was speaking to at least two others they could not see, discussing something about Suzanne's nephew and his interest in acquiring properties.

Eriq motioned to Catherine to keep going. She did, slowly, but then paused when she spotted across the room a partially finished painting of a woman reclining in a chair, her gray hair piled atop her head and a diamond necklace around her neck. With a start, Catherine realized that the woman in the painting and the woman in the chair talking about properties were one and the same. Given what Suzanne had just said about the portraits being made, she realized this must be Madame de Maintenon.

That was exciting enough. But then an older man suddenly came into view, elaborately attired in a white wig, silver coat, and high-heeled shoes. He was looking at the woman, but then he raised his head, noticed Catherine standing there, and smiled, wrinkles spreading around his mouth and eyes.

King Louis XIV. *Le Roi Soleil.*

Paralyzed, Catherine could only stare in return until Eriq grabbed her hand and pulled her away, out of sight.

CHAPTER TWENTY-ONE
Renee

The next morning was the reunion's closing event, the big Talbot family church service, which was held in one of the ballrooms of the hotel. With such a large group of people, there was always plenty of ministerial talent to choose from for this event, and the whole thing ended up being lovely, with music provided by a Talbot quartet and a great sermon from a distant Talbot cousin. Rejected from yesterday's ceremony, somehow Aunt Cissy had wormed her way onto the slate today, but even she was not so bad—thanks mostly to the huge room and a faulty microphone that went strangely quiet almost the moment she started to sing.

As the service drew to a close, my thoughts kept going back to one of the Bible verses the pastor had quoted, from Proverbs: *The wicked flee when no one pursues, but the righteous are bold as a lion.*

I wanted to be bold as a lion. But most of the time I was about as bold as a Malayan tapir, whose best defense when pursued was to dive underwater and wait for its predator to go away.

So many times in my life, I had hidden rather than stood up for myself. I had failed at being brave as a child when I ran screaming from the sight of a dead body and then later when I had not been able to convince a single adult of that fact. I had failed at being brave as a teen-ager, when I learned what a good hiding place a science lab could be. Even now, as an adult, I was still afraid, still hiding, still always watch-ing for danger around every corner.

I couldn't even be brave for love, I realized as I stood there sur-rounded by the chattering crowd. Just as Danielle had said the other day, none of my relationships ever worked out. I always picked the same type of guy: cerebral, polite, nonthreatening men who were easy to get to know and easy to keep at a distance. Anytime things became too serious or my feelings began to grow, I'd find a way to cut the guy off. I stayed aloof. Insulated. Free from the entanglements of love. Which kept me protected, yes, but also kept me isolated and lonely.

Until a few days ago, that is, when Blake Keller came along. The polar opposite of my usual type, he was big and muscular and physical, not to mention headstrong and stubborn and quick. He was also a lot smarter than I'd first given him credit for, and I was attracted to him despite myself. Yet that meant stepping outside my comfort zone and actually risk getting to know the kind of man who would never toler-ate being kept at a distance.

Yesterday afternoon in my grandfather's study, we didn't lock in a date or share a kiss. But we did make a plan for the biggest thing I felt was standing in our way, a plan that would unfold tonight, out in the Dark Woods at the cabin.

After the service, everyone went through a half hour of goodbyes and why-don't-you-come-for-a-visits and it-was-so-great-to-see-you-agains. Then the crowd began to thin until finally our time with the ballroom was up and we had to go.

Lunch for the immediate family was back at Nana's, once again catered. But with cold cuts, sandwich fixings, and various salads, it was a simpler affair than Friday night's fancy dinner. Some had to eat and run so they could catch their flights home, but some stayed for hours, aunts and uncles and closer cousins I hadn't really had a chance to visit

with yet because I'd been so busy with the pamphlet. The whole afternoon, in fact, was all about family. But when the crowd had thinned
down a bit, we got out a board game and played as if we were children
again, having a blast.

Danielle and Maddee each slipped out for a while, but when they
came back they indicated with a subtle nod and a thumbs-up that they
had managed to work things out so they could stick around till tomorrow. I was so relieved. This way, not only could we all find out together,
but my cousins and I could face the source of our biggest fear head on,
hand in hand, which was long overdue.

If only Nicole could be there with us too. First thing this morning,
Maddee had texted her and told her what was going on, adding that
we'd missed her at the reunion but we wouldn't hassle her about it if
she wanted to show up tonight just for our experiment with the luminol. Several hours later came a single-word reply: *Maybe*.

Whether she came or not, the plan was to meet up with Blake at the
tennis court at eleven p.m., long after all of the other relatives and the
staff had gone and Nana was in bed. After such an exhausting weekend, I felt sure she would sleep soundly from the moment her head hit
the pillow until the next morning.

I suppose I should have felt bad about not telling her our plan, but
I had never felt *less* guilty in my life. My cousins and I agreed that it was
to be a top secret venture—until we knew the results, that is. If blood
really was detected at the scene, then we didn't care if the whole world
found out. But if for some reason the test failed—not because the body
hadn't been real, but simply because too much time had elapsed or the
area had been contaminated in some way—then we would never tell
a soul what we'd done tonight. Even all these years later, not one of us
could handle a fresh round of accusation, ridicule, and doubt.

At ten thirty, half an hour before go-time, I found Danielle and
Maddee standing in the living room of the guesthouse with no lights
on, looking out through the sliding door across the expansive lawn.

Considering we were just three days shy of a full moon, we'd expected good visibility, but currently the sky was overcast, the moonlight obscured by a thick layer of clouds. Whether it was bright enough to see the Dark Woods or not, we all knew they were there.

"Here, I got us these," I said softly, walking to the table and setting out the contents of my plastic shopping bag: bug repellant wipes and five small LED flashlights.

Coming over, they each grabbed a flashlight, tested it, and shoved it in a pocket. I grabbed two, one for me and one to give to Blake. We opened the wipes and began rubbing the disposable cloths over every inch of exposed skin, trying to ignore the fifth flashlight still sitting there, the one I'd gotten for Nicole, just in case. We'd never heard another word from her, which wasn't a good sign.

Knowing we might need some time to acclimate ourselves for what lay ahead, my two cousins and I had decided to head out a little early. We planned to do nothing more than sit on the tennis court and take in our surroundings. After twenty minutes of darkness, I figured our eyes would be nicely dilated, our ears would have adjusted to the night's noises, and perhaps our nerves would have settled a bit as well.

The nerves part was what I needed most right now. Suddenly, just the thought of walking out that door nearly sent me into a panic attack.

"Y'all mind?" I asked, but before they could even reply I grabbed their hands, bowed my head, and said a quick prayer for strength, guidance, and protection.

"Amen," we all whispered in unison, then we dropped hands and just stood there for moment, looking at each other.

"Guess it's now or never," Maddee said.

"Yep," Danielle replied with false bravado. "Let's do this thang."

Then she led the way to the door. I grabbed the wipes, and before Maddee turned to follow, she impulsively scooped up the fifth flashlight.

"You never know," she said to me sheepishly as she tucked it into her pocket. "She still has twenty minutes."

Then we headed out.

At least the moonlight seemed a little brighter once we were outside, which was a good thing because we didn't want to use the flashlights unless we absolutely had to, lest someone notice and call the police or come to investigate for themselves.

When we reached the tennis court, we pushed open the fence gate, wincing at the rusty squawk, and then walked all the way to the middle and sat, cross-legged, on the ground. The night air was surprisingly cool and pleasant, but the clay surface radiated its stored warmth from the day. As we sat there, we didn't really talk much. We were each lost in our own thoughts, searching for whatever inner strength we could muster.

Coming early had been a good idea. We jumped at every new sound at first, but by the time we heard footsteps heading our way, we weren't flinching at all.

"Guess Blake is here." Danielle got to her feet and we followed suit.

"I can't believe she didn't show," Maddee said sadly as she brushed dirt from her jeans.

I reached out to place a comforting hand on her arm, but as I looked toward the sound, I realized the shadowy figure moving toward us was short and petite and in no way resembled Blake.

"Ready or not, here I am," Nicole said softly, stepping through the gate and coming to a stop.

Even in the dim moonlight, I could see she was not looking good. Dressed in olive green army pants and a brown T-shirt, she was at least suited for the task. But she seemed thin and pale, her arms like sticks and her blond hair bleached to a vivid yellow.

Still, she had come.

Stifling our squeals, we ran to her and pulled her into a group hug, and though she responded stiffly at first, by the time we let go, a grin was on her face.

"Where you been, cuz?" Danielle whispered, reaching out to stroke her hair. Nicole was the youngest and tiniest of our foursome, and we all tended to treat her like our little pet. We even used to tease that she was our mascot.

Nicole shook her head. "No hassles. Y'all promised."

"No hassles," Danielle replied. "We've just missed you, is all. We were worried about you."

"Well, I'm here now," she said.

I could tell she was uncomfortable, and I had to give her credit for coming, especially making the long drive all by herself. Staring off toward the main house, she smacked at her arm, which reminded me of the bug wipes. I handed them over. She took them gratefully, and by the time she was done using them, I could see Blake coming our way.

He was dressed in dark clothes, a camera bag slung over his shoulder, a tripod in one hand and a black case about the size of a toaster oven in the other. No doubt that held the chemicals and the spray bottles. Knowing the luminol's properties, I had a feeling it had to be mixed at the scene and used right away rather than being prepared ahead of time.

As he came through the gate, my heart skipped a beat. From the smile he flashed my way, I had a funny feeling he felt the same in return.

I introduced Nicole, and though Blake had learned enough about her from me to be surprised that she was here, he didn't let it show. Once the greetings were done, he set down his things and quietly laid out the plan.

Soon, the five of us were moving single file over the footbridge with me in the lead and Blake bringing up the rear. There was only one path in and out, so despite the dark it wasn't hard to find our way—except for the fact that we were still trying not to use flashlights at all, at least not until we were farther in. As we walked, I'm sure we each had our own worries. Mine vacillated between apprehension about seeing the cabin again and fear of running into a snake or some feral night creature. The farther we went, though, the more I began remembering, the more I found myself going back to the last time I made this hike when I was only a child.

Even at ages nine, nine, eight, and six, the four of us knew the trek well, so well we could have done it that year with our eyes closed. But we didn't. There were too many birds to watch, too many familiar smells to take in—the crispness of pine needles, the humid sweetness of summer moss.

Thinking back now, I could still remember the sounds of our hike, the crunch of boots on dried leaves, the sucking kiss of mud when we stepped in it. That sound, in fact, so entranced little Nicole that she'd been slowing us down the whole way, pausing at every muddy patch we encountered to squish one foot into the brown muck and then pull it out again with a loud and satisfying *schlurp*.

"Hurry!" Maddee had scolded from up ahead. She pointed to the sky through the trees. "We're losing daylight here."

Of course, it was only about noon at the time, if I remembered correctly, and the cabin was just half a mile away, but that was Maddee for you.

"It's all right," said Danielle in her usual calm, peacemaker voice. She and I were always mediating between the two sisters—when we weren't cracking up at the ridiculousness of their arguments.

"Well, I'm not waiting around anymore," Maddee snapped. Then she turned and started hiking again, expecting the rest of us to fall in line.

Danielle and I stood there on the path, suspended between Maddee's directive and Nicole's stubbornness, a place we often found ourselves. We didn't mind. We four were only together one weekend a year and we treasured every bit of it, even this.

"Fine," Nicole snapped, making one more *smush* in the mud then running to catch up. "We'd better not keep Her Highness waiting."

Chuckling, Danielle and I let Nicole pass and then fell in after her.

We'd been coming to these woods for a couple of years, ever since we were old enough to go off on our own without parents. The first time, Nicole had been so small she was barely able to keep up. She complained the whole way. But she had wanted to explore as badly as we did—and we never left each other out of anything. So she'd tagged along, and when the trek got really bad we took turns carrying her.

Our destination was always the same, the old cabin buried at the very center of the woods. I had a feeling it had once been a hunting cabin back before the area had grown more populated and hunting in those particular woods was prohibited. After that, it had slowly fallen into disrepair with vines growing up its sides, its old boards slowly rotting, its roof losing shingles till it looked like a dog with patches of mange.

But it was our favorite place in the world. In our imaginations, we were pioneers in the big woods, settlers at Jamestown, conductors on the Underground Railroad.

The day of the Incident, our hike started out like every other one had. As we came around the bend and the cabin loomed into view, we all paused together to take in the familiar sight. Then we made our way to the window beside the front door—if you could call a square hole with shutters but no glass a window. The shutters latched from the inside, but this one had always been easy enough to open with the aid of a small but sturdy twig. All we had to do was insert it at the center and slide it upward, forcing the hook out of the loop. Once that was done, if we'd had longer arms, we probably could have just reached through far enough to unlock the door. As it was, we'd had to come up with a different approach.

"You know the drill," Maddee said, stepping closer and placing her right leg forward, bent at the knee. Then Danielle did the same on the other side, and I stood behind Nicole and helped hoist her up until she was standing on their legs. Then she slid her arms inside the hole, and we lifted her, feeding her body inside, head first—but slowly enough that she didn't get hurt. As our resident gymnast and daredevil, she didn't mind all that much.

She did mind how hard it was to get the door unlocked. We could hear her on the other side, griping and pulling and trying to get it open.

"It's too dark in here," she complained, rattling the knob. "And there's a weird smell too. Like rust."

Finally, we heard a click and then the door swung open, letting fresh air into the dark space that had stayed closed up way too long.

"What do you know," Maddee said as she stepped inside. "Nicole wasn't exaggerating for once. It does smell in here."

"Let's get all the windows open. That'll help," I offered. We started with the window at the front, the one Nicole had climbed through. There were hooks on each side, and as soon as we latched open the shutters, a breeze fluttered in. Light came in as well. Danielle and I handled the window on the right and the sisters got the one on the left. By the time we had three windows latched open, we could actually see in there.

That's when we turned to go to the last window, the one on the back wall, above the old cot.

Only then did we see that we weren't alone in the cabin.

We didn't scream, not at first. Maddee gasped. Danielle clutched my arm so hard I was sure her nails would leave a mark. Otherwise, the four of us just stood there in shocked silence, each one willing the other to speak.

On the cot just a few feet in front of us lay a man, an old man with a withered face and gnarled hands. Dressed in a tan shirt and dark pants, he was on his back, his legs stretched out in front of him as if he'd just laid down for a quick nap. But from the middle of his body protruded the wooden handle of a long knife. The rest of it, the shiny sharp metal part, was buried almost all the way in his chest.

The second big thing I noticed after the knife were his eyes, which were open. Glassy and clouded, it seemed as if they had once been blue, but it was hard to tell. His mouth was twisted open as well, almost as if he'd died midscream.

And there was no question he was dead. Not just because of the knife and the eyes and the stillness, but because of the blood. Lots and lots of blood, way more than a body could spare. Even at nine, I knew enough to realize the knife must have pierced his heart or maybe sliced some artery, because it was everywhere. Pooled on his chest, splattered on the wall behind him, soaked into his clothes, puddled on the floor below.

"Do you think he's sleeping?" Nicole whispered, startling me from my observations.

I stepped closer, looking for signs of movement, for a chest rising and falling, but I already knew. This man was not asleep.

I felt the three of them behind me, watching, waiting for me to do something, anything. I was the oldest after all, even if only by a few months. But I didn't know what to do. In the distance, a robin sang. A chipmunk chattered from a tree. And the four of us just stood there, staring down at the grisly sight.

"Wake up, mister," Nicole said. Then she stepped forward, reached out, and patted him on the shoulder.

Somehow, I don't think she'd comprehended the knife before then, or the dead open eyes, or the blood. But when she looked down, she realized she was standing in a dark syrupy puddle, the tip of her boot coated in red as if she'd dipped it into a jar of finger paint, and then she began to scream.

That's all it took.

In an instant, we were all screaming, all hysterical, all certain that whoever killed him was going to kill us next.

Nicole ran to the door and then out, and we had no choice but to take off after her, even though we knew at the moment we were probably safer inside, where no killer was lurking, than outside, where surely he was lying in wait, ready to strike again.

We'd never run so fast. You would think by being the smallest that Nicole would be the slowest, but it was all we could do to keep up with her. The hike that had taken us maybe half an hour coming in couldn't have taken more than ten minutes going out.

At least we never saw anyone, never heard anyone behind us, never spotted any lurking killers anywhere. We burst out of the trees and headed for the footbridge, pounding across as our screams started up again, running toward the rest of our family, who were still eating and enjoying the sunshine as if nothing was different, as if our four small lives hadn't been changed forever.

Hearing the ruckus, our parents came running to meet us. I flew into my father's arms and just held on and sobbed, my body trembling violently as I tried to tell him, between gasps, what we'd seen. Around us, my cousins were explaining to their parents as well, and soon a whole group of concerned and angry Talbot men were preparing to go see exactly what this was about.

It took Granddad to talk them all down, saying it wouldn't be safe, that the killer could still be lurking nearby, that they simply had to wait for the police. Only when they finally agreed to wait, albeit grudgingly, did he head for the house to call 911.

It took forever for the police to get there, but when they finally arrived and had questioned us and were ready to venture into the woods, they allowed only the three fathers to go with them. Everyone else—including us girls—had to stay behind.

They were gone a long time, maybe half an hour, and I knew the moment they came back and I saw the weird expression on my dad's face that something was wrong. Much of what followed was a blur to me now, but a few parts I could still remember. The shock of being told there was no dead body in there, no blood. Just a pile of blankets and a stick and a puddle of rainwater.

I remembered becoming angry, really angry. I marched over to Nicole and demanded, "What do you call this then?" as I pointed down to her bloody boot.

Only the blood wasn't there anymore. It must have washed away as we ran down the muddy and puddle-ridden path.

I remembered Maddee and Danielle sobbing, Nicole curled up in her mother's lap sucking her thumb—a habit she'd given up long before. I was the only angry one, the vocal one who refused to believe what they were saying. Eventually, reluctantly, the men agreed to go back to the cabin one more time and bring us with them.

Once there, the sight in front of us was even more shocking than the old dead man with the knife in his chest: the *lack* of anything remotely resembling the grisly scene we'd encountered when we were here before. No body, no blood, no knife. Just a scene that had been staged to make it look as if we were idiots, children so caught up in our imaginations that we didn't know the difference between a pile of fabric and a recently slaughtered corpse.

It wasn't long before we were the laughing stock of the reunion—at least in snickers and whispers and appraising looks. A few of the boys dubbed us the Liar Choir, a name that stuck for years.

My mother gave us the benefit of the doubt, but only to the extent that she thought perhaps a practical joke had been played, that someone had created a fake grisly scene and then removed it again once we were gone. But even that infuriated me.

There had been nothing fake about any of it. I knew it then, when I was nine.

I still knew it now, whether tonight's test proved it or not.

"I think we're getting close," Maddee said, startling me from my thoughts.

Suddenly, I wasn't a child anymore. I was an adult. My three cousins were adults. And for the first time since that horrible day, we were almost back to the scene of the crime, at the cabin in the woods.

I felt my heart surge with righteous indignation, pushing away the fear. It was high time we did this. I was ready.

As soon as we came around the final bend, there it stood. The cabin. During the walk, the clouds had drifted away, letting the moonlight through. Now it shone down on the place, which was smaller than I remembered and so ramshackle by this point that I wasn't sure if it was even safe to go inside.

But Blake didn't seem to share my concern. I felt a warm hand on my back, and I turned to see him next to me now.

"You okay?" he asked softly.

I nodded.

"Good. Still want to do this?"

I nodded again.

"Good." He let his hand drop, and then he stepped forward to address the group.

"I'll go in alone first and check for structural integrity. If it looks okay, I'll come get Renee so she can help me set things up. You three should probably wait outside until we're ready to spray the luminol, but then we'll call you in so you can watch as we do it. Sound good?"

My three cousins nodded, their expressions somber.

He and I began moving toward the cabin. When he reached the door, he pushed at it, but it didn't budge.

"You know the drill," Maddee said, teasing Nicole.

"Yeah, right. I'm not y'all's trained monkey anymore."

We all smiled.

I was wondering how we might get the door unlocked without having to repeat the old method when Blake surprised us by giving it one swift kick, knocking it open.

"If we'd known it was that easy," Danielle said, "we could've done it like that all along."

"Be right back," he said before carefully making his way into the blackness.

While he checked things out to make sure the place wasn't going to collapse on our heads, I took in the full sight of the cabin and tried to render it down to size. I had thought of this place as my enemy, of sorts, for nineteen years, but I realized now it was about to become my friend. If it really had held on to its secrets all this time as we hoped, it might even be one of my best friends.

"Okay," he announced, suddenly appearing in the doorway, framed by an odd reddish glow. "No flashlights."

Sucking in a deep breath, I took one last glance back at my cousins and then stepped into the old cabin. My eyes went first to the opposite wall, to the spot that still haunted my dreams, but it was empty. Only the cot remained, with not even a mattress on it anymore, much less the blanket. Or the stick.

"We can mix this over here," Blake said easily, knowing the perfect antidote for my current terror would be to engage in a little science. Directing my attention away from the far wall, I realized the red glow was coming from a nearby lamp, providing just enough light to see by while still maintaining our night vision for when we sprayed the luminol. Clever.

Blake led me to the rickety wooden table and told me what to do, and then he turned his attention to setting up the camera and tripod. As instructed, I went to work combining the luminol with some potassium hydroxide and water, and then I poured that into an empty bottle and added in an equal amount of hydrogen peroxide. Then I screwed the sprayer onto the top and told him I was done.

So far, so good.

When he finished with his task, he gave me an affirming smile before moving to the doorway and inviting my cousins inside.

They entered one at a time and huddled together off to the left, to a spot Blake indicated.

"You sure there are no snakes in here?" Maddee asked, stepping gingerly.

"I took a look when I first came in and didn't see any," he replied, which wasn't exactly a no but better than nothing.

"All right, here's what's going to happen," he told us. "We're going to turn off the red light so it's completely dark, then Renee is going to start spraying the luminol on the floor and the wall. If we're lucky, some blood will still be here, it'll react, and we'll see a blue glow. Okay?"

We nodded.

I held my breath as Blake stepped over to man the camera, which was on the tripod, pointed down at the floor.

Then he gave me a nod and I turned off the red lamp.

Plunged into darkness, my heart began pounding so hard I could barely breathe. Trying to hold my hands steady, I pointed myself in the direction of the blood, steeled my nerves, and squeezed the trigger. With a steady *swish-swish*, I sprayed the luminol.

Almost immediately, like the Milky Way bursting to life on a planetarium sky, little blue dots began to flash and glow on the floor in front of me. More spray, more glowing, the incessant snapping of the camera. Soon the wall and the floor were lit up like a Christmas tree, blue sparkling everywhere, especially where the puddles of blood had once collected.

"Look!" Danielle cried, and though I couldn't see her in the dark, I realized what she was talking about, an odd glowing splotch a short ways off. Spraying and moving, I managed to illuminate five similar splotches total, leading toward the door.

"No way," Nicole whispered, sending shivers down my spine.

It was the print from the toe of her bloody boot, from when she was only six years old.

The luminol had worked. The blue glow all around us was the proof.

And for the first time in nineteen years, I knew how it felt to be truly vindicated.

As we set off back down the trail toward home, equipment in hand, we decided we weren't going to wait one more minute to get this on the record. We were going immediately to the police station, even if it was the middle of the night.

Though I could tell Blake would have rather waited till tomorrow, he agreed to come along, and soon all five of us were piled in his SUV and heading down the empty roads toward the station in town.

We were there for maybe two hours, each of us taking turns in a small room with a uniformed officer and a recording device, telling our version of the story, then and now. The officer was very nice, very polite, though not all that captivated by our tale until he saw the photos of the luminol and spoke with Blake about our procedure.

He said a detective would be in touch with us tomorrow and take it from there. In the meantime, he would write up our statements and assemble all the information so the case could proceed. That was their next step. Ours was to tell Nana all about our experiment first thing in the morning before she heard about it some other way.

Blake drove us home, and once we got back to the house, my cousins practically leaped out of the car the moment it came to a stop, obviously so that he and I could be alone. I was embarrassed by their actions, but he just laughed, saying we probably did need a few minutes to ourselves after all that had happened.

He turned off the car and we both settled back in our seats, a deep calm overtaking me as I gazed through the windshield at the night sky. We didn't speak at first, but it was a good silence, especially when he reached out and took my hand.

"There's no way on earth I can ever thank you for what you did tonight," I said finally, my eyes still on the stars. "Not just for me but for my cousins too."

"I was happy to do it."

More silence, and then he added, "Though you know my efforts weren't entirely altruistic, right?"

I smiled. "Yeah, I know. You were hoping to make copper nitrate."

"Oh?" he said with a chuckle.

I turned to him as I explained. "Simple chemical displacement. Do you know what happens if you mix copper with silver nitrate?"

"Refresh my memory."

"The copper knocks the silver out of the way so it can bond with the nitrate and become copper nitrate."

I let him think about that for a moment, and he didn't disappoint.

"So I'm copper," he said slowly, "you're nitrate, and that cabin and all the baggage that came with it is silver. Am I on the right track?"

"You got it."

"Well?" he asked with a sly grin. "Are we a compound yet?"

My pulse surging, I met his gaze.

"I do believe displacement has occurred," I replied, giving his hand a squeeze. "Silver took a hike the second that first blue dot began to glow."

By the time I went inside, my roommates were in bed and sound asleep—all three of them, I realized, my heart filled with joy at the sight of Nicole there too.

I knew that I would probably be awake for hours—but I didn't care. My first date with Blake Keller was scheduled for tomorrow evening at six.

Ignoring the Pandora's box that our actions tonight had opened, I settled in under the covers and closed my eyes. All the questions that lay ahead—Who was the dead man back then? Who killed him? Why? Where did his body go?—were important, but they were for another day. For now, I would revel in the fact that after almost two decades, we finally had the proof we'd always wanted.

Chapter Twenty-Two
Catherine

*T*hat was him! That was the king!" Catherine exclaimed as they pushed through the door into the courtyard. She had been surprised by the man's smile. She had not expected that at all.

"And Madame de Maintenon too!" Eriq said, grinning.

They moved through the courtyard of the palace and onto the grounds, giddy from the sighting.

"Too bad we don't have more time," Eriq said, gesturing around them. "We will not be able to see it all in half an hour."

"Then let us see as much as we can," Catherine responded, lifting the skirt of her gown and hurrying forward. They covered as much of the grounds as they could, scurrying past fountains, statues, and the Orangerie, where perfectly manicured lawns, bushes, and trees lined the pathway.

Catherine couldn't help but think of the crowded slum on the edge of town, of the destitute throughout Paris and the entire country, but then she pushed the thoughts away.

By the time they reached the canal, her mind was only on the beautiful view—a ship with three masts, gondolas, and rowboats all moored close by.

Eriq linked his arm through hers. "It's amazing, is it not? They have turned a vast, dry area into a garden. Like Eden."

"*Oui*. It is beautiful."

He laughed. "*Non*. It is magnificent!"

Catherine didn't say anymore. She did not know what to say. But as they walked back to the palace, she felt a little dizzy. It was beautiful, but all so much. So vast.

A wave of homesickness passed over her. Here she was, in a place she had long dreamed of visiting, and she was left feeling uneasy even with Eriq at her side.

"Lyon has nothing for us," he said. "Not compared to Paris. Not compared to this." He stopped and took her hand. "Your uncle hinted at the possibility of my working for him."

Catherine took in a sharp breath. "But what about our families?"

"We cannot keep waiting for Pierre and Jules to make a decision, can we? Besides, your grandmother could come here too."

"She would never agree to it. Neither would Amelie," Catherine answered. Amelie would not want Valentina raised in Paris.

Eriq squeezed her arm. "But you could still decide to come. You like Paris."

Catherine wrinkled her nose. "We would not be safe here. Besides, I am still hoping to go to London."

"You heard your grandmother talking to Suzanne. She never said a word about London. It sounds as if she plans on either staying in Lyon or following Jules to the Plateau. If those are your options, would you not rather live in Paris?"

There were things she liked here, that was true. "But we would be identified as Huguenots. You are the one who said the Temple at Charenton will soon be burned."

Eriq shrugged. "Your uncle had some ideas about all of that. You should speak with him."

The sun was nearly overhead. "Let's go back," Catherine said. "It would not do for us to be late."

When they reached Suzanne's suite, the duchesse stood and beckoned Catherine over. "Would you copy this for me, dear? Your hand is so much steadier."

Catherine took Suzanne's place at the desk and copied the document twice. Then she stood again and gave the seat back to Suzanne. Taking quill in hand, she signed both copies then dripped wax at the bottom and pressed her ring into it.

"*Merci*," Catherine said, admiring the seal. "That is lovely."

Suzanne stood and walked toward Grand-Mère with the letters, saying, "In return, I may be asking a favor of you soon—for you to keep safe a valuable piece of artwork for me." She handed Grand-Mère the pages. "If you end up staying in France, let me know where you relocate." Then she motioned to the door at the far end of the room. "We will move into the dining area now."

As they all followed, she said, "We are going to have a special guest for dinner, my nephew Anton." She flashed Catherine a mischievous smile.

With a start, Catherine realized the duchesse might be playing matchmaker. She could not help but remember that in a letter Suzanne had said she wanted to see what Catherine "had to offer." Was she hoping now to make a love match with her nephew?

By the time they reached the table, a thin young man in a black wig stepped into the room. He kissed Suzanne's cheeks and then she introduced him as, "My fourth nephew, Anton, the youngest brother of the Duc de la Rochefoucauld. "

Suzanne introduced Grand-Mère as Baronness Gillet.

Anton kissed her hand.

"And this is the granddaughter of the baroness," Suzanne said. "Catherine." In a low voice, she addressed her nephew. "Is not she exquisite?"

"*Oui*." Anton took her hand and kissed it, murmuring, "*Enchanté.*" His eyes smiled up at her. "What a lovely top-knot you are wearing." She couldn't tell if he was serious or being facetious.

She simply murmured, "*Merci*."

"You know Sir Delecore," Suzanne said. "And this is Monsieur Talbot, who is in business with the Gillets."

Anton greeted the men warmly. During the meal, he addressed questions to Catherine directly, first asking how she liked Paris and then how she liked Versailles. She said she appreciated all she had seen of both, so far.

When the meal was finished, Anton led the way back down the corridor, although now the door to the room where Madame de Maintenon and the king had been was closed. They turned and headed along another corridor, one lined with curtained alcoves. "This is where lovers have their privacy," Anton said. Catherine could not tell if he was teasing or not.

"Look at this," he said, opening the door to a large room. The walls were also covered with gold wallpaper, and red velvet draped the windows. Over the fireplace was a huge painting. "It is the king with his *famille*—the queen, long before she died of course, and son and grandchildren," Anton said. "Jean Nocret painted it. He was the father of the artist Madame de Maintenon is currently sitting for."

The king looked larger than he had in real life. "Is he that much taller than his son?" Catherine asked.

"*Non.*" In a whisper Anton said, "He manipulates everything to make himself look better. Taller. Thinner. More muscular. Apollo, *oui*?" He stood up straight, squared his shoulders, and smiled. "That is your prerogative when you are the Sun King, I suppose."

In the painting, the king, draped in gold cloth, sat on a throne. His queen, mother, daughters, only son, and grandchildren all surrounded him.

"This way," Anton said. Catherine and Eriq followed him out of the room.

Once they were back in the corridor, Anton asked about Lyon, saying he had never been there. "I have heard it's quite lovely."

Eriq described the two rivers and the land in between.

"And what business are you in?" Anton asked.

Eriq told him about the print shop.

"Sounds fascinating. As the fourth son, I am trying to figure out exactly what my livelihood is going to be." Anton laughed. "The bad luck of the draw, *oui*?" He nudged Catherine with his elbow. "Ladies do not have to worry about such things."

"*Non*," Eriq said. "They just have to worry about the position of the man they want to marry."

"Believe me," Catherine said. "We ladies have plenty to worry about."

Anton laughed again. "If it were up to me, you would not have a single trouble in the world." Then he said, "I do a bit of traveling. If I make it to Lyon, I will be sure to look you up. I may be going sooner rather than later..."

His gaze made Catherine feel uneasy for a moment, but then she regained her manners and smiled back. It didn't matter what his intentions were, or Suzanne's. She wouldn't see Anton again after today. Even if he came to Lyon, she would most likely be gone by then—preferably to England and not the Plateau. Or the galleys.

"How long will you be staying in Paris?" Anton asked now.

"Just a short while," Catherine answered.

"Could I call on you?"

"I am betrothed."

"Betrothed is not married." Anton's eyes twinkled. "Besides, I am sure I would be the better option."

Flustered, Catherine said, "We should be going back."

They returned to Suzanne's apartment without any further discussion of the matter, though as they parted Anton gave it one last try.

"I definitely will visit you in Lyon," he told her. "But don't be surprised if I show up on your great-uncle's doorstep first."

Catherine's face grew warm. Anton laughed. "Your pink cheeks match nicely with your purple gown, Mademoiselle."

She blushed even more. She hated to make a scene, but she did not like Anton. Not at all.

That night, back in their suite at Uncle Laurent's, Catherine was finally free to ask Grand-Mère the questions she had held inside during the three-hour ride home and the light supper afterward.

"Were you able to procure any additional help from Suzanne? Passage to London, perhaps?"

"I obtained what I needed."

"But I thought we agreed London would be the best place to go, *oui?*"

"I entertained the thought but never felt at peace about it."

Catherine shook her head. "Grand-Mère, why would you make such a decision based on emotions? Our very lives are at stake!"

"Catherine...I'm sorry, but I cannot explain it."

Taking in a deep breath, Catherine turned toward the window. The shutters were closed. The only light was the candle on the washbasin stand. As Grand-Mère moved across the room, her shadow leaped along the wall. "Are you coming to bed?"

"*Non.*" Catherine took a second candle from the drawer of the stand and lit it. "I think I'll stay up for a while."

While Grand-Mère slept, Catherine wrote by the light of the two candles about everything that had happened—her growing friendship with Eriq, Grand-Mère's childhood home, the new gowns, the dinner at the café, the trip to Versailles, and Anton's attention. Last, she wrote about Grand-Mère rejecting the plan to go to London. She consoled herself with the thought that at least they had the letter of protection, which should get them to London if Jules could untie enough money to finance the trip and help establish them once there. Perhaps Amelie would be strong enough to travel soon. Otherwise, Catherine could not imagine what they would do.

When she finished, she dragged the feather absently across her face and then put it away and prayed for the first time since their visit to the Charenton temple. "God, please get us to London," she whispered, but then her thoughts fell to Pierre. Were he and her brother betraying their people in Lyon, as Eriq suspected, while she was here, enjoying all that Paris and Versailles had to offer? A pain grew in her stomach.

"God," she whispered again. "Show me what the truth is. Show me what to do."

The next morning, after dressing in her new rose-colored gown, Catherine made her way downstairs. Grand-Mère sat in the dining room with a cup of tea, staring into a mirror across the room. Eriq was nowhere in sight.

"*Bonjour,*" Catherine said.

Grand-Mère looked up, her eyes still far away for a moment before they focused on her granddaughter.

Catherine sat down beside her, poured herself a cup of tea, and took a pastry from the tray. "Where's Eriq?"

"Out. He's upset with me."

"Whatever for?"

"We are leaving tomorrow."

"Why so soon?"

"We have what we came for. And there is no reason to stay."

"How about to spend more time with your brother?"

"We are only putting him at risk."

"Do you not want to see more places from your childhood?"

Grand-Mère shook her head. "We will walk by the convent and Saint-Germain today. Otherwise, *non.*"

For some reason, Catherine wasn't nearly as disappointed as she might have been. She was surprised to realize that a part of her was ready to go home as well.

The two women headed to Saint-Germain later that morning. Catherine was eager to see the Catholic church Grand-Mère had attended when she was young. On the way, they paused outside her old convent school. "The nuns were kind. They disciplined us, true. But they were good to us."

"Do you ever wish you would have stayed in Paris and remained part of the court?"

Grand-Mère shuddered. "I cannot imagine anything so dreary compared to the life I have had in Lyon." Without even taking the time to go inside, Grand-Mère turned and started walking again.

Catherine stepped quickly, trying to keep up. "Do you really mean that?"

"I do, with all my heart. Don't be deceived by appearances, *chérie.* It is all a charade." She led the way across the street and then increased her pace. Concerned, Catherine took her grandmother's arm to stabilize her should she trip. By the time they reached Saint-Germain, she was nearly out of breath. They pushed through the front doors, but instead of entering the sanctuary, Grand-Mère turned to the right through a rustic door into an empty chapel.

"It's so simple," Catherine said. Even more so than their temple had been.

"*Oui.* I know we can worship God anywhere, but this is where I first felt Him."

"Not in the cathedral?"

Grand-Mère shook her head. "In here. Parts of the building have burned over the years, but this original chapel is more than a thousand years old."

Lyon had ruins that old, and older, but not any existing buildings.

"I would come here to pray," Grand-Mère said. "The simplicity always appealed to me." With a smile, she added, "Perhaps I was always Huguenot in my heart, *oui*?"

Catherine smiled in return. Certainly, this was the most Huguenot-like Catholic chapel she had ever seen.

"I always felt God's hand on me, especially in here," Grand-Mère continued. "I knew He had plans for me and I just had to be open to His guidance. Then I met your grandfather and learned about his faith, and it all made sense. I never had any doubts, even when my family nearly disowned me. I knew it was my destiny, what God was pointing me toward all along."

A shiver ran down Catherine's spine. "How did you know for sure?" she whispered.

"I had never known anything with such certainty in all my life." Grand-Mère turned the ruby ring on her finger. "This ring your grandfather gave me reminds me of my decision every day." She started toward the front of the chapel but stopped and turned back to Catherine. "And now I need certainty again. I am going to pray. You can join me if you like."

Sensing that Grand-Mère would prefer to be alone, Catherine said she would go into the cathedral. It was impressive with its paintings, ornate woodwork, and high, vaulted ceiling. When she was finished looking around, she stepped back into the chapel. Grand-Mère was still kneeling at the front, but she was not alone. A priest was kneeling by her side, a hand on her back. The two spoke for a few minutes, and then the priest helped the older woman to her feet. "You are always welcome here," he said. "Your family. Your kind."

"*Merci.*"

"I despair over what is happening," the priest said. "It is always on my heart. I do what I can—"

"*Merci,*" Grand-Mère said again. "God is in control. We will persevere."

The priest nodded and said, "Go in peace." Then he headed toward the door, smiling at Catherine as he passed.

Grand-Mère did not speak until they were back outside. "That filled my soul," she said.

After a long moment, she added, "The priests here are opposed to the way we are being treated while those at Notre-Dame are supportive of the king."

Catherine thought for a moment. "But Uncle Laurent attends Notre-Dame. Does that mean he supports our persecution?"

Grand-Mère sighed sadly. "That is my concern."

Catherine tried to absorb such a thought.

"I believe my brother may be in debt," Grand-Mère continued. "I noticed a stack of bills on his desk. And I overheard him raising his voice with someone, a creditor, I am afraid, in his office."

"But why would he spend the money on our clothes and on the dinner for Eriq and me if he owes others money?"

"To impress you, I imagine."

"But why?"

"He wants something," Grand-Mère answered. "He is cunning, Catherine. Always thinking ahead." She sighed again. "We cannot trust him."

Catherine's face warmed.

"Appearances can be deceiving," Grand-Mère said softly, almost to herself. Catherine thought of the painting of the king and his family, so filled with deception. She thought of Pierre and Jules, who pretended to be good Huguenots but were possibly betrayers instead.

Grand-Mère folded her hands together. "I have one other concern. Suzanne suggested that Eriq plans to woo you, which caught me off guard. But now I am worried about that too."

When Catherine did not answer, Grand-Mère added, "Eriq and Pierre may be brothers, but they are not interchangeable."

"You're right," Catherine replied. "Eriq has vision and ambition. And he has a sense of adventure, unlike Pierre. Also, he is not unduly influenced by my brother." She took a deep breath and exhaled. "I will admit that I'm frustrated with Pierre."

"And perhaps a little angry?"

"*Oui.*"

"We tend to become the angriest with those we love the most."

Tears flooded Catherine's eyes. "I am afraid I am feeling the anger much more than the love these days."

"Catherine..."

"Papa always said he would never pressure me to marry. That it would be my choice."

"I know, but not so long ago you and Pierre seemed to be ready to wed."

Catherine swallowed hard, afraid her feelings had shifted. "Well, he changed."

Grand-Mère stopped walking. "We've all changed this last year, at least those who have been paying attention to what is going on."

"I've been paying attention."

"And that is why you think the only answer is to get out—now."

"So many are doing that, Grand-Mère. Monsieur and Madame Talbot. The cobbler. Lots of others."

"Do you think they all went just like that?" She whisked her hand in front of her face. "Do you think they went without *months* of planning?"

Catherine stiffened. Her grandmother had never spoken so harshly with her.

And apparently she was not finished. "Just because your brother shields us from what is going on does not mean we should not be grateful for what he does."

"I am grateful."

Grand-Mère looked at Catherine as if she were still the little girl who lied about stealing a pastry set aside for her brother.

"And I do not plan to marry Eriq either." After a moment, she murmured, "At least not anytime soon."

Grand-Mère just shook her head and resumed walking.

Chapter Twenty-Three
Catherine

That afternoon, while Grand-Mère rested, Catherine wandered over to the park by herself, stopping at the pond. A boy pulled a boat on a string across the water. Two swans floated near the middle.

"Catherine."

She turned around. Eriq stood behind her. "I thought this is where you would come on your last day in Paris."

She smiled at him. "What have you been doing today?"

"I saw Monsieur Olivier and Anton."

"Why?"

"I met your uncle at the café at noon. Anton was there. We all ate together. He said to tell you hello. He was in the city for just a few hours, otherwise he would have stopped by."

"Oh." Catherine was not sorry she had missed him.

Eriq stepped closer to her. "I know we could find the right buyer for the business—for all of it, if only we were staying in Paris as long as we had planned."

Catherine turned toward the pond. "Would you go to Switzerland then, to your parents?"

"*Non*," Eriq said. "I do not know where I would go, but not there." He smiled at her. "London still sounds right to me."

They watched the toy boat on the water. Catherine told him about Saint-Germain and the kind priest. She felt comfortable with Eriq, nearly as much as she once had with Pierre. But all of that seemed so long ago now.

That evening, Eriq and Uncle Laurent holed up in the office. Catherine couldn't help but wonder what they were talking about.

The next morning, the fourth Saturday of Easter, Eriq was gone when Grand-Mère and Catherine got up. "I sent him on an errand," Uncle Laurent said.

"But you knew we were leaving," Grand-Mère replied, frowning.

"He will be back."

The carriage had just arrived when Eriq hurried into the house with some documents. He gave them to Uncle Laurent, who thanked him.

Grand-Mère, her cape on and a basket of food in her hands, asked Eriq if he was ready to go.

"I need to gather my belongings," he said, hurrying up the stairs.

Catherine was annoyed with Eriq but thanked Uncle Laurent for his hospitality and the new clothes.

"I pray you will return to Paris and I will be able to buy you more," he said.

Catherine curtsied, thinking of his debts. Grand-Mère kissed her brother and thanked him too, but there seemed to be a rift between them.

Eriq thundered down the stairs, his bag in his arms.

"Yvonne, please reconsider," Uncle Laurent said. "I can offer care for Amelie and the baby. For all of you. If the men refuse to come, let me at least care for the women in the family."

Grand-Mère shook her head. "We are trusting the Lord for what we need."

"The Lord and Suzanne."

"The Lord, Laurent. Whom He uses is up to Him."

"Then let Him use me."

She shook her head and started out the door, saying over her shoulder, "You ask too much of us."

"Do not be ridiculous, Yvonne. I cannot let you leave like this, unprotected."

"We have Suzanne's letter."

He shuddered. "Do you think that will save your lives?"

"Our lives belong to the Lord. We have asked for as much assistance as prudent, and we will now trust our Maker with our destinies."

Uncle Laurent shook his head. "You are a foolish woman."

Grand-Mère merely shrugged.

Uncle Laurent turned to Eriq. "It is now up to you to change the minds of the women in this family."

Eriq nodded, solemnly. "I shall do my best." Then he offered his own thanks.

Uncle Laurent clapped him on the back, saying, "It was my pleasure. I look forward to...seeing you again."

Catherine stepped around the men and hurried to catch up with her grandmother, wondering exactly what Eriq had been up to. By the time they reached the carriage, he was right behind them. Once they were all settled, the driver pulled onto the street and then away from the Jardin du Luxembourg and toward the Seine.

By the time they had reached the countryside, Catherine put her doubts about Eriq aside. He had been assisting Uncle Laurent with some business. It was the least he could do for their host. Eriq used good judgment—she knew that. She had no reason to doubt his integrity.

They stopped at the same inns on the way home, but Eriq did not speak with fellow travelers as he had before. He seemed reflective, but he was also fun and playful on occasions, teasing Catherine that she had better hide her new dresses and top-knot before they got home or Jules would not let her leave the house. The last night, Catherine and Eriq walked down to the Saône. The breeze blew through the cotton-woods and a flock of swifts flew up into the sky, above the river, and then swooped back and settled in the trees. Eriq put his hands on her shoulders and gazed down into her eyes. Her heart raced and she turned her face toward him.

"It has been a wonderful trip," he said, looking deeply into her eyes. "Absolutely beyond my expectations."

"*Oui*," she answered, remembering what Grand-Mère said about the brothers not being interchangeable. Of course they were not. They were as different as could be. And she could not help but appreciate Eriq's determination.

He leaned toward her, as if he might kiss her. She stepped away, her thoughts on kissing Pierre in the vault.

"Catherine," Eriq said, his head dropping.

"It's nothing," she said. "I'm tired." And confused. She started back to the inn and Eriq quickly followed, not seeming upset in the least.

Regardless of whether she married Pierre or not, she still owed him her respect. Maybe they would never marry, but she was not going to insult his dignity. Time would tell which brother was right for her. It was not up to her to rush the decision—nor to kiss any other man in the meantime.

On the road the next day, after Grand-Mère nodded off, Eriq apologized for being too forward. "I would be honored to have your affection, but I don't mean to rush you."

"*Merci*," Catherine answered. "I don't want to be rash." At least not more than she usually was. She had enjoyed spending time with him in Paris. He had been a good friend to her, and she couldn't discount that, not at all.

Grand-Mère stirred, and Catherine wondered if she had been asleep or merely resting. Eriq didn't say anything more on the subject and neither did Catherine.

The travelers returned home on the last Tuesday of May, the sixth Tuesday of Easter. Monsieur Roen met them in the courtyard.

"How is everything?" Grand-Mère asked him as he helped her down.

"There have been some changes with the staff."

"Oh?"

"Cook will tell you." He extended his hand to Catherine.

Eriq jumped down next and helped Monsieur with the trunk as the women went into the house. Cook was not in the kitchen.

"*Bonjour,*" Grand-Mère called out as they continued into the house.

"*Bonjour,* Madame!" Cook exclaimed, scurrying down the hallway with bedding in her hands. "We received your message you were coming early, but it only arrived yesterday."

"Is everything all right?"

"Amelie has not been feeling well again. Not gravely ill by any means, but not well."

Grand-Mère passed Cook in the hall. "Where is the housekeeper?"

"Gone, and so is the footman."

Grand-Mère froze. "But you are still here."

"*Oui,* and Monsieur Roen too. We told you we did not plan to go anywhere."

Grand-Mère's voice wavered as she spoke. "What about Estelle?"

"She is here, nursing the babe and caring for Amelie, and also helping with the cleaning and the wash. Doing all she can."

"*Merci,*" Grand-Mère said. "To all of you." She continued on to her rooms.

When Catherine reached the bedchamber, Grand-Mère was hovering over Amelie, her hand on her forehead. Estelle stood at the end of the bed with the baby.

"Catherine," Grand-Mère said. "Send Monsieur Roen for the physician. And get cold water and rags."

As Catherine spoke with Cook in the kitchen, Eriq came in carrying the trunk. "Amelie is ill again," Catherine said. "Leave the trunk in Grand-Mère's sitting room."

He nodded and kept on going.

"Is Jules at the shop?" Catherine asked.

"*Non.* He and Pierre left for the Plateau last week," Cook said. "I had a message from them too—Amelie read it—that they should be back soon."

"Why did they go when she was ill?" Catherine asked.

"She was better when they left. And Father Philippe assured them there would be no problems with the dragoons for a few weeks—and he was right." Cook shrugged. "Although I'm not so sure that others have not had difficulties. Several more in your congregation have disappeared."

"Who?" Catherine's heart began to race.

"The butcher and his family, for one."

"Did they disappear before or after Jules and Pierre left for the Plateau?"

Cook placed her finger on her chin. "Let me see…just before, I believe."

Catherine inhaled sharply. That did not mean anything, not really. Eriq had to be mistaken. "Perhaps the butcher and his family fled?"

Cook shrugged. "I hope so, but the less we all know when the dragoons return, the better."

"They are returning for sure?"

Cook nodded. "That is what Father Philippe said. He tried to get them reassigned, but to no avail. They destroyed your temple, and then they gave your people a chance to convert. Now their plan is to return and to clear Lyon of the Huguenots completely."

"Oh, dear."

"*Oui*. Believe me, it was an answer to my prayers to have you two come back ahead of schedule."

"What about the Berger family?" Catherine put her hand on the table and leaned toward Cook.

"They are still here. Madame Berger came several times to check on Amelie, but now their boys are ill."

Catherine sighed. So many trials and tribulations. "How about the guards from the convent? Did they come back?"

"*Oui*, after Jules and Pierre left, but Monsieur Roen marched them down to the cathedral and Father Philippe chastised them. They haven't been back since."

Catherine couldn't help but smile at the thought. God bless Father Philippe. He was a true friend to them. He loved the way the Lord commanded.

Eriq came back through the kitchen and said he was going to the shop to see how things were there. "Then I will go back to our house and see if we have any staff left." He started toward the door. "I am guessing we do not."

The physician arrived in the late afternoon, listening to Amelie's heart, his ear against a cloth spread over her chest. "It has weakened more," he said. "I am afraid I will need to do the bloodletting after all." He turned toward Grand-Mère. "I will need help."

"Of course."

"Grab the basin." The physician took a lancet from his bag. "I will cut her foot."

Catherine felt herself grow faint and turned to go. She remembered the smell of the bloodletting of her mother when she was a girl. She hurried out of the room and down the hall, breathing deeply as she did.

Without saying anything to Cook, she made her way into the courtyard and collapsed under the chestnut tree. First her mother, then her father, and then her uncle. Surely not Amelie too. Tears filled her eyes. Death was part of life. She knew that. But not her sweet cousin.

She swiped at her tears. She would have to be strong. It would be up to her to care for Valentina. Grand-Mère's eyesight was worsening, and as much as Catherine longed for her grandmother to never die, she would not live forever either. Even though Jules would be Valentina's legal guardian, he knew nothing about children, especially little girls.

She stood and leaned against the tree as the courtyard door scraped open, followed by the neighing of a horse. She turned toward the street as Jules and then Pierre rode into the courtyard.

Her brother nodded at her while Pierre broke into a grin, but as he neared his expression fell. "Is everything all right?" he asked, dismounting his horse as Jules continued on to the stable.

Remembering what Eriq had shared in Paris about his suspicions, she stepped back. She felt a distance from Pierre she had never experienced before.

"What is it?" he asked.

No. Eriq had to have been mistaken. Pierre didn't tell her everything, but he wouldn't be involved in anything as sordid as betraying their own people. She put those thoughts aside, welcomed him, and then told him about the change in Amelie's health.

He stepped closer, his expression empathetic, but he didn't reach out to her. Perhaps he too was aware of the distance the last few weeks had put between them. "I'm sorry, Catherine." He smelled like the road—dust mixed with fresh air and the sweat of his horse.

"I have something for you," he said. She hadn't brought him anything from Paris. He stepped toward his horse, opened a saddlebag, retrieved a small packet, and handed it to her.

She untied it. Inside was a silver cross on a chain, a Huguenot cross like the one on the banner that Basile had burned when he set the temple on fire.

"*Merci*," she said, meeting his blue eyes as she tried to fasten the chain around her neck.

"Let me help." He stepped behind her and saw to the clasp, his hands lingering for a moment. She turned to face him again, her fingers on the cross.

"It's beautiful."

Pierre nodded and smiled again. "The Plateau is magnificent. La rivière Lignon is small but it has its own rugged beauty. And the people—they are kind and caring. Good, good people."

Catherine stepped back. "It appears Jules has completely manipulated you, then."

"*Non*," Pierre said. "It's just not the desert that everyone makes it sound." He met her gaze. "God is there."

She let go of the cross.

"We will be returning to the Plateau soon," Pierre said. "Jules is still hoping to buy the paper mill—and we have already started building the warehouse. He hired a manager to see that the work continues."

None of it made any sense. "Why would he do that?" she asked as her brother approached.

"Do what?" he asked. Before she could answer, he turned to Pierre. "I told you not to discuss this—"

Insulted, Catherine crossed her arms. "*Bonjour*, Jules," she said to her brother, her voice tense.

"*Bonjour, ma soeur*," he answered, placing his hands on her shoulders and kissing her cheeks, even though her arms were still crossed. "I trust your trip went well."

"*Oui*," she answered. "But Amelie took a turn for the worse again after you left."

He cringed and released her. "How is the baby?"

"Good."

He turned and hurried toward the house.

Catherine tucked the cross under her dress. "It looks as if we still differ regarding the future," she said to Pierre.

He simply nodded. Perhaps Eriq was the right Talbot for her after all.

Amelie seemed better after the bloodletting. Grand-Mère doctored her foot every morning, noon, and night, and the lancet wound healed quickly.

On the day of the Ascension, the last of May, the family gathered in the lounge for Scripture reading and prayer, and Amelie was strong enough to join them. Once they were finished, Catherine and Estelle spread thin sheets of fabric over the furniture and then did the same in the dining room. From now on, the family would meet together in Grand-Mère's sitting room and take their meals in the kitchen. It was too much work with too few hands to clean the unnecessary rooms.

On the seventh Friday of Easter, Pastor Berger arrived at the house, asking for Grand-Mère. He was obviously ill and said Madame Berger was worse. "She is delirious with fever. So many have left that I do not know who else to ask. Could Catherine come and nurse Madame?"

Grand-Mère said she would go herself. Catherine protested, but she knew she would not do Madame much good. Grand-Mère insisted. "Send someone for me if Amelie worsens. Or if the dragoons return."

The day after Pentecost, as Catherine tried to think about the coming of the Holy Spirit into the world, the dragoons showed up. Basile was as noisy and obnoxious as ever. Catherine immediately sent

Monsieur Roen after Grand-Mère, but he returned without her. "She has fallen ill," he said. "You are to stay in her apartment with Amelie and Estelle."

The next day, before he left for the print shop, Jules announced that he and Pierre would be leaving for the Plateau in two days. "Eriq is going to come and stay here."

Obviously Eriq had not said anything to Jules about his feelings for Catherine, and she certainly wasn't going to. "Do you think he can handle the dragoons?"

"I have spoken to Father Philippe. He will help if needed. Monsieur Roen knows to summon him if anything comes up. And Eriq is maturing. I'm impressed with the connections he made in Paris. One has worked out for our benefit."

Catherine cocked her head. "Oh?"

"He is proving himself," Jules said. "I have no doubt he will protect all of you."

Catherine nodded. Eriq would be as much—or more—of a protector than Jules. But she could not help thinking of Eriq's suspicions that Jules and Pierre had been betraying Huguenots to the dragoons. "He had some...concerns...about you and Pierre that he voiced to me in Paris."

"Concerns?" Jules shrugged. "He was probably testing you to see how gullible you are—"

"Perhaps." Catherine answered. "But—"

Jules stepped toward the door, cutting her off before she could say more. "I'll be staying at the shop late tonight and tomorrow."

Catherine did her best to stay hidden as the dragoons were in and out, but the next evening, on the Tenth Wednesday in Ordinary Time, Basile followed her back to the suite after she had returned the dinner tray.

She scurried through the door, shoving it shut behind her, but he managed to get his foot in the way. "Leave me alone," she hissed.

He laughed. "It is not you I am after."

She hoped he was not transferring his affections to Estelle. Catherine knew she was fond of Waltier.

She pushed on the door harder. "Go away."

He heaved back and came crashing through, sending her to the floor. Trying to scramble to her feet, she stepped on her gown, stumbled, and yet managed to block the doorway to the bedchamber.

"How is your cousin feeling?" Basile asked.

"She is ill."

"I am not particular." Basile pushed against Cathcrine with his firearm, breaking her hold on the doorjamb. He forced his way past her into the bedchamber. Estelle, huddled in the corner with the baby, cried out. Waltier must have been in the hallway because he rushed through the sitting room into the bedchamber too.

Estelle turned away from Basile, protecting the baby.

"Sorry," Waltier muttered.

"Stay," Catherine begged, positioning herself between Basile and Amelie, who sat up in the bed.

Basile shook his head at Catherine, and she sat down beside her cousin, completely blocking Basile's view.

"I ran into the guards from the convent today," he said. "They told me about your escape."

"It's none of your concern," Catherine said.

"Oh, it is," Basile replied. "The baby needs to be returned."

Catherine sat tall. "*Non*. She was baptized into our church."

Basile laughed. "Prove it."

Catherine opened her mouth but then closed it. Pastor Berger probably had not recorded it, and even if he had, the records would have burned. "The baby belongs with her mother," Catherine said.

"You are right, she does," Basile said. "Under my protection. If Amelie marries me, the baby stays here. If not, I take her to the convent."

Amelie groaned. Estelle yelped. Waltier's face turned ashen.

Basile was being ridiculous about marrying Amelie, but perhaps not about taking the baby. Catherine stood and stepped toward Basile. "When?"

"Immediately."

Catherine's palms grew sweaty. Why was Grand-Mère not here to guide her? She faced Basile, shaking her head as she did. "Weddings do not happen in a day. Give us two." She needed to buy some time so she could get Valentina to Father Philippe.

As if on cue, the baby began to cry.

Basile backed away.

"Now go," Catherine said, before he could reply. "You have upset her."

"Two days," he said as he left the room. "No excuses."

Catherine and Amelie conversed long into the night, going back and forth about what should be done. Amelie wanted to wait for Grand-Mère to come home, but Catherine said they didn't have time. Finally, Amelie fell asleep. Just after daybreak, as soon as Catherine heard the dragoons leave, she hurried down to Jules's office, but he was not there.

She rushed to the kitchen, asking Cook if she had seen her brother.

"He left a half hour ago. He wanted to be on his way before the dragoons were up."

Catherine sank down on a kitchen chair.

"What is the matter, Mademoiselle?"

Catherine sat up straight. She wouldn't have time to speak with Jules about her plan, and he probably would have just torn it apart anyway. "I need you to take Estelle and Valentina to mass with you and then put them in Father Philippe's care. Tell Monsieur Roen you need to go in the carriage."

Cook didn't ask any questions but scurried out the back door. Catherine returned to the apartment, telling Amelie she planned to take Valentina and Estelle to Saint-Jean-Baptiste.

Amelie had a minute with the baby while Estelle dressed. "What if Basile goes to the cathedral?"

"He cannot take the baby from Father Philippe. He won't allow it."

Amelie rubbed her lips over her daughter's soft hair. "Go with them," she said to Catherine.

"*Non*. I'm staying here with you."

"I'll be fine. The dragoons have left, and you will be gone a short time."

Catherine shook her head and glanced toward Estelle. "Valentina is in good hands."

Tears filled Amelie's deep brown eyes. "But I need to hear from you that Father Philippe understands the situation and will protect her. Otherwise I will be terrified that someone else might turn her over to the dragoons."

Catherine took a deep breath.

"That is far more important than me being left alone for a short time."

Catherine hesitated and then said, "*Non*. I will have Monsieur Roen and Cook stay with you. I will take Estelle and the baby."

Amelie frowned. "I would feel better if at least Monsieur Roen went with you."

"*Non*," Catherine said. "We will hurry."

Getting out the door took longer than Catherine expected. Finally, they made it as far as the courtyard, only to have Estelle say she forgot something. She came back with a handkerchief that Catherine suspected Waltier had given her and the thin silk blanket Grand-Mère had bought the baby for the warmer weather.

By the time they had walked to the cathedral, Father Philippe had already started down the aisle. Estelle and Catherine scooted into the back row. A few people gave Catherine funny looks, but Estelle sat tall and stared them down. Catherine held the baby until she began to fuss, and then Estelle reached for her and the little one gave out a sigh as she settled against her nursemaid, the silk blanket wrapped around her.

From the pulpit, Father Philippe's eyes fell on Catherine for a brief moment. When the service was over, they waited until the parishioners filed out.

Father Philippe returned to their row and greeted the two women. Then he turned to Catherine. "What do you need of me?"

She explained the situation. "We are looking for sanctuary. For the baby, along with Estelle."

"Of course," Father Philippe said. "Tell Amelie she has my word."

"*Merci.*" Tears filled her eyes.

"Go in peace," the priest said.

Catherine thought of the verse her father used to quote, the one from Galatians, *There is neither Jew nor Greek, there is neither bond nor free, there is neither male nor female: for ye are all one in Christ Jesus.* She felt that with Father Philippe—neither Protestant nor Catholic, but one in Christ.

She hugged Estelle. "You have been God's gift to our family."

Estelle hugged her back and then told her goodbye.

Catherine hurried home, racing as fast as she dared. Relief flooded her when she reached the courtyard—until she realized the coach was gone.

"Cook!" she called out, running into the kitchen. She was nowhere in sight. Catherine guessed she had sent Monsieur Roen on an errand while she attended to Amelie. Catherine ran down the hall, past Jules's office, and to the corridor, hurrying on to Grand-Mère's apartment. The door was wide open. The sitting room was vacant. So was the bedchamber.

Amelie was gone.

CHAPTER TWENTY-FOUR
Catherine

Catherine searched every room of the house, certain Amelie must have been frightened and hidden herself somewhere. But she was nowhere to be found.

Consumed by despair, Catherine slid down the wall in the hallway outside of Jules's office to the floor and put her head in her hands. Basile must have discovered her plan to save the baby and taken Amelie for spite. Or perhaps he had dragged her off to force her to marry him. Not to Father Philippe but to some other willing priest.

Catherine stood—she would go from church to church until she found her cousin. She rushed to the back door, but before she reached it Basile came crashing into the kitchen, followed by Waltier.

"I am not waiting any longer," Basile said.

"What have you done with her?" Catherine backed up to the table in the middle of the room.

"Done with her?" Basile held his firearm high. "Nothing, yet."

"She isn't here. I...I went out, and when I came back she was gone."

"Do not try to fool me!" Basile shouted as he stormed by Catherine. "It is only right I get something out of this assignment."

Catherine did not bother to follow him. Waltier waited in the doorway.

"She really is gone," she said.

"I believe you."

"And I have no idea where." She swiped at a tear. "I thought Basile had taken her."

Waltier raised his eyebrows. "What about Estelle?"

"Gone too."

"But you have an idea where she is, *oui?*"

Catherine inhaled sharply and then nodded.

"I will not ask anymore."

"*Merci*," Catherine murmured, stepping to the other side of the table so she would have a good view of Basile when he returned. It didn't take him long.

"Where have you hidden her?" He stormed around the table and grabbed Catherine by the arm, yanking her as he continued to clutch his firearm in the other hand.

Catherine tried to jerk away from him. "Nowhere!"

"Basile," Waltier said, his voice as harsh as Catherine had ever heard it.

"Shut up," Basile sneered.

If only *he* would shut his mouth—and go away.

Catherine tried to wrench free. She needed to get to her horse. But where would she go?

Basile tightened his grip and pulled her closer. His breath reeked of wine. "One cousin is the same as another to me," he said, his nose nearly touching hers. "As long as the house comes with the bargain."

A voice came through the open door. "What is going on here?" It was Eriq.

Basile tightened his grip. "Official business of the king."

"Release her," Eriq demanded. "A friend of His Majesty's is here to visit me, and I have brought him to see Catherine."

She yanked her arm away just as Basile let her go. She stumbled back toward the fireplace.

"Catherine?" Anton, dressed as if he were in Versailles with his ruffled blouse and gold jacket, stood behind Eriq in the doorway. "Are you all right, *chérie*?"

"*Oui*," Catherine answered, surprised at the strength of her voice. Her heart beat in terror.

"Show me your papers," Basile demanded, stepping to the doorway.

"Don't be ridiculous," Anton said. "I am the brother of le Duc de la Rochefauld. I have been residing at Versailles with the king for the last several months."

Catherine couldn't help but note the exaggeration. He had been staying in an apartment in Versailles, but that was hardly the same as residing with Louis XIV. Perhaps that finer point would be lost on Basile. And Anton definitely exuded a confidence of being in command.

"Monsieur Talbot and I are on official business. We're inspecting properties, including this one."

Basile squared his shoulders and raised his firearm. "The owners are heretics of the faith and traitors of His Majesty." His voice grew louder. "Unless there is a marriage—" certainly he did not still think he could force Amelie to marry him, "—or a conversion, this property is being confiscated. Tomorrow."

"Nonsense," Anton said. "How can it be confiscated when I am buying it? I have just left my deposit with the owner's solicitor. And while I am here I will be looking at the estate west of town too."

Catherine gasped. All along she thought Jules should sell the home, but now that it was a possibility she felt sick. And to Anton?

Basile lowered his firearm and looked at Waltier, who said, "We should consult with the captain."

"*Oui*," Basile said. "We will return with the captain."

"Will you be all right?" Waltier asked Catherine.

"*Oui*," she answered, wanting to laugh. She would be fine as soon as Basile was gone. Once they were out the door, she said, "I am leaving too. Amelie is gone."

"Gone?" Eriq stepped closer to the table.

"I ran an errand this morning, and when I came back she had disappeared."

"Who was with her?"

"Cook," Catherine said. "She is missing too, and so is Monsieur Roen."

"What about the nursemaid and the baby?"

"They are at the cathedral with Father Philippe. Basile was going to force Amelie to marry him."

"That is ludicrous." Eriq crossed his arms.

"*Oui*. But I need to find Amelie. I do not know where she is or if she is in harm's way."

"Wait for just a moment," Anton said, reaching out and touching Catherine's arm.

Catherine turned toward Eriq. "What is going on? I don't understand."

"Of course not," Anton responded. "I have not gotten to the best part yet. I have a proposal for you."

Catherine stepped backward.

"A proposition, actually, with much to gain on your part. A place in the court. A life of meaning. Time with Suzanne and even Madame de Maintenon, another woman with a Huguenot background who changed her destiny."

"What are you talking about?" Catherine asked.

Anton smiled, but his eyes narrowed as he reached out to her. "You were much more amorous at Versailles."

She jerked her hand away. "Amorous? I was no such thing!"

She looked to Eriq, expecting him to be as shocked and angry at Anton's words as she was. But he wasn't even looking her way. Did he not care? Had his affections for her been a lie?

"You were, *chérie*," Anton insisted. "Aunt Suzanne said so too. She could think of no reason why you would not accept me."

"No reason? We only just met. We conversed for a short time. How could anyone know…" She stopped. Anton was no better than Basile. He wanted her family's property too, but all of it for as little as possible.

"You're not making this easy on me." His voice was calm. "Could we start anew? With me telling you how beautiful you are." He reached for her hand again and raised it toward his mouth.

She shuddered at the thought of his lips on her skin. "I need to go."

He grabbed her wrist. "Catherine, I'm asking you to marry me."

The pressure of his hand alarmed her. He appeared sane, but his force was almost as much as Basile's.

"Eriq?" Catherine sought his eyes, pleading for his help.

Their eyes locked for a long moment, and then Eriq said, "What can I do? I have to look out for myself."

She was dumbfounded. "You betrayed me," she whispered, scarcely believing it.

"*Au contraire.* This is what is best for you too."

"That is a lie and you know it."

He shrugged. He didn't care. Why had she ever trusted him?

She turned toward Anton. "Why would you want to marry me?" Catherine stepped closer to him so the pressure on her wrist loosened.

"I can afford your home but not your land. I need to be a true nobleman." He lowered his voice. "And you will be my lady. You will have a much better life than you would tied to a wheel. We will live here some but spend as much time at Versailles as possible."

Catherine shook her head. "The land, all of it, belongs to my brother, not me."

"Not if you convert," Eriq said.

Catherine spun toward him, pulling away from Anton. "And what do you have to do with all of this? Did you work with Monsieur Olivier to make the arrangements?"

Eriq shook his head. "*Non.* With your Uncle Laurent. He drew up all the papers. Monsieur Olivier just gave us the idea."

Catherine shook her head. "And Uncle Laurent will receive a cut, I presume."

"Of course."

Catherine put her hands to the side of her face. "My brother agreed to selling the house?"

"*Oui,*" Eriq said. "He is up to all sort of surprises. I was right about him and Pierre turning in Huguenots to the dragoons."

"*Non!*" Catherine's hands fell to her sides. How could Pierre look her in the eye and bring her a cross as a gift if he was betraying their own people? Her hand went to her neck.

"It's true," Eriq said. "The butcher and his family. Even his apprentice. You saw the vault in the warehouse. That's what they are using it for." Eriq chuckled. "Why do you think the dragoons were not so bad to you and Amelie?"

She took a deep breath, thinking they had been horrible. But she knew it could have been much worse. "What about you, Eriq? Who have you been helping?"

"I am the one who got the cobbler out. And, of course, my parents too. At least my brother had the decency to let them leave. I arranged the sale of this house to help Jules with his latest project, still hoping I was wrong about my misgivings. But, tragically, I have learned how correct I was. And there is more. It seems he has been smuggling contraband."

"What kind?"

Eriq shrugged. "I don't have the details, and it doesn't matter. He has what he wants. Money from the dragoons. Money from the house. He will buy the paper mill on the Lignon from the Audets. He is probably planning on turning them in next and getting his money back—and perhaps he has already betrayed Amelie."

"Don't be absurd."

Eriq shrugged. "All I know is that I have lost my brother."

Catherine swallowed hard. She had lost Pierre too.

Anton cleared his throat. "It sounds as if there are many reasons for you to marry me and be under my protection, Catherine. What is your answer? I saw how fascinated you were with the glamour of Versailles. I think we have a lot in common."

"Could I have a few minutes?" she asked. "To clean up?"

"Of course," Anton said, smiling. "And put on some decent clothes. If I had seen you dressed all in gray in Versailles, I would not have given you a second glance."

To think she had been so excited about the new clothes, paid for by an uncle who had no qualms about arranging a marriage and betraying her.

Catherine led them through the kitchen to the hall and then to Jules's study. "Wait here," she said.

As she hurried down the corridor she wondered at the truth in all of it. Eriq was in alliance with Uncle Laurent and Anton. He had no love or concern for her, even though he had presented himself otherwise. Was Pierre as coldhearted? Could no one be trusted except for dear Grand-Mère?

She dressed quickly, putting on the skirt of her riding habit first instead of her underskirt, and then pulling the purple gown over the top of that. Next she put on the headpiece. Then she grabbed her satchel, made sure the copy of Grand-Mère's letter of protection was inside, and collected her journal and slipped it in too, along with quills, a bottle of ink, the flint from the fireplace mantle, and her purse with several coins.

As she turned away from the desk, she saw her small Bible behind the jar of quills. She slipped it under the headpiece, securing it in her bun as Jules had once suggested, and took Grand-Mère's small dagger from the drawer of the desk, slipping the scabbard into her stocking. Finally, she took the Huguenot cross Pierre had given her from around her neck and tucked it into her purse.

Then she opened the window and the shutters at the very end of the room and lowered her satchel to the ground.

A few moments later she stopped in the doorway of the study. "You must be hungry," she said to Anton and Eriq. "I apologize that we have no cook. I will prepare some food myself and be right back."

In the kitchen she wrapped a loaf of bread and the end of a block of cheese into a towel and then tiptoed out the back door, retrieving the satchel and then hurrying to the stable.

Her horse was the only one left. "Hush," Catherine whispered soothingly, grabbing a saddle blanket and then the saddle.

Once the mare was ready, Catherine led her through the courtyard to the street and mounted quickly. The bells of the cathedral began to toll.

As she passed Janetta's shop, the girl stepped out into the street.

"Catherine, what are you doing?" she called out.

"Starting a new style," Catherine replied with a wave. Janetta laughed, and Catherine turned her horse toward the river and the warehouse. If Jules did have something to do with Amelie's disappearance, that was where he would have taken her.

Chapter Twenty-Five
Catherine

Catherine put her horse in the stable and tried the back door of the warehouse. It was locked. She hurried around to the front to the shop. She banged on the door and finally heard footsteps. The oldest of the printers, a man who had worked as a boy for her grandfather opened it.

"*Bonjour*, Mademoiselle," he said, peeking out the door. "No one is here but me."

"When did Jules leave?"

"A while ago."

"Was he by himself?"

The printer shook his head. "Monsieur Talbot was with him."

"No one else?"

"Not that I saw." The man's bushy white eyebrows furrowed as he spoke.

Catherine hesitated. "I may have left something in the warehouse. May I come in and take a look?"

He shook his head. "I'm sorry, but Monsieur Gillet gave me strict instructions..."

She looked up at him. "But he didn't know I was coming." She felt unsettled about her deception, but she had no other choice.

He glanced back into the shop as if trying to guess what Jules would want him to do. He finally arrived at a decision. "Come in."

Catherine thanked him and hurried forward, but then she remembered she would need a light for the vault and headed to the fireplace. She grabbed a stick out of the crock Jules kept for tinder and held it to an ember until it caught fire. The man watched but didn't say anything.

As soon as she reached the warehouse, she lit the lantern on Pierre's worktable and then stamped out the stick on the stone floor. She bent down, pushed the lever, and then held the lantern high as the pulleys lifted the door. The room, in the shadows from the light, was empty. Her heart fell.

Surely Jules would not have risked taking Amelie to the Plateau. Catherine turned to go, but a white object on the floor of the vault stopped her. Valentina's blanket! She snatched it up and hurried back through the warehouse, blowing out the lantern and leaving it on the table. Someone must have taken the baby, and most likely Estelle too, from the cathedral soon after she left. Perhaps Father Philippe was working with Jules and Pierre. Perhaps all of them were deceiving her.

She hurried back into the print shop. "Found it," she called out to the printer, quickly holding up the blanket and heading out the door.

Once Eriq realized she was gone, he would either come to the shop looking for her or go to the Bergers. As much as she longed to see Grand-Mère, she couldn't risk going there.

When Papa, Uncle Edouard, Amelie, Jules, and she had gone to Le Chambon all those years ago, it had taken them two days, and she was sure she could do it again. She remembered the route, the stops. She reached the stable, led her horse out, quickly mounted her, and headed back across the bridge to the other side of the Saône. She needed to get out of town as quickly as possible.

On the outskirts of Lyon she passed three dragoons she didn't recognize. She kept her head up and dug her feet into the flanks of her horse, holding her breath as she urged the horse forward. In her purple-and-gold gown, she certainly didn't look like a Huguenot woman. The dragoons did not follow.

Still Catherine's legs began to shake. She wouldn't be safe along the road. Women never traveled alone, but what other choice did she have? Either Jules and Pierre were both deceivers and had captured Amelie, who now needed Catherine's help, or else they had a plan up their sleeves to save them all—and in that case she needed to find them. Perhaps she should have dressed as a man, but there was no going back home now to find a pair of Jules's trousers. Besides, if she disguised herself as a man and then was found out, the consequences might be even worse. She determined to keep on going. Traveling alone was by far the most foolish thing she had ever done, but she would do it anyway.

She rode along green fields, with the Rhône always nearby. The warm weather had dried out the road and dust blew around her skirt. She tied the baby's blanket around her neck, pulling it up over her mouth and nose, adding to the look of the ridiculous headpiece and the riding dress under her gown. Perhaps looking like a madwoman would keep people away. She stopped at the fountain in Oullins, the first village she came to, to water her horse and for a drink and then veered west toward the next village.

She stopped at that fountain too, in the shadow of the steeple of the church, and ate some bread and cheese. A group of little boys pointed at her top-knot and giggled. She simply smiled and mounted her horse.

She rode on. From the position of the sun, Catherine guessed she had three hours until dark and thought she could easily make it to Saint-Étienne. She would not sleep under the stars—that would be far too foolish. Perhaps there would be a temple there, and she could find a Huguenot family to stay with. Or an inn. Surely the community had some sort of accommodations.

The road grew steeper. She stopped along the river, dipped her hand into the water to drink, and then ate the rest of the cheese and more of the bread. Dusk began to fall as she saw the abbey on the hill ahead. With another turn of the road, the village of Saint-Étienne came into view.

When she reached the first houses, she asked a woman herding a small flock of sheep if there was an inn in town.

The woman was taken aback. "You are not traveling by yourself, Mademoiselle, are you?"

"I am following my brother," Catherine answered, which was true. "I'm hoping he's lodging in this village." It was improbable, but she could hope.

The woman said there was an inn near the cathedral.

"*Merci*," Catherine said. "Are there any Huguenots in Saint-Étienne?"

The woman hesitated and then said, her voice low, "They have all left. Most have gone to the Plateau. Others have fled France altogether."

"*Merci*," Catherine said again and kept riding. By the time she reached the inn, it was nearly dark. She tied her horse to the hitching post and started up the stairs, but when she reached the door she heard a woman say, "I told you we are full. Now be on your way."

Two dragoons appeared in the doorway. Catherine stepped back toward her horse, adjusting her headpiece. As the soldiers staggered down the stairs, she turned as if she were looking for someone to arrive. The dragoons kept going.

Catherine sank against her horse. She was too tired and sore to climb on again. Her mare needed a rest and she had nowhere to go anyway. Even if she were foolish enough to sleep under the stars, the temperature was falling fast, and lighting a fire would bring attention to herself. She had no choice but to petition the innkeeper. Straightening her satchel on her shoulder, she started up the steps. A woman holding a broom met her at the door. "No rooms are left," she barked.

"*Oui*, I heard, but I was wondering if you would be so kind as to allow me to sit at the table for the night. I will still pay."

The woman squinted in the dim light. "Surely you are not traveling by yourself!"

"I became separated from my brother. I believe he is not far from here, though."

The woman shook her head slightly. "It is not safe."

"I know," Catherine said, holding her head high.

The woman glanced toward a long plank table and benches behind her. A half dozen men sat at the far end. "I cannot protect you."

"Still, it's safer than sleeping outside," Catherine answered, her knees weakening. She would have to sit by the fire all night, awake.

The woman nodded toward the table and named her price. Catherine took the coins from her purse. "*Merci.*"

The woman slipped the money into the pocket at her ample waist. "I will have the stable boy take care of your horse. You may wash in the back room."

When she was done, Catherine made her way to the other end of the table, closest to the fire, hoping the men would assume someone would soon join her.

The woman brought her a bowl of soup and a piece of bread. Catherine forced herself to eat slowly. Two of the men left, going out the front door. Another headed to the second floor of the inn. The other three asked for more ale, which the woman delivered.

Then she took Catherine's empty bowl, built up the fire, and settled it with the poker. The woman turned toward Catherine, the poker still in her hand and made eye contact. Then she buried the tip of the poker in the embers of the fire. She left the room without saying anything.

Another of the men went upstairs. The remaining two men's voices grew louder. Catherine sensed them looking her way from time to time. She stood, her back to the fire so she could see them, but she soon tired.

All she wanted to do was put her head down on the table and sleep. She sat back down on the bench and took some paper from her satchel. Perhaps writing would keep her awake. She took out her quill, sharpened the point with the dagger she pulled from her stocking, and then dipped it in the ink, trying to remember everything that had happened since the last time she had written. Grand-Mère had gone to the Bergers...

She was so lost in her journal that she didn't notice that only one man remained until he stood and walked toward her. He swayed a little. Catherine reached for the dagger just as a log fell in the fire, causing sparks to fly. Wrapping the baby blanket around her hand, she stood and stepped to the fire, grabbing the poker and turning slowly around toward the man. His white shirt was stained and his jacket was torn. His breeches hung loosely on his hips.

"Mademoiselle." He took a step backward, bumping against the bench, his hands up. "I have no ill intentions."

She did not believe him and stood her ground, wondering what she would do if he stayed until the poker cooled.

He ran his hand through his greasy hair and then without saying any more turned toward the stairs. Catherine held the poker until she heard a door close above and then, after returning the poker to the fire, collapsed at the table.

All she could do was return to her writing. When she finished, she paced up and down the room, struggling to stay on her feet. Every muscle of her body ached. How could she possibly stay awake? Finally, she took off the headpiece and wriggled her Bible from her bun, slipping it into her satchel.

By the middle of the night, she dozed, her dagger in her hand and her head on the table, but at the faint first light through the high dirty window, she placed her Bible back in her bun, put on the headpiece, and gathered her things.

Noise from the kitchen meant someone was up. As Catherine made her way around the table a mouse scurried across the floor and then another. She stopped at the kitchen door.

The woman was kneading dough on the table. "Looks as if you survived."

Catherine nodded. "*Merci*," she said. "For placing the poker where you did."

The woman smiled. "It's just one of many tricks of mine. I hope you didn't burn your hand."

Catherine held up the blanket and returned the woman's smile.

"How about some food for the road?"

"*Merci*," Catherine said again as the woman handed her an end of a baguette, a hunk of cheese, and wrinkled apple.

The innkeeper dug her hands back into the dough. "God be with you, child."

"And with you."

⁓

Before she reached the edge of the village, a voice called out to her to halt. For a moment she considered trying to outrun whoever it was, but when she glanced over her shoulder she saw it was the two dragoons from the night before.

She pulled her horse to a stop.

"It's you," one of the dragoons said as he dismounted.

"*Bonjour.*"

"Where are you headed?"

"Le Chambon-sur-Lignon."

"Alone?" he asked, dumbfounded.

Catherine shook her head. "My brother is ahead. I should catch him soon. He has business there."

"What kind?"

"He is buying a paper mill."

The other dragoon dismounted. "Huguenots own the mill there."

Catherine nodded. "That is true."

The first dragoon smiled and laughed. "No doubt he is getting a good price then." He nodded at her satchel. "Just let me have a look at what you are carrying and then you can be on your way."

Catherine handed it to him.

As he pawed through it, the other pointed at her headpiece. "What kind of hat is that?"

"A gift from a friend in Versailles. The Duchesse de Navailles. Have you heard of her? She was a lady of honor to the Queen Mother." Catherine touched the lace of the headpiece.

"It is not exactly riding attire," the dragoon said.

Catherine smiled. "You're right about that. I would not be surprised if it ends up alongside the road soon."

The other dragoon handed back the satchel. She took it, making sure the letter of protection was still inside. It was.

"We have had Protestants smuggling all sorts of things through here. People, for one, but also Bibles."

"Oh," Catherine said, resisting the urge to touch her top-knot again. "Where are you headed?"

"We are going as far as Firminy."

"May I ride with you?" she asked, taking two coins from her purse, careful they could not glimpse her cross as she did. "And pay you for the protection."

The dragoon smiled. "Of course."

"*Merci.*" Catherine remembered Firminy from her trip with Papa and Uncle.

The dragoons kept up a fast pace, but Catherine stayed with them. It was midmorning by the time they reached the village. She stopped at the fountain to water her horse, calling out a thanks as they rode on to the largest of the churches.

Back on the road, the terrain grew steeper and steeper. She reached Pont-Salomon by noon but only stopped for water and to eat some of the cheese and bread. Her body ached and she was saddle sore. Months of not riding were taking a toll now. She forced herself to mount her horse and go on.

As the road climbed in altitude the broadleaf trees gave way to more evergreen. Her mare slowed until she was merely plodding along. She was tired too. Catherine pulled her to a stop beside a creek and dismounted. A short rest would do them both good.

Tired of the headpiece, Catherine took it off. Then she took out the Bible too and placed it in the satchel, and shook down her hair, running her hands through it and then repinning her bun as her horse drank. She wrapped the baby's blanket around her head like a scarf.

When she finished drinking, the mare stepped away from the creek, limping. Catherine's heart sank as she examined the horse's swollen ankle and then pulled up her skirts and led the mare back into the creek, hoping the cool water would help.

There was nothing to do now but rest. She could not ride the horse. Her weight would be too much.

God had turned His back on her, she was sure. Perhaps because she longed for the finer things in life. Or because she wanted the easy way out—a quick trip to London to resume a life close to what she had always had, cared for by her family's money and with no sacrifice on her part.

Now she had lost everything. Her family. Her home. Her betrothed. Her security. Her church. Her people.

After she led the horse out of the water, Catherine sank to her knees. She was a young woman, alone. With no protection and no options.

Then she remembered when Basile lit the temple on fire and she had said all was lost. *Au contraire,* Grand-Mère had said. *Nothing is lost. We are the Lord's temple.*

Catherine knew that did not mean she would be spared or kept safe. Huguenots—men, women, and children—had been tortured and killed.

As girls, Grand-Mère had required Catherine and Amelie to memorize what God had said to Moses before the Israelites crossed the Jordan River. *Be strong and of a good courage, fear not, nor be afraid of them: for the Lord thy God, he it is that doth go with thee; he will not fail thee, nor forsake thee.*

Even in the face of death, Grand-Mère said that God did not forsake His people. Catherine reached into her satchel and retrieved the Bible, flipping to the book of Deuteronomy. She reread the verse and then thought back to her childhood again. Grand-Mère made the two girls recite their catechism, from John Calvin's Church of Geneva, over and over too, starting with, *What is the chief end of human life?*

The girls would answer, in perfect unison, *To know God by whom people were created.*

Catherine clutched the Bible to her chest, feeling a measure of peace. Her free hand fell to her purse and she took out the Huguenot cross. No matter the outcome, the Lord would not fail her. She would be devoted to His glory, as best she—

The rattling of a wagon interrupted her thoughts. She scrambled to her feet, still clutching the Bible and the cross. She expected a company of dragoons until she heard the sound of singing. She stepped onto a stump. Two horses came into view and then a lone driver. It was a rag cart—a wagon, actually. Perhaps one that belonged to Jules. She scrambled up to the road, waving her arms to the ragman.

But it was not a ragman at all. It was Pastor Berger.

CHAPTER TWENTY-SIX

Catherine

She left the top-knot behind, grabbed her satchel, and slipped the Bible and necklace into it. Leading her horse with her free hand, she hurried to the road, calling out, "*Bonjour*, Pastor Berger!"

He squinted into the overhead sun as he pulled the horses to a stop.

"It is I, Catherine Gillet!" she called out. "My horse is going lame."

Pastor Berger hopped down. "Catherine? What in heaven's name are you doing out here?"

"It's a long story."

"You can tell me on the way." He offered her his hand, and she stepped up to the bench, recognizing the wagon now as the newest addition to Jules's fleet. He and Pierre had made it themselves, and it was larger than his other rag carts, its bed wide and deep.

The pastor led her mare to the back and tied the reins to the wagon. He took off the saddle and blanket, and put them on top of the rags.

Then a muffled sound, like a giggle, erupted from somewhere below.

"*Chut*," Pastor said.

"Who is back there?" Catherine asked.

He glanced around before putting a finger to his lips.

Catherine faced forward. When Pastor Berger climbed back up on the bench, she asked where he was going.

"To Le Chambon. Jules is storing rags there for the paper mill."

"It could be a trap. Eriq said Jules has been turning Huguenots over to the dragoons."

Pastor rubbed his chin. "I doubt that."

"I hope it's not true, but there have been so many secrets, so much deception that I'm not sure who to believe anymore."

"Baroness Gillet trusts him implicitly, Catherine."

"Grand-Mère? How do you know?"

He nodded toward the back.

"She is under the rags?" Catherine's stomach flipped at the thought of her discomfort.

"No, there are hidden compartments below the wagon bed."

"Is she well?"

Pastor nodded. "She recovered enough to come along."

"And your family is back there too?"

He nodded again.

He will not fail thee, nor forsake thee. Perhaps they would all die together.

They spent the night in the forest, Catherine and Grand-Mère huddled together, joyous to be reunited. The sun was high overhead the next day when they arrived in Le Chambon. Modest houses and businesses lined the streets, and Catherine recognized the village square from her previous visit, along with the fountain and the common area where the women washed laundry, a usual feature in rural villages. To the right was the river, and Pastor Berger turned that way. Ahead was the temple—a good sign, indeed, that it was still standing. They turned and traveled parallel to the river. Ahead was a warehouse, facing the water, that looked identical to the one in Lyon.

She gasped. *How* identical was it?

Scaffolding stood on one side, and scraps of lumber littered the area around the building. The windows had shutters but no glass.

As Pastor Berger pulled the wagon to a stop, Catherine jumped down and headed toward the warehouse, counting on it being identical in every way, including the hidden vault, where she prayed she might find her cousin at last.

"Wait," he said, motioning to her. She stopped. "We need to get everyone inside, into the—"

"Vault?" She turned toward the warehouse again. "I will be right back."

She hurried through the door, rushing into the storeroom and finding the lever. Sure enough, the wall began to rise.

"Mademoiselle!" Estelle exclaimed, squinting at Catherine from the darkness inside. She held the baby. Amelie, wrapped in a blanket, sat propped in a corner.

"Is she all right?" Catherine stumbled toward her cousin.

"She has taken a bad turn," Estelle said. "Jules has gone for the healer." Catherine knew it was rare for a village to have a physician.

Amelie opened her eyes but did not respond. Catherine felt her forehead. She was burning up.

Catherine turned to Estelle. "Why are you in here?"

"Jules is afraid the dragoons will come after Amelie."

"He is not hiding Amelie here to turn her over to them?"

Estelle's eyebrows furrowed. "That doesn't make any sense. Why wouldn't he have just turned her over in Lyon?"

"I know," Catherine said. "But Eriq—"

Estelle shook her head. "Surely you would not believe him over your brother and Pierre?"

Catherine inhaled.

"If so, you are an *imbécile*," Estelle said.

Catherine did not know what to believe.

"Jules is good. So is Pierre," Amelie whispered, her eyes closed again. "They saved me…"

Catherine heard a strange noise then, like the sound of a pulley. She thought perhaps the doorway to the vault was descending, but it was not. Instead, on the opposite side of the room, a small square in the floor was sliding open. Then Jules's head appeared, and he climbed up into the vault. So this place was not exactly the same after all. It had a second entrance through a hatch in the floor.

He started at the sight of his sister but then turned his attention to Amelie.

"We have to go," he said, sliding the hatch door closed again and crawling toward his cousin. "The dragoons are close, and I'm sure they know about the vault, thanks to Eriq."

Quickly, Jules scooped Amelie into his arms and carried her from the vault, exiting through the sliding panel into the storage room and the warehouse beyond. Turning to Estelle, Catherine unwound the blanket from her head and draped it over Valentina.

"*Merci*," Estelle whispered.

Then they both followed, Catherine pausing to press the lever and close the vault door before hurrying through the storage room after the rest.

As they raced down the hall, Catherine asked Jules why he had not told her he was taking Amelie, Estelle, and the baby.

"I told Eriq to tell you," Jules said. "I thought I could trust him."

"But now you think—"

"I do not think. I know."

She nodded. She knew too. Eriq was the real traitor.

"We will wait for the healer to examine Amelie and then we will slip out the back," Jules said. He laid their cousin on a worktable in the main part of the warehouse as Pastor Berger, his family, and Grand-Mère came through the front door, followed by Pierre and a woman Catherine assumed was the healer. She stepped to Amelie's side.

Only then did Pierre notice Catherine. Dirt was streaked across his face and a strand of hair had worked its way out of its leather tie. He brushed it back, his eyes lighting up when he saw her—until Eriq and the dragoons burst through the door.

Basile yelled, "Under order of His Majesty, this property is confiscated along with the paper mill, the residence in the village of Le Chambon-sur-Lignon, the estate west of Lyon, and the print shop in the city, all under the name of Jules Gillet."

When no one responded, he continued. "It's also my responsibility, in the name of the king, to take into custody the *enfant* and her mother and return them to the convent outside of Lyon, along with claiming her share of the aforementioned properties. Father Philippe has no jurisdiction over the guardianship of the child."

"Let me see your orders," Jules said, stepping toward Basile. The dragoon opened his bag and took out a thick package, handing it over. As he did, Catherine glanced toward the woman, who had already begun to examine Amelie.

Jules studied the pages, flipping through them one by one. "All of these orders are under the assumption that I am not in compliance with the king's religion."

"*Oui*," Eriq said. "You are not."

"So you *can* speak," Jules said. "I thought you were aiming to have Basile do your dirty work."

Eriq shrugged. "Anton decided he wanted the estate and the print shop too."

"And you figured you could steal them from me?"

Eriq smiled, but his gray eyes narrowed. "I need to make my living somehow. I will be compensated handsomely. And Basile will profit from Amelie's share."

"It has been transferred to me," Jules said.

Eriq laughed. "It doesn't matter. We'll get it all anyway. You have no recourse."

"Except," Jules said, holding up the documents. "All of these are void. I'm in compliance with the king's religion. I converted the day before yesterday."

"*Non*," Eriq said. "I do not believe you."

"I have my certificate of baptism right here." Jules pulled a piece of paper from the leather pocket around his waist. He handed it to Basile, who handed it to Eriq.

Eriq studied it for a moment and then pronounced it a forgery.

Jules shrugged. "Take it back to Father Philippe and ask him yourself. His signature and seal are at the bottom."

"We will bring the child and mother with us," Basile said.

The volume of Jules's voice increased. "*Non*, you will not. I am the legal guardian of both."

"Not if your conversion is not true," Basile said.

"If you cannot read Father Philippe's name, at least recognize his seal," Jules countered.

Catherine's heart raced. Jules must have weighed his reasons carefully. She didn't agree with him, but she understood—especially when it came to the safety of Amelie and Valentina.

Basile's face grew red as he turned to Eriq and said something too low for Catherine to hear.

Eriq looked to Pierre. "And you? Have you converted as well?"

Catherine swallowed hard, dreading Pierre's answer.

He shook his head. "*Non.*"

Her heart swelled with relief.

Eriq grinned triumphantly. "Then all of the property in the Talbot family will be transferred into my name. We have additional orders."

"Hate to tell you, little brother," Pierre replied, "but there is nothing to be had. Before Father left for Switzerland, he sold everything to Jules, promising that once he was settled, he would reinvest that money into a new print shop, and then both businesses would be co-owned by the two families."

The smile faded from Eriq's lips.

And from Catherine's. *Oui,* it was a good plan, but, as with so many other things, Pierre had kept this a secret from her too. She truly had lost him.

"This is lunacy," Eriq said. "I don't believe it."

"We have the documents," Jules said.

"Then they are also forged," Eriq shouted.

Pierre remained calm. "I will go summon the *agent de justice* of the village to get his opinion."

Basile told Eriq and Waltier to stay at the warehouse while he accompanied Pierre. After they left, the Berger boys ran outside and Catherine turned her attention to Amelie, Grand-Mère, and the healer. Jules followed her.

The healer turned toward them and spoke softly. "Keep her warm and comfortable. Her heart is very weak."

"Would bloodletting help?" Catherine asked.

The woman shook her head.

"It seemed to when the physician did it."

"Sometimes it can cause an ill person to rally briefly, but there is no long-term benefit for her. That procedure does not strengthen the heart. I am sorry, but hers is beyond repair. Get her to a comfortable place as soon as you can."

Tears stung Catherine's eyes.

"Let us take her out to the wagon for now," Grand-Mère said.

Eriq bristled as they headed to the door, but Waltier overrode his objection. "Let them go."

Once all of them were outside and Amelie was in the back of the wagon covered with blankets, the *agent de justice*, Pierre, and Basile arrived.

The agent looked over the documents and then said to Eriq and Basile, "They appear legitimate to me, both the certificate of baptism and the sale of the business." He turned toward Jules. "But I cannot say for sure. Why will they not believe you?"

"They are after my holdings and have been for quite some time." Jules turned toward Eriq. "It seems the younger Monsieur Talbot has been scheming since a trip to Paris."

The agent scowled. "Do you two have any other evidence? Anything to substantiate your claims."

"Only our word," Jules said.

"*Non.*" Grand-Mère stepped forward. "We have Catherine's account."

Catherine clutched her satchel. "*Pardon?*"

"Your account...your journal. Did you not record Eriq's dealings in Paris, where he went and whom he spoke to? And our conversations with Suzanne and Anton? From the beginning, even when Suzanne invited us, I believe she was hoping Anton would benefit from our property."

"Did you write it all down?" the agent asked.

Catherine nodded.

"May I look?"

"Of course," she said, pulling the relevant papers out of the satchel and arranging them so the meeting with Suzanne was on the top. "It begins here and goes through yesterday when Eriq brought the youngest brother of le Duc de la Rochefauld to our house." She exhaled. "He proposed I marry him so our property would belong to him." She turned toward Jules. "Of course he had no idea my brother had already converted."

"Did you know?"

"*Non*," Catherine said. "Not until now."

The agent leaned against the wagon, skimmed through the pages, and then handed them back to Catherine. He turned to Basile. "I am in favor of these people, but my opinion carries no weight as far as the property in Lyon—or the mother and child. Take the documents back to Lyon and have them verified with the priest if you are suspicious. Consult with your captain too, and then come back."

"We need you to detain the suspects here while we are gone," Eriq said.

"*Non*," the agent replied. "I do not have the facilities. This is your problem. Leave one of your men to watch them." The agent turned to go, calling over his shoulder, "You have taken enough of my time."

Basile consulted with Eriq and then said, "We will take Estelle and the baby to Lyon."

"You cannot," Grand-Mère said. "I have a letter of protection."

Basile groaned. "Another forged document?"

Catherine pointed at Eriq. "He can verify this one. He was there, in Versailles, when it was written."

"I am afraid she is correct," Eriq said. "This one is legitimate. The baby stays with Baroness Gillet. And that means Estelle does too."

Basile groaned again. "Where do we lock up the others?"

Eriq turned to look at Jules. "This warehouse is identical to the one in Lyon, *oui*?"

Jules nodded.

"Then into the vault it is. Let's go."

Not bothering to reply, Jules paid the healer and then scooped up Amelie yet again and headed for the vault. Pastor Berger rounded up his family and shooed them into the warehouse as well.

"What about food and water?" Catherine asked.

"Estelle will help Waltier see to that," Basile said. "Eriq and I will be back in three days."

"Speak for yourself," Eriq said. "I am leaving for Paris with Anton. The arrangements have already been made." His eyes fell on Catherine. "Once this is all sorted out, and we discredit Jules and Pierre, Anton will have to decide what he wants to do next. And you will have to choose which life you prefer—a short one on the wheel or a longer one of style." He leaned closer. "Don't be a fool."

Catherine stepped away.

It was crowded and hot in the vault, a single lantern the only thing keeping them from complete darkness. Grand-Mère had Amelie's head in her lap, while Catherine knelt beside her cousin. Estelle, who could have been allowed to wait outside, insisted on staying with Amelie and Valentina. Pierre sat closest to the hatch.

The adults whispered quietly while the three little boys kicked each other. Pastor gently scolded them, reminding them how ill Amelie was. Catherine motioned for Jacob to come sit beside her, and he did.

"When can we get out of here?" Catherine whispered to Jules.

He scooted closer. "When we know for sure Basile and Eriq are both gone. There is a boat waiting for us at the river. Once the coast is clear, we will all go out through the hatch and make our way there."

It sounded like a good plan, but she saw one problem. "What of Waltier? If we disappear on his watch, he will be held responsible. But he has been kind to all of us. Surely we cannot repay him in this way."

"I agree, but we have no choice. Anyone who has no plan of converting needs to be on their way as soon as possible whether it gets him in trouble or not."

"*Pardonez-moi,*" Estelle whispered, scooting toward them, "but I couldn't help but overhear. Waltier wants to help no matter the cost. I already told him about the hatch door. He said he will come for us that way once the others are gone and it is safe."

Her throat full with emotion, all Catherine could do in response was give Estelle a big hug.

They agreed to wait for Waltier. In the meantime, once Estelle scooted away again, Jules reached for Catherine's hand in a rare gesture of affection.

"You know if I only had responsibility for myself, I would have left for Switzerland months ago. But I had to think of our employees, of Grand-Mère, of Amelie, of Valentina—of you."

Catherine nodded. She understood.

"So now I must ask if you have any plans to convert."

She swallowed hard. "*Non.* I have absolutely no conviction to do so."

"I thought that would be your answer." He sighed. "In that case, Catherine, you must leave."

"What about you, Jules? Will you stay here or go back to Lyon?"

"We will continue to go back and forth as we have been doing," he said, gesturing toward Pierre.

We? Catherine's stomach lurched. Once again, Pierre's loyalty was to Jules and not to her.

She grew silent after that, a sharp pain encircling her heart. From time to time she glanced at her betrothed. He did not meet her eyes but sat with his head down as if deep in thought.

An hour later, the hatch slid open and Waltier appeared. He said it was safe to come out, but to stay quiet and move carefully.

At Jules's direction, one by one they dropped down through the opening into the short tunnel below. Pierre handed Amelie through to Jules and then came out last, pulling the hatch closed behind him.

They made their way down to the river and climbed into the boat, which was barely big enough to hold them all. Pierre untied it and grabbed two long, sturdy sticks, tossing one to Jules.

"The river is a little deeper here," Jules said, pushing off from the bank. "And up to the mill too. The plan is to store the paper in the warehouse and then ship it out by wagon. The first load goes out on Monday, all the way to La Rochelle."

"Why so far?" Catherine asked.

"I have a buyer in England. It will go by ship from the harbor there."

Catherine pursed her lips as she began guessing at her brother's plan. How could she have doubted him? "Sounds like a good idea," she said, imagining herself hidden among crates of paper.

Then it dawned on her. The way he seemed to have everything under control, the newly established commerce routes that just happened to lead out of France, the special wagon with its hidden compartments...Her brother wasn't just going to smuggle her out of the country. He had *been* smuggling out other Huguenots as well all along—more than likely with Pierre's help.

They weren't traitors. They were heroes.

Swallowing hard, she couldn't help but remember Pierre's many entreaties to trust him. She should have listened. She would know better now.

Five minutes down the river, Jules and Pierre maneuvered the boat to a landing. Catherine knew what was up the trail—the childhood home of her mother. By the time they reached the door, Cook had it wide open, hugging each person as they passed through. "You don't know how much it pained me to leave without you," she said to Catherine, giving her a second hug.

"Is Monsieur Roen here too?"

She nodded. "We traveled through the night to make it. Jules and Pierre rode ahead on their horses holding lanterns to light the way."

Relief flooded through Catherine for the faithfulness of Cook and Monsieur Roen to all of them.

Grand-Mère and Catherine concentrated on laying out a pallet on the floor in the front room and then getting Amelie settled there. The rest congregated in the dining room and kitchen.

"Where is Valentina?" Amelie muttered.

"I will get her," Catherine said. Estelle was in the kitchen nursing the little one while Cook stoked the fire.

As Catherine waited for her to finish, she listened to Waltier and Jules talking. It sounded as if their plan was for Waltier to break from the dragoons and hide deeper in the Plateau.

"You can stay with a farmer I know," Jules told him. "You should be safe there."

Waltier gestured toward Estelle.

"Of course she is free to go, but I hope she will wait until the baby is weaned." Jules sighed. "We are indebted to you, Waltier. All of us are. I will do whatever I can to help you."

"*Merci*. But what about you? What happens when they come back?"

"What can I say? My conversion documents are genuine. There is nothing they *can* do."

"But Basile—"

"Basile is all talk, fueled by wine and his ego, but that is it. There is no way I would have let him claim my cousin's hand or allow that buffoon from Versailles have any right to my sister."

Waltier smiled.

Catherine took the baby from Estelle to burp. As she patted the little one's back, she turned to Waltier. "You have my gratitude too. You were a friend when we were children, and you have remained so."

He bowed his head toward her, and she stepped into the dining room with the baby. Pierre and Pastor Berger were deep in conversation. Madame Berger pushed up from the table. "I'll see what I can do to help Cook." Before she left, she told the boys they could go outside as long as they stayed between the house and the river.

When Catherine reached the front room, she paused and looked down at Amelie, so beautiful, so pale. So ethereal.

Blinking away tears, Catherine knelt and placed baby Valentina into the crook of her mother's arm. Amelie smiled slightly in response but that was all. She didn't open her eyes again or utter her daughter's name. Holding back a sob, Catherine knelt beside mother and child, smoothing the hair from her beloved cousin's feverish forehead. She watched as the baby wriggled for a moment before falling asleep. Catherine settled beside them, lying down and wrapping her arms around them both like a shield against a storm.

She stayed there for a long while. She stayed even when Valentina awoke and grew fussy and was taken away by Estelle. She stayed as Amelie's breathing ceased and her soul slipped off to heaven. She stayed even as Grand-Mère began sobbing at their loss.

Early the next morning, on the Sunday of the Solemnity of the Holy Trinity, Pierre and Jules dug a grave in the flower garden. The group gathered around as the men carried Amelie one last time and lowered her body into the ground. Grand-Mère and Estelle clung to each other in grief. Pastor Berger gave a short funeral sermon, praying for Valentina and all of them, asking God to direct their paths. Catherine cradled the infant in her arms, her heart aching but her mind clear. Amelie's legacy would live on, that much she knew.

In the end, love would be stronger than death.

CHAPTER TWENTY-SEVEN
Catherine

ook roasted a chicken and root vegetables for dinner, but Catherine had no appetite. Neither did Grand-Mère, who teared up several times during the meal. Dabbing at her eyes, she said, "It is Amelie, *oui*, but it is also the baby. If Basile does not bring the letter of protection back, I have no documentation to protect her." She turned toward Jules. "You will have to go back to the house and get the second copy."

He shook his head. "I can ask for it, but I doubt I will get it. I sold all of the household goods too."

Catherine shot him a look of frustration. He could have at least told her so she could have collected some of her things. Then she sighed. Perhaps he had entrusted Eriq with that bit of information as well. She addressed her grandmother. "I brought the second letter. It's in my satchel."

Grand-Mère's hand flew to her chest.

"We can use it to go to England. You, Valentina, and me."

Jules shook his head. "The baby is too young."

"I am her godmother," Catherine said.

"And I am her godfather, as well as her guardian," Jules countered.

"I will not agree to having her raised outside our faith," Catherine said. She could not bear the thought of leaving Amelie's baby behind.

"I am not going to England," Grand-Mère said. "This is far enough. My eyesight is too bad and, besides, I have no desire to leave my homeland. I would rather live in the wilderness than abandon my country. I will assist Jules in raising Valentina, using my letter of protection to ensure my safety and the little one's too."

Jules nodded. "I will still raise her in our faith in the privacy of our home. My conversion is as thin as the piece of paper it is written on. My heart has not changed."

"Am I to go to England alone then?" she whispered.

"Your only other option is to stay here," he said. "But to do that, you must convert. Are you sure you won't change your mind?"

Catherine was grateful that Jules was giving her a choice. Many guardians would not.

"*Non*," she said. She had no reason to stay except to be with her family. She could not bear the thought of leaving them, but in her heart she felt certain God had another plan for her.

"Do you want to go farther into the Plateau?"

She shook her head, tears filling her eyes.

"Then England is your best option," Jules said. "I have set aside some money for you, and I've made a contact in Dartmouth. There is already a community established there. It's not London, but it should afford some opportunities for you."

Catherine nodded. God would go with her.

"Monsieur Roen is driving the shipment of paper, leaving tomorrow," Jules said. "You can speak with merchants once you are in England and perhaps find more business opportunities for our family."

She nodded again, at first startled by his words but then deeply pleased. How far he had come in his opinion of her. She could only hope she would prove to be worthy of his expectations.

Taking in a deep breath, she breathed in the mountain air, finding her courage but also feeling suddenly very much alone.

Then Pierre cleared his throat and began to speak. "I would like to go to England too. With Catherine." He stood and turned toward her. "As your husband."

She lifted her face toward his blue eyes. "You would have to want me as your wife."

"That is all I have ever wanted."

Her heart stopped for a moment and then began to race. She had once loved Pierre. Did she love him still? "We need to talk. You and me, alone."

He stood. "Let's go down to the river." He took her hand and led her out the kitchen door, around the house, and down the trail, past the Berger boys throwing pine cones at one another under the trees.

Once they had reached the bank, he spread out his coat for her to sit on. Sunlight reflected off the water, and the breeze danced through the boughs of the pines overhead.

"You imagined us marrying," Pierre said. "Is that not correct? Before everything fell apart."

She nodded. "Since I was a girl."

"And then you did not."

"I didn't know what to think, Pierre. Everything felt so secretive. You weren't honest with me anymore."

"I know. I'm sorry."

"Is that the way it was for you too? You hoped we would marry someday and then you did not?"

He shook his head. "*Non.* I've always wanted us to marry, although lately I *feared* we would not."

She shifted away from him. "I need to know what happened, why you didn't trust me. Why you wouldn't tell me what you were doing." She needed an explanation. She couldn't marry him if there wasn't trust between them.

He reached for her hand. "We didn't want you at risk. Jules made up that story about you talking too much as an excuse."

"He was partly right," Catherine admitted.

"Well, sure," Pierre said with a small smile, "but our silence really was for your protection. I didn't want the dragoons suspecting you.

And if you didn't know what was going on, you wouldn't act in a suspicious manner." He leaned toward her. "You have always been so honest, Catherine, which is something I respect. It's one of the many things I love about you. I just didn't want it to harm you or those we were smuggling in and out of the warehouse."

"Eriq said you and Jules were turning people over to the dragoons, for money. I was afraid it was true." She thought of her horrible, lonely ride toward the Plateau, no longer knowing who her brother was. And not knowing who Pierre had become.

"We purposefully made it look that way. We hoped people would think that and start rumors. It kept the dragoons from suspecting us of sneaking our people out."

Catherine met his eyes. "Did you convert?"

"*Non.*" He exhaled. "I wasn't sure about it the way Jules was. He said it was his cross to bear."

"He carries it more like a crown," Catherine said.

"What do you mean?"

"He seems to have no regrets."

"*Oui,*" Pierre said. "I'm sure he does not. He methodically weighed his options and decided what was best."

"He plays by his own rules," Catherine said. He always had. She remembered refusing to play games with him as a child, protesting against *les règles de Jules.* "He is always right," she said.

"*Non,*" Pierre interjected. "He has his doubts, his fears. He takes his responsibility deeply. But he is logical. He doesn't move on emotions."

"Not like me."

"You and your brother are very different people. Do not try to understand him. Just know he has had your best interests in mind."

Catherine nodded. She knew that now.

Pierre leaned toward her. "I didn't feel good about deceiving you." He paused, his eyes growing brighter. "I couldn't talk to you because I had secrets from you. None of it felt right."

Catherine's heart swelled. She swallowed hard, anticipating her last question.

"Do you plan to convert?"

He shook his head. "Never. It's not my calling."

She nearly collapsed in relief. *Merci, Seigneur.* "What about your parents? Shouldn't you go to Switzerland?"

"We'll write to them and ask them to come to England instead. We'll start a business together there."

That was as it should be. "What about Eriq?"

He leaned back. "I will pray for Eriq, for his soul, because he truly has a heart of deception. And of greed." Pierre shrugged. "But he is my brother. I cannot help but wish him well. Anything else?"

She hesitated. "Eriq said you were smuggling contraband."

Pierre shook his head. "What a *caméléon.*"

"Were you?"

"*Oui.* Bibles. Lots and lots of them. You know the small ones, like you have?"

She nodded.

"Jules printed off hundreds of those over the last year. He is afraid no one will have access to Bibles, so he smuggled them out in the rag carts. And then women smuggled them farther in their buns, under their caps."

Catherine smiled. Jules hadn't made that up when he'd suggested it to her.

"They are all over the Plateau now, and making their way down into the south too."

Catherine sighed, saddened that she had ever considered Eriq's stories.

"Anything else?" Pierre whispered.

Catherine hesitated again but then smiled. "*Non.*"

He reached for her hand. "I have something I need to say. You were right to complain that I have tended to follow your brother too blindly, without always thinking for myself."

She nodded, biting her tongue to keep from speaking.

"But I've decided I will not do that anymore. I am my own man, and I have come to realize I can be a loyal friend and yet still disagree with him, standing firm on my own decisions and convictions."

He paused for a few moments, maybe expecting Catherine to say something, but for once she was speechless as her heart raced. But then she found her voice. "No, you haven't been the puppet I accused you of. You didn't convert. You adhered to your own convictions when it truly mattered."

Pierre smiled. "You were right. Jules followed his convictions, but until now I was simply following him." He took her other hand and met her eyes. "Will you forgive me for deceiving you about the other things?"

"*Oui*," Catherine said. "Of course I forgive you, Pierre. And I thank you for the work you have done on behalf of our people." She squeezed his hands. "But what of those who still need to be helped? Once you're out of France..."

"Then I will carry on that work from England, God willing. Jules and I have not been acting alone, Catherine. We are part of an entire network of sympathizers. I can be just as useful there as I have been here. Perhaps even more so."

She gazed at him, seeing for the first time in a long while the man he truly was.

Looking deeply into her eyes, he whispered, "Will you marry me, *mon coeur*?"

She met his eyes. "*Oui*. I want nothing more."

She respected him. Once again, she trusted him. She loved him. He was the man she wanted to marry. There was no one else she could imagine building a new life with.

That Sunday afternoon Grand-Mère pulled Catherine aside and took her upstairs to a small room. "I found this dress," she said. "It's much nicer than your purple-and-gold gown, *oui*?"

It was gray with a white collar. Catherine picked it up and held it to her chest. It looked to be a nearly perfect fit. They would need to take in the waist some, but that was all.

Grand-Mère took her hand. "This is a day full of sadness but also full of joy. Amelie would want you to be happy. She would be thrilled you are marrying Pierre. That is what she wanted. That is what I wanted too."

"I know."

"Life goes on," Grand-Mère said. "Valentina is proof of that. So is your marriage to Pierre. Despite the tragedies, *Dieu est bon*."

"*Oui*," God was good. He'd been faithful even as she had doubted. He had cared for her even though she had been foolish.

Next, Catherine, Jules, and Pierre worked out the marriage contract. It was simple. The dowry her father set aside for her would be sent by Jules from Lyon once Catherine and Pierre were settled, and Catherine would work with Pierre and his parents to establish a business, most likely a print shop. The couple would honor God and each other, striving to glorify the Lord in all things.

Catherine wrote it out, and then she and Pierre both signed it. As her guardian, Jules did too.

"I don't have a ring for you," Pierre said regretfully.

Catherine touched the cross around her neck. "It's all right. This is all I need."

Before the sun set, Pastor Berger married Pierre and Catherine along the river. She wore the gray dress, a white lace head covering, and the silver Huguenot cross around her neck.

Pastor Berger read a passage from Isaiah. *The wilderness and the solitary place shall be glad for them; and the desert shall rejoice, and blossom as the rose.* The Plateau was often referred to as the wilderness, the desert where the persecuted fled, where they were exiled. With her family here, it did not feel like a wilderness to Catherine, not anymore. It felt like a place of safety. For a moment she wondered if she and Pierre should stay, but she knew in her heart it was not where God was leading them.

Versailles, in all its opulence, felt far more like a desert than the Plateau. Dry. Unsustainable. Full of facades. A place of danger.

As Pierre repeated his vows, she held his hand. They would be refugees and strangers in a new land.

"Do you, Catherine…"

For all those years she had thought she would marry Pierre. And then she did not. And now she was.

"…take Pierre Talbot?" the pastor asked.

"*Oui*," she answered. It *was* what she wanted. In that moment she felt the starry-eyed wonder of her youth again.

"Do you have a ring?" the pastor asked.

Catherine shook her head, wishing they had asked him to take the question out.

"I do," Pierre said, taking something from his pocket. He held it in his fingers until he slipped it on her finger.

It was her grandmother's ring, the one with the ruby her grandfather had given his wife all those years ago. Catherine turned toward her.

"It would have been yours anyway someday," Grand-Mère said. "It's better coming to you now from Pierre."

"*Merci*," Catherine said, looking at her grandmother and then her husband.

"You may kiss your bride," Pastor said.

It was a gentle kiss, sweet and tender with a hint of the passion that was yet to come.

After the service, Catherine wrote out the marriage certificate under Pastor Berger's direction and they all signed it. When it was done, he said that he and his family would not be going to England with Pierre and Catherine after all. "We would rather go farther into the Plateau," he explained. "I think that will be a life better suited for our boys."

Jules said he would send them with Waltier the next day. "I have arranged for a wagon full of hay to be taken to a farmer I know just beyond the village of Portes. He's expecting it."

Madame Berger had a smile on her face.

"Dress accordingly," Jules suggested.

"Oh, I will," she answered. "Wrapped in a blanket. And praying I don't sneeze."

The others drifted into the front room of the house while Pierre and

Catherine stayed at the table, their marriage certificate and a bottle of wine between them.

"Do we need to talk more?" He reached for a lock of her hair that had escaped from her lace head covering and then leaned toward her.

"*Non*," she said, smiling at him. "Maybe."

"About?"

"I don't know."

He took her hand again, but this time led her up the staircase. Instead of going down the hallway, he stopped on the top step and pulled her down beside him, putting his arm around her and pulling her head to his shoulder.

Tears filled her eyes. "I'm sorry for doubting you," she whispered. She had been tricked by Eriq's bravado and by his deceit. And it had made her doubt the person she had loved most in all the world.

"Don't be sorry. It couldn't be helped."

"But I am. And I am sad for all it has taken from us."

He put a finger under her chin, lifting her head. "Things will be better than they were before. We'll be together with no secrets between us. We have survived adversity. We have changed, but it has made us stronger and better prepared for what is ahead."

He no longer smelled of paper and ink, but of smoke and wine, mixed with the mountain air. She relaxed against him for a moment, taking in his warmth and his wisdom. He was right. They had both changed. Her heart surged as she turned her face up to his. He drew her into an embrace as they kissed, his hand on the nape of her neck. When he released her, she stood, pulling him up to the landing and then toward the bedroom.

Before dawn the next morning, Catherine lit the candle at the desk and wrote a bit more in her journal while Pierre—her gentle, generous, passionate Pierre—slept in their marriage bed behind her. After she recorded the details of her wedding and hopes for their future, she stacked the pages in order and tucked them safely into her satchel.

Grand-Mère would not be able to read this record of her life until now and her private thoughts about all they had gone through recently, but someday Valentina would. Catherine knew what it was like to lose a mother. She hoped Amelie's daughter would find a measure of comfort in this glimpse of her own mother and an understanding of what led her family to Le Chambon-sur-Lignon.

At dawn, on the eighteenth of June—the Eleventh Monday of Ordinary Time—Catherine told Cook and Estelle goodbye. Then Grand-Mère and Valentina. Finally, she turned to her brother.

As she reached to kiss him, he interrupted her by thrusting a pamphlet into her hand. Puzzled, she examined it. It was one she had seen in the print shop on Thursday of Holy Week, titled *A Collection of Verse for the Encouragement of Young Men and Women.*

"This awful thing?" she said, flipping through the pages. "Why are you giving it to me?"

"*Excusez-moi?*" Jules replied, feigning deep offense. "Pierre and I worked very hard on that."

Her brow furrowed. "What? The two of you made this? Why?"

Pierre explained. "It's one of the ways we have helped guide our people to freedom. What looks like an ordinary pamphlet actually contains information about how to make it safely out of France—including various routes, safe houses, and secret allies along the way."

Stunned, Catherine flipped through the pages but saw nothing of what he described. It was merely a collection of drawings and poems. "Where?" she demanded. "How?"

Taking it from her, Pierre turned to the page featuring the poorly rendered sketch of the horse. "For example," he said, "if you look closely, you'll see a map hidden in the animal's flank."

She stared at the drawing for a moment and then gasped. "This line here, this is the escape route?"

"*Oui*, one of them," Jules replied. "And here, where the poem refers to 'Galloping in the noble meadows by moonlight before coming to rest in a grand place that fits like a glove'? What that says is that it's safe to move quickly through the rural areas outside Grenoble as long as you travel at night. Your goal should be to find a Monsieur Grand at the glove factory, where you will be given food and safe shelter for a day."

"Really?"

"Trust me, the information is all there in the words if you know what to look for. 'Noble' means 'Grenoble.' 'By moonlight' means 'only at night.' Those who have been given the pamphlet have been instructed what to look for."

"And this works?"

Both men nodded.

"Just last week, for example, I got a letter from one of the families we recently helped with it," Jules said. "It was a drawing by one of their children—a picture of a house with a yard and a stable and a rope swing—and at the top, they had written, '*Bonjour* from Bern. *Merci beaucoup.*'"

Catherine shook her head, truly amazed. As a work of art or poetry, it left much to be desired, but as a hidden key showing the way to deliverance, it was a work of genius.

"*Merci beaucoup* from me too," she said, clutching the pamphlet to her chest. "I will treasure this."

Pierre put an arm around around her. "I'm so sorry, *chérie*, but once we reach England we will have no choice but to burn it. Because it can incriminate sympathizers and get them thrown in jail, we have had to guard it carefully and insist that it always be destroyed the moment those who have been using it reach safe haven."

"Actually," Jules corrected, "I think we should let this one copy survive. We should preserve it for the future so generations can better know how their forbearers managed to escape. Always keep it safely hidden, but eventually give it to your children, for their children."

Pierre nodded in understanding and Catherine reached, again, to kiss her brother's cheeks. This time he cooperated.

As he pulled away, he winked at Pierre and said, "Besides, this particular one is special. It has a coded message to my sister inside."

Then Jules looked to her, and for the briefest of moments a smile flickered in his eyes, the old smile she knew when they were young and he had not shut her out of his heart.

Astounded, she thought of their code-breaking game from when she was a child. She looked again inside the pages, this time spotting the familiar circles. One last message from her brother. She would decode it tonight, once she and Pierre safely reached their first stop.

She looked around at the faces of family once more, committing the moment to memory. The time had come to be packed into the wagon among crates of paper with her beloved Pierre—her husband!—and be driven by Monsieur Roen on the overland journey to Rochelle, where they would then board the ship for England and their new life together.

Wherever God may lead them, she knew they were safe within His hands.

CHAPTER TWENTY-EIGHT

Renee

On Monday morning, the morning after our big discovery in the Dark Woods, my cousins and I got ready for the day and then went to the main house to talk to Nana together. We were feeling nervous but also excited—not to mention more than a little defiant. We had no idea how she would react, but now that the four of us had been vindicated, we didn't really care that much.

Or at least that's what we told ourselves.

We had three surprises for our grandmother. First, that Nicole was here; second, that we'd gone out to the cabin late last night and done some testing; and third, that said testing had essentially proven the validity of the claims we'd been making for nineteen years. And though we knew she'd be thrilled by the first bit of news, the second would likely make her peeved for having been kept in the dark, and the third…well, we weren't sure how she was going to react.

On the one hand, she would probably be glad to know that her four granddaughters weren't raving lunatics. On the other hand, she would surely feel terrible for not having believed us back then. Complicating matters was the fact that this finding now opened up a huge can of worms that she would be stuck dealing with more than anyone because of her home's proximity to the murder scene. I'd already heard from the detective, who was coming over soon for a visit that would officially kick off the investigation.

There was nothing like dumping a mess on your grandmother's lap and then leaving town.

We found her in the solarium, sitting at her little rattan writing desk, no doubt penning thank-you notes and other follow-up correspondence from the big weekend. The four of us entered the room together, but she was so absorbed in what she was writing that she didn't pay much attention at first.

"Good morning, girls," she said, her eyes still on the page in front of her. "There's fresh fruit and muffins in the kitchen if you haven't had breakfast yet. The staff's off today, but I think we can manage on our own, don't you?"

Stifling smiles at her obliviousness, we looked to Nicole, who quipped, "Hey, Nana. Sorry I'm late."

Our grandmother's head whipped around, and the look on her face was one of confusion followed by pure joy. "Nicole!" she cried, rising and moving toward her youngest granddaughter. If she was startled by the girl's bleached locks and gaunt appearance, she didn't show it. She simply took her into her arms for a long hug.

Of course, once their greeting was complete, the questions began— "How did you get here?" "When did you arrive?" "Didn't you realize the reunion ended yesterday afternoon?"—and so on. I jumped in lest Nicole have to break the big news herself. I suggested we all sit because we had something we needed to explain. Soon we were settled, with Nana in one side chair, me in the other, and my three cousins side by side on the couch.

I began our tale, laying out the situation as succinctly as I could and explaining how Blake and I had been talking on Saturday about the science of chemiluminescence and how it can be used to prove the existence of blood stains, even really old, cleaned-up, long-gone bloodstains. From the stricken look on Nana's face, I could tell she realized where I was going almost immediately. She didn't speak, however, so

I pressed on, telling her the whole story, ending with our trip to the police station last night.

"We didn't say anything to you ahead of time," I added, "because there was a chance the test might not work, and we just couldn't risk a repeat of nineteen years ago, if you know what I mean. I'm sorry, but that's how we felt about it." With that, I clasped my hands together in my lap and looked over at her, waiting for a response.

She didn't give us much. In classic Nana fashion, she took a long moment to process the news and then seemed to draw up inside of herself, her posture growing erect, her diction precise.

"This is all very interesting, though I do wish you girls had come to me first before going to the police."

"We were too excited to wait," I replied.

"What difference would it have made?" Nicole asked.

Nana looked at her, flustered for a moment. "I...well, I suppose I'm just feeling a bit blindsided, is all. Did you say a detective is coming here? Today?"

We all nodded.

"Very well. If you girls will excuse me, I have a phone call to make."

"Wait, what?" I said.

Nana sighed. "I need to contact my lawyer to discuss the situation. I'm just being prudent. It did happen practically in our laps, you know." With that, she rose and left the room.

Eyes wide, we all gaped as she went, stung by her utter lack of remorse or sensitivity. Where was the apology for not having believed us all those years ago? Where was the shock and joy over our new discovery? Where was the hope that this nineteen-year-old mystery could finally be solved and laid to rest?

"If I didn't know better," Danielle said softly, "I'd think...well..." She shook her head.

"You'd think what, that there's something she's not saying?" Nicole replied. "Me too."

"Sure does feel that way," Maddee agreed. "It's almost as if she knew already. She wasn't the least surprised."

"At least not about the results of last night's testing," I agreed. "She seemed a lot more startled at the thought of a detective coming over. What's up with that?"

Our eyes met, but none of us had a clue.

Nana made the call from her bedroom upstairs, so while we waited for whichever came first—her return or the detective's arrival—we headed for the kitchen to avail ourselves of some breakfast. We'd just about finished our muffins and fruit when the doorbell rang.

"I'll get it," I said, wiping my mouth with a napkin and heading for the entrance hall as my cousins quickly cleaned up our mess and then followed.

The detective was younger than I expected, a woman in her mid-thirties with black hair, dark eyes, and a pleasant-looking face. She introduced herself as Detective Ortiz, and despite her age, over the next hour I came to realize that her calm demeanor and laser focus seemed to suit her perfectly to the job.

We spoke in the living room, my cousins and I answering her questions by repeating pretty much everything we'd told the police last night. She took a lot of notes and seemed to have a good grasp of the situation, and I was eager for her to finish her part of things so we could ask our own questions in return, namely, what the next steps in the investigation would be and how long it would take to get DNA results on the blood.

Once we finally reached that point, Detective Ortiz responded by laying out the general plan, saying that they would start this afternoon by bringing in a forensics team to do a thorough examination of the cabin and the surrounding woods, though after all these years they likely wouldn't find much evidence other than the blood our test had revealed last night. As for that, she said, they would run a few more tests of their own to verify our findings and to get a better look at the spatter patterns. They would also attempt to recover enough residue for DNA testing if possible. "But even if we can't get DNA," she added, "there are other ways to go about ascertaining the identity of the victim."

"Wait," Maddee said, "what do you mean if you can't get DNA? If there's blood, doesn't that mean there will be DNA?"

The detective shrugged. "There has to be enough for testing, which may not be the case in this situation. Trust me, if it's there, we'll find it, even if that means dismantling pieces of the cabin's walls and floorboards and bringing them into the lab. But it's not a guarantee by any means."

Maddee nodded, her expression dejected.

"Remember," the detective added, looking to all of us, "there are a lot of variables here. We are talking about nineteen years of exposure in an uninsulated, untended cabin." She counted off on her fingers. "Extremes of temperature, potential contamination by animals and other people, dilution through flooding, absorption rates of the structural materials, and so on. On the other hand..." Her voice trailed off as she flipped through the file folder at her side and finally pulled out an enlargement of what I recognized as one of Blake's photos from last night. "Tell me more about these shoe prints," she said, setting the picture down on the coffee table. "These were made by one of you?"

Nicole held up a hand, as if she were in a classroom. "Me. Though they were boots, not shoes. I stepped in one of the puddles of blood that day and then ran off, apparently leaving those footprints behind, even if they were wiped away by the time the cops got there."

Detective Ortiz nodded. "And the boots themselves? I don't suppose you still have them? Because there's always a chance some residue could be up inside the treads."

Nicole looked crestfallen. "No. I was so traumatized I made my mom throw them away. I used to love wearing those boots, before. But after, no way. I never even wanted to see them again."

The detective nodded, making a note, and we all grew silent until Danielle spoke.

"I do have my drawings," she said softly. "I know it's not as good as DNA, but maybe you could use them the way you would a police sketch."

"Drawings?"

Danielle nodded. "Of the old man. The cabin. The blood. The knife. I have dozens. Guess I sort of worked through the trauma by drawing pictures of what I'd seen. Eventually my mother made me stop, but I still kept making them. I just didn't let her see them."

"How old were you then?" the detective asked skeptically. "Just nine, right?"

"Yes," I interjected, "but Danielle was a real prodigy. Trust me, at that point she was better than some artists twice her age." I remembered the sketches she'd made that first night and how realistic they were, how disturbing.

"I see. And you still have these?"

"Sure do. I'll have to dig them out, but I know I have them. They're with a bunch of my old papers."

That thought gave us all hope. Maybe even if police couldn't produce enough DNA samples for testing, they would be able to track down the victim's identity using the old drawings instead. Surely someone somewhere might recognize the man's face—or perhaps police could even run an image or two through their computer using some sort of facial recognition software.

Either way, I felt sure that learning the victim's identity was the best next step in answering the many questions that surrounded the Incident—which sounded like an important element of the detective's plan as well.

As for Nana's odd reaction, she seemed much more herself when she came back down the stairs. Joining us in the living room, she settled into her usual chair and answered the detective's remaining questions with grace and honesty. I couldn't imagine what all that had been about before, but it bothered me enough that it was the first thing I asked once we were done and the detective was finally on her way.

"Not that it's any of your business," Nana replied, looking first to me and then to my three cousins, "but I needed to make sure I was legally protected. You girls may not realize this, but that land next door is part of this estate. If indeed a man was murdered there, I feared that I could be liable in some way because I'm the property owner. That's all."

My cousins seemed to accept her answer, but it only served to confuse me more. The Dark Woods were a part of this estate? Owned by my own grandparents? Why hadn't I known this? More importantly, when I called Granddad four years ago and asked him for the owner's name so I could get permission to have someone investigate there, why hadn't he said as much then? Instead, he'd just become quite upset and told me to let it go.

Had he really been more concerned about some liability issue than his own granddaughter's emotional well-being?

I couldn't imagine such a thing, but now that he was gone, I couldn't exactly ask him about it. All I could do was give him the benefit of the doubt and assume he hadn't been avoiding the question so much as reacting to the notion that I wanted to dig up this matter from the past.

For now, I needed to turn my attention to farewells. It was time for all three cousins to hit the road, and though I was sorry to see them go, I knew this was a different goodbye than ever before. So much had changed in the course of a single night. Even if we did have more questions than answers, at least this first hurdle had been cleared. What we'd always known to be true was now proven at last.

They told Nana goodbye inside the house, and then I walked them to their cars. As we went, I put an arm around Nicole and gave her thin shoulders a squeeze.

"One question," I said softly. "Otherwise, I promise I won't bug you."

"What?" she huffed, though I could see she was smiling.

"Why did you skip the reunion this year? Are you doing okay?"

"That's two questions. But yes, I'm fine. I promise."

She sounded so young, more like a belligerent teenager than a woman of twenty-five. I held my tongue, waiting for her to fill the silence that followed with an answer to my other question.

"I just couldn't..." she said finally, blinking away sudden tears. "This was the first one without Granddad, you know? I couldn't stand the thought of it, all those people laughing and playing games and having fun, like life went on as usual. It was just too much. I figured it'd be easier to stay away for this one. I'll come next year, I promise."

"Good. 'Cause it wasn't the same without you." With a smile, I added, "Not to mention you missed a killer solo by Aunt Cissy."

Then the four of us drew together for a group hug, and we were laughing and crying all at the same time. I promised to keep them posted on any new developments that might happen while I was still here, but otherwise we'd have to depend on someone local—whether Nana or Blake or maybe even Detective Ortiz—for our updates.

Of course, I should have known better than to bring up Blake, because instantly the topic turned to the question of him and me, starting with whether or not he had kissed me last night in the car. I could feel my cheeks burning as I tried to deflect their interest.

"It wasn't the right time or place," I admitted at last. "But we're going on our first date in a couple of hours, soooooo...we'll see."

That earned catcalls and whistles as the group dispersed. I hugged each cousin in turn, starting with Nicole and then Maddee and then finally Danielle. I'd miss her most of all.

Their two cars headed out and I was left standing alone. Turning, I looked up at my grandmother's big, beautiful home and then walked alongside the garage so I could see beyond it to the wide, expansive lawn behind. Detective Ortiz had told Nana that police would be using the footbridge as their access point to the Dark Woods, and I was pleased now to see that several cars were already parked down on the grass next to the tennis court. I felt sure Nana wouldn't be too happy about them driving across her lawn, but I wasn't going to be the one to tell her.

I continued to the guesthouse, intending to go online and see if any work-related issues had popped up in my absence. I also wanted to do some research about code breaking so that I would be ready when Blake and I heard back from the Smithsonian.

First, however, now that I was the only one left, I took a few minutes to straighten the kitchen, bathroom, and the Cousins' Room. I also started a small load of laundry to get me through my unplanned days here and so that I'd have something cute to wear tonight. For my date, I planned to dress *my* way, not Nana's, which meant I'd be in jeans for the first time since last Wednesday. Hallelujah.

The next few hours passed uneventfully. I was wrapping up things online and about to start getting ready for my big evening when I heard from Dr. Underwood. He was calling to say that the folks from the Smithsonian had already finished finding all of the circles throughout the text, phase one of what they had dubbed "Project Pamphlet."

"Phase two, decoding the letters, hasn't started yet," he added, "but they went ahead and sent me the list for now."

I gasped. "And?"

"And I'm forwarding it to you as we speak. I'd love to take a crack at decoding the thing myself, but I'm tied up tonight with a function. If you have a chance to play around with it and manage to make any progress, do let me know."

The email came through as we were ending our call. Holding my breath, I opened it up, took a look, and nearly fell over at the size of the list. I'd expected to see about twenty letters, maybe fifty at the most, but this was far more than that, at least five or six hundred. All this time, hundreds of circles had been inside that pamphlet, just sitting there faded from view, waiting to be discovered. Amazing.

I couldn't wait to tell Blake. And though it would have been more fun to spring this on him in person, I knew it would be smarter to call him now. If we wanted to do any decoding, we'd need a hard copy of the list, and that would require a printer, something I didn't have.

He answered on the first ring, and I jumped right in, giving him the news. He sounded equally thrilled, readily agreeing to bring a printed copy tonight. He gave me his email address so I could forward the document to him ASAP. I quickly typed it in and hit "Send."

"You have to promise you won't try any decoding on your own first. No cheating. Just download it, print it out, and bring it tonight so we can do it together."

"Renee," he replied, sounding genuinely hurt. "I wouldn't do that. The whole point is to decode it *with you.*"

I smiled, pleased that he, too, wanted this to be something we shared.

"It just came through," he added. Then he opened it and read aloud the note at the top of the page from the Smithsonian. "'Update day one, Pamphlet Project. Finished identifying all circled letters. Full list below. Have forwarded along to NCM for decoding. Will keep you posted.' Huh. What's NCM?"

"The National Cryptology Museum. I think they're affiliated with the NSA."

"The NSA?" He sounded incredulous. "To crack a code that was originally created for a nine-year-old girl?"

I chuckled. "Well, remember, it's in seventeenth-century French—and it's really long."

"Let me see..." His voice trailed off as he scrolled down to view the entire list. "Nah, piece of cake."

I laughed. "Yeah right."

"I'm serious. You just wait, Renee. A little thinking, a little tinkering, and the two of us will crack this baby wide open."

Blake hadn't told me where we were going on our big date. He'd just said to dress casually and comfortably, to wear sneakers, and to bring bug spray. I couldn't imagine what he had in mind, but as long as we could carve out some time to work on decoding the secret message, I was happy to leave the rest to him.

As it turned out, where it took us at first was about ten miles up Huguenot Trail to a small park on the James River. Though the place was picturesque, it didn't seem like anything special. Still, the trees were lush and the water was sparkling in the afternoon sun and there was a picnic table nearby in the shade of an old oak tree. Between that and the insulated tote bags Blake pulled from the backseat, I assumed we were here for a picnic. But when we reached the table he kept going, all the way down to the water, where a man was standing on the bank holding on to a rope connected to a small boat floating nearby. As we got closer, the man turned, and I realized he was Ingles. Looking nothing at all like the uniformed guard from Friday, he was now dressed in the cutoff jean shorts and old gray T-shirt of a weekend fisherman. Completing the ensemble was a hunter-green life jacket, which he began to unbuckle and remove as soon as he saw us.

I had no idea what was going on here, but once we reached him, I was surprised to see Blake trade the keys to his Durango for the rope to the boat.

Then, turning to me, he asked if he might interest me in a little trip down the James River.

I was startled but also quite pleased, and I answered his question with a nod and a smile. I loved boating—though my usual jaunts on the water tended more toward sailing on Lake Washington than john-boating on the James.

"Do we have time, though?" I asked, glancing toward the sky. It was almost five thirty, which meant there were only a few hours of daylight left.

"Sure do," Blake said, stepping toward the boat, setting the totes inside, and pulling out a pair of matching green life jackets, the smaller of which he handed to me. "We're only going a little past Robius Landing. Dinner for two on the deck at River Mill restaurant sound okay to you?"

"Sounds wonderful."

"Great." Turning to Ingles, he added, "I'll text you when we're close, and you can meet us there to trade back."

"All righty. See you folks later," the older man replied. He tossed his life vest into the back and walked away.

"Should we invite him to join us?" I whispered. "I feel rude."

Blake smiled, explaining that it was a trade-off. In return for Ingles's help tonight, he was going to borrow the boat for the entire weekend.

"Gotcha."

"Besides, I figure we can do our decoding over dinner."

I smiled. A boat ride along the James River with a handsome and interesting man, followed by decoding and dinner? Sounded like a dream date to me.

As I buckled the vest and tightened the straps, I took a good look at our vessel, which was an eleven- or twelve-foot gray metal craft with a double bench seat and a small trolling motor mounted on the back. This part of the James River could get pretty shallow in places, but I knew that with our flat bottom we could easily glide on through.

Blake took my hand and helped me aboard before settling in beside me as we floated toward the middle of the broad waterway. The afternoon sun was hot, but as soon as he started up the motor and we began chugging forward, the breeze picked right up, lifting the hair from my forehead and fluttering at the fabric of my blouse.

Somehow, I realized suddenly, this was exactly what I'd needed. After all the hard work of the reunion and the emotional upheaval of the blood testing, the simple joy of a boat ride along a scenic river next to a handsome man on a lovely afternoon was just what the doctor ordered. Giving in to the experience, I allowed myself to be in the moment, to take in my surroundings, and to let my heart soar like the great blue heron that sailed alongside us in the sky.

After about fifteen minutes, as we rounded a bend and the waterway stretched out straight in front of us, he slowed down and then cut the engine. We drifted in silence for a while, Blake occasionally correcting our course with a paddle he'd pulled from under the gunwale. I did the same on my side. Otherwise, the current was our only propellant.

And it was sublime.

"So how exactly did you know this would be the perfect choice for our first date?" I asked, shifting in my seat to fix my eyes on the man beside me.

He shrugged, suddenly shy. "Best cure I know for when life gets crazy. Couple hours in a boat can bring a person back to himself—or herself, as the case may be."

I sighed, tilting my head to look up at the blue, blue sky. "Crazy is an understatement," I said. "Between the pamphlet and the reunion and the luminol and the detective—"

"And the new man in your life," he added, smiling.

"And the new man in my life," I repeated. Then I turned to meet his gaze, my own smile fading. "What are we doing, Blake?" I asked softly. "I live in Seattle. You live in Virginia. I'm only here for a few more days and then we'll be three thousand miles apart. What's the point?"

"Ah, that," he said, busying himself with the paddle to avoid a stump up ahead.

"Yes, that," I replied. "Aren't we being a little unrealistic?"

He was quiet for a moment before speaking. "For starters, Renee, I'm not exactly married to Virginia."

"What do you mean?"

He shrugged. "I love it here, but I've lived a lot of places that I loved. I'm always open to change."

Even as he said it, I realized there was much I didn't know about him. Where had he lived before this? We'd been so focused on me—my pamphlet, my weekend, my ancestors, my relatives, my crisis, my dead body in the cabin—that I hadn't ever taken the time to focus on him instead.

I apologized for my self-centeredness and then said it was time for him to start talking. "Tell me everything about you, Blake. Go ahead. Pretend we just met the other day."

He chuckled. "We did just meet the other day," he replied, and then we both laughed.

"Sure doesn't seem like it."

His eyes met mine. "You can say that again."

For a moment, I thought he might kiss me. But then we realized we'd drifted too far to the left, and the spell was broken as I grabbed the paddle and worked us back out to the middle. The moment having passed, I repeated my request.

"Only if we eat while I talk," he replied, reaching for the tote bag and pulling out its contents, producing a delightful array of before-dinner snacks and a thermos of sweet tea.

As our little johnboat drifted along with the current and I nibbled on fresh strawberries, I listened to the facts of Blake Keller's life. How his father's job as a special envoy to the United Nations had given Blake a childhood lived in numerous exotic locations—all of which had been temporary. How he continued the pattern himself once he graduated from NYU and went to work for Eagleton Trust, advancing through the ranks but repeatedly refusing the biggest promotion because it would keep him in one place rather than allow him to travel on special assignments as he did now.

He went on to say how lately he'd begun to realize that he was tired of all that shifting around, that maybe the life his parents had handed him wasn't the one he wanted for himself now that he was an adult.

"My company has a branch in Seattle, actually," he added, causing my pulse to surge. "You never know. I could end up taking that promotion and talk them into basing me out of there. Under Eagleton's tuition reimbursement program, I've also been planning to go to UVA law school, but I could do the University of Washington instead."

I gaped at him, astounded that he would even consider such radical changes to his life for a woman he'd known less than a week. Then again, he seemed to understand, as I did, that this might not turn out to be an ordinary relationship.

"Maybe the first step would be for you to plan a trip out there to see what you think," I said evenly, not wanting to get my hopes up.

"Already working on that," he replied with a grin. "How's two weeks from Friday? There's a conference in Tacoma my boss has been wanting me to attend. Maybe I could add on a few extra days after and shift myself up to a hotel in Seattle. Get a peek at your world."

I gazed into his deep green eyes. "In other words, you're willing to do what you can to give this a shot."

"To give *us* a shot," he replied softly with a nod.

That's when he kissed me at last, moving his lips to mine ever so slowly, pausing partway to gently cup my cheek in his hand. When our mouths finally met, we were tentative at first and then quickly grew more passionate. As he slid both arms around me and pulled me even closer, we kissed hungrily, as if we couldn't get enough, could never get enough. My hands pressed to his rock-like chest, my heart pounded with a fierce rhythm, and all I could think was, *I have found you at last.*

When it was over, we sat back against our seats, our fingers entwined. The current continued to carry us slowly along, but inside my heart was coursing through rapids—and I was ready for whatever lay ahead.

"So what do you think of the scenery through here?" Blake asked suddenly, gesturing toward the overgrown bank on our right.

"Beautiful. Lush. Verdant. Just like the rest of the river."

He nodded. "Good. Because that's the Dark Woods."

"What?"

"Beginning right about there at that dead tree and running all the way to the bend. That's one reason I wanted to bring you out here, to give you some perspective."

"How incredibly sweet," I replied, squeezing his hand, "but to be honest, all of that changed last night the moment the luminol began to glow."

"Oh, I'm sure it did. But I thought you should see the place from here too, to understand that these woods are neither foe nor friend. They're just another stretch along the river."

After gazing at the dense foliage for a long moment, I settled into the curve of his arm, realizing he was right. This place that had loomed so large in my mind for so long was simply one more scenic element in a region filled with beauty. That was all.

We drifted on past, and once we'd made the curve it was my turn to point something out to him. Gesturing toward the left, I told him I was pretty sure we were looking at the original land grant where sixteen-year-old Emanuel Talbot first got his start in Virginia more than three hundred years before. Of course, the acquisition of his own property on the opposite side of the river, the eventual building of the paper mill, and then the family printing business came later. But this was where it all began.

"Wow, that's really something," Blake said, scanning the wooded shore. Then he turned to me, eyes sparkling. "I don't know about you, Renee, but I don't want to wait till dinner. You feel like decoding right now?"

I laughed, gesturing at our surroundings. "Sure, though it might be kind of hard to concentrate. I don't want to crash into a downed log or something."

"No problem. I got this." He turned on the motor and brought us downriver a short ways, around a bend and then over to the left bank, where we puttered to a stop at an abandoned dock. Most of the horizontal slats were gone, but the vertical posts remained, and that's all we needed. He tied the boat to one of those and then settled in beside me, our little vessel held fast as the water lapped gently at the hull and the breeze kept us cool.

As Blake dug in his bag for the printout, I told him how I'd done some research on breaking simple codes. I began rattling off some of what I'd learned online this afternoon, describing grid ciphers, the Cesar shift, and polyalphabetics. But then he interrupted me to make one very good point.

"Remember what the journal said? Jules designed the code to help Catherine with her counting, handwriting, spelling, and reading. To decipher it, she had to count off and cross out certain letters. That's not a substitution cipher. That's an elimination cipher."

"Elimination?"

"Yeah." He finally produced from the bag a pencil for each of us and not one copy of the list but an entire stack of duplicate copies. "Here's how I see it. The reason there are so many letters is because we're going to be crossing most of them out, until all that remains are the letters that make up the words. Like this."

Across the margin on the top page, he wrote R W E O N P E M E L.

"Now, assume this is an elimination cipher, and your instructions are to delete every other letter. What does that leave you with?"

I did as he said, reaching out with my pencil and crossing off the W, O, P, M, and L.

"Oh." I laughed. "It says 'RENEE.'"

"Exactly. That's what we're dealing with here. Except that it won't be as simple as every other letter. The pattern will be more complicated than that, like count five and cross out one, then count three and cross out one, then count one and cross out one, and so on. Or it could require multiple passes, like go through and cross out every tenth letter, then go through the remaining letters and cross out every fourth. Like that."

I sat back, exhausted at the very thought.

"How can you say this will be a piece of cake? Do you know how many potential patterns there are for counting off and crossing out? Good grief, Blake. This could take forever."

He smiled, clearly enjoying the moment. "First of all, you don't have to try out patterns on the entire thing. You just do the first line or two, enough for a potential word to stand out. Once you have that, then you can try feeding it through the rest to see if works."

I shook my head. "But I wouldn't even know where to start."

"Well, think about what you learned online. What's one of the first things to look for when decoding?"

I thought for a moment. "You determine *e*. That is the most frequently used letter, so you look for whatever seems to be popping up the most and assume that particular letter probably stands for *e*. But that's with substitution ciphers."

"True, though the same principle can apply here. Try to find counting patterns that allow most of the *e*'s to stay. Of course, that's for English. I'm not sure about letter frequency in French."

I pulled out my phone, did a quick search, and we looked at the results together. In the French language, the most frequently used letter was also *e*, followed by *s* and *a*.

With that in mind, we divvied up the pile of copies and then set about trying various patterns, counting off and crossing out to see if what remained made any sense. I didn't have much luck, but eventually Blake seemed to hit on something promising.

"I have words," he said excitedly. "I tried a one, one-two, one-two-three, one-two-three-four, one-two-three, one-two, one pattern and that left this."

I looked at his page, where he'd written down the letters *nousavons*. With a space, that made *nous avons*, French for "we have."

I gasped.

"Keep going," I said, watching as he counted and crossed, counted and crossed. Excited, I flipped my stack of papers over and wrote down each of the uncrossed letters from his page. Soon I had added a long string, which I broke down into words. *Nous avons tous nos croix à porter.* "We all have our crosses to bear."

My pulse surged. "That's it! That's it! Keep going!"

Eventually, we got through the whole list, and for the most part were able to figure out the correct spacing that would turn the remaining string of letters into words. There were five places, however, that made no sense, three *vvv*s or three *ppp*s in a row. Stumped, we both stared at those for a moment until it hit me.

"Punctuation. What's the French word for 'period'?"

"*Point*," he said, so quickly that I shot him a glance.

"Did you major in French or something?"

He smiled. "No. We lived in Marseille for a few years when I was a kid."

"Well, there you go." I changed each trio of *p*s to periods. That seemed to fit. "So what's French for 'question mark'? Does it start with a *v*?"

"*Point d'interrogation*. No *v*."

I thought for a moment. "How about 'comma'?" As soon as I asked the question, I remembered the answer.

"*Virgule!*" we both cried at once.

Then I made the change, replacing each of the triple *v*s with a single comma. Together we gazed down at what our efforts had wrought. Two sentences, one short and one long. Forty-four words total.

"Okay, Mr. Marseille," I teased. "Why don't you say it for us in English."

"Sure. So this was the secret message that Jules gave Catherine via the Persecution Pamphlet. Ready?"

I nodded, handing him the page.

His face grew serious as he took it from me, held it high, and began to translate. "'We all have our cross to bear as well as our crown to cherish. My cross is light compared to the sacrifices of many, especially our Savior, and my crown is filled with many jewels, including having you as my sister.'"

"Okay, so this is Jules's parting message to his sister." He held up the page and began to read in his deep baritone. "'We all have our crosses to bear as well as our crowns to cherish. My cross is light compared to the sacrifices of many, especially our Savior, and my crown is filled with many jewels, including having you as my sister.'"

I breathed in the words like fresh air. *My crown is filled with many jewels, including having you as my sister.* How wonderful to know that, after all their conflicts, in the end Jules and Catherine parted lovingly. I wasn't sure what happened to him after that, but given that the Talbots were able to come to America and eventually set up a paper mill here in Virginia, my guess was that Jules Gillet and his descendants continued to have an ongoing influence within the family, including the branch that immigrated to America.

Taking back the page, I folded it up, tucked it carefully into my pocket, and then helped him gather the other pages, which he returned to his bag along with the pencils.

"Thank you for helping me," I said earnestly.

"Thank you letting me help," he replied.

We shared another long, deep kiss, one that somehow managed to pull me in close and send me somewhere far, far away all at the same time.

With a sigh, I settled back against the seat as he untied the boat and brought us out to the middle of the waterway. As our journey continued downriver, hands entwined, we alternated between chatting and laughing and falling into comfortable silences. How *easy* he was to be with, I thought. How perfectly suited our temperaments were.

It wasn't until we were nearing our destination that Blake mentioned he'd recently given this vessel a name. "It had one on it when I bought it," he added, "but I've been trying to think of something different, something of my own. Then this morning, it came to me."

Intrigued, I turned in my seat and got up on my knees, leaning toward the back until I could see where he'd painted it on. There in black hand lettering was the new name:

$Cu(NO_3)_2$ 4Ever

Copper nitrate forever.

A laugh burst from my throat. Turning, I gave him a big kiss on the cheek.

"Like it?"

"*Love* it."

"I wasn't trying to be presumptuous with the forever part," he added, looking a little embarrassed. "It worked with the formula."

"Works for me too," I said, hugging him again. I hoped it just might prove to be true.

Looking ahead, I could see the restaurant up on the right, its outdoor deck sparkling with twinkle lights in the gathering dusk. As Blake reached behind us to turn on the motor and putter in toward shore, I couldn't help but gaze at him and at the beauty that surrounded us.

Events of the past week had served to remind me of my eleven-greats grandmother, Catherine Gillet, and the treasure that was her journal. Though she lived more than three hundred years ago, her actions and honesty inspired me.

Now that her story had been brought to mind, I realized it was time for my own to begin. And though I wasn't sure where it might lead, at least I was finally willing to take a leap and find out.

Discussion Questions

1. *My Brother's Crown* takes place in two different time periods, alternating between Catherine's story in 1685 and Renee's in the modern day. Did you like this format? Why or why not? How did the structure allow these concurrently unfolding narratives to inform and enhance each other?

2. Before reading this book, did you know much about the struggle of the Huguenots in seventeenth-century France? If so, did this story provide new insights? Do you feel that you have a better understanding of that era and the situation now that you've read *My Brother's Crown*?

3. When Renee and her cousins are young, they come upon a grisly scene in the woods that has somehow been cleaned up and rearranged by the time police arrive. Which part of that event do you think would be more damaging: witnessing something that horrific at such a young age or having no one else believe that it was ever actually there?

4. A running theme in the historical portion of *My Brother's Crown* involves the decision of where to relocate if forced to leave France. Catherine longs for city life in London, while her brother and fiancé both seem to be leaning toward the Plateau, one of the most rural parts of France. Which location would you prefer? Why?

5. How did the life of Suzanne de Naivailles as a member of the court of King Louis XIV differ from Grand-Mère's life as a Huguenot living in Lyon? Which lifestyle would you have preferred?

6. As a scientist, Renee has a very unique perspective of the world. Did you find her various science-related thoughts and dialogue contributed to her characterization? Which did you find to be the most memorable?

7. Grand-Mère was raised Catholic but became Protestant as a young woman. Did the authors handle this dynamic with sensitivity? What were some of the things Grand-Mère appreciated about her Catholic upbringing?

8. Catherine is by nature—and by circumstance—a brave person, while Renee considers herself to be the very opposite. How do you think our experiences in life play into our levels of courage? What impact do our personalities have on our bravery?

9. In what ways was Jules pragmatic? As you were reading the story did you find yourself agreeing with Catherine's frustration toward him, or did you believe he had a viable plan to save his family and care for his employees? Did you agree with the decisions he made by the end of the story? Could you do the same? Why or why not?

10. Did you empathize with Catherine's helplessness and lack of rights as a woman in the seventeenth-century? How do you think you would have dealt with the limits put on women in that era if you were in her shoes?

Don't Miss

My Sister's Prayer

Book 2 in the Cousins of the Dove Series
Coming Soon to Your Favorite Retailer

Continue the discovery of what truly happened in the Dark Woods
and join the next generation of Talbots as they come to America,
only to be met with a shocking turn of events.

ACKNOWLEDGMENTS

Mindy thanks

John Clark, my husband, who never ceases to amaze me with his infinite skills, support, and love.

Emily Clark, my older daughter, who always helps during the writing process but really went the extra mile on this one.

Lauren Clark, my younger daughter, who has an uncanny gift for helping me think my way to the answers I need.

Tara Kenny, my ever-helpful assistant.

Joey Starns, my brother, and Andrew Starns, my nephew, who are always quick to respond to my cries for information and input on book-related issues.

Charlotte Hrncir of the Smithsonian Institution in Washington, D.C.

The helpful staff and volunteers of the Smithsonian's National Museum of American History and the National Portrait Gallery.

The Smithsonian American Art Museum, in particular the gifted experts at the Lunder Conservation Center.

Leslie thanks

Peter, my husband, for his enthusiasm and delight as he traveled with me to gather the needed elements for the historical thread of this story.

Linda Mordell Letsom, a reader and friend, for sharing about her Huguenot heritage.

Anaïs, Francois, Evan, and Deborah Edom, for their hospitality, love, and inspiration in Lyon, and also for the French language help. (Any mistakes in the story are mine and mine alone.)

Jean-Louis and Sylviane Theron, for taking us to Le Chambon-sur-Lignon and the paper mill in Annonay (along with many other sites), answering my endless questions, and sharing stories of their own ancestors, both Huguenot and Catholic.

Monsieur Vincent de Montgolfier, for the tour of the Museum of the Paper Mills, Canson and Montgolfier, in Annonay; the lesson in old-fashioned paper making; and for answering my questions. (The Montgolfiers have owned paper mills in France since the mid-sixteenth century. The Canson family was added to the enterprise by marriage. We knew none of this when we first came up with the story of the Gillet and Talbot families, but learning the history of the Montgolfiers and Cansons confirmed that a centuries-old business that crossed the Atlantic was, indeed, a possibility.)

Laurie Snyder for reading an early version of the historical thread and for her continued encouragement and support.

Mindy and Leslie thank

Chip MacGregor, our agent, for all his efforts on our behalf.

Kim Moore, our editor and friend, for her expertise and encouragement.

All of the fine folks at Harvest House, for their hard work, dedication, and much-appreciated support.

About the Authors

Mindy Starns Clark is the bestselling author of more than 20 books, both fiction and nonfiction (over 1 million copies sold) including coauthoring the Christy Award-winning *The Amish Midwife* with Leslie Gould. Mindy and her husband, John, have two adult children and live in Pennsylvania.

Leslie Gould is the author of twenty novels. She received her master of fine arts degree from Portland State University and lives in Oregon with her husband, Peter, and their four children.

To connect with the authors,
visit Mindy's and Leslie's websites at
www.mindystarnsclark.com and www.lesliegould.com.